Don't Ask, Don't Tell

Don't Ask, Don't Tell

M.T. Pope, Tina Brooks McKinney,
Brenda Hampton, and Terry E. Hill

www.urbanbooks.net

Urban Books, LLC
78 East Industry Court
Deer Park, NY 11729

ISBN 13: 978-1-60162-338-6
ISBN 10: 1-60162-338-0

First Trade Paperback Printing March 2012
Printed in the United States of America

10 9 8 7 6 5 4 3 2 1

*This is a work of fiction. Any references or similarities to
actual events, real people, living, or dead, or to real locales
are intended to give the novel a sense of reality. Any simi-
larity in other names, characters, places, and incidents is
entirely coincidental.*

Distributed by Kensington Publishing Corp.
Submit Wholesale Orders to:
Kensington Publishing Corp.
C/O Penguin Group (USA) Inc.
Attention: Order Processing
405 Murray Hill Parkway
East Rutherford, NJ 07073-2316
Phone: 1-800-526-0275
Fax: 1-800-227-9604

A DISHONORABLE DISCHARGE

By M.T. Pope

Chapter 1

Kyle

Yes, Sir!

"Drop down and give me twenty!" I looked at him in his eyes, face to face, as stern as I possibly could. The front of his uniform was adorned with all types of medals and badges. He was not to be fucked with and I knew this. He was a thoroughly built muthafucka and I didn't want him angry at me for not obeying a direct order.

"Yes, sir!" I saluted him and did as I was told. I got down on my knees in front of him and slowly unzipped his pants. I reached in and pulled out his flaccid dick. He was in charge of our sexual sessions and he decided when he wanted to fuck me or just for me to blow him.

I took him in my mouth the first time. "One." I sucked half of his five-inch flaccid dick and then looked at him with pleasure in my eyes.

"Two." I sucked again; this time I took him all in my mouth.

"That's right, soldier." His hand palmed the back of my head like most men did when they were getting head. "Aaahhhhhh . . . Yeahhhhh . . . I need another honorable discharge today." I looked at him before I took on his now fully erect nine-inch dick.

"Yes, sir!" I immediately took him in my mouth again, with a plan to give him the discharge of his life today. I didn't want to, but I did as I was told, and in this army and under his leadership you did what you were told with no questions asked.

You see, the man I was going down on was my wife's father. Yes, that's right; my father-in-law and I were getting it on. My problem was that I had had a past with men and my wife was one to look past my past. She did make it known to her parents, though, and both her parents were outwardly skeptical about it. After we got married and had kids the entire ruckus about my past dissipated, and we were one big happy family. That was, until one evening with her father on a fishing trip, when he turned me into his sex slave.

Sergeant Harris, my wife's father, used my past against me. I couldn't tell my wife or anybody in her family. Who would believe that this sergeant in the army was using me for sex? Mind you, I was stationed on the same base with him. He would call in sexual favors all the time and anytime. Nobody knew the type of freak this bastard was. Here I was a twenty-five-year-old sex slave to my wife's forty-five-year-old father. We were in his office and here I was giving him oral pleasure like my life depended on it. He held my family, career, and future in his hand.

"Oh, yeah! Do that shit to daddy," he moaned. The "daddy" resonated in my hearing as he palmed the back of my head and pushed me down harder. He was my wife's daddy and he shouldn't have been mine. I gagged on regret and his dick because the truth and his dick were a little too hard to swallow at the same time. But I managed.

"Look at me while you suck on my little soldier." I did, and the smirk on his face was filled with satisfaction. "Umm hmm . . . You like this dick, don't you? You sorry piece of shit." His verbal abuse was nothing compared to the same shit I told myself after every encounter we had had thus far. *You low-life bastard!* Yeah, that was what I said to myself most of the time and maybe a little more depending on my guilt level. They say no one can treat you worse than yourself, and they never lied about it.

"Yes, daddy," I said in between slurps. "I love this dick."

"I bet you do, you slut. Now finish what you do so well." He thrust in my mouth, once again hitting the back of my throat. I gagged again and spit dripped from the sides of my mouth.

"Yes, you're a good little cum sucker, aren't you?" He was sounding so fucking sexy and I wanted to hold back on my skills, but I just couldn't. I hated it and loved it all at the same time. I had to be all that I could be in every situation including this, as wrong as it was.

"Get the fuck up!" he commanded me. Again, we were all alone in his office. No one could hear him disrespect me. I did as I was told and stood up. My little soldier was at attention as well, because while I was sucking him off I had managed to pull my dick out of my zipper and pull at it. He wasn't the only one who was going to get a nut out of this.

"You should be fucking ashamed of yourself, taking advantage of your father-in-law like this." He was a sarcastic muthafucka. He grabbed my dick in his hand and let it throb in his hand. I stood there and looked at the wall and focused my attention on his awards. I wanted to be a decorated officer like he was one day. I just didn't think it would take this. He had made me some promises about looking out for me when it came to my army career and I hoped he would keep his promise. "I don't know how my daughter would marry a wimp like you." He was still massaging my dick and playing with the pre-cum on the tip of my dick.

"Okay, soldier, bend over that desk and spread that ass. It's time for corporal punishment." I pulled my pants down and bent over the desk like he instructed. I had to admit I shamefully wanted to feel his warm dick in me. I looked back and watched him strap on a condom, and then he spit on his dick and slid in me easy like Sunday morning. He started to grind in me with his hand pushing down on my back. I gripped the edge of his desk as he worked up a pace. I laid my head down on the desk and took it like a man. It was one for the team as they say. And I was staring at my team right now. The picture of my wife and our two sons stared me in the face as I was being passionately fucked.

"Ummmm . . . ummmm," I moaned as I bit down on my bottom lip because my father-in-law now had one leg up on the desk, pushing his entire dick in me.

"Take it, take it, take it," he grunted and thrust into me. "Damn, you got some good ass," he whispered in my ear, as he was now leaning over me giving me a slow, long, deep stroke.

Minutes later, he collapsed on me as he came.

"All right, get up and get dressed, soldier; it's time to get out of here and home to my wife. You're holding me up." I looked at him in disgust, because he must have forgotten that he was just fucking me and not the other way around. I quickly pulled myself together and waited by the door, because I had a weekend pass and he was my ride home. My car was in the shop.

The whole ride home all I could think about was our pact that my wife and I made when we decided to get married: to never try to play both sides of the fence. She said that it was an automatic divorce.

***

About an hour later . . .

We pulled up to the front of my house and he honked the horn, letting my wife know that he was outside.

The front door to my house opened and my beautiful wife came out with one of my sons in her arms and the other one walking beside her. It was a sight to see my wife and my kids coming to greet me as I came home. Even though it happened every time I got a weekend pass, the feeling never changed. I felt like a complete man.

I got out of the car as my wife, Tasha, approached. Her smile was so radiant. I loved me some her.

"Hey, baby." I kissed her on the cheek, mainly because I just had her father's dick in my mouth about an hour or so ago. I had gargled with a travel Scope on the drive home, but I still felt dirty.

"Hey, honey. I'm so glad to see you. I missed you," she pouted. My heart melted and then I looked at my offspring and quickly scooped them up into my arms.

"Hey, boys." I beamed with pride as I looked into their eyes. We had a three-year-old and an eight-month-old baby. Kaynon and Farrow: my pride and joys.

"Daddy!" my wife squealed as she ran around the car and into the arms of her father. She was a true army brat and a spoiled brat.

"Hey, baby girl. How's my sunshine doing?" He picked her up and squeezed her like she was a rag doll. He was a big guy and my wife was a petite little thing. She was about the size of Jada Pinkett-Smith.

"I'm good, Daddy . . . Just missing my two favorite men." She kissed him on his cheek.

"Daddy missed you too." He smiled and then looked at me. I quickly gave my attention back to my boys like he wasn't even there anymore. I was home and I was focusing my attention on my sons. I needed to see them more than anything right now. They were my foundation along with my wife.

"All right, you guys. I have to get home to my wife. I am pretty sure she is waiting on me to get home." He smiled.

The sorry bastard! I felt sorry for his wife, because she was such a nice lady. She didn't deserve to be treated like this.

"Okay, Daddy. I'll see you later." My wife walked back around the car and onto the curb. We watched him get into the car and pull off down the road.

"You okay, baby?" Tasha asked me because I was in a daze for a few seconds as I watched the car disappear around the corner.

"Yes, baby. I'm home, so I'm great." I didn't know how much longer I could take this. The army's policy of "don't ask, don't tell" was spilling over into my household and I couldn't do a thing about it. "Let's go into the house. I'm beat."

Chapter 2

Tasha

Home, Sweet Home

"Baby, put your stuff by the door and I will wash it and have it ready for you to go," I instructed my husband, who was behind me, as he had Farrow in one arm and his duffle bag in the other at the front door. He set his bag down and made his way into our living room. I had Kaynon by the hand as I too walked into the living room. Kyle plopped down on the sofa like he was dead tired. He had a worn-out look on his face and his shoulders slumped. I was pretty sure he had a busy week on the base. I was so glad that I took my mother's suggestion. I suggested to him four years ago to go into the army instead of working like a slave at a regular job like he was doing.

"Kyle, watch them real quick. I have your food warming up in the oven." I walked into the kitchen and picked up the phone.

The phone rang several times before it was answered.

"Hey, Ma."

"Hey, Tasha."

"I was just calling to let you know that Daddy just dropped Kyle off and he is on the way home."

"Okay, baby. I'll get his dinner heated up and ready to go." My mom loved to be a housewife. She lived and breathed it. I followed in her footsteps and took all the instructions and lessons she taught me. My mother was my best friend, besides my husband, in the whole world.

"All right, talk to you in the A.M. Muah!" I hung up the phone and pulled my husband's plate out of the warm oven and walked it into the dining room then placed it on the table.

"Baby, your food is ready."

"All right, I'll be in there in a minute." Just like he said, he was in the dining room not long after with the baby, Farrow, in his arms and our toddler, Kaynon, following him.

"Wow, baby, you really outdid yourself this time. Barbecue ribs, red potatoes, greens, and cornbread. Ummmm, baby, you are too good to me."

"Nothing is too hard for the man of the house." My mother always taught me to treat my man like he was the king of the castle, and I did it to the best of my ability.

"Thank you, Tasha." He handed me the baby and sat down at the table to eat.

"No problem, baby." I kissed him on the cheek. "I'm going upstairs and run you some bathwater. You want bubbles in it?"

"Sure, baby. Do what you do so well." He was smiling hard as he picked up a rib off of his plate and sunk his teeth into the meat. "Damn, baby, this meat is so tender."

I walked away with a smile on my face. I loved my husband, our kids, and my life.

Chapter 3

Kyle

A Night Out

Feeling like the king of the castle only lasted a few more moments of being in my house. I sat at the table and devoured my food with a lot on my mind. I looked around my dining room at all of the things I had accumulated with my wife and felt good about it. Even after I divulged my past to her she still gave a brother a chance. I can't even explain how happy I was when she said yes when I proposed to her only after a year of dating. My mother always told me that the Bible says, "When a man finds a wife he finds a good thing," and I wanted to please my mother so bad. But most of all I wanted to be complete. My sexuality wasn't my choice.

On a night, days after graduating from high school, a few homeboys and I were celebrating in a buddy's basement with some liquor and marijuana. My mother and father were no-nonsense parents and I was on a tight leash up until I graduated high school. I did nothing without them knowing about it. My mother or father would pick me up and drop me off to school every day without fail and on the weekends I had little interaction with children in my neighborhood. My parents said that most of the kids would end up no good in the end because their parents were so loose with their dis-

cipline. I didn't see it that way. I literally felt suffocated
when I was in my house with my parents. They drilled
me about diligence, prosperity, and perseverance.

So when they did let me go hang out with one of their
friend's kids I was a little hesitant, because all of their
friends were just as strict as they were. When I found
out that the guy's parents had to leave for an emergency and trusted us in the house by ourselves, I was
shocked. This was a first for me. No adult supervision.
I knew it was because all of us had good grades and
manners.

"Hey, yo! They gone?" one of my buddies asked Jerrold, the guy whose house we were in. I felt like there was
something different about Jerrold but I just couldn't put
my finger on it. He had some things said about him in
school, but I didn't know if they were true. Mind you, I
went to an all-boys school and the things said about him
were not flattering, to say the least.

"Yeah, they're gone. Y'all ready?" He smiled as he
came down the stairs to his basement that we sat in. It
was a basic basement with some furniture and a big-
screen television. They had some nice stuff and you
could tell they lived well. There were four of us sitting,
looking at each other. When Jerrold put the bag of
weed and the liquor on the table, all of our eyes got big
as saucers. I knew what it was, but I didn't know how
he got it. All of us went to the same school and had the
same classes.

"Fuck! Where'd you get this shit from?" One of the
other guys spoke up before I could.

A smile eased across Jerrold's face before he spoke.
"A man never gives up his sources; besides, one of you
goody two-shoes might rat my ass out when you get
home. I can't chance that shit."

"When are your parents coming back? This shit could get us grounded for life." I spoke up with nervousness in my voice.

"They're going to be gone for a minute." He smiled. "My aunt is having twins in the hospital on the other side of the state." We lived in Virginia so I knew that traffic was horrible and they could be there for hours. I eased up and relaxed my shoulders.

Thirty minutes later, we were all, as they say, "lifted." I tried to get up but the room spun, so I laid my ass back down on the chair I was laid out on. Everyone else was doing the same thing. There was some music on now, but I couldn't have told you what it was. I was gone and so were the others. Before long, I had passed out, and awoke to my shorts being pulled off.

"What the fuck is going on, man?" I looked at Jerrold in his eyes. His were red as a stop sign. I could only assume my eyes were red as well. I looked around the room to see that the other two guys were gone and it was just us two left in the room.

"Chill the fuck out, man, and let me do this." He pushed me back down on the chair with force. He was a thicker guy than I was so it wasn't hard to handle me.

"Nah, man. I'm not with this shit," I protested.

"Bitch, shut the fuck up and sit back!" he threatened me with his fist held high. That didn't deter me though. I was not into the gay shit at all.

"Man, you're going to have to beat my ass in this muthafucka before I let you do anything to me." I pushed up off the chair again, and that was when I felt the hardest punch in my life land against my jaw. It sent me back down on the sofa like a brick out a window.

"Ah fuck nah, man." I felt a bruise on my jaw. I got up and started swinging and holding my own, until he got me with a haymaker that knocked me on my butt for the last time.

I was weak, dazed, and confused, but I still tried to fight back. It was a futile effort, because he flexed his arm like he was going to hit me again and I flinched with the memory of the last punch on my mind. I gave up.

"That's what the fuck I thought." He hovered over me for a second before he pulled my shorts all the way down and flipped me over on my stomach and propped my butt in the air. He stuck his face in between my butt and started to lick savagely.

"You like that?" I didn't answer. I was praying to God for this to be over fast or to have someone interrupt us.

"You hear me, muthafucka?" He swung and connected with the back of my head. "Answer me, bitch."

"Ahhh uhhhh," I moaned in pain and shame.

"I bet your soft ass do." He spoke in between licks. "I've been looking at this juicy ass all school year. I wanted to see what it tasted like and now I am. You got you a nice bubble butt." He smacked it before he dived in again. I couldn't describe the feeling of what I was going through with too many words, but one came to mind: shame. I knew then that what people said about him was true, but I wondered how many of the guys who were here experienced what I was presently experiencing. I would never know now because I was definitely not asking around.

When it couldn't get any worse he stuck a finger in my asshole.

"Ahhhh." I was almost screaming like a girl.

"If you don't shut the fuck up I will beat your ass again. You're going learn to like this shit right here."

My pride wouldn't let me cry, but I sure enough wanted to. I was still a virgin and I didn't think my first sexual experience would be this. I wanted to be with a woman. The way some of the guys talked about pussy in school made me thirst for it. I lay in bed thinking about it constantly. Now I was in a basement ass out, literally.

"I'm about to fuck this tight ass right here." He stuck two fingers in and smacked it again. I bit on to the sofa cushion in anger. I heard some paper rustling behind me and then I felt what I knew was his dick pressed against my asshole. I squirmed as much as I could until he punched me in my side, almost knocking the air out of me.

"That's right; bite on that muthafuckin' pillow. I'm about to punish this fresh ass."

The pain that I felt in that next moment made tears come to my eyes. I had never felt pain like it in my life. It was like having your whole hand slammed in a car door repeatedly.

"Damn, you tight," he said as he forced all of him in me slowly. The pain was causing me to tremble and shake involuntarily, but he didn't stop. "You shaking now, but in a few minutes you'll love it." I seriously doubted it. I didn't know how men did this on the regular. It was pure torture.

"Yeah, there we go." He started pumping me slowly. He was leaned over me with his tongue licking my ear and face. I was silent as I could be. "Damn, this ass is good." He moaned and then he ground his hips into my butt.

"You like this dick?" I nodded to appease him. Truth was it was still killing me each second. "I bet you do."

He began to pick up the pace and pump me harder. Minutes went by and he was still fucking me. And yes, eventually the pain went away and then "it" happened. I began to like it, but I didn't let him know that. He eventually pulled out and he released on my back. I lay there for a few more minutes and then I slowly eased myself up. When I went to sit on my butt I winced in pain.

"It will go away by the time you get home." He offered me some consolable words that I really didn't care about at that moment. "Call your parents and let them know you are ready to go." He walked out of the room like what just happened didn't happen. I was flabbergasted and baffled. *This couldn't have been the first time he did this.*

I called my parents and mustered up a straight voice so that they wouldn't think that anything was wrong.

Before they came I went into the bathroom and looked at my face. There was a small scrape on my face, and I was glad that nothing else showed up on my dark skin. I also threw back some Listerine for my breath and some Clear Eyes to get rid of my red eyes that I had from the weed. I didn't need my parents questioning me about anything. And if they did I just would say that we were roughhousing and one of the guy's class rings grazed my face.

My parents came and picked me up and they asked me how my day was. I faked a bright, cheery smile and told them it was the best time of my life. I knew that I didn't want to ever go over to Jerrold's house again and each time my parents suggested it, I declined. That didn't last long, because one day they had to go out of town for a funeral, which I hated attending, and I had to stay over at Jerrold's house once again. They didn't trust me in the house by myself. They went on and on about parties, sex, and all of that stuff. I couldn't believe that I was an eighteen-year-old still being bossed around by my parents. It was either a funeral or Jerrold's house. I chose the latter, because I knew that Jerrold's parents would be home. I knew that he wouldn't try anything with his parents' home. I was wrong. The parents were traditional parents too; we had to sleep in his room and not on the living room sofa or floor like I wanted to do, alone. You can't believe how many times Jerrold violated me those nights in his room. He made me do the same things that he did to me weeks earlier and yes, knowing that it was wrong, I enjoyed them. That whole summer we were butt buddies and even after I went to college I continued to be sexually involved with men.

That was, up until I met Tasha in my sophomore year at Virginia State University. I was interning at a software company and she was too. We both complained about the job and how we were both looking for something else. We hit it off immediately and got serious fast. She was my first girlfriend. From the first day we met we clicked. I told her about my family and she did the same. She was an only child and an army brat. She was the one who suggested that I go into the army instead of pursuing my career in computer technology. Since her father was a sergeant in the army, I talked to him a few times and then I dropped out of college and enlisted in the army. My parents were livid. Mainly my mother, because my father thought it was a good idea. He always thought I was too soft, because I never really played or liked sports. That was six years ago, and now I'm a happily married man with two kids and a wife.

"Honey, your water is getting cold," I heard my wife yell down the steps at me.

"I'll be right up." I cleaned my plate and made my way upstairs to where my family was. I had to find a way to get my father-in-law to back off of me. I just didn't know how.

Chapter 4

Christine

Same Ol', Same Ol'

"Hey, baby." I kissed my husband on the cheek as he entered the house. I had waited in a chair by the door for him to arrive, and when I heard his car pull up the driveway I opened the door to let him in. He looked exhausted. I took his jacket and hung it up on the coat rack. He walked into the dining room and sat down at the dining room table.

"How was your day, baby?" I asked as I bent down to take off his shoes and replace them with his slippers.

"Same ol' same ol'." He frowned. "Ordered some ingrates around and kept everything in order—like I always do." My husband had worked hard in his military career. He was a much-decorated officer and everyone took him seriously. He was a force to be reckoned with. On my few trips to the base, everywhere we walked people saluted and gave him his due. I was proud to be his wife and even prouder to take care of his home. He was the man of the house and I made him feel that way every day that he walked through that door. They say good men are hard to find, but I knew that I had one. My husband was a good provider for me and Tasha and he never let us down. He took the army pledge to be all that he could be to his heart for his country and his family.

"Awww . . . Baby, I'm so glad you are home." I rubbed his cheek with my hand and slid it under his chin and kissed him on the lips. "Let me go and get your plate of food out of the oven." I sashayed into the kitchen, pulled his plate out of the oven, and poured him a big glass of sweet tea. I walked back into the dining room with a little more switch in my hip. I was forty-four years old but I still had some sexiness in me that rivaled any twenty-something beauty.

"Babe, what would I do without you? You are still the prettiest thing in this whole wide world," he spoke, and I grinned as I set his plate down in front of him. He always knew how to sweet talk me. In fact, that is how we meet.

Twenty years ago, I was waiting tables in a restaurant in Hampton, Virginia when he walked in the door. He was all decked out in his army attire looking all dapper and well put together. I was working in one of those diner-type restaurants so I had to work the counter as well. He plopped down at the counter and that was when I looked into his big brown eyes and fell in love. He had a million-dollar smile that lit up the room.

"What can I get you today, sir?" I asked as I poured another customer some coffee.

"Well, beautiful, what do you suggest I eat? I'm pretty sure your sweet self could pick something right tasty for a man to eat." He had a deep Southern drawl so I knew he was new to this area.

"Well, thank you, kind sir. I would recommend our feast for a king meal, since I know a big, strapping guy like you has to serve our country on a full stomach. I couldn't have you out there on the line without proper nourishment." I smiled.

"All right, Chrissy. I'll take it." He called me by my nickname, which was on my name badge. "And let me have a cup of that fine coffee I know you put your heart into."

"Sure thing." I grabbed him a cup and poured him a cup. "Cream and sugar?"

"Cream, yes . . . but I got enough sugar from your sweetness to last me a lifetime."

I couldn't help but blush. We talked as he ate and in between me waiting on tables. I found out that he was from Tennessee and he was stationed right here in Virginia. He was an only child and an army brat. I filled him in on me and from that day forward he would come into the restaurant and order the same meal. We started dating shortly after that and within a year we were married. Over twenty years later and we were still as happy as could be.

"Baby, I'm going upstairs to run you a bath, don't take too long. I don't want the water to get cold on you."

"I won't, babe. I'll be right up after I finish."

With that I walked out of the living room and up to the bathroom to prepare his bath. I loved being a housewife, and taking care of my man and his house was a full-time job.

My husband made it upstairs in a few more minutes. I had his bathwater ready and he eased down into it. I was kneeling down beside him with a sponge, ready to wash him up.

"Aaahhh, boy. What a day." He leaned back in the tub and I began to wash him up with a sponge. Some people probably thought that this was too much for a wife to do, but my husband provided well and it was my wifely duty to supply all his comforts when he got home. I enjoyed washing up my husband.

"I know you are tired, babe. That's why I'm going to give you the treatment you deserve." I worked up a lather in the sponge and washed up his whole body, from his feet all the way up to his chest. "You have fun today whipping all of those soldiers into shape?"

"Sure did." He smiled. "One in particular I had to make an example out of. I gave him some special punishment." His smile was wide across his face. He then closed his eyes, lifted his arms, and put his hands behind his head. I washed his underarms and then he leaned forward so I could get to his nice, strong back.

"You work him over good, baby? Showed him who was in charge?" I loved when he was happy. It made me happy. There is nothing like a happy and content man making a living for his family.

"Yes, I sure did." He nodded his head. "He's stubborn, though. I might have to work him over on the regular to get him into shape."

"Do what you got to do, baby." I got up off of my knees, grabbed a towel off of the towel rack, and waited for my husband to get out of the tub.

"You know I will," he said as he got out of the tub.

He stood there in the middle of our bathroom as I dried him off.

"Thanks, babe." He kissed me on the forehead and left the bathroom for our bedroom. I already had his undergarments out on the bed, waiting for him. He put them on and then we both got into bed to get a good night's sleep for the next day.

Chapter 5

Kyle

Bonding

Lake Chesdin is in the east-central part of the state, in Petersburg, Virginia, and that was where we were headed again. It was just a couple of weeks past our last encounter at his office. The sergeant and I were on one of our sexual excursions once again. The first time we came to this lake was a year into my marriage to his daughter, and he said that we should do some male "bonding." His words, not mine. I didn't think that that was to be taken literally, with his dick bonded to my ass, but that is what happened. That shit still played in my head like it was yesterday.

We were sitting in a boat with our lines out on the water, waiting for a bite. I never knew that the sergeant was waiting for his opportunity to bite as well. His being gay was the last thing I would have thought about him. In fact, he was belligerently flagrant with his gay slurs before my wife told him about my past. I was hesitant, but I manned up and did the right thing. I wanted to go into my new life with everything on the table.

"Son, go on ahead and take a shower first, and then I'll take one. We got to get up early again tomorrow to get us some more fish." This was hours after sitting on the lake and catching a few fish. I had to admit the conversation was pleasant. We talked about sports a lot and my future in the army. He said that I had a promising career and I believed him. Even after I came clean with my past it seemed that he embraced me as the son he never had. That was, until later that night when I was sound asleep in my bed.

I was sleeping good, thinking about my wife and our newborn son, who was delivered only a month earlier, when the sergeant slipped into my bed and under the covers and snuggled up to me. His warm body pressing against my naked back shocked me like I was dipped in freezing cold water.

"What the fuck!" I bolted out of the bed and quickly turned on the lights to the room.

"What's wrong, son?" He was butterball naked. Can you imagine a man the size of the big black brother in *The Green Mile* in the bed naked? Well I had a full view that night. To say I was shocked is an understatement.

"You don't like what you see?" He smiled and pulled back the covers to expose his entire naked body. I shook my head in confusion.

"Huh?" was all I could get out.

"Don't act as if you don't want this." He grinned and stroked his dick, which was bigger than average, but not huge.

"What?" I tried not to look at his dick. I focused on his face. But my eyes quickly went back to his erection. "What the hell is going on? What's wrong with you? I'm your daughter's husband. You can't be in here like this. This is wrong."

"It's wrong and I don't want to be right." He laughed. I didn't see anything funny at all.

"Sir, you have to go. This is not going to happen." I spoke with authority and confidence.

"On the contrary, it is going to happen and it will happen all night long." His facial expression had change from happy to firm. I knew this look all too well. It was his no-nonsense look that he got when we were on the base. I had seen dudes reduced to tears when he got like this. But I was not going to budge on this one. I had left my past in the past and I wanted it to stay that way.

"Sorry, sir, it's not." I opened the door to the room and pointed out into the hallway. "Go!"

He got up and sat on the side of the bed and looked at me for a few seconds.

"Boy, I didn't think you had those types of balls in you." He smiled.

"Well, I have to do what I have to do." I spoke like I had won a big war.

"Too bad I have to bring you to your knees." He looked at me with the serious face again. At this point, I was thinking he was a lunatic and I needed to get my ass out of there before he tried to kill me or something.

I turned to go out of the door.

"If you so much as cross that door seal, I will have your ass dishonorably discharged for indecent exposure and disorderly conduct by an officer. You know there is a quiet but standing policy in the army. You know what that is?"

I remained quiet. I didn't want to say the words.

"Answer me, soldier!" he barked. "What is it?"

"Don't ask, don't tell," I mumbled.

"I can't hear you." He spoke like I was in an army lineup.

"Don't ask, don't tell," I spoke louder.

"Right. That policy keeps faggots like you safe. You like being safe, don't you, officer?"

I nodded my head.

"I thought so." He smiled again. "Now get over her and get on your knees for your country."

That was the beginning of a sex-filled night. And to make matters worse, he had a DL brother on the base record me giving a couple of guys blow jobs against my will. He made me watch it and the only thing that was shown was me giving head to some blocked-out faces. So, like I said before, he had my life, career, wife, and kids in his hands. On these trips I just blocked out what we did and tried to keep a positive attitude. And that was so hard to do. It brings to mind that passage in the Bible that says, "For what I want to do I do not do, but what I hate I do." I just needed an out and anyone would do right now. I loved my wife and children and my career. And now I was falling back into some very dangerous territory with the sergeant. I didn't want to start to get messy and lose everything I worked hard for.

"You ready to have some fun?" He reached over and squeezed my thigh, breaking me out of my trance. We had pulled up to the cabin. I looked out at the lake that was about a hundred feet away and thought about running and jumping off of the end of the long pier and letting myself drown, but the vision of my two boys brought me back to reality. I had live and fight my way out.

"Yes, sir." I reached for the door, opened it, and walked around to the back to pull out our fishing gear from the bed of the truck. Even though we did do some fishing, they were mainly for show for our wives.

After sitting on the boat for a few hours and just looking out into the water, I decided to see if I could get some information from the sergeant about his past and how he came to be who he was right now.

"Sir, can I ask you, how did you come to be gay?"

He looked at me for a few seconds and then burst into hearty laughter. I just sat there and looked on, waiting for him to answer me.

Chapter 6

Henry

The Stairs

"You want to know how I became gay?" I asked him after I had finished laughing my head off. This little bastard had a nerve to want to know my business. "Son, I don't think you are ready for that type of conversation. And I'm not gay. I'm just experimenting with the same sex."

"Try me," he countered.

"Don't say I didn't warn you." I laughed, but was serious on the inside. "My life growing up wasn't a fairytale and it will definitely give you nightmares if you're not stable in the head. But you've been taking my dick in the ass, so you just might be able to handle this.

"I was about eight years old when my first 'experience' happened. I had a very good day playing in the hot fields of Monroe, Tennessee. I was a big, strapping young lad like you see before you, just younger. I had dreams of being an airplane pilot or an astronaut like any other normal kid. But that shit was ripped from me the night my mother came into my room and ripped the thin blanket that covered me on my twin-like cot off of me and onto the floor. We didn't have much, but we made do as the older folks used to say. My mother was heavily intoxicated and she reeked of anger. My

father must have stayed out again this night like he did
so many other times.

"'Get yo' buffoon ass up. Didn't I tell you to clean
them steps before you went to bed?'

"'Y . . . yes, ma'am.' I nodded as I sat on the side of
the bed still half asleep.

"'Well, that shit ain't done.' She staggered a little
as she pointed out of my door and toward the steps.
'You . . . you just like you lazy-ass fatha. Good-for-
nothin' bastard.' Spit managed to fly from her mouth
and land on my cheek. I dared not move or try to
wipe it off. The last time I did that I woke up the next
morning on the front porch by the dog licking my
face.

"'What are you still sittin' there fo'? Get yo' ass and
do it now.' From my recollection, I did do the steps before I went to bed, but I was not going to say anything.
I just went on ahead and did as I was told.

"Go on with yo' big, lazy ass," She pushed me out the
door as I passed by her. I tripped and went face first
into the door post and hit my head.

"'Uhhh,' I moaned in pain as I felt my lip that was
split and slightly bleeding.

"'Get blood on my flo' and you will be cleaning that
up too." She grabbed me by my arm and helped me out
the door.

Kyle shook his head as he listened to me talk. I continued so he could get the full effect of my story.

"I hurried up my pace a little, walked down the steps,
and grabbed the wooden bucket that was in the corner.
I marched toward the kitchen to fill it with water and
grab the scrub brush for the steps. I grabbed some
Ajax from under the cabinet and hurried toward the
steps. The less time it took to clean the steps the less
she had to see me. The more she saw me and less of

my father the more she would take her frustration with him out on me. I looked like him so I must be like him: her words, not mine. We only had, like, ten steps so it wouldn't take me long to get it done."

"I started at the top and worked my way down. She sat in a chair at the bottom and watched me do every step. I made sure I got every nook and cranny. When I got to the last step, I picked the bucket up, getting ready to empty it out off of the front porch like I usually did.

"'Where do you think you going?' she hissed as I made my way toward the door.

"'To empty it out, Momma.' I had on the most pitiful look I could muster up.

"'Get yo' ass in that kitchen and scrub that floor, and I mean on your hands and knees.'

"I must have huffed or something, because before I knew it, Momma was on top of me breathing like a fiery dragon. 'Boy, you sassing me?'

"'N . . . no, ma'am, I'm not. I was just breathing.' I managed to get out.

"'Get in there.' She pointed with the liquor bottle still in her hand.

"I was in the kitchen in seconds and on my knees, scrubbing.

"'Look at you, shaking your ass like a li'l sissy. Yeah, you just like yo' soft-ass daddy. You probably want somebody to fuck you too, like your sissy father.'"

I paused in telling my story to give Kyle some pertinent information. "Now this was in, like, the mid-seventies, and I didn't know what the hell my mother was saying. I didn't know that 'sissy' meant men who liked men. All I knew was that I didn't like being called that in school because none of the other boys like to be called it, and most boys would fight at the mention of it. I just continued to scrub the floor so I could go back to bed."

"Back to the story," I continued.

"'You like boys?' she asked me as I continued to scrub.

"'Yes,' I answered, because I didn't know that there were two kinds of likes.

"'I knew that shit. I knew it,' she hollered. We had a farmhouse so no one could hear her holler at me.

"'Get the hell up. I'ma break you in before you can start fucking all them boys in school. You won't be having them people calling me, looking at me funny. When I get finished with you, you won't like boys no mo'.'

"I did as I was told and stood in the middle of the floor.

"'Bend over that muthafuckin' table.' She pointed. 'Yo' ass is gonna learn not to fuck with me, Ronald.

"Ronald was my father's name." I looked at Kyle and then continued my story.

"'Momma, my name is Henry,' I said as she left the room and came back into the room with the plunger.

"'I know yo' fucking name. I said Henry,' she hissed.

"I didn't even try to correct her, because I knew that she was drunk and not listening. She walked over to me and yanked down my Fruit of the Loom underwear.

"'I'ma teach you,' were the last words I heard before she forced the wooden part up my rectum. The scream that I let out was unheard of. It was so loud that I was hoarse the next day. That was the first of many nights that my mother would violate me. Each time my father wouldn't come home I got the same treatment. Pretty soon I was taking it like I was supposed to. I would whimper so she would stop, but she would continue to do it. One day my father just didn't come home and my mother just gave up. She found my father's revolver in a closet and took her life. I guess she just couldn't take the fact that she lost her husband to another man. I later found that out from one of my cousins, who had overheard my aunts talking about it one day. I was passed around from family member to family member until I was old enough to enlist in the army, and that I did.

"Oh and when I was with my older cousins, they heard about my father and thought the same thing my mother did. They continued in the footsteps of my mother, only they didn't use a plunger, they used the real thing. When I got into the army the "don't ask, don't tell" policy was in full effect, it just didn't have a name until 1993, and it has been in my life as a standing motto at work and home from then on."

All Kyle could do was shake his head and look out into the water.

I didn't tell him the story to make him feel sorry for me; it was quite the opposite. I wanted him to fear what I could do to him, because of what was done to me so long ago. It was like prey becoming the predator and I was good at it, too. I had nothing to lose by tormenting him anyway. He just didn't know what he married into. Poor sap. I almost felt sorry for him. We went back to shore and into the cabin to do what we always came to do: fuck.

Chapter 7

Kyle

At Ease

"Everybody get your stinking, rotting ass up and at attention," Sergeant Harris barked, startling everybody awake. It was, like, four in the morning and I was sleeping really well. The story about his childhood was two weeks old in my memory but it still resonated freshly in my mind as I got to my feet and stood at attention. He came from a long line of sick bastards.

He walked down the line as each of us men stood waiting for his next fiery instruction. I needed some really solid evidence to get his ass off of my back, figuratively and literally. He was a thorn in my side. People on the base knew that he was my father-in-law and thought that he was treating me differently because I was family. And I don't mean in a good way; he made me do shit that was extremely petty.

"You maggots make me sick." He breathed heavily into the face of a guy two guys down from me. We were all used to it, but none of them had the close encounters that I had had with him. I was sure of it. "Get all of your shit in order and line up your sorry asses outside in ten minutes."

I breathed a sigh of relief, because usually five minutes was the limit. *He must be in a good mood or maybe just in a better mood.* You just couldn't tell with his sadistic ass.

Within the time limit, we were all outside, standing at attention, but I was the last one to show up.

"What's wrong with you, you can't tell time?" he barked in my face.

"Yes, I can, sir," I spoke back with authority.

"Are you talking back, soldier?" He was really close to my face.

"No, sir, just answering your question, sir." I knew that he was horny and this was his way of getting me in his office. I could have kicked myself for going back and brushing my teeth real quick.

"I think you are trying to make a fool of me, officer." He paced away from me a few steps, and with his back to me he then said, "I don't like to be made a fool of, officer."

In my head, I was calling him all kinds of bitches and muthafuckas but none of them crossed the seal of my mouth. He was trying to make this bigger than it really was. I didn't want to push him too far. Like I said before, he would do something that would show that he wasn't giving special favors since I was his daughter's husband. Most of the other officers knew that I was his son-in-law and he was dead serious when he said he didn't like to be made a fool of.

"Do I need to make an example of an officer who makes a fool of me?" he said as he walked down the line and back toward me. No one answered. It was fear of punishment that made most of the men fear him. He was infamous for making you serve the whole base in your underwear with "maggot" written on your chest for all to see, or the ever popular punishment of singing "I'm Every Woman" while washing trucks out in the open for all to see. I had seen it done and I didn't want any part of any of it.

"Do I?" He was back in my face again.

"No, sir!" I spoke up.

"I think I do," he countered. "So, officer, meet me in my office for your punishment at the end of the day."

"Yes, sir!" I wanted to spit in his face.

"Any of you other maggots want to make a fool of me?" he barked as he went back down the line.

"No, sir!" the other officers chimed in at the same time.

"Well, get your sorry ass out of my face and over to the mess hall for chow. Get out of my face."

We all did as we were instructed to do.

"Damn, Kyle, the sergeant really be digging in yo' ass." One of the few men I spoke to on base joshed as we both sat down at one of the tables to eat out meals. "You must not be fucking his daughter good enough."

A few of the guys nearby laughed as well. I smiled slightly, because I didn't want to let on that I wasn't really feeling like discussing the issue with people who had no idea what was really going on.

"I don't know what his problem is." I turned serious. "I do know that I don't know how much I can take. This is getting to be a problem."

"Nah, man. That nigga needs to get some pussy. That's his problem." The guy I was sitting with spoke up. "He's so mean his dick even scared to get hard."

Again, everyone burst into laughter. I played it off like I loved the joke. They didn't know that his statement was far from the truth. His dick had no problem getting hard.

"Shit, maybe he wants you to suck his dick." The comment came from one of the guys behind me. I didn't know who said it but it made me spit out the water that I just put in my mouth.

"Y'all some crazy mofos for that one," said my buddy, Clifton, in front of me.

"Sure the hell is," I seconded his statement.

"Dude, don't worry about it, just keep your head up. I'm sure he will ease up." A guy who was sitting at a table near us spoke up. "All that huffing and puffing is for show. Soon as a newbie comes along, you'll be out of his radar. Believe me, I know."

"I hope so." I shrugged.

That evening I met him in his office and, sure enough, we did what he loved to do: fuck.

Two weeks later at home . . .

"Baby, how well do you know your father?" We were laid up in bed, looking at some reality show she liked. I wasn't really interested in the show; my mind was too focused on the secrets that I was holding. I didn't know if I could talk to my wife about this and have her believe me. She loved him like he was one of her legs or something.

"What do you mean?" She looked at me curiously. She was such a vision of beauty. I really didn't want to bust her bubble about the perfect father she thought she had.

"Well . . ." I paused to think about how I was going to ask her this question. "I think he's not the man you all see and know."

"Kyle, you are treading on very serious territory now. What are you talking about?" She grabbed the remote, muted the television, and sat up to look at me while I was still laid on my pillow-top bed with my hands tucked behind my head.

"I mean I think your father has some really serious mental issues." I chickened out with the "gay" question. She wasn't ready for the truth. I seriously thought that my wife would choose him over me if an altercation between him and me came about.

"Mental issues?" She looked at me and shook her head like I had some as well. "Kyle, my father is *very* grounded in his thinking. I think you need to back off this topic before you cross a line you don't want to. As a matter of fact, you already did. What the fuck is wrong with you?" She was now standing, looking at me like she didn't want to know me. I had never seen this side of her before. I was a little taken aback.

"Baby, you don't see the way your father treats me on the base; he is a lunatic. I mean I am all for being tough, but he is sadistic and nasty to me and a few others."

"Kyle, you're in the army. I think you need to man up and take whatever is being thrown at you. You know . . . Serve your country and be all that you can be. Real men don't whine about stuff; they get over it and keep it moving."

"Real men?" I hopped up off the bed like my butt was on fire. I was in defense mode. "What are you trying to say?" I almost called her a bitch, but she was my wife and I didn't want to disrespect her. *I know she wasn't questioning my manhood. Was she?*

"I'm sorry, baby, wrong choice of words. I meant to say . . . Never mind that. Daddy *can* be a *little* hard, but just ignore him and get the job done." She walked over to me and faced me. She pouted her lips and then wrapped her hands around my neck. "Don't pay Daddy any mind. I'll talk to my mother and see if she can talk to him."

"I don't know about that. I don't want you discussing our business with your mom. It's my problem, I'll handle it." I knew she would do it anyway though.

"Okay, baby, whatever you say." She kissed me on the lips and before long we were making out on the bed.

Chapter 8

Christine

Schooling

"Hey, baby," I said as I entered my daughter's townhouse. It was the spitting image of mine. She had everything in place and it was neat and tidy. Good home training and foundation were things that I prided in teaching my daughter. Keeping her home happy meant keeping her man happy. So when she called me to tell me that Kyle was upset about how my husband was treating him, I decided that it was time for me to make a house call and get things in order.

"Hey, Ma." She smiled, but I knew that she had a lot on her mind from the worry lines on her forehead.

I walked into the living room to see my two grandchildren sitting on the sofa: one in a car seat and the other on the sofa.

"How are Nana's babies?" I gushed with pride as I sat down in between the two on her Tiffany sectional. When my daughter said she was pregnant the first time I thought that I was going to burst I was so happy. I had my doubts about Kyle's fidelity and lifestyle commitment, but he came through and most of the doubt left as soon as my first grandchild arrived. When she said she was pregnant again I put any and all small reservations that were left out with the next day's trash.

I picked the baby up out of the car seat and cuddled him in my arms. He was the spitting image of Kyle. I couldn't help but say I was glad with the way that my daughter's life had turned out. She had everything that I pushed her to have: home, family, husband, stability.

"So, how was Kyle acting when you talked to him today?" I posed the question to Tasha, who sitting in a chair diagonally from me, as I cradled baby Farrow in my arms, kissing and nuzzling him.

"He seemed . . . better." She shrugged. "I don't think he is over me insinuating that he wasn't a real man."

"You what?" My voice escalated and startled Farrow to the point that he started to cry. I rocked him as I spoke my next words. "You said he wasn't a real man? How could you? That was low."

"Well, I didn't mean it, Momma. He was just going on and on and it slipped out. I didn't mean it. You know how I was raised: with tough love."

"That doesn't even matter. The fact that you even hinted at it might mess everything—I mean, your marriage—up. How could you be so careless?"

"I'm sorry, Momma. I don't know what I was doing." She slumped over a little bit. I could see that she was worried. I would be too if I called my man's manhood into question. Knowing his history he could . . . well, you know.

"You sure as hell don't." I was a little pissed. "Look, I'll take the kids on the next weekend he gets leave and then you can try to smooth it over with him. Girl, you better put it on him and sex him like you never have before. Before he thinks too much and ends up in somebody else's arms." I didn't want to say a man, but she knew it, because that would not be pretty. I needed to let her know what was at stake here. I was always about the truth. Always.

"I know." She shook her head. "So are you still going to talk to Daddy about his temper?"

"Mamma will work her magic and see. No promises though."

"Thank you, Ma." She got up off of her chair and came and kissed me on the cheek. *The things that a parent will do for their child are so immeasurable.*

Chapter 9

Kyle

Mr. Telephone Man

I lay in my bed thinking about my life and all that I had been through. My wife calling me out like that the other night really made me think about my past now, and how things had gotten so messy over the last few months. I couldn't even call anyone. My parents disowned me when I told them that I was gay. I told them the first week that I moved onto the campus of Virginia State. I never thought that they would cut me off but they did. They cut me off like a chicken's head before its deep fried. I had no one I could go to so that I could get things off of my chest. Even when I proposed to Tasha and called them and left them a message on the answering machine they never responded. I guess they may have thought that I was pulling their leg or something. Being an only child and a castaway was not a good look at all. I felt so all alone.

I got up out of my bunk, threw on some sweatpants and a T-shirt, and went outside. Even though we weren't supposed to be walking around the base at night, I did anyway because I needed to get me some fresh air. I looked up at the sky as I walked and wished that everything in my life was a little different. But I knew that I was only asking for the easy way out. I knew that that was not going to happen.

Have you ever gone down memory lane in your life and seen nothing but confusion? That was how I saw it right now: misery. And, as they say, misery loves company. I just didn't want to be a part of that company anymore. I was mainly talking about the sergeant at this time. He was miserable and I knew it. I don't know what was going on between him and his wife, but I knew that he was messing with things between me and my own. I walked over to one of the only pay phones on the base and dialed my house.

On the fourth ring my wife picked up.

"Hello." She sounded groggy, but still sweet to me.

"Hey, babe." I was huddled up on the pay phone like I wanted to be with her at this moment. "What are you doing?" I knew that she was half asleep but I asked anyway.

"Dreaming about you." She spoke softly. I heard a hint of seduction in her voice.

"Really?" I asked because I wanted to be sure. As a man, I needed that assurance of being needed and wanted. After what she said to me the other day I felt like the truth was seeping out of me somehow. I mean, I didn't want it to be the truth, but it was. I was having sex with her father. When you are doing dirty things and playing the role of innocence, things begin to unfold without your permission, and that was what I was thinking when she said "a real man." Not that I didn't think that I was a real man, but because the world set the criteria for how a man should act and what a man should do. But I knew that I was a real man, because I took care of my home and my family. I just had some issues, just like the next man.

"Yes, Kyle." I heard her shifting in the bed. "You are my man." She said it with such authority and confidence. A brother sure was turned on right now. I shifted my growing erection in my pants.

"I know that's right." I smiled. I felt a lot better hearing that she was dreaming about me, no matter how corny it was. "You making me horny, you know that?"

"Me too, baby," she whispered into the phone. "Can you guess what I'm doing right now?"

It didn't take a rocket scientist to know that she was pleasuring herself.

"Damn, baby. You got me hard out here at this phone booth."

"Pull your dick out for me, baby," she moaned. "I want you to fuck me over the phone."

I did as I was told and pulled out my dick right there at the phone booth. It was after midnight and I knew that nobody was around. I just hoped that there were no cameras around to catch me, because I didn't want to get into any trouble for doing what I was about to do outside.

"You got it out?" she asked.

"Yeah. I got him out."

"Now, pull on him and imagine him digging deep into my baby girl." That was our nickname for her womb.

"Okay." I closed my eyes and thought of her on the bed and me on top of her putting myself into her. I had the phone in between my shoulder and my ear. I stroked my dick slowly like I did her all the time.

"Baby, I'm putting you in me right now." She gasped like she really felt me entering her. "Damn, baby, you thick and warm. Stroke me, baby. Stroke me!" Her voice escalated a little. I could tell she was working her clit overtime.

"I know . . . I feel you too, baby . . . I feel your tight walls around me." I was rocking as I stroked myself. "You . . . feel . . . so . . . goooood!" I moaned loudly as I stroked my dick intensely.

"Right there, baby, right there." She was gasping for air. I could tell she was about to come. "Work the middle, Kyle. Work the middle, baby." I imagined her on her back and fingers inside of her and the other hand working her clit while her torso was lifted off of the bed.

"Take this dick, baby . . . take this dick . . ." I thrust as I pumped my dick. Being outside had totally left my consciousness. I was at home, stroking my wife full speed ahead.

"I'm taking it . . . taking it . . ." Her voice was gruff. She was real close to coming. It caused me to stroke even faster.

"I'm coming . . . I'm coming . . . uhhhhhhhhhhhhhh," she exploded, and then there was silence.

"Ahhh . . . Ahhh . . . Ahhh . . . Ahhh." I came all over the ground around the phone. There was silence on both ends for a few more seconds.

"Damn, baby." I huffed a little. "That was some serious fucking."

"I know, right." I could see her smiling face and her body stretched out across the bed. It was just like I wanted to be right now.

"We got to do that more often," I spoke as I tucked my dick inside of my pants. I looked around to see that I was still alone.

"We will, because Momma is taking the kids on your next leave."

"Really?" I perked up even more than before. I mean, I loved my kids, but every parent knows what a real break is, especially an overnight break.

"Yes, and we are going to have the house all to ourselves."

"All right now . . . I can't wait."

"Me either, baby. We are going do all the lovemaking we want to do and anywhere we want to do it, too." My wife giggled as she spoke. She was a freak by nature. One thing I loved about her, among other things.

"Look, baby, let me get off this phone and back to bed. I am going to sleep like a log after that nut you just gave me."

"I bet you will." She giggled again. "Night, baby."

"Night." I hung up the phone and went to bed a happy man.

Chapter 10

Henry

Lightening Up

"Hey, babe." I kissed my wife on the cheek as I entered my house and followed the same routine as we had become accustomed to since day one. I sat in my chair in the dining room, slipped off my shoes, and waited for my dinner to be served to me.

"Dinner will be ready in a moment." She walked off and into the kitchen.

"All right," I said, and then I picked up the newspaper that was sitting on the table waiting to be read by me. "Let's see what's going on in the world today."

"Hey, baby. Here's your dinner." She set my plate of meatloaf, asparagus, and brown rice in front of me. It was one of my favorite dishes. She really did treat me well.

"Thank you, babe."

She sat down in a chair diagonally across from me and watched me eat. She smiled ever so brightly. I knew that she had something up her sleeve.

"All right." I set my fork down and focused all my attention on her. "What's wrong?"

"Nothing, babe." She was lying and I could tell. Her eyes darted away from me momentarily and that was all I needed to see.

"Chrissy, spill it." I spoke with authority.

"Well, since you asked." I didn't know why she was acting this way, but I knew she was conniving as could be at times. I didn't know that until after I married her, but that was a topic for later on; I needed to know what she wanted now.

"Is everything at work okay?" She reached out and put her hand over mine.

I looked down at it and smiled. "Christine, why are you asking me about this?" My appetite was spoiled now. Hungry and angry was not a good combination on me. She knew this, too.

"Well, I got a call from Tasha and she said that Kyle kind of had some issues with the way you were treating him."

"Oh, really." *That sniveling little punk can't handle a little bit of pressure.* I was beginning to regret fucking him.

"Yes." My wife nodded her head. "She said Kyle is really upset about it. I think that you should ease up on him a little bit. Give him a little slack."

"Ease up, huh?" I was talking to myself but looking at her. At this moment, I was pissed beyond belief. I felt betrayed to have a man call on his wife and mother-in-law to come to his defense. *If he thought that I was rough on him, wait until he gets a load of me when we get back to the base. He hasn't seen anything yet.*

"Yes, please, babe. Do it for Tasha. Do it for me." She got up and walked over to me. She walked behind me and blew on the back of my ear. She thought that she would soften me up with some sex, but I just wasn't for it tonight. "Will you do it for me, soldier?" She now had her tongue in my ear.

"Not tonight, babe, I'm exhausted." I got up from the table, removed my napkin from my collar, and walked out to the living room, up the stairs, and into the bathroom to get in the shower. I stripped down until all of my clothes were off. I folded them and placed them on the top of the wicker hamper and turned on the shower. Truth of the matter was I was turned on by Kyle wanting me to ease up. It meant I had control. I loved control. I breathed it more than I did air. I stepped into my shower after measuring the temperature with my wrist. I lathered up with some Irish Spring body wash and began to wash all over. Kyle's plump behind popped into my head and pretty soon I was massaging my dick to a full erection. I leaned up against the wall of the shower and worked myself up really well. I even moaned Kyle's name a few times. I knew that my wife was downstairs cleaning up after me and doing her housewife duties. I was up here alone. It didn't take long for me to shoot my load onto the floor of shower and watch it go down the drain.

"Damn." I shook my head at the intensity of my session with myself. I was truly spent. I finished washing up and got out of the shower. I heard footsteps in the next room and assumed it was my wife getting ready for bed as well. I walked into my bedroom with a towel around my waist. She had a big smile on her face.

"You ready for bed, baby?"

"Yes, I am truly exhausted." I went over to the bed and grabbed the underwear and T-shirt that she had laid out for me. As I sat there on the edge of the bed, she came over with some lotion and worked my arms and legs over really good. I rolled over and went to sleep a happy man a few minutes later.

Chapter 11

Kyle

The Quiet One

I was in the base's barbershop getting my hair trimmed up, with a lot on my mind. Mainly how my day was going to go. For the last couple of days my father-in-law had been a little nicer to me than usual. I knew that my wife had something to do with it, and even though I told her not to, I knew she still talked to her mom about it. That was the one thing about my wife and her mother that bothered me the most: the closeness of their relationship. I mean, I knew that a mother and daughter were supposed to be close, but these two took it to a whole new level. They talked on the phone every day, they shopped together, cooked the same meals, and wore some of the same outfits. I mean, that was just plain ridiculous and too much for two people. I didn't say anything most of the time, because I knew that being a military wife could be lonely with me being gone weeks at a time. And even though we only lived two and a half hours away from the base, she still couldn't just pop up when she felt like it. All she had was her mom, the kids, and the phone calls during the week to get her by until I got off on leave.

"All right, soldier, you're done." The soldier cutting my hair broke me out of my train of thought. "See you in a few weeks."

"Okay, see you then." I got up out of my chair and walked over to one of the mirrors on the wall and surveyed my fresh cut.

"Nothing like a fresh cut." The usually quiet soldier who spoke up in the mess hall spoke to me. The other day when the other guys were teasing me about how hard my father-in-law was treating me, he was the one who said that it would get better as soon as someone else new came along. After that, I started to notice him a little more around the base. It let me know that I needed to open my eyes up and pay more attention to my surroundings. He looked like a cool brother. But looks were deceiving, especially around here. I planned on staying a loner. It was better that way.

"Yeah, man, that is so true," I spoke while still looking in the mirror. He was in another mirror looking at his fresh cut. He must have been in another chair at the same time I was. Again, I didn't notice that until now. I rarely went into any part of the base and just stared brothers down. It was just something you didn't do. In here, "don't ask, don't tell" was in full effect. You had to act a certain way, walk a certain way, and talk a certain way. Any deviation would send up red flags in people's heads. Don't get me wrong, I knew that there were some brothers on the base who were gay; you could see it in their eyes. I, being someone who had had experience with it, could tell. It takes one to know one, as they say. I kept it all to myself.

"Take it easy." I breezed past him and out of the door. I was a computer tech on the base and I had a few that needed to be inspected today. A few feet away from the door, the guy jogged up to me.

"Dude, what's the hurry?" He walked beside me and spoke.

"I have some work to do." I looked at him briefly and then continued to walk and look straight ahead. "I need to get it done and over with."

"Sarge must really be on you. You don't play when it comes to your work and getting it done. I have noticed that about you. You like to be seen and not heard."

"Is that true?" I was talking about the "Sarge being on me" part, when I stopped walking and looked at him.

"Yeah, man, you do 'how high' real well when it comes to Sergeant Harris." He was smiling like it was a joke. I didn't see it as funny.

"So what you're saying is that I'm a topic of discussion around here?"

"Nah, people just take notice after a while."

"Private Bryant," I said, reading his name badge. "I mind my business in here, plain and simple. I would appreciate it if you and whoever else has me as a topic of discussion would mind your business as well. I'm on this base to do my job and not make friends. Tell them that." I walked off and left him standing there with a dumb look on his face.

As I made it to one of the offices on base, the one I was supposed to be working in, I walked in with yet another problem on my mind. *Is minding my business and staying to myself really bad for my army career?*

I had been this way all of my life. It was the way that my parents raised me to be. A child is to be seen and not heard. I planned on passing those same ideals on to my boys. I was an observer and I was taught who to deal with just by watching people every day. *I am so confused right now. Do I really need to be more outgoing?* I thought that I was. I always smiled and spoke when I entered a room. I had brief conversations with my buddy Clifton. You know, wife and kids stuff and maybe a little talk about sports, but that was it.

I thought as I worked. The more I thought the less work I got done. After a while, I was just sitting at a desk by a window looking at the activities that where going on around the base: marching troops, Jeeps driving to and fro, and even some joggers running around the base.

"I wonder what secrets these guys have got locked up in their heads." I spoke my inner thoughts out loud. I was always curious whether all men functioned the same. I mean secret wise. Keeping them bottled up until it or they exploded. I wondered if women were better at keeping them than men.

A few minutes later, I cleaned up the small mess that I made and made my way back to my barrack. I wasn't sure how this thing called life was going to work out, but I hoped that it would get better soon. I didn't know how long I could remain "the quiet one."

I had a book in my locker that was calling me to read it and I did just that. I read until I was sleepy. Tonight I went to bed hoping for a better tomorrow. It sounded clichéd but, hey, it's the truth.

Chapter 12

Tasha

Family Time

"La de da . . . la de da." I hummed to myself as I folded some of my husband's and children's clothes in our laundry room. I was in a good mood. No, I was in a great mood. They all were upstairs watching television and playing while I was down in the basement doing my duty. A proud mother and wife was what I was proud to be.

I was glad that things had smoothed over for Kyle and my father. My mother assured me that everything was going to be okay and I knew that from previous experience I could trust her. "Momma knows best" was my motto. I was one now and I knew that I had to be a good example to my children, like my mother was to me.

My parents were coming over later on for a family dinner and family time. I loved having everybody at home and things going just right. Life couldn't get any better than to have a good family and great food on a day like today. What more could I ask for?

I grabbed the wicker basket filled to the top with clothes and made my way back upstairs to put them away in the appropriate homes.

"Hey, babe." My husband turned and looked at me on the sofa as he bounced the baby on his lap. I smiled inside when he said that. My husband was the perfect father. He was so good with the kids. "You need help with that?" he asked as he sat the baby in the baby swing.

"No, baby, I'm fine. It's very light." The truth was, my back was hurting a little bit, but I knew that this was a part of my job as a wife. I had to make it easy for my man since he was off working so hard to keep his family fed, clothed, and housed. "Thanks for asking though." I leaned over really quickly and gave him a peck on the lips. The softness of them made me want to sex him really good later on tonight when my parents left and the children fell asleep.

I climbed the stairs and walked into the baby's room to straighten up and then I did my room as well. Forty minutes later, I was downstairs in the kitchen, preparing to start the meal for the day. Meatloaf, cabbage, baked ziti, and rolls were on the menu, so I had to get started right away. It was 2:00 P.M. and my parents would be here at five o'clock sharp. We were an army family and we did everything on time.

I was in the kitchen putting the finishing touches on the dinner. I already had the table set for four plus the children's highchairs when I heard the doorbell ring.

I gracefully put down the potholders and made my way to the front door. I heard Kaynon call out, "Nana" as I walked past the living room and opened the front door. This happened often and he knew like clockwork that his Nana was at the door.

"Hey, Ma. Hey, Daddy." They both kissed me on the cheek as they entered. I took their coats and put them in the coat closet by the door. They immediately went into the living room with Kyle and the children.

"Dinner will be done in a few." I peeked in momentarily and then headed back to the kitchen to finish up. Just as I got in the kitchen the timer for the rolls chimed, letting me know that they were done and ready to be pulled from the oven. I carefully removed them and placed them on the counter for a few minutes to let them cool. I grabbed the main dish and the sides and took them into the dining room and placed them in the center of the table.

I smiled as I walked into the living room to get everyone for dinner. "Dinner is served."

"All right, baby girl." My daddy smiled. I loved seeing my daddy smile. It meant he was proud of me. I smiled inside too. I prided myself on honoring my parents and making them proud. They were my first foundation, next to my husband.

"Smells good, baby girl." My father sat down at the head of the table, while Kyle sat down at the other end. Momma and I were in the middle. She had Farrow and I had Kaynon.

I fixed Kyle his plate and my mother fixed Daddy's. We did the same for the children.

"You sure are your mother's daughter, because this meatloaf is a delicious." He dug into his meatloaf and savored it with a satisfied moan.

"Thanks, Daddy." I was floating on cloud nine.

"She sure is," my mother chimed in.

Chapter 13

Henry

Let the Games Begin

We all sat at the dining room table savoring the great meal that my daughter had cooked. I looked over at Kyle across the table as he solemnly ate his food. We shared a few glances as the women were feeding the children. Lust made my dick stiff against my thigh as I thought about fucking him again. I wanted some ass today, right now. Only his ass would do.

"Kyle, you're kind of quiet over there." A sinister smile covered my face. "Is everything okay?"

"Yes, sir." He looked at me plainly. "Everything is just fine."

It had been a few weeks since our last sexual encounter and I knew that he thought that he was home free. I was just playing cat and mouse with him. I told my wife that I would let up on him and I did, but that was getting old. An old man like me needed some adventure, something to help me deal with the everyday stress. My son-in-law was the perfect scapegoat for my outlet.

"Oh . . . okay, I was just asking." I grabbed a roll from the bread basket and took a bite out of it. "The game is coming on later, how about you and I retire to the basement and look at it on that big plasma television while the ladies tend to the children and the dishes?"

"Oh, Daddy, that is a good idea," Tasha chimed in with a bright smile. She didn't know that she was sending her husband downstairs to be manhandled by me. I should have been ashamed of myself, but I wasn't.

"I'm not really up to any *games* today." He looked at me with a smile. He was a smart mouth little bastard. That was a turn-on for me. Didn't he know by now that playing hard to get only made me play harder and for keeps? When would he ever learn?

"Awww, come on baby." Tasha gave him the puppy dog face that I knew would break him down.

He was quiet for a few seconds, but he eventually gave in.

"Okay." That was all he could mutter in defeat. He faked a smile, but I knew that he was not feeling this situation. He knew that I was going to lay down the pipe when we got down in that basement. It was inevitable. I had two condoms in my wallet just for that purpose. The dinner was great, the kids were excellent, but free sex with your son-in-law was priceless.

Fifteen minutes later, we were down in the basement with the game on. I made a suggestion to Tasha and Christine to take the children to the park since it was such a nice day outside. They agreed and as soon as I heard that front door shut it was on between me and Kyle. I could feel his warm insides already waiting for me to make my way into his man hole.

"Daddy, we're leaving," Tasha yelled down the stairs at us. "You guys don't have too much fun."

"All right, baby girl." I had already unzipped my pants and had my dick out as soon as she shut the door to the basement.

"You know the drill." I looked over at Kyle, who was sitting in a La-Z-Boy recliner, acting like he was watching the game.

"Nah, man. It's not going to happen." He didn't even look at me when he spoke. He was pissing me off. I couldn't whip his ass in his house because that would leave too much to be explained.

"Boy, if you don't get over here . . . Don't forget you're in my fucking army now. You're my little soldier and I am breaking you in every chance I get."

"Damn, muthafucka, why can't you find somebody else to fuck? I'm tired of this shit. You don't care anything about your damn wife, your daughter? What about my children, man? Think about them, your grandchildren." He sounded like he was on the verge of a breakdown.

"Am I fucking them?" I asked him.

"Your grandkids?" he asked, confused.

"Yes, muthafucka. I am not fucking them, I'm fucking you. Be concerned with me right now and not them."

"Damn, you are a cold muthafucka." He shook his head in disgust. I probably would have been disgusted too but, hey, I was running the show. I had nut in my sack waiting to be let loose.

"Yeah, man, whatever. Think about that shit while you sucking my dick. As a matter a fact, take that shit out on my dick. Put all that energy you using now into giving me some serious head. Do that."

He got down on his knees and took me into his mouth and did just that. Within minutes I was cumming on his face; a record for an old man like myself.

I fucked him for almost an hour before I was exhausted. I took a nap on the sofa upstairs and was awakened by Kaynon jumping on my lap.

"Pop-pop." He kissed me on the cheek. Instantly it made me feel like shit. I didn't know how I could be so cruel. I guess the saying 'hurt people hurt people' comes into play. I picked him up and cradled him in my arms. I stared at him for a few seconds and my rocky childhood came flooding back. I put him down and patted him on the butt to send him over to his grandma. She had a blank look on her face.

"You ready to go, baby?" she asked as she looked at me intensely. "You look tired."

"Yes, babe. I sure am."

"Tasha, we're leaving." She was in the mini bathroom down the hall changing the baby. I got up and walked down the hall to where she was and gave her a kiss and a hug. My wife grabbed our coats and we made our way home.

Chapter 14

Kyle

Getting to Know You

I was back on the base and it was a few days from the last encounter with my father-in-law at my house. Staying away or avoiding him on base was damn near impossible. Although, lately he had been busy with some new recruits and had little time to harass me. I just hoped that he found some fresh meat in this bunch and left me alone for good. I knew that it was a selfish thing to ask but I felt myself slipping. The more I had sex with him, the more I wanted to do it with other men. It took me a long time to get away from my past and it seemed like my future with my family was slipping through my hands. I began to look at men in *that* way again and I began to have "gaydar" again. I needed an out and in a hurry. I was seriously thinking about a transfer to a different base in another state that was far, far away from her father and his drama. That was the only option that I could think of, but convincing my wife was a whole different story. She literally would have a mental conniption for sure. If I even mentioned pulling her away from her parents and to an unknown state with no family to support her she would die. It didn't help that I would be on the base a lot of the time. I was between a rock and a hard place.

It was the afternoon and I was hungry. I did my work for the day and all I could think of doing was getting a hot meal from the canteen and laying myself down. It was last call when I walked into the canteen so I quickly grabbed a tray and made my way toward the food service area. The place had a few folks in it eating and socializing. I went through the line, selected my food, and found me a corner to eat in. I had a lot of thinking to do and I really didn't want any bother. I nodded my head a few times at some brothers I associated with from time to time.

The food wasn't all that like my wife's cooking, but it did what it was supposed to do: fill me up.

"Hey, what's up, soldier?" It was the quiet dude again. He was standing in front of me with his tray of food in hand. He wasn't quiet anymore. "Can I have a seat?"

I looked around the room for a second. I wasn't really sure what dude's MO was but I decided to give him another chance after what happened the other day.

"Sure." I nodded my head. *He's not a bad-looking dude,* I thought. I didn't notice that before.

"I wanted to apologize for the other day." He had an apologetic frown on his face. "It was uncalled for and unprofessional."

"Okay."

"That's all you have to say is okay?"

"Yes." I nodded.

"Another one-word answer." He shot back at me a look like, "What's up with this dude?"

"Not much really for me to say," I countered.

"Sergeant Harris must really have you wound up."

The thought of his name made me tense up. The hairs on my arm stood up and my breath labored a little. I never had a panic attack before, but I knew the signs.

"Humph," was all I could get out as I leaned back in my chair and breathed out a frustrated breath. I looked around the room again and noticed that a few of the people who were left inside had gotten up and left the canteen.

"Dude, I have something that could take his ass out of this muthafuckin' army for good. I'm talking about a muthafuckin' dishonorable discharge." He was leaned over the table with a hushed tone. He had a dead serious look on his face. I perked up instantly.

"Oh, really." I seemed interested but not overly so.

"Yeah, man. I got some stuff that would blow this base up. His ass wouldn't even be able to show his face up in here ever again."

"Is it really solid evidence?" My stress level immediately went down. I was on the beaches of Hawaii right now—basking in the breeze of freedom from Sergeant Harris. Yep, I was already there. I could see me and my wife rolling around in the sand while the kids made sandcastles.

"It's as solid as you and me sitting right here right now." His assurance was written all over his face.

"So what do I have to do to get this evidence and why are you so eager to help me out?" I wasn't anybody's fool. I knew that there was a catch with this.

"Well . . ." He paused and then leaned over toward me again. "Four words: 'don't ask, don't tell.'" A smile crept across his face.

"What's that?" I played dumb. I didn't know him from a bag of rocks. He wasn't pulling out any information from me and then putting me on blast. Hell nah.

"Ha ha ha," he laughed a little to himself. "You are very good."

"That I know." I smirked.

"Okay, let's stop playing games. I know about you and I know you know about me."

"Come again?" I said, playing dumb again.

"Your ass is like Fort Knox with the personal business."

"I like it that way." I smiled.

"I know you like it other ways, too." He smiled harder than me. "I like it that way too."

"Okay." I folded my arms in front of my chest. "Where are you going with this?"

"I need me *some* in order to get you what you want."

"*Some?*" I raised my eyebrows in curiosity.

"Yep, I think two helpings of *some* would suffice."

"Let me think about it."

"Don't think too long. Things have a way of disappearing around here." He got up from the table and turned around and bent over to tie his boot. He didn't bend his knees. He had a very nice ass, to say the least. Think about giving him some had taken up residence in my mind and I knew that it was going to happen. *Why not get me some in the process of taking Sergeant Harris down or the threat of it? It's going to be one of the last times I do it anyway.*

Should I feel guilty for even thinking about ending a man's career? I mean this could really hurt my wife since she is a daddy's girl. I didn't want to hurt her, but I knew I had to do this. I had to at least get him to back up off of me. If I showed him the proof maybe he would leave me alone. He had a proof of my activities and I soon would have proof of his. We would be even. I hoped.

A few minutes later, I put my trash in the trash and made my way back to my sleeping quarters. I was almost happy enough to skip my way back. Almost.

Chapter 15

Henry

Old Times

"What's going on, soldier?" I was sitting in my car in the army parking lot getting ready to leave as an old acquaintance walked by. He had a tight, little bootie in his fatigue pants. I was always a sucker for round boy ass.

He froze like a deer caught in headlights. He was petrified, I could tell. I always had that effect on my boy toys. I needed them afraid of me and afraid to cross me.

"Good day, Sarge!" He saluted me. His smile was weak and fake. I didn't care because I needed some ass and he was next in line.

"Where you headed to?" I inquired, not really caring about the answer though. I already had a change of plans for him.

"With you?" He already knew the deal.

"You know it." I unlocked my passenger door so that he could get in. I was going to take him to the motel a mile or two from here and fuck his brains out and then go home.

"Nothing like old times, eh!" I smiled as I pulled off. He didn't have on the happiest face, but I didn't care. His faggot ass was scared to be outed and I used that against him as well. I always said that it was best to not keep secrets that you didn't want anyone to use against you. Yeah, I know what you are thinking, he could easily find my wife and tell her about us, but I would then have to call his father—that was, a well-known anti–gay rights congressman—and let him know that his son has been taking little soldiers down his throat. How would it look for a congressman who could be our next president having a son who spent more time on his knees than a preacher? Our little secret was safe for sure. I had no doubt that he would keep quiet.

We got to the motel and I waited in the car while he paid and got the key to our room. I never let anyone see my face when I came out to do these types of things. I had a reputation to keep and a job as well.

When we got into the room he immediately did what was expected.

"Ahhh." I rubbed the top of his head and then palmed it as he took me into his mouth. His mouth was so warm, almost hot as an oven. It was just like riding a bike; because once you learn how to suck a dick there is no way to unlearn it. My dick fit into his mouth like O.J. Simpson and that bloody glove: tight like a muthafucka. "Damn, you still got it." He ignored me as he continued to assault my piece with his mouth.

I was thrusting and thrusting into his mouth. I sat down on the bed because I was a little tired from my day's work.

He was giving me the head of my life and then I felt my phone ringing on the side of waist.

"Hello," I answered the phone. My breathing was a little labored. He was sucking me like a Hoover vacuum.

"Hey, baby." My wife spoke sweetly into the phone. "Is everything okay? You're breathing hard."

"I'm just training another soldier."

"This late?"

"Yes, this late," I countered. "Is there a problem?"

"No, no." She backed down quickly. "I was just ask-ing. I'm sorry, baby."

"Yeah, okay. Don't let it happen again." I was lying back on the bed while talking to her. The job the soldier was doing on my dick caused my midsection to rise up off of the bed involuntary. "Look, I have to go. I'll see you when I get home." I hung up the phone.

She knew not to disturb me when I was at work and to wait for me to get home. She was only to call me in times of emergency. We were going to have a talk when I got home.

The soldier in between my legs hadn't stopped for one second while I was on the phone. He was a good little soldier.

"All right, soldier, off of your knees and onto the bed." I got up and watched as he did as he was told. He stripped down to his birthday suit and positioned himself on all fours. That's what I liked: a man who knew how to play his position and played it well. Kyle could learn some-thing from this soldier. I hadn't played with him in a while. I guessed I would give him a day or two more of rest and then continue with my fun. There is nothing like a man and his toys. I loved being a big boy with toys.

I strapped a condom on my dick that was still hang-ing out of my front zipper. There was no need for me to undress. I was going to fuck him and head on home to the misses. I loved being in control.

I pulled up to my house totally famished. The sexual tricks that boy could do wore me out. My legs felt like

Jell-O when I walked out of that motel room. He was such a loyal bootie hole. I needed to whip Kyle into the shape that I had in him. I loved total submissiveness in a sexual partner.

I got out my car and walked up to the door and, like clockwork, my wife opened the door, looking very beautiful and adoring. She was always there for me and keeping me together and happy. I couldn't ask for more.

"Hey, baby." She kissed me on the cheek as I entered our house. A neat and clean environment to live in was a must and she never let me down. She and I had some agreements when we got married and she had been keeping up her end of the bargain on all of them, plus some perks, too. That one slip-up today was forgivable, but I had to let her know that it was unacceptable to happen again. I was the head; she wasn't.

"Hello, dear." My tone was even and plain. I wanted her to have to guess at how I was feeling. I hated to make her feel guilty for my stuff, but hey, it was a part of the territory with me.

"I just wanted to say that I am sorry for earlier." She spoke to me as I walked to the dining room and sat down in my usual chair and waited on the meal I knew that she prepared. Again, I had it good. I was having my cake and eating it, too. There was nothing like it.

"It's okay, dear." I put my hand on her waist as she was now standing in front of me. She looked sorry enough for me to forgive her. "Just don't let it happen again."

"I promise it won't happen ever again." She smiled. I had to admit that I loved her in a way. Her smile was beautiful. It just wasn't enough for me. I had other needs that she could not meet.

"Good." I smiled back. "I'm famished from a busy day. Is my dinner ready?"

"Yes, it sure is." She made her way to the kitchen and before long my plate of hot food was sitting before me. I finished and made my way up to bathroom and then to bed. I had it good.

Chapter 16

Kyle

A Done Deal

"Okay, I'll do it." I spoke to myself in the mirror after I had brushed my teeth. I had to do what I had to do. I just hoped this deal was worth it. I had been going back and forth with doing it and not doing it. I just didn't want to hurt my wife, but the truth hurt and I knew I had to do it. But I would only do it if I felt like I had to do it. This proof was as a last resort. An option . . . It took me about a week to get up the nerve to say yes. I felt a little apprehensive about this, because it would officially mean that I was cheating on my wife. I know what you are thinking: I was cheating when I started messing around with her father, but my logic was that it was not solicited on my part so it wasn't officially cheating. I was doing it to keep my life together. But the same argument could be said for why I was meeting with this guy now. "This shit doesn't make a lick of sense to me." I shook my head in confusion. It was just one big mess that I hoped ended with my life intact.

I walked out of the bathroom feeling fresh and refreshed. I had washed every orifice of my body because I had a feeling I was going to be going all in on this brother. I for once was in control—well, partially anyway. If I was going to do this I was going to get it in good for the very last time. I just hoped he wasn't playing me for some dick. There was no way to tell so I had to see it out to the end.

I pulled up to a sleazy-looking motel a couple of miles from the base and made my way to the room that dude told me earlier. I was a little nervous as I walked down the long balcony that stretched across the second story of the establishment. I looked around nervously, because I wasn't used to this sneaky type of living. I just wanted this to be over with.

I knocked on the door three times like he said and then the door opened. There was soft music playing as I entered the shabby room. He had a couple of candles lit. His trying to create ambiance was lost on me because I was here on a mission. Even though I had a small side mission of physical gratification he didn't have to know that. Every man likes a good nut and I was no exception.

"You ready, soldier?" he said as he walked over to the bed and crawled across it on all fours. He was totally effeminate now, nothing like he was on base. Every bit of his quiet, hard exterior was gone. He looked like a queen as he stuck a finger in his mouth and slowly pulled it out. Part of me was turned on and the other part wanted to get the fuck away from this queen. "I've been thinking about this all of the time you made me wait. I secretly had a crush on you. I wanted you from the day I saw you. I didn't think that you and I would ever hook up because you always stayed to yourself. But here you are and here I am." He rolled over on the bed onto his stomach and then onto all fours. He had a nice, round butt that he popped to let me know that he wanted to be fucked and fucked good. A little drool eased out of the side of my mouth as I watched him gyrate and bounce. I had never experienced a gay man of his caliber. He was extremely flamboyant and open. Again, a complete contrast to what he showed on base. It made me wonder what I was really missing being on base. Who else was like this behind closed doors?

"Yeah, I'm ready," I said as I started to unbutton my shirt. I was a little thrown by his appearance and it showed as I fumbled with my shirt.

"Let me get that." He hopped up off of the bed and seductively sashayed over to me. His hips switched just like a woman's. Could have put my wife's head on his body and I would have thought it was her walking toward me. He had it down. Again, I was in awe. Most of the men I encountered in my short gay life, which were few, never acted like this. I almost didn't want him to touch me because he was so over the top.

He slowly unbuttoned my shirt and pulled the rest that was tucked in my pants out and threw it onto the floor. Then he pulled my white T-shirt off over my head and threw that on the floor as well.

Then he did something that I never saw before. He started to lick my pecks and suck on them like they were his mother's and he was an infant. The sensation that I felt made my dick harder than it already was. A few moans escaped my mouth as he stroked my dick in the process.

"You like?" He looked up at me and then eased his way down my chest to my navel and then to my dick. He started to lick the impression of my dick through my pants. He softly bit it, which drove me wild. My mind was racing with exhilaration. He unlatched my belt and pulled my pants down to my ankles. He took off my shoes and I then stepped out of my pants. I was standing there with my tight boxer briefs and my dick lying hard on my thigh. You could see where his saliva had soaked through my pants and underwear. My thoughts were, *where they do that at?* but I continued to let him do what he did best.

"He looks so happy." He was talking to my dick like it had a mind of its own. I could tell that he was a dick connoisseur and he loved it. He sucked on it through my underwear once again. I was in a small trance with my eyes closed. I felt him stop and I opened my eyes. He got up and guided me to the bed. He aggressively pushed me down on the bed. I fell back and the control that I thought I would have or wanted was long gone. He had me gone. I was not expecting this. He pulled my underwear off of me and my dick stood up at full attention.

He took me into his mouth fully and engulfed me on the first slurp. I was amazed at his prowess and control of his gag reflexes. He was a professional for sure. My mouth involuntarily opened as he bobbed up and down on me. He was sucking so hard that the bed moved with every bob. He was fucking my dick with his mouth which was another new thing for me. Then I felt myself about to cum. I exploded like I had never before.

I lay there because it felt like my legs were paralyzed. His ass needed to be a porn star or something. Skill like this was a gift. I couldn't say from God, because well . . . you know.

"Are you ready for some more?" He had on a bright smile as he stood in front of me with a condom in his hand. "I am going to ride the rest of them babies out of your balls."

I was almost scared, if that was possible.

"Sure." That was all I could muster up along with a fake smile. Sex like this should have been illegal. Shit, it was! Again, I liked a good nut like any man, but damn. He took dick loving to the extreme. He climbed onto the bed and took a sumo wrestler's stance over my torso. I breathed in hard because I knew this brother was going in for the kill. He took my dick in his hand and then guided it into his bottom and a few strokes were all it took for him to get a good rhythm going. I was holding on to the sides of the bed and my inexperience showed.

"You like it, daddy!" He bounced and bounced and smiled.

"You good as shit," I huffed. "A muthafuckin' pro."

"Being . . . all I . . . could be . . . didn't start . . . in the army . . . for me." He was talking and bouncing at the same time. "But that's . . . another story . . . for . . . another . . . time."

I just nodded my head as he rode and ground into my hips. I could only concentrate on what was happening below my waist. All that he was saying was going in one ear and out of the other. I felt the build-up in my balls letting me know I was about to explode. He must have sensed it because he hopped up off of me and got on his knees in front of the bed. I hopped up and stroked until I came on his face.

I sat down on the bed, totally exhausted. He went into the bathroom and came out with a washcloth and proceeded to wash off my genitals and the surrounding area.

"You have to take care of him," he said as he kissed my flaccid dick and then got up.

"It was good." I smiled. I so wanted to be out of here in the next five minutes. "You got what I came for?"

"Damn, you right to the point, aren't you?" He looked a little disappointed. I wasn't looking for anything, especially a friend-with-benefits package. Most of the time those benefits were counteractive and I didn't need nor want anything else to set me back. I already had to live

with the fact that I had to do him and go home to my
wife and kids, pretending that nothing happened.

"No, I just have to go home to my wife and kids. They
are expecting me to be home at a certain time." I tried
to look as remorseful as I could. I didn't know dude at
all. He could have been a basket case or something like
that.

"Oh, I understand. I got a little one at home too."

"Huh?" My mouth hit floor. I would have never
guessed that in a million years. I have truly seen and
heard it all. It was official: I was leaving this shit behind
me for sure.

"Don't look surprised. I can have a family and secrets
too." He burst my bubble. If I didn't know it before, I
knew it now: he and I were the same. Sleeping with
men and going home to your family was the same if you
were feminine or not.

"You're right." I nodded my head in acceptance. I
didn't know why I thought I was better than him, but
he brought me back around fast.

"I'm sorry," I apologized. "I'm not used to this. I just
needed to get what I came for so I can go."

"I hear you loud and clear. 'Don't ask, don't tell' is a
bigger burden than most know and it started way before the army pegged it."

"True," I concurred

He went to a bag in the corner and pulled out a disk,
which I assumed had my evidence on it.

"Here's what you came for." He handed me the disk.
"And don't worry about the second helping of *some*."

"Thanks," I said somberly. I proceeded to pick up my
clothes and put them on. I was out of the hotel room
and headed home within fifteen minutes after some
more brief chitchat. I didn't know what was on the disk
but I knew that it was going get me a get off free pass
with Sergeant Harris.

Before I got home, I went to the liquor store and got me some hard liquor to drink. It was out of the norm for me but I needed something to get the edge off. I didn't know how Sergeant Harris was going come off at me when I showed him this disk that I had.

The other dude said that I could tell the sergeant who gave it to me because he was shipping out tonight to a base all the way in California. He also told me to tell him to "kiss his warm, tight ass good-bye." The sergeant must have treated him very badly for him to want to come at him like that. I didn't even ask what happened; I just got what I needed and bounced.

After getting my drink, I sat in my car a couple of houses down from mine and drank my liquor in peace. I knew my wife was not going to be happy and I knew that she would be suspicious, but I would just tell her that we had a sendoff party for one of the boys on the base. I just hoped she believed me.

I pulled up to the door and I put the CD underneath my seat compartment for safe keeping until I figured out what to do with it. I grabbed my duffle bag and headed into the house.

Chapter 17

Tasha

Out to Lunch

"No, no, no, no way. No way I'm living without you." I sang Jennifer Hudson's version of "And I Am Telling You" to the baby with the spoon that I had stirred my lunch with a few seconds ago. It was a normal day during the week and my home was spotless. I had my days when I would get bored around here. And sometimes I would think about finding me a job and putting the kids into daycare, but I always shrugged it off. I enjoyed doing what I did.

My husband would be home later on and I was taking my kids over to my parents' house so we could get some more one on one, hopefully make me that little girl I always wanted. I couldn't complain because I loved my boys, but I always wanted to have a little girl who I could place the same values in that my mother placed in me.

My husband and I discussed it a few times and we thought it would be better when he got a little higher in rank and on a bigger pay scale. He was moving up the ranks a little; soon he would go from private to specialist. I just hoped it was soon enough. I wanted my little girl soon, because I wanted all of my children close in age so when they headed on out into the world it would almost back to back that they left the house. Yes, I was planning my children's exits. I was a planner by nature and I loved to have goals set in place.

When Kyle got home he was drunk as a skunk. I had never seen him this way before. I was a little shocked, to say the least. My husband was not the type to be inebriated the way he was or at all. I had never seen him take a drink in the whole time of us being together. Well, we had had wine with dinner once or twice but that was it. Something wasn't right with this situation. I was going to get to the bottom of it.

"Baby, what's going on?" He was stretched out on his back across our sectional. Thank goodness the kids were taking a small nap. I didn't want him breathing his smelly breath all over them. He smelled like he could give them liquor poisoning by just looking at him.

"No . . . Nothing is wrong. I'm the happiest . . . happiest . . . happiest . . . happiest . . . man on the whoooooole wide planet." He had on the silliest smirk on his face, like a drunken joker.

"Okay." I looked at him, puzzled. I didn't know what to think right now. "Where did this drinking come from?"

"Oh, some of the fellas from the base and I went out for some drinks. One of the guys is transferring to another base. We sent him off with a . . . ooooh, shit." He sat up real quick, startling me. I was on the other end of the sectional as I watched him vomit on my nice carpet.

"Oh my God, my carpet." I yelled a little. I covered my mouth so I wouldn't wake the children I had the baby monitor on my hip while I cleaned the house a little.

"Damn, baby, I'm sorry. This is the first time in a long time that I have been this fucked up." He wiped his mouth with the back of his hand. I was sick to my stomach just looking at the pile of vomit on my carpet.

"That's all right, babe," I said, getting up out of my seat and headed toward the utility closet. "I'll clean it up. Just go on upstairs and get in the shower, because you have throw-up all over you." My face was frowned up because adult vomit and baby vomit were too different types of vomit. Adults' vomit smelled far worse than babies' vomit.

"Thank you, baby." He slurred as he got up, staggered a little, and then rode the banister all the way upstairs. I watched him bobble a little when he got to the top. I prayed that he would make it to the bedroom without waking the kids. I didn't hear anything after a few seconds so I assumed that he made it. I just hoped he didn't vomit in my bed. I was going to hurt him if he did.

"Crazy self." I shook my head and went back to cleaning the carpet. "Eww," I mumbled as I got on my knees and began to spray and scrub. A couple of minutes later I was finished. I was thinking that I would do a second scrub on it but decided against it. It was six in the afternoon and I usually didn't leave the house this late with the kids, but I decided to get out of the house and take the children over to my mother's house for the rest of the evening and let Kyle have a peaceful slumber. I didn't want the boys to be getting loud and wake him up. I had had a hangover once and loud noises were painful.

It didn't take me long to clean up the house a little bit more and then get the boys ready to go.

I took them both out to Kyle's car, with Farrow in a car seat and Kaynon walking beside me while I held his hand. I took Kyle's car because I didn't want to drive the minivan, or the mommy mobile, as I called it. Kyle's car was faster and I love the way I looked in it. I was superficial at times. I got them both into the car and headed over to my parents' house.

I pulled up to my parents' house about twenty minutes later, got the boys out of the car, and headed up the walkway to the door. Instantly, the door popped open and my father appeared with open arms as he took Farrow from me. Kaynon scurried into the house really fast.

"Pop-pop," Kaynon cooed with his arms stretched up toward my father. My father smiled and then bent down to retrieve him. I loved to see the look on my father's face when he had the kids in his arms.

"Hey, baby." My mother was coming out of the kitchen with a dish of food in her hand. "You made it."

"Yes, ma'am." I hugged her and then put down the small diaper bag I had with me. "Just in time, too." I loved my mother's cooking and hospitality; she was such a good homemaker. That was why I patterned myself after her.

"I bet," she chuckled. "Have a seat. You better be thankful I made extra." I giggled because I knew that a home-cooked meal was just what the doctor ordered. I loved to be served every now and then too.

Daddy brought the children into the dining room with us and we all sat down to eat. We ate and talked for the next two hours and then I decided to make my way back home. Surely, Kyle would be in a deep sleep now. He was going to feel it in the morning.

I pulled up in front of my house, all ready to get the kids of the car. I decided against leaving the kids over at my parents' house, because after thinking about it, I didn't want to have drunk or hangover sex with my husband. That was not the best idea of sex to me.

Farrow was wide awake and decided to launch his pacifier at me, which fell in front of me and rolled under my car seat. I fumbled and reached underneath the seat trying to reach it, but in the process I felt something else that was attached to the bottom of the car's seat. I pulled out what looked like a DVD in a clear, crystal-type case.

"What is this?" I wondered out loud. The DVD didn't have any writing on it so it made me curious about what was on it. As a woman, I was very meticulous in the things I did and saw. My stomach started to lurch a little, letting me know that something wasn't right. With all the sex tapes that these celebrities were having nowadays my stomach got even sicker. I was actually scared to watch it, but I knew now that I couldn't do anything until I did. I hated situations like these; they left you bound in suspicion and curiosity until you got to the bottom of the situation. I stuffed it in the baby's diaper bag, grabbed the kids, and went into the house.

When I got in the house I was, as they say, "out to lunch" in my head. I was gone. I was in overdrive with the possibilities that could lie on that disk. I thought about my husband's past and the tears welled up in my eyes. I didn't want to go through this. I shouldn't have been going through this.

"No," I moaned a little in despair. I didn't know what I was going to do if I had to leave my husband. I didn't have a job, and Lord knows I couldn't tell my parents what was going on. I think my father would kill him. There would a dead man and a dead woman walking if my father found out. He was so adamant about being careful about Kyle and his history, but my mother convinced him otherwise.

I assumed Kyle was still asleep, because I didn't hear any stirring going on upstairs. I was in the living room trying to put the children to sleep. The whole time my focus was on the diaper bag and the disk.

"Hush little baby don't say a word, momma's going to buy you a . . ." I paused the singing I was doing as I was rocking Farrow in my arms. I sobbed a little because my heart was breaking. I knew what the truth was already. I knew it. As a woman, I knew it. I didn't like it and I definitely didn't want to see it, but again, I had to look. I had to see. I had to know.

After an hour both of the kids were asleep. I carried both of them upstairs one by one and then I went into our bedroom and looked at Kyle sprawled out across the bed, with one leg in his pants and the other out.

"Why?" I stood in the doorway and watched his chest heave up and down repeatedly. His mouth was wide open. He was out for the count. I loved my husband, but at this moment I wanted to grab a pillow off the bed and put it over his face and end his life. I wanted to watch him fight and fight and fight and fight to breathe. I wanted to watch his arms flail in the air as the air he so desperately needed escaped him. I wanted to watch him claw at the bed as I sat on top of him and pushed down harder and harder, watching his life dissipate from his body. And after every ounce of life was gone I would spit on his face for lying to me about not ever betraying me for his past. *'Til death do us part . . . for better or worse . . . in sickness and health*. We'd had better, but was this the worse that I was waiting for? Anticipating? Pleading with to pass us by? I wasn't ready . . . I couldn't handle this . . . right now. But this was my hand that the dealer had dealt. He wasn't partial in his dealing; he just shelled out the cards and you got what you got. Here I was in this life-changing situation . . . hesitating about the inevitable.

I walked out of the room, down the steps, and into the living room. I sat down on the floor in front of the bag and just looked at it for a few minutes. It was just me and it. There was quiet all through the house. My heartbeat was the only thing that could be heard and it sounded like the police beating on a door right now.

Finally I pulled myself together and removed the disk from the bag. My hand trembled as I walked to the basement door, opened it, and closed it behind me. I felt like I was going to the showdown at the O.K. Corral. It didn't take me long to get to the bottom of the steps and place the disk into our Blu-ray player. The screen to the television came on. I didn't want to sit, but standing there in the middle of the basement seemed odd. I watched a blue screen for a few seconds and then the "movie" started.

I gasped at what I saw on the screen. A scream was what normally came out when you watched what I was watching right now. I tried to scream but nothing happened. Everything in me was dying right now. Everything. My life had drained from my legs and I collapsed onto the floor. I lay there almost paralyzed as I continued to watch the scene play out in front of me. Then I began to heave and heave and then vomit all of the food that I had eaten today.

I blacked out and awoke to a dark room. The disk had stopped and I was on the floor lying in my own liquids. I must have pissed myself as well because I felt wetness beneath me.

"Oh God, why? Why me?" I sobbed. "Not my life." I wanted the floor open up and swallow me. I wanted to die right then and there. I couldn't confront this. I didn't want to do this. How could this be happening to me? I thought that I was a good person. I thought I was exempt from this type of pain. It was now clear that I wasn't, because here I was in this situation.

After a few more minutes of wallowing, I got up and barely made it to the sofa that was against the wall. I didn't know what to do with what I had; I didn't know if I wanted to expose the truth. I wanted to go to my computer, make a copy of the disk, and put the original back where I found it, but what kind of woman would I be to do that? What kind of wife? What kind of mother? So no, I had to expose it. I just didn't know how. And then it popped into my head. I was going to do the unthinkable. I had to do it and accept the consequences.

Chapter 18

Kyle

Hung Over

I woke up the next day, as hung over as I possibly could be. I was so glad that it was a Saturday morning and I didn't really have to do anything. I felt around the bed and then snuggled up to my wife, who was sleeping like a baby.

"Morning." I kissed her on the nape of her neck. She didn't respond. I assumed she was tired, because being a full-time mother was no joke. I didn't take all that she did around here and what she did for my children for granted. So hangover and all I decided to get up and check on the children. I wobbled a little into their room and peeked into Farrow's crib and then over at Kaynon on his race car bed. They were still sleeping, but I knew that soon they would be awake, so I picked them both up and carried them downstairs. It was time for me to give my wife a break for a change.

When I got down to the kitchen everything was in order and I really didn't know where everything was located. I almost never cooked in the kitchen, because I let my wife have total control over how it was run. I wasn't the best cook, either.

My wife was a beast with organization, very detailed. We had a small kitchenette table and chair set in the kitchen so I grabbed the high chair for Kaynon and strapped Farrow into his little car seat. I was going to whip us up some good food to eat: scrambled eggs, potatoes, and ham sounded good. That was really the best thing I could cook to tell you the truth. I grabbed a bottle out of the refrigerator and heated it up in the microwave for Farrow, and gave Kaynon one of those toddler breakfasts, and prepared the meal for me and my wife. Again, I wasn't the best cook, but I did what I could in the kitchen today. I was in my robe and slippers and I had some soft jazz playing as I cooked. I was a happy man. I had evidence to get the sergeant off of my back for good. I planned on watching the tape soon to see what was on it so I could describe it to the sergeant and threaten to go to his wife and my wife if he didn't back up off of me.

While I was cooking I heard my wife sloshing down the steps in her slippers. She sauntered into the kitchen with a plain look on her face. It was completely drained and void of emotion.

"Hey, baby." I walked up to her as she just sat at the kitchenette table and played with Farrow whimsically.

"Hey." That was all she said as she looked at me with a faint smile. I could tell something was wrong. It looked as if she was more hung over than I was. I went back to cooking our food.

"Is everything okay?" I had the spatula in my hand as I turned from cooking our food. "You don't look too good."

"I'm okay." She got up out of the chair and walked over to our back door and peeked out of the curtains. She was beginning to worry me.

"You sure?" I knew that as her husband if I didn't show her that I was totally interested in her wellbeing that there would be hell to pay. My wife wasn't the typical wife; she let a lot of my foolishness slide. As a man, I knew that I could be hard to deal with and my quietness was not always a turn-on, so I knew now that communication with all people, especially my wife, was key to getting along in this world. "Babe, go in to the dining room and I'll bring you in a plate of food."

"Sure." She walked right past me. I went to kiss her on the cheek and she flinched. I was a little thrown by it.

"What's wrong?" I grabbed her by her arm lightly, and pulled her toward me. "Something's not right." I looked her in the eyes and her eyes shifted away from me. I didn't know what was going on with her, but I knew something wasn't right.

"I'm . . . I'm just not feeling well." She put her hand on her stomach and a tear slid out of her left eye. "I think I'm coming down with something."

"Really?" I asked with the sincerest concern possible. My wife almost never got sick and when she did it was not pretty. "How long have you been feeling this way?" I felt her forehead and it was slightly warm, but not feverish.

"Just a day," she mumbled. It was as if she had no energy. I let her go and she walked into the dining room. I immediately went to take-care-of-my-wife mode. She was always there for me, even at my weakest, and now it was her turn to be tended to.

I finished the food and fixed her plate. I quickly went into the dining room and placed it in front of her. She was just sitting there with a blank look on her face. I swiftly went back into the kitchen, and grabbed my plate and Farrow. I sat him close to her for a second while I went back in the kitchen to grab Kaynon and his high chair. Both of the children were bubbly and giggly at this point. This seemed to perk her up a little as a smile crept across her face as Farrow blew some spit bubbles her way. We were having a family moment and I was feeling it. It seemed liked my hangover was nonexistent as I sat there in the midst of my family.

She began to eat and so did I. She even complimented me on my fried potatoes. I was beaming on the inside. I couldn't have been any happier at that moment. I played with and tickled Farrow as he chewed on his teething ring.

It took me back to when she first had had Kaynon and we were in the hospital. It was the proudest moment of my life. I couldn't even really describe holding my son in my arms for the first time and the glow that my wife had on her before and after she had him.

I was on cloud nine that day; it seemed like all of my prayers were answered and all of my problems disappeared when he was pushed out of her womb. The only thing I didn't have was my parents to share it with. I left them a message saying that I had a son, but they never returned my calls. I assumed they were still heartbroken when I told them that I had a gay lifestyle for a few years. Again, I would call them from time to time and each time the phone would ring and go straight to voice mail. But after my son was born I washed my hands of them. It was their loss and my gain. I had a new life and I was happy. Then came the sergeant and his mess. I shuddered at the thought of him. A thorn in my side he was. *I like that . . . was.*

Then all of a sudden my wife just burst into tears and started sobbing uncontrollably. She got up and ran upstairs and then I heard the bathroom door slam shut. *She could be pregnant.* That would be a nice thing. I went back to entertaining the kids. I was hoping she would be in a better mood by tomorrow, because it was family night and her parents were coming over for dinner. I didn't want a repeat of the last time we had dinner and the sergeant wanted a special dessert.

Chapter 19

Tasha

All Cried Out

I sat on the toilet in the bathroom and sobbed uncontrollably for what seemed like hours, but in actuality it was only fifteen minutes. The looks on my family's faces this morning almost made me regret what I was going to do tomorrow.

I got up and looked at myself in the mirror. I gasped a little, because I almost didn't recognize myself. My eyes were swollen and my hair was disheveled. I looked like the ghost of Tasha and not myself. I felt like I was lost inside of myself and I was trapped in my head; my head was full of scenarios and scenes that a director controlled and not I. So much could happen tomorrow and so much would change. The truth would be revealed and I didn't know how to deal with what I saw the outcome to be. Have you done something that you *had* to? No matter the consequences you had to say it and be strong when you did it. I wanted to run; run away from all of the problems, people, pain, hurt, and dismay, but I had to stay and live for my babies and keep my head up. No matter what I had to be strong.

"Girl, get it together," I spoke to myself in the bathroom mirror.

I cut the water on and doused myself in the face to really wake me up. I grab some Bioré facial scrub off of my vanity mirror and scrubbed my face really quick.

I had to wash some of the tears and pain away.

"Serenity now, serenity now," I chanted a little as I prepared to open the bathroom door and head back to my family. I was going to make the best of this day because I didn't know what was going to happen tomorrow.

I opened the door and right in front of the door was my husband with Farrow in his arms and Kaynon standing next to him, looking like they had lost their way. My heart melted and instantly felt like there could be hope in this situation.

"How long have you been standing there?" I asked with faint smile.

"A couple of minutes." He had on that What-can-I-do-to-fix-this face.

"I'm better now." I picked up Kaynon and headed back downstairs and into the living room.

I sat down on the couch and let Kaynon play in the middle of the floor with his toys. I cut on the television so that he could have something to look at as well. *SpongeBob SquarePants* was on Nickelodeon and he was watching and playing with his toys back and forth. Kyle had come down and sat on the floor with and played with Farrow in his baby seat. I tried not to focus on the kids, but my mind wandered back again to when I was a little girl. I would play with my dolls just like my son was playing with his GI Joes right now.

When I was a little girl my mother bought me some dolls and a dollhouse. It was so big and it had all of the furniture in it. It was my favorite toy to play with. Barbie would always be waiting for GI Joe at the door to come home and have his dinner fixed and ready for him to eat. My mother would sit and play with me sometimes and for some odd reason she would always have two GI Joes from time to time in the house with Barbie. I didn't know what was going on then, but now it struck a nerve in me and I wanted to know the truth. I didn't know if I could handle it. What I was thinking the truth was made my heart beat faster and faster. It couldn't be the truth . . . It just couldn't.

"I'll be right back." I got up and went upstairs for a minute. I went to a box of old pictures I had from my childhood in my closet. I pulled it out and looked at a couple of pictures and all of them were the same. My hands started to tremble and shake and before long a couple of tears streamed out of my eyes and down on my face.

"No . . . No . . . No." I shook my head from side to side in fear of the truth. It was staring me right in the face. I threw the box and the rest of the pictures across the room and fell onto my bed face down. I sobbed and sobbed uncontrollably. I couldn't handle this and I couldn't live like this. It was driving me insane. Was my whole life a lie? What was really going on? Did I really know anything? I began to have a fit in the bed. I kicked and punched the pillows and bit into them and screamed into them. I thought I would lose my mind. I didn't know when I did, but I fell asleep and was awakened by husband calling me from the steps.

"Babe, I need you to watch the kids while I step out to the store real quick."

"Okay, I'll be right down," I answered. "Just give me a minute."

"Okay." I heard him go back down the stairs and then I sluggishly got up and went into the bathroom. I splashed some water on my face for the second time today, combed my hair a little, and then went downstairs to tend to my kids.

Chapter 20

Kyle

Lost and Found

I hopped into my car and pulled off. I couldn't help but think that my wife was acting really strange lately. She just wasn't herself. I mean I watched her while we were in the living room together and she was totally zoned out. She tried to look cool, but I knew that she was going through something. I knew my wife; she was happy all of the time. There was a pattern change and I picked up on it. At first I thought she was pregnant, but that wasn't it. I just didn't know what was. She looked so withdrawn and out of it. And when I went upstairs to check on her she was wrapped up in the comforter on our bed like it was thirty below zero. Her hair was a mess and all. My wife kept it together all of the time and this behavior she was having for the last couple of hours was out of character.

I drove for about ten minutes until I got to our local Wal-Mart and pulled to the parking lot. I ran into the Wal-Mart and went straight for the electronics department.

"Excuse me, where are the portable DVD players?" I asked the attendant of that department.

"Three aisles over and in the middle." She pointed. I walked down the aisle and spotted the section. I grabbed the first one I saw and picked it up to purchase it.

I went to the counter and waited my turn to be rung up. The line wasn't long so I was in and out in a few minutes. When I got to my car I ripped the box open and plugged the DVD player up with car charger that came with it. I felt under the seat to retrieve the disk that I placed there last night. I felt around and felt around but I couldn't feel the disk. I got out of the car and got on my knees and stuck my hand all the way under the seat. It wasn't there. I opened the back door, thinking that maybe it had slid back to the back of the car. That was no such luck.

"What is going on?" I wondered as I sat in the driver seat with my body halfway in the car and the car door open. "I know I put this disk in here." I was drunk at the time so maybe I just thought I did.

"I hope I didn't lose that shit." I was still in the parking lot and a few people looked at me like I had lost my mind. "I couldn't have lost it." I scratched my head in wonder.

Then it popped into my head that my wife had left the house for a little while yesterday. I was drunk that day, but I did get up to take a piss and get something to snack on. The whole house was empty so I knew she had taken the kids out to the park or something like that.

"She couldn't have found that disk," I tried to convince myself. The disk wasn't there and I didn't have it. *Maybe she looked at the disk. Maybe she knows everything and is waiting for the moment to kill me. These types of situation always end up with somebody getting hurt or killed. Is that the reason she was acting so weird? She could have seen the disk and is waiting for a time to strike.*

"Shit." I banged on the steering wheel. "I should have just come clean the first time her father approached me. I should have just put his ass on blast. I wouldn't be going through any of this right now."

I didn't know what was on the disk. If she watched it and something implicated me I know she would have approached me by now. The tension I was feeling eased up and I instantly felt better about the situation. Then I thought about what if the quiet guy got me for some sex and gave me a blank disk. He could have played me. One thing I knew was that I damn sure couldn't go home and ask her if she found a disk in the car. I wasn't even going to bring it up.

"Why does your past always have to come back and smack you around in life?" I said as I fully got into the car and started it up. I pulled off of the parking lot and made my way home.

Before I got home, I stopped by 7-Eleven and got her some roses. I thought it was a nice gesture. She deserved them and it had been a minute since I showed her that I really care. Part of me was also doing it because she may have known something and been waiting to take me out. I was hoping the flowers would make her smile and feel better about whatever she was going through, because it just may have been something else and didn't have anything to do with me. My drunken ass just could have lost the disk or something. I hoped.

When I got home I got in the house and the aroma of good cooking was in the air. I was all for a good meal.

"Honey, I'm home," I said as I closed the front door.

Chapter 21

Christine

If I Had Listened

I was in my bed tossing and turning all night long. I felt so uneasy on the inside. My husband was on the other side of the bed, asleep like a log. I sat up, grabbed my nightgown off of the back of the bed, and slipped into my slippers. I got up and watched my husband shift a little and then stop moving. I looked at him and then left the bedroom. I walked down the stairs and into the kitchen. I pulled a tea bag out of the container that I had on the counter and put it into a mug that was always waiting on me in the middle of my kitchen table. I grabbed a pot and boiled some water. I needed some chamomile tea to get me to sleep. The demons of my past had me up and I knew it. Every so often I would sit up this late and think about my life and how it all turned out. Now in my mid-forties, I felt like there was so much that I could have done in my life if I had only done what my parents told me to do. I wouldn't be where I was right now. I hated myself so many times of the day and no one really knew what was going on but me. People don't know when you're really going through some things, even your family. They think that you have it all together and you don't. There were days that I really wanted to just explode and/or kill myself. But that would be the easy way out.

One day I was going have to come to terms with my past and let go of some lies. I wasn't ready to do that just yet, though. I was not strong enough to handle what may have come if the lies came out of the closet. All I ever wanted was to love and be comfortable in my life. I wanted the house, the family, and the man. I had it all, but a whole lot more than I bargained for.

Now that I sat there and thought about it with my tea, I asked myself, was it really worth it? Was being stable financially really worth all of my lies and secrets? I rationalized and justified it all of my life, but now it was too late. I had to keep up the shame for the rest of my life. I had to. I wasn't forced into it by anyone but I accepted it for my own comfort.

I found out some secrets in my youth that my mother swore me to keep secret and here I was acting the same. What could I do? It was too late. If I had only listened to myself and not mimicked my parents then I probably would have had a different life now. I always wondered what would have happened if I had listened.

The way Henry talked to me sometimes always triggered this mood that I was in right now. Sometimes he could be just . . . ugh! Impossible: that was the word I would use to describe him sometimes. But I couldn't really complain about it. I was impossible at times too.

"What am I going to do?" I spoke out into the air expecting the answer to come back to me. I thought that it was going to just float into the room, pop into my head, and then everything was going to be all right, but I didn't believe in fairytales and today I wasn't going to start. There was no white horse, no man in armor, and no pot of gold at the end of the rainbow. I knew that I was on borrowed time and every day I just woke up again and asked to borrow some more time to live out my existence of lies and pain.

I finally finished up my cup of tea after sitting at the table for almost a half hour. I went to bed thinking about my parents and all I was taught. I thought I was different. I thought I had it down. I was going to be in control of my life and I was going to be in control of the people in my life. And I did what most kids did when their parents told them what to do and not to do: I didn't listen. I had a plan and I knew that I was going to get what I wanted my way and not theirs, because theirs seemed so outdated and boring. Now I wished I had listened. I didn't need an "I told you so" from anyone right now, because it was self-evident that had I listened I wouldn't be in the situation I was in now.

Chapter 22

Tasha

This Is It

"This is it," I said to myself as I was in the kitchen preparing possibly a farewell meal. I knew I was saying good-bye to someone today, but who was the question.

I had been up almost all night going over the scenario in my head. I walked into my children's room at about midnight last night trying to gather strength from their sleeping bodies. Children have that resilience that some of us adults really needed to pay attention to. I was hoping that I would be able to bounce back no matter what happened. Lord knew I sat in that room, in the rocking chair that was given to me as a baby shower gift, and sucked in the peacefulness those two breathed out. It was so serene and calm. They had no cares . . . no worries. It seemed like I had the world on my shoulders; well, my world anyway.

Here I was now in this kitchen doing what I did best: cook. I had the recipe for the food I was cooking, but the full recipe to solve my family's problems eluded me. It was missing the truth and that was the most important part. My husband did his usual part and entertained the children until my parents arrived.

I was cooking a roast, red potatoes, fresh-seasoned string beans, linguine with shrimp, and cornbread.

And for dessert there was devil's food cake with Dutch chocolate icing.

I had the stomach for none of this. I couldn't even hold down a saltine cracker on my stomach, that's how stressed I was at the moment.

"How are things going in here?" My husband walked into the kitchen with Farrow in his arms and Kaynon following them.

I had a knife in my hand when I turned around to answer him. He flinched like I was going to cut him. "It's going great." I had a deep smile on my face. I was smiling so hard my jaws trembled. "Everything will be ready by the time my parents get here. Did you need something?" I waved the knife in my hand a little as I talked. My eyes were fixed on his eyes and his eyes were fixed on the knife.

"Oh, no, nothing for me." He was a little jittery as he spoke. "I just came in here to check on you and get something to drink for the boys."

My son reached for me and instinctively I reached out for him. I placed the knife on the counter and took him into my arms. I cradled him and cooed at him a little and then handed him back to his father. Kaynon stayed by his daddy the whole time because he was a daddy's boy.

"All right now, y'all go ahead back in the living room while I finish cooking."

They did as they were told and marched on out. I continued to cook and finish my meal.

Two and a half hours later the food was just about finished when I heard the doorbell ring. I jumped a little because I was startled. *Showtime!*

I heard them come in and they all did the pleasantry/ greeting thing and then I heard my mother say she was headed to the kitchen to help me out.

My stomach was churning even harder now and I had to steady my hand because it started to shake some. *Get it together, girl!* I coached myself in my head.

"Hey, baby." My mother greeted me with a kiss on the cheek. "You really have it smelling good in here. Is there a special occasion or something?"

"No, ma'am, just a good meal." I shrugged my shoulders. "I thought it would be nice."

"Oh, okay." She patted me on the shoulder. "You need help with anything?"

"Well, Mom, could you set the table for me real quick? I'm running a little behind," I said over my shoulder. I dared not look at her in the eye. She could always tell that something was wrong when she looked at me as a child and I knew that trait didn't just disappear with age.

"All right, baby, Momma got your back." As soon as she left the room with the dishes in her hand I let the tenseness in my body relax.

Pretty soon all of the dinner was on the table and everybody was seated. My mother and I both served our men and the boys and then fixed our own plates. My father said grace and then we all began to eat. The only sounds in the room were that of food being eaten and the boys making noise while they ate. All of the adults were completely quiet.

"Baby girl, this roast is so tender." My father picked a piece off of his plate and stuck it in his mouth.

"Thanks, Daddy." I smiled.

"Yes, it is," my mother agreed, "I think she is trying to outdo her mother. The student surpassing the teacher is such an honor."

"Thanks, Ma," I said as I put a spoonful of potatoes in my mouth. I was praying that it stayed down.

"I can't wait to get a piece of that chocolate cake in the kitchen." My husband spoke as he cleaned his plate. No one at the table had a clue that I was about to drop a bomb in a very short time.

Everybody ate and had seconds. I went into the kitchen and cut a few slices of cake onto a serving platter and brought in some cake plates and put them onto the table. By this time, both of the boys looked full too and they looked like they would fall off to sleep at any moment. It was perfect timing for me because I needed the boys to be sound asleep when all the "festivities" started.

After another ten minutes everyone was sitting pretty and full and I decided to make my move. It was now or never.

"Daddy, Kyle, how about you go downstairs and get things ready for movie night? Could you also take the boys and put them in the basement nursery, too?" We had a small nursery for the boys in the basement for when I was doing laundry and we had company over. It was set up just like their room upstairs.

"Okay, babe." My husband grabbed Farrow out of his seat and proceeded to go downstairs, and my father did the same with Kaynon.

"We'll be down in a few after we finished cleaning up the table," I said as they disappeared down the stairs.

"So what movie do you have planned for tonight? I hope it's not one of them sappy love stories. I need something a little rough, like a Bruce Willis flick or something."

"Believe me, Mom, it's not a love story at all, and yes, it is rough, but Bruce Willis is not in this one." My mom did have a small crush on Bruce Willis. I thought he was handsome too.

"Okay, I just hope it don't put me to sleep." She laughed as I put the last of the dishes in the dishwasher.

"Oh, I think you will be wide awake for this one." I smirked.

"Okay, honey," she laughed.

"Mom, go ahead on downstairs because I have to go upstairs and get the movie."

"Okay, baby." She too disappeared down the stairs and I was left alone in the kitchen. I turned from the dishwasher and leaned on the kitchen table for support. My stomach started to turn and wrench in pain. I knew that it was the stress of what I was about to do.

I went upstairs and retrieved the disk and made my way back downstairs toward the basement door. I stood there and breathed a few times; my mind told my feet to move but they weren't cooperating. Then it happened, I started walking down the stairs. It seemed like forever as I walked to the bottom. My parents were seated together on the love seat I had downstairs and my husband was seated on the sofa that was sitting on an angle facing the television. They all watched as I walked over to the Blu-ray player and put in the disk. I walked over and sat next to my husband just as the blue screen came on. After a few seconds, the show was playing on the screen. There was no sound but we all knew that they were enjoying themselves. We all watched my husband and my father have sex in his office.

I looked at my mother and she had a blank look on her face. And then I looked at my father, whose face was also blank. And last I looked at my husband, because I knew this shit had to be his doing. He probably started all of this shit.

Chapter 23

Kyle

Ah, Damn!

I looked at my wife as she looked at me for an explanation. It didn't take a rocket scientist to tell me that she found my disk and I didn't lose it. I kicked myself for not taking it in the house with me, but that was neither here nor there. I was caught red-handed.

"Baby, I'm sorry." I reached for her hand but she instantly snatched it away.

"Don't," she warned me. "How could you do this to me? To us? To them?" She pointed to pictures of our sons on the walls.

"Tasha, you don't understand," I pleaded. "I didn't want to do it. Your father made me, he blackmailed me."

"Now how did he do that?" She looked unconvinced. She had a banner up for her father that said she was sold out for him and he could do no wrong.

"Tasha, he threatened to have me dishonorably discharged if I didn't do what he said. He said that he would tell you that I was sleeping with men on the base. I didn't want to lose you. You and the boys are everything in the world to me . . . everything."

"So why didn't you come and tell me about this?" she proposed. She looked very angry.

"Tasha, would you have believed me if I did come to you and tell you that your father was gay?" I proposed. She was stumped. She didn't say a word for a few seconds.

I continued, "He's not the man you know and the husband you know." I looked at my mother-in-law and then back at my wife. "He's a tyrant and an arrogant, selfish, sex-crazed maniac. This has been going on for two years and I promise you that I didn't want to continue in this foolishness, but I was only thinking of you and the boys the whole time."

"Oh, really." She folded her arms with attitude. "So you're saying that when you and my father were fucking you was thinking of your wife and kids."

"No, that's not what I meant. I was doing it for you. I didn't want to lose my career and the support it gave us."

"Ma, you hear this fool over here trying to rationalize having sex with my father and God knows who else?"

Her mother remained silent the whole time.

"So you're not going to address your father in this situation?" I was pissed off now. "You're going to blame all of this on me. None of the blame goes to your father."

"He didn't have this problem before you came along." She said matter-of-factly.

"Tasha, a man don't just develop these habits overnight, it's not that simple. He probably was doing this all along. He just didn't get caught until now."

Sergeant Harris now had a silly-ass smirk on his face as he watched his daughter and my wife defend him to no end. I truly couldn't believe that my wife was taking his side as if he weren't even in the video at all.

"You saw the video, Tasha. I was not sucking Casper the Friendly Ghost's dick and your father was enjoying himself. Explain that."

"No need to explain; you're the one with the history, not him."

"So you're taking his side?" I asked.

"Kyle, he's my father and you had these issues before."

"I can't believe this shit." I stood up, pissed off and disgusted. "I can't believe that you are so gung-ho for your father that you wouldn't even acknowledge his part in this."

"Oh, no, I am going to ask him about his side of the story." She turned and looked at her father. "Daddy, did Kyle blackmail you or something to get you to have sex with him?"

"Yes, baby girl. You know your daddy wouldn't do anything to intentionally hurt you. I love you."

"Well, there you go, Kyle. What do you have to say for yourself, before I toss your sorry ass out on the street?"

"Ain't this a bitch." I got down on my knees in front of my wife and pleaded with her. "Baby, I love you; why would you put me out over some lies? He's lying, baby . . . He's lying."

"Kyle, it's over, get your shit and go." She didn't even look at me. Some tears fell out of her eyes. I knew she was hurt by this. I was too. I didn't have any evidence to prove her wrong so I had to go. I had to leave my wife and my sons. I was extremely hurt and devastated. I wanted to go over there and beat her father's ass but I didn't. I got up and walked toward the steps with my head down. I didn't know where I was going, but I had to go.

Chapter 24

Christine

You Didn't Ask and I Didn't Tell

"Wait! Kyle, don't leave," I called out just as he was about to go up the stairs. "I can't let this happen."

I looked at my daughter, who was crying, and her husband as they were about to end their life together.

"What? What do you mean, Momma?" Tasha turned and looked at me. "What's going on?"

"It's . . . it's . . . it's not Kyle's fault," I stammered.

"What?" Tasha looked at me, confused. "I'm confused."

I looked at my husband and then at my precious daughter. "Kyle didn't pursue Henry. It was the other way around."

"What!" She looked shocked. "Daddy?" She looked at him with so much hurt in her eyes. "How could you?"

"Tasha, I'm not finished. He's not your father, either." Saying it broke my heart, but knowing that the truth was out made me feel a lot better.

"You're not my father?" Henry shook his head no. "Momma, why didn't you tell me?"

"You didn't ask me so I didn't tell you."

"How the fuck I'm supposed to know to ask that question?" Spit was flying from her mouth as she spoke. She had a temper and she was using it now.

"I'm sorry, baby. I was doing what was best for us," I rationalized.

"So you knew that my fath . . . I mean, Henry, was fucking my husband all along?"

"Yes, it was the only way I could keep him happy. When Henry found out that Kyle had a past with men, he said if I didn't let him have him he would leave me. I didn't have a choice."

"You didn't have a choice?" Tasha shot up out of the chair she was in. "Bitch, how about you choose your family." I was taken aback by her calling me a bitch, but I let it slide because she was angry and rightfully so.

"Baby, you don't understand. Your father walked out on us and I had to work really hard. I needed some help, some stability, so when Henry came along and said he would take care of me I married him. I found out about him being gay when I found a tape of him have sex with a soldier. I confronted him and he threatened to leave. I just couldn't go back to work and you were already calling him Daddy. I had no choice but to let him do him to keep food on the table. All I had to do was be a cover for him and he would take care of us."

"You sick bastard!" She hauled off and slapped the taste out of his mouth. "So your telling me to marry Kyle was so I could have stability?"

"Baby, I just wanted you to have a good life. I wanted you to be stable."

"I can't believe you . . . You're crazy . . . both of you." She looked like she wanted to spit on us both. "You know this don't ask, don't tell shit is inexcusable. Is there anything else you holding back on? Are you my mother?" She looked as serious as a heart attack.

"No, Tasha. That's all of it. And yes, I'm your mother." I looked at her. "Please forgive me."

"How could I forgive you? I will forever think about what if I never found this disk, would you still have lived this sham to the end? I can't believe this shit. I was about to put my husband out and lose my mind all because you wanted to be stable. Get out! Get the fuck out of my house. I don't want to see either of you again."

"Tasha, No . . . I'm sorry. I didn't mean for it to turn out like this." I stood and went to her so I could grab and hold her. I knew she was hurting inside and it was my fault. She backed up and put her hands up, signaling me to stop.

"Get . . . out!" she yelled. She picked up a vase and threw it against the wall. We watched it shatter into pieces. Both Henry and I headed toward the steps in a hurry. Kyle moved out of the way so we could go up the stairs. He shook his head in shame. I couldn't blame him. I would have done the same thing.

We grabbed our coats and headed to the car in silence. There was nothing to say; we were caught and it was over. The question that floated in my mind several times as I drove was, *was it really worth it?* I was so delusional to think that I could trade my daughter's life for my own happiness and stability. Henry sat in the passenger's seat as quiet as a mouse. I didn't know what he was thinking about, and if he was feeling any kind of remorse he sure didn't show it.

The thought of losing my daughter and grandchildren was overbearing and it brought me to tears as I drove. *I lost everything in a blink of an eye.*

We were on the highway and the speed limit was forty-five but I was doing sixty-five. I pushed the pedal some more and watched the speedometer creep up and speed faster and faster.

"What are you doing?" Henry grabbed my arm and edged the car over farther to the side of the road. I saw a big pole up the road and decided that this was my way out . . . our way out. I knew that Tasha meant every word she spoke. I was never going to see them ever again. It was dark out and the road was almost clear. Henry wrestled with me for the wheel but tonight my strength outmatched his, and we drove head first into this massive telephone pole.

Kyle's Epilogue

I sat in the living room chair and held the kids in my arms. I watched my wife place her mother's urn and her father's urn on the mantle. I still couldn't believe that they were gone. One suicide and one murder. I shook my head in shame. I would have never thought it would have ended like that. My wife took it really hard. She was a wreck at the memorial service. I knew she blamed herself for it, but I assured her that it was not her decision. Her mother made that decision for her and her husband. I knew that she still felt guilty for putting them out after the discoveries. I reminded her that she could only control her actions and not anyone else's. Her mother was going to have to answer for those deaths, not her. After a while she agreed, but I knew that the pain of it all would still be there. Who wouldn't mourn the deaths of their parents and the tragic way their lives were ended? Even with all the lies and deception I still shed a tear at the memorial. It didn't have to end that way, but it did.

My wife and I had a nice long talk after her parents left two weeks ago. She apologized and apologized for not believing me. I apologized for not confessing to what was going on sooner. We both decided that we needed counseling so we could work through our problems. We both agreed that there would be no more lying or secrets, and we would take our love for each other more seriously for our children. She also told me that she understood about my past, but she couldn't tolerate another bout with me sleeping with men. And at any time I felt like I wanted to do it, I needed to respect her enough to say it. She said she expected me to be a man of the house and that she would respect every decision I made.

She also found out that she was pregnant. We were both hoping for a girl. She said if it was a girl that she would name it after her mom, because it would be like giving her mother a second chance at life. I agreed.

Anyway, while at the memorial service for her parents she grieved really hard. She didn't think that it should have ended the way it did. I held her and promised her that I would do my best to never let her down again and that she didn't have to worry about my past anymore. I told her that I would be straight up with her from now on no matter what.

Ironically, a few days after her parents were killed; my mother called me and asked me if she and my father could come see their grandkids. Everything in me wanted to say no, but I said yes and today was the day that they would be coming by.

"Baby, come sit down and rest." I patted the cushion beside me. "Take a load off."

"Okay, but not for too long. Your parents will be here in a few hours and I want to have dinner ready."

"Baby, you don't have to impress them. Just be you. You're all that matters to me." I kissed her on the cheek.

"I'm just nervous though." She smiled weakly.

"Tasha, if they can't accept you as you are then we won't have anything to do with them."

"Okay." She laid her head on my shoulder.

"You know, baby," she spoke after she picked her head up off of my shoulders. "I want to go back to work."

"Really?" I looked a little shocked because she never really talked about working.

"Yes, I would really like to get out of the house. I mean I love my kids and being a mother, but I was living my mother's life, not my own. I want to be happy and stable in my own way. I think after I have the baby I will start looking for a job."

"Do you, baby, I'm one hundred percent behind you all the way."

"Okay, then that is what I am going to do." She picked Farrow up out of his seat and nuzzled his nose and hers. I was so elated that I still had my family.

"Tasha." I looked at her seriously once she started to rock Farrow in her arms. "I need to say something to you."

"What is it, Kyle?" She looked a little nervous. "Is something wrong?"

"No, I just want to tell you thank you for giving me and us another chance. Only a real woman and wife would take back her man after all of this. I mean I am truly grateful for you. I can't even describe how I really feel about you and my boys. This whole gay thing is not for me. I know that it's easier said than done, but I know that I can grow and change with you. I already did it before and I know I can do it again. And if I ever get to the point where I want to step out on you again, then I will stay gone. Agreed?"

"Agreed." She nodded her head.

"This is a new start for us. I see us getting old and these boys changing our diapers. I can see it." She laughed at the last comment and so did I.

I was not going to say that everything was perfect, but we were a family and that was a good start. A lot people in this world doubt that a person who has slept with the same sex can be changed. But I was going to step out on the faith that my parents instilled in me. Because I knew that God could do anything but fail. I had proof and it was my family. They're all the proof I needed.

Other Books by M.T. Pope
Both Sides of the Fence
Both Sides of the Fence 2: Gate Wide Open
Both Sides of the Fence 3: Loose Ends
Anna J. Presents: Erotic Snap Shots Vol. 1 (e-book only)

Author Bio
M.T. Pope is a native of Baltimore, MD where he currently resides. He is a store manager of a bookstore. He is hard at work on future titles. He welcomes the feedback and comments of readers. Also, feel free to check out his other works of fiction.

M.T. Pope's e-mail:
chosen_97@yahoo.com

M. T. Pope's Web sites:
www.facebook.com/authormtpope
www.twitter.com/mtpope
www.wix.com/mtpope/bothsidesofthefence

BETTER NOT TELL

By Tina Brooks McKinney

Chapter 1

Lauren Burns

My hands were shaking when I opened the letter with the official army seal, addressed to me. Ever since I walked into the recruiter's office and signed on the dotted line, I was prickling with anticipation.

"What does it say?" Tiffany snatched the letter from my hands. She was so fast, I couldn't stop her. I was afraid she was going to tear it up, especially since she was less than happy about my decision to enlist. As she read the letter, I waited for the explosion I knew was coming.

"It's official. I got my marching orders, pun definitely intended."

"You bitch. How can you do this to me? What am I supposed to do while you're off playing GI Joe?"

Both questions were rhetorical and I didn't want to touch either one of them. Especially today, since Tiffany was in a bitchy mood. Tiffany was my girlfriend/lover, but she was also my drama queen. Lately, we weren't seeing eye to eye on most things so I figured time apart would do us both some good. Apparently Tiffany didn't see things the same way and when she didn't get her way, Tiffany tended to get mean. I loved her, but I didn't like her very much, which made it easier for me to leave. But there's a right and a wrong way to do things; this was why I told Tiffany my plans before I signed up.

When my mother left my dad, she ran off in the middle of the night, leaving a jacked-up note. I wanted us to remain friends so I opted not to treat her badly. With the way things were going, I had to constantly remind myself we were friends before we became lovers and I wanted to at least maintain a fraction of our relationship.

"Come on, Tiff, we talked about this. After I do the ten weeks of basic training, I'll only have to go two weekends a month." I thought we both knew a lot could happen in ten weeks, but I wasn't going to be the one to say it. We were at the point in the relationship where we would either have to fight to stay together or walk away, so I was looking forward to the time away to help me decide what I wanted to do.

"That's almost three months! What am I supposed to do while you're bunking down with fifty other fucking women? You won't even be thinking about me." She was pouting and it confused me because she rarely did it. Throwing things, cussing up a blue streak, or storming out: those were things she did when she was upset. Although we never physically fought, we'd come pretty damn close to it on a number of occasions.

"Why are you acting like this? We talked about this and you said it might do us some good."

"That's because I didn't think you were going to do it. What if I said I don't want you to go?" She balled up my letter and threw it in the trash, which was a childish move on her part.

"Well it's too late now, I'm supposed to report in two weeks." I didn't mean to sound lackadaisical or like I didn't care about her feelings but I was sick of her theatrics.

"I think you need to pick up the phone and tell them you made a mistake." I heard the threat in her voice and I felt things were about to get ugly. I was sick of the drama. Even if it were possible to change my mind, I wouldn't do it. I was tired and I was looking forward to the break. I knew it was possible I'd get to boot camp and regret my decision but anything would have been better than the hell we'd been living.

Tiffany grabbed a vase off the dining room table and winged it at my head. It was a good thing I had anticipated the move or she would have knocked me the fuck out. I tried to talk myself out of getting upset because this was typical Tiffany behavior.

She stared at me, her eyes blazing a trail on my skin. "Fine, I hope you get shot right in your fat ass!" She walked out the door, slamming it behind her. She didn't even bother to check to see if I'd gotten hit with any shards of glass. However, this tantrum was mild compared to some of our other battles and I thanked God for its simplicity. I could replace the vase . . . and her too.

"Congratulations, sis, I'm proud of you." James leaned into his computer screen and put his hand up against his monitor. I mimicked his actions, placing my palm against his. It was the closest I'd been to my brother in months. He was also military and doing a tour in Iraq.

"Thanks, I'm excited. I can't wait to see Dad's face when he sees me in my uniform."

I noticed the flash of annoyance on my brother's face. He wasn't a big fan of my father even though he chose to follow his lead and join the military. But I understood his reaction. My dad didn't approve of my life choices and had disowned me. We hadn't talked in a few years but I was still hopeful he'd come around. James thought my father was an ass and had no qualms letting him know it.

"You don't have anything to prove with him. If he can't accept you for who you are, you don't need him."

This was one of the reasons James was my best friend. I could tell him anything and it never changed his opinion of me.

"I know, but you can't blame a girl for trying. I miss him even if he is a jerk."

"You ain't never lied about that. It's a good thing Mom isn't around to see what an asshole he turned out to be."

My smile lost a bit of its luster. I didn't want to talk about our mother. She didn't like being an army wife so she left. The problem was, she didn't take me with her and I had to figure out where I fit in between my dad and my two brothers.

"Don't be like that, Lauren, you look just like her."

"Whatever." I didn't want to be reminded of how she looked; I saw it every time I looked in the mirror or when I accidentally came across her picture. Kissed by chocolate, I had the same slim, athletic build as my mother with light brown eyes and two piercing dimples.

"Why do you give Dad so many breaks and have zero tolerance for Mom?"

"At least he stuck around. How about that? Why do you insist upon defending her?" All my earlier elation disappeared and I was ready to quit my Skype conversation with my brother.

"Because every time I look at you, I'm reminded of her. If I hated her, I'd ultimately end up hating you."

I never thought about it that way. James and I had a special connection unlike the one I had with my younger brother, Matt. He was more bullheaded like my father and wouldn't know an original thought if it slapped him in the face.

"Fine, forgive me if I don't share your sentiments. When was the last time you heard from Dad?"

"He sent me a postcard a few weeks ago but I didn't respond. He's retired now and thinking about settling down."

I shouldn't have been surprised by this revelation but I was. It was a damn shame I had to find out news about my father from my brother, but I refused to live a lie just to make him happy.

"It is what it is."

"So what did your girlfriend say when you told her you were enlisting?"

"She pitched a bitch, threw a vase at me, and walked out. I haven't heard from her since."

"Good, you didn't need her anyway. That bitch is crazy."

James didn't think Tiffany was the right girl for me and here lately I was starting to agree with him. He didn't like her mood swings and thought she was bipolar but I didn't want to talk about her either. I wanted to get back to happier thoughts.

"Have they said anything about when you're coming home? I would think since bin Laden is dead, more troops would be coming home?"

"Naw, sis, just the opposite. We're on red alert just in case someone wants to retaliate."

"Well I hope the war is still going on when I get there. I can't wait to have a weapon of my own." I'd been shooting since I was twelve so I was anxious to show off my skills.

"Oh you'll get a gun, believe that, but being in the army ain't so much about shooting a gun. You got to make sure you have your mind right before you get here or you'll be all messed up. The army gets in your head, that's what they do, and if you're fucked up to begin with, you can bet your ass they will find a way to use it against you."

"Are you trying to tell me that you don't think I have what it takes?" I was stunned and offended. I never expected criticism from my only ally and it hurt.

"No, that's not what I'm saying at all. I'm saying you need to resolve your issues before you get here because if the army finds your weaknesses, they will use them against you, especially in boot camp. They figure if they weed out the problems early, it's one less disability check they have to write later."

For a second my computer went dark but a little red window appeared letting me know it was trying to reestablish the connection. This happened sometimes with Skype; it wasn't perfect but it was the best game in town for video chatting.

"Damn, I thought I lost you for a minute."

"I know right, it's all good now. But I didn't understand what you were talking about when you said issues. What issues? Being gay is no longer an issue."

"Yeah, I know, but just because those rules have changed, don't be surprised if everyone doesn't embrace them. Look how long it took to abolish segregation, that's all I'm saying. You can't come in waving a sexual equality flag and not expect to get some flack about it."

"Well this is my pussy and I can give it to anybody I want to."

"I hate it when you speak to me like that. Jeez, I don't even want to think about you having a pussy let alone using it. You're my baby sister, for Christ's sake. All I'm saying is be careful about who you trust with your personal information. The army dismissed a lot of people because of their sexual orientation but they ain't gonna apologize for being ignorant. Their job is to tear you down by any means necessary so they can build you up the way they want you to be. Don't give them any ammunition to use against you, that's all I'm trying to tell you."

"Damn, you got it sounding like a cult."

"I ain't never heard it called that before, but the army does brainwash you into believing certain things. They call it stinkin' thinkin'. They have a hard job taking a group of strangers from all walks of life and teaching them to live like family and die like soldiers. Trust and believe the bonds you make in boot camp will last a lifetime. You are going to be spending a lot of time with those folks so bring your A game and you'll be all right," he said, laughing.

"Yes, Big Brother *Capitaine*." I saluted my monitor and even though I was joking, I appreciated his honest advice.

"What are you going to do about your apartment?"

"I was going to let Tiffany move in while I was gone but the bitch might get a wild hair and set my shit on fire!"

"You said a mouthful. Lock it down or put your things in storage is your best bet; it's what I did. Listen, I got to go. Let me know where you're stationed and I'll make sure to drop you a line. For me, one of the hardest things to get used to was being cut off from everything I knew. I'll make sure you get a package every day if I can do it."

"You'd do that for me?" I felt my throat close as a small lump rose in it. I knew James loved me, but it meant so much more now.

"Of course I would, but I've got to get ready for the morning. Love ya, sis."

"I love you too. And, James . . . Thanks for being my brother." I ended the call with a big-ass smile on my face. James was twenty-seven, just two years older than me, but he acted like a much older man. He was such a loving person, I wondered why he never married. He's good-looking, kindhearted, and had a great head on his shoulders. I would never butt into his business, but if he ever wanted to talk about it, I promised myself I'd always be there to listen the same way he was there for me.

Chapter 2

Anji Foster

As I sat in church, I made mental notes of all the things I would never do again once I left Jackson, Mississippi. At the top of the list was weekly Bible Study. Don't get me wrong, I was just as religious as the next person, but enough was enough. I thumped Bibles with the best of them and I needed to have something else drilled into my head besides hell and damnation. I was ready to experience some of the fun things in life without peeping over my shoulder to see if God was going to set fire to my behind. I would never bake another pie for the church raffle or volunteer to be a judge for another bake-off where I had to lie just to protect somebody's feelings.

I was not going to hold another ugly baby and call it cute. Or consider Wal-Mart an "outing" worthy of getting dressed up for. And I would never, ever, ever wear another dress that came down to my calves. This was my short list of "won't dos" but the list was growing the longer I thought about it.

I was looking forward to a clean break from small-town living. I'd come back to visit, of course, but I never planned on living there again. My friend Rita claimed I'd changed, but I called it growing up. If I stayed in Jackson, my dad would forever keep me a child. I didn't have any marketable skills or talents so I had limited options available to me. I knew his views on the army and I was certain he would never approve of my desire to enlist. He didn't believe in killing even if it was for our own country. But my dad had a long list of stuff he didn't believe in. I could have argued with him until I was purple, but he would've used the Bible against me and made me feel like a heathen for even considering enlistment.

After church service, I caught up with my friend Rita before she got in the car with her parents.

"Rita, can you do me a big favor?"

She looked around to see who was watching before she responded. "I guess so, what is it?"

"Nothing major. I just need you to give this note to my dad tomorrow while I'm at the fair."

"Why can't you give it to him yourself?" Rita was nice as she wanted to be but could be dumber than a box of rocks sometimes.

"Because it's a surprise. Will you do it for me?" I was nervous. I needed her help but I didn't want to answer any questions.

"Yeah, sure." She stuck the note in her pocketbook.

"Promise me you won't forget to give it to him and you won't peek in it?"

"I promise." She giggled as she waved at me and climbed in the back seat of their car.

"Bye." I waved back. Part of me was sad that, come morning, I would be leaving her behind too, but the feeling didn't linger long. I chose to believe I wasn't leaving her so much as I was moving forward without her.

If everything went as I planned, tomorrow, instead of going to the fair, I would catch a bus to St. Louis and join the army. I'd already qualified; I only needed to sign my paperwork to make it official. I refused to spend the rest of my life in Jefferson County with a population of fewer than 10,000 people. I tried talking to my father but he simply didn't want to hear it. He told me I needed to pray to the good Lord for deliverance. To this day, I didn't know what he wanted me to be delivered from but I was determined not to find out.

For once, I wanted to go to the movies without running into at least ten people who knew the first, last, and middle names of my parents. I wanted to enjoy a meal in private without everyone on the block knowing what I had to eat, and I wanted to kiss a boy who hadn't already kissed half of my friends or wasn't related to me. I wanted to go someplace where a trip on the information highway wasn't affiliated with shopping at Wal-Mart.

Even though I planned to shed many of my antiquated thoughts and ideas at the bus station, I had no intentions of changing the core of who I was. I was excited and nervous but I was looking forward to what my tomorrows would be like.

As I packed what little clothing I wanted to take with me, I was nervous. It wasn't much because where I was going, I would have no need for long dresses and short, stubby heels. I was gonna get me some booty shorts I saw on television and a slinky top I could wear without a bra. I curled my copper-colored hair, something I only did on holidays. I normally wore my hair in a ponytail but tomorrow was a holiday as far as I was concerned. I was moving on to what I hoped would be exotic people and places.

"Anji, turn that light out and get some sleep. You have to get up early in the morning and I don't want no mess out of you," my father shouted from outside my door. For a second I thought he was going to try the knob but I relaxed when I heard his steps moving away from my door.

"I'm going now. Good night, Dad." I wasn't expecting to get choked up when I said good night, but I did. I
wanted to fling open the door and wrap my arms around
my dad while I showered him with kisses, but I knew he
would suspect something if I did. So I rocked myself to
sleep with visions of the things I'd get to see and do running through my head.

We boarded a motor coach from St. Louis to Fort
Leonard Wood, Missouri. There were seven guys and
three women and I thought I was in hog heaven. Already the odds of finding a man were in my favor as I
eyed the candy in front of me. The guys were kinda cute
but they weren't for me. If they were on the same bus as
I was, they had to be small-towners too and the man of
my dreams was from the city.

There was an excited buzz on the bus that was hard
to ignore, but I did my best to appear to be unaffected
by it. I refused to get caught up in the conversations
and eventually fell asleep. I woke as the bus pulled up
to what would be my home for the next ten weeks.

"Wow." The base was bigger than I had imagined. I
wasn't dumb, nor was I naïve, but I'd never seen such
organized madness in my entire life.

"Good afternoon and welcome to Fort Leonard Wood.
I would like to personally thank each and every one of
you for giving back to your country. This is the reception
area and the first stop on your journey. When you exit
the bus, I will need for each of you to line up on the right
and wait for further instructions. Make the most of this
experience."

I was impressed with the welcome, and felt encouraged by the decision I made. This place was a beehive of
activity and it seemed like everyone was going in differ-

ent directions, but there was a method to the madness. I tried to keep my mouth closed as we were shuffled from one post to another, collecting our gear, but there was so much to see I kept forgetting.

It didn't take long before my enthusiasm began to wane. The gear we were given was heavy, forcing me to use muscles I didn't even know I had. I kept waiting for someone to show us where we could stow the gear but they kept giving us more stuff. I didn't want to complain but I was beginning to get annoyed. I tried not to let my irritation show but my face read like a road map. As organized as they were, it seemed ludicrous to me that they didn't plan better to accommodate for all the things they decided we needed to have. I felt more like a mule instead of a woman, and I was not a happy camper!

Our first break came at lunchtime. I was starving and looking forward to having an opportunity to relax for a moment. Up until this point, I thought most of us were too shell-shocked to talk so after we grabbed our trays, a few of us started getting to know each other. With a full belly, I began to unwind. We'd been so busy, I hadn't had the time to worry about how my father reacted to my leaving. I didn't want to hurt him but I knew he would never understand my reasons for leaving, so I didn't try. However, when the realization of what I'd done finally sunk in, I almost started to cry. I was his only child; what was I thinking?

"Are you okay?" a woman next to me inquired.

"Yeah, I'm good. Just feeling a little homesick."

"Girl, we just got here." She chuckled.

"I know. Crazy ain't it, but I've never been away from home before."

"Well you better figure it out quick because the last thing you want to do is have someone riding your ass about it."

I was slightly offended by her language but she was right. I didn't want to be a Debbie Downer especially on the first day.

"Thanks." No matter the delivery I understood what she meant so I tried to pull myself together. I was ready to find my bed and stretch out. They couldn't possibly have anything else to give us so I was ready. If I'd known ahead of time what was coming, I might not have been so eager to get to it.

"No problem. My brother is in the army so he pulled my coat about a few things."

"Oh yeah, well when are we going to be able to put away some of this stuff?" I was looking twice at my newfound friend. If she knew some of the ropes, she might not be a bad person to have around.

"I hate to bust your bubble, but I think we're going to be stuck carrying gear the entire time we're here."

"Are you serious? That bag is heavy." I hoped my friend was pulling my leg but she wasn't laughing and I started to get worried.

"You've got to be kidding me. Where did you think you were going, a country club?" She laughed but if she was trying to be funny, I didn't get the punch line. I saw no benefit to toting the added pounds and it kind of soured my first impressions of the military life.

"No, but I don't see the point of carrying that big old bag." I felt myself getting angry.

"Welcome to the army." She was a little to stuck-up and rude for my taste. I didn't even know her name but already I didn't like her or her pompous attitude. I turned my back to discourage any more conversation with her. Besides, I wasn't there to make friends with females anyway: too much drama. My plan was to meet some hot guys, flirt and have fun, fall in love and settle down, the end.

"Attention. On your feet, maggots. This picnic is over so stow your trays and line up now."

Everyone leaped to their feet and rushed to dispose of their trays. It was mass confusion and a little bit messy as everyone tried to balance their trays and gear as quickly as possible.

"Shut up," the officer yelled.

"Who is that?" I whispered to my friend.

"Someone you don't want to piss off: the cadre."

The cadre was a little woman but she had an awfully big mouth. I didn't have to be told twice to tread lightly. I wasn't trying to attract that kind of attention this early in the game while I was still trying to figure things out.

Chapter 3

Lauren Burns

Thanks to James, I wasn't surprised when the cadre came into the mess hall shouting. He told me that for the first couple of hours everyone would be nice, but after we were divided into platoons things would change. He said they would typically pick out the recruit they thought was going to bail and ride their ass until they did it. The cutie sitting next to me looked like a likely candidate, so I quickly grabbed my tray, trying to get as far away from her as I could. If her simple ass was going down, she would do it without me.

"Hey, wait up."

"Shush!" Shit. I knew this chick was going to be trouble the second she started bitching about her bag. I had to shut her down quickly or she was going to bring heat down on both of us.

She mumbled under her breath, "She doesn't have to be nasty."

The cadre stopped me from responding. "Shut the fuck up. I don't do repeating myself; am I clear?"

"Sir, yes, sir," I shouted along with a few other recruits. I looked around to see who else had a fucking clue, because those were the folks I wanted to make friends with. However, there were at least one hundred people in the mess hall so singling out a few voices would have been next to impossible. I was going to have to play it by ear for now until I had a chance to watch more.

"When I call your name, file into four lines." She pointed to an area next to the wall. We were about to be separated into squads and I said a prayer that I wouldn't get picked with a squad full of losers. My brother told me a squad was only as good as its weakest link. If one person failed, we all failed. The army was big on teams and team building. If they weren't trying to teach us how to stay alive, they were working on our people skills.

"Fuck," I mumbled. God was showing His or Her sense of humor when He or She put me in the same squad with the spaz. Normally, I didn't like to prematurely judge anyone, but my gut told me this cutie was going to be trouble and I should tread lightly with her. It wasn't my physical attraction to her that scared me; it was almost like she was forbidden fruit. I knew boot camp would difficult enough, so I wanted to get through it as stress free as I could. If this meant I was going to have to check ol' girl, I would.

"What's going on?"

"Shut up."

What planet was she from that she didn't understand a simple order? Clearly this bitch could tell this was not the time for twenty-one fucking questions. I allowed her to push me to the edge but she wasn't dragging me over.

"Private, do you have something you want to say?" the cadre asked.

I felt like a giant spotlight was beaming down on me. I was busted and I was going to beat the brakes off that chick the first chance I got for causing me to get called out in formation. The cadre got right up in my face.

"Do you have a problem with your hearing?"

"Sir. No, sir."

"Then how come you didn't keep your trap shut when I gave you a direct order? Are you stupid?"

"Sir. No, sir." As much as I wanted to turn around and point a finger at the real culprit, I knew better, so I sucked it up and hoped my punishment wouldn't be so bad.

"Obviously something is wrong with your retarded ass."

The silly one raised her hand. "Excuse me, sir, it wasn't her fault. I asked her a question."

"Oh, so you're hard of fucking hearing too?"

"No . . . uh."

She was making it worse for herself and I just wanted her to shut the hell up. The rest of the squad was totally silent as they should be, why didn't she get a clue?

"Drop and give me twenty," the cadre shouted.

I knew the drill and if my new friend didn't, she pretended real well as she fell to the floor and performed her pushups with me. I felt like I was living through a rerun of *Gomer Pyle*, an oldies sitcom my father used to enjoy. I was hoping this would be the last time I took a punishment for my newfound friend because if it wasn't, we wouldn't be BFFs for long. When I finished my reps, I got to my feet and waited for further instructions. I was winded but believed I did the pushups in a timely manner. However, as long as I had the cadre in my face, she demanded my utmost attention. I prayed the dumbo standing next to me knew it too.

"Get a good look at the person standing to your right. This is your battle buddy, your twin for the next ten weeks. You will eat, sleep, and shit with your battle buddy. Fall out," the cadre yelled.

I could barely lift my feet as we ran to the barracks. We had five minutes to change clothes, stow our gear, and form another line outside the barracks. It was like a fucking bad dream and it was only the first day. I didn't waste time. I unpacked my clothes and placed them in the drawers next to my bunk. Even though we were given a short amount of time, I knew not to make a mess. I quickly shed my civilian clothes and donned my uniform for the first time. Despite my rocky start, I felt a sense of pride. I didn't have time to admire myself in the mirror since I did not want to be the last person in formation. Taking one last look around my bunk, I rushed back outside.

I wasn't first to arrive, but I certainly wasn't last. I was okay with that but my relief was short-lived when I realized my disastrous mistake. I was outside without my battle buddy. Where the fuck was she? I was so annoyed to have gotten stuck with her, I ignored her the entire time I was getting dressed. I ran back inside but didn't see her anywhere and her bunk was a hot frigging mess. She'd pulled out her uniform but failed to stow the rest of her gear. Where the fuck was she? We had less than a minute to get outside. Franticly, I raced into the bathroom and found her.

"What the fuck are you doing?" I was beyond mad, I was ready to fight.

"What does it look like I'm doing?"

Oh no, she didn't get an attitude with me. I was ready to kick her ass. "I don't know what your problem is but if I have to do another fucking pushup because of you, there's going to be a fight up in this bitch. Now get your ass out there!"

"You are going to stop hollering at me or you won't have to wait for a fight." She stood her ground but now was not the time to argue. I grabbed her arm and dragged her outside, fussing the entire way.

"You haven't heard hollering yet." I pushed her in front of me and stood at attention. Her shirt was improperly buttoned and her bunk was still a mess, but we made it before the cadre came back outside. We all stood at attention and waited in the hot sun until she finally emerged from the building.

"Every squad has one, never fucking fails." She was walking the line with her hands behind her back. I felt tiny beads of sweat trickle down my back and I fought the urge to scratch or fidget.

"Never fucking fails. There's always one." She didn't have to call any names because I knew exactly who she was talking about.

"Foster!"

"Sir, yes, sir."

She stepped forward and I let out a short sigh of relief when Foster addressed the cadre correctly; however, my relief didn't last long.

"Do you have a maid at your house?"

Even though the question sounded all nice and innocent, I could tell right away where it was going. If Foster had a lick of sense she would deny everything and take whatever punishment was dished out to her in silence. One thing was for sure: this was not a good way to start out.

"Sir, no, sir."

"Then why did you leave my bunk looking like a pig sty? Do you live with pigs, private?"

"Sir, I ran out of time, sir."

I heard a hitch in Foster's voice and I prayed she would keep it together in front of the squad.

"Is that supposed to be acceptable to me, private? Is that your final answer?"

"Uh, no . . ." Foster's confusion was written all over her face, and against my better judgment, I began to care about her.

"I can't hear you!" The cadre got so close to Foster they shared the same breath. It was intense and I was sure everybody in the squad felt it too.

"Sir, no, sir."

"I thought so. Since you think we should have a maid, you and your battle buddy will be our maids for the week. How about that?" She nodded her head up and down. "Yeah, I think I like that." The cadre smiled for the first time since meeting us. The bitch was gleaning sick pleasure out of Foster's mistakes.

I stepped forward. I didn't want to do it but I didn't see where I had a choice. "Sir, yes, sir." If I could have whacked Foster across her windpipe and gotten away with it, I would have.

"Glad to hear it. Schedules have been posted in the barracks. This is free choice unit. If you feel like you've made the wrong choice, I invite you to step forward and I will be happy to see your ass out of my unit."

She looked right at Foster and, by default, me. Part of me wanted to shove Foster forward and help pack her shit. It would certainly make my life easier. But the other half of me felt sorry for her. I was not going to fail and if I had to drag Foster along with me to succeed, then I would.

Chapter 4

Anji Foster

I couldn't sleep. Not only was I in an unfamiliar bed, I had nine other women in close proximity and all of them were strangers. Things didn't go quite the way I'd planned them and I was beginning to doubt my reasoning for signing up in the first place. Compared to this joint, I was living in the lap of luxury. The only thing expected of me was Bible Study and a few household chores, but other than that it wasn't so bad in retrospect. The hardest part of my life was church. We went to church six times a week. Every single day except Saturday. On Saturdays, I cleaned house while Daddy went to church. In hindsight, it wasn't such a bad life.

Lying on the uncomfortable bed confirmed my suspicious that I'd made a mistake and I was racking my brain on finding a way to fix it. By now, my father was sure to know I wasn't coming back, but I was hopeful he would forgive me in time. I needed to find out how badly a dishonorable discharge would affect my future. Would I be able to find another job? All this and more was running through my head when I should have been sleeping. I wanted to wake my battle buddy up to ask but I had a feeling she was ready to punch me dead in the face already. Waking her up might be the only justification she needed to actually do it.

I was homesick and heartbroken. I expected things would be different here, but I never realized how different it would be. Based on our accommodations, it was clear how little America thought about its soldiers. Our bunks were uncomfortable, we had zero privacy, and our commanders talked to us like crap. The hardest pill for me to swallow thus far was the privacy issue. I couldn't pee in front of strangers and heaven forbid I had to take a poop. I didn't know what I was going to do. Even if I waited until the barracks were empty, I'd still have to deal with my battle buddy since she had to be with me at all times. If I risked the punishment to be alone, my battle buddy would probably kill me in my sleep.

Dressing in front of strangers wasn't new to me. I struggled with it as a child in high school, and I thought I'd outgrown it. My own mother, God rest her soul, didn't get to see me naked a day after puberty. I didn't consider myself a prude, it just didn't seem natural to me to walk around nude. It bothered me to see the way these women pranced around the room naked. It was downright sinful. They ran around slapping each other on the butt like children but I didn't play that. I already knew what was going to happen the first time someone struck me on the butt. I'd be going to jail. The other thing I was having a hard time adjusting to was the bad language the women used. They cussed so much, you would've thought we were bunking with a bunch of men instead of women.

I tossed again trying to get comfortable on my tiny bed with its super thin mattress. I would have thought the army would've spent a little more money on comfort to make sure their soldiers got a good night's rest. But that's just me. I wasn't expecting a deluxe suite or anything like that but this cot was a step above sleeping on the floor. The pillow felt like two sheets folded and stuffed in a burlap sack. Back home, we had farm animals that were treated better than we were.

"You should get some sleep. We've got to get up real early and we definitely don't want to be late anymore."

I was surprised that Burns, my battle buddy, was even speaking to me after having to clean the bathrooms and mop the floors before we were allowed to sit down. I didn't know if I would have spoken to her if the shoe were on the other foot. But just because we weren't doing anything physical, it didn't mean I was resting. My mind was very active and my thoughts were all over the place, causing me to toss and turn on my stupid mat.

"It's too quiet in here. I usually sleep with the radio on when I'm at home."

"Well you ain't in Kansas no more, Dorothy."

I heard the sarcasm in her voice, even though she was whispering. Her smart remark offended me. I understood we got off on the wrong foot, but I hoped we weren't going to spend the rest of our time together sparring with each other.

"I'm sorry I got you in trouble." She didn't say anything for a few seconds so I assumed she'd fallen asleep.

"Are you asleep?"

"No, I'm trying to stay out of trouble."

We weren't supposed to talk after lights out but we hadn't been able to say anything all day, and I felt like I was going to bust if I didn't talk about what I was feeling. "Sorry." I punched my pillow again and tried to force my brain to be still so I could go to sleep.

"Don't think for a minute that just because the schedule says five o'clock doesn't mean they won't come in here earlier."

"Expect the unexpected, right?" For some reason it sounded ominous to me so I laughed.

"Shut up." An angry voice, from the other side of the room, reminded me we weren't alone.

I didn't appreciate being told to shut up, but decided to keep my peace for the time being. The last thing I needed was another person who had reason to hate my guts. I rolled over a final time and silently mouthed my prayers. I asked God for patience and understanding. I also prayed the women in my barracks would find Jesus and put on some darn clothes!

Today was payday, and as a special reward, we were allowed to go to the on-base store. Armed with a list of things the army "suggested" we get, we had our first taste of semi-freedom. I didn't appreciate them suggesting anything for me, especially after the way we'd been treated over the past several weeks. Apparently the army believed an idle mind was the devil's playground, because they made sure when we hit the rack we went to sleep.

The first couple of days, we learned what sleep deprivation felt like. It seemed like they woke us up every fifteen minutes, but it was probably more like every few hours. Every time the bell tolled, we were expected to run out outside and stand in formation until we were dismissed. After the second time, I wanted to keep on my clothes but my battle buddy told me it would paint a target on my back for being a smart ass. Whatever their reason for those drills, I thought they were stupid.

"Are you going to pick something up or are you going to keep walking around in damn circles?"

Lauren could be nice when she wanted to be but today wasn't one of those days. She acted like she was PMSing. She'd been snapping on me all day and I was about to tell her off.

"I'm trying to find the right stationary. You know, something unique to me."

"For crying out loud, it's fucking paper. You personalize it with your words."

I glanced in her basket and noted that she had only purchased some notebook paper, a box of envelopes, and the other recommended items the army so thoughtfully suggested.

"You write your letters your way, and I'll write mine my way." She had a good point about personalizing the pages with words but I wasn't about to say it to her.

"Suit yourself. You're going to spend ten dollars for ten sheets of paper and envelopes. That's a buck a letter. I'll be writing for weeks on the same dime while you'll be back here buying more stationary."

"Fine, I'll get the stupid notebook paper." I couldn't argue with her logic, so it did make sense to stick with plain paper.

"Don't do me no favors. If you want to waste money be my guest." She reached over me and grabbed the stationary I had put back on the shelf and tossed it in my basket.

"I said I'd get the darn paper, didn't I?"

"Yeah, but you got a little shitty attitude, too. I ain't trying to hear your mouth for the rest of the day because you didn't get what you wanted."

"Then go away. This is free time, so be free." I shooed her away but she wasn't budging.

"Haven't you learned anything since you've been here? For all you know, this could be another damn test. Regardless of whether or not we're on duty, we're expected to be together like flies on shit."

"Why do you cuss so much? Can you go five minutes without cussing?"

"Yeah, I could if I wanted to but I happen to like cussing. It's liberating."

"It is not. It's a sin."

"You've got to be kidding me. Have you read the Bible? There is cussing all throughout the Bible."

"I'm not talking about 'hell' or 'damn.' I'm talking about the B word and the F word. You say those a lot."

"So? Why you clocking what I say? You think you're better than me just because I cuss a little?"

"No, but you think you know everything." I brushed past Lauren, going to pay for my stuff. I tried not to let her know she'd gotten to me. I'd heard this from too many people to shrug it off as a random thought. I didn't put on airs and I never tried to act like I was better than someone else, so I couldn't understand why people continued to say this to me. If this person who I'd spent so much of my time with in close quarters didn't get me then what did that say about me? I wanted to get out of the store and if I didn't need some of the items in my basket, I would have left without them.

"Hey, slow down. I didn't mean to step on a nerve."

"Forget you," I said as I slapped my items on the counter. Lauren started laughing and it only made me madder.

"What's so funny?"

"You, you're funny."

She stepped to the other register and paid for her items. I wanted to slap her in the back of the head like we'd been trained to do but she probably would've slapped me back. I didn't understand Lauren half the time. One minute she could be as sweet as a sun-kissed watermelon, and the next a dried-up lemon: bitter and tart. I waited until we'd left the store and were heading back to the barracks before I broke down.

"Why?"

"Huh?"

I didn't know if she was just playing dumb or had legitimately forgotten what we were talking about.

"Why am I so funny to you?"

"Oh, well, if you'd have said fuck you instead of forget you, you would've felt better."

She walked ahead of me, which further pissed me off. Lauren was a loud-mouthed, big-headed heathen who probably didn't even believe in God. I smiled when I thought of her clinking glasses with the devil; she'd change her tune then. But it'd be too late, which was sad though because other than a potty mouth, she seemed like a good person. Maybe I was a little better than her, but she could still work on it, real hard. We walked the rest of the way back in silence. It was the first time in days we weren't running and I wanted to relish it. I didn't get why we had to run everywhere we went, only to stand in another darn line. Patience was not one of my virtues so I made a mental note to add it to my prayer list. I knew prayer delivered all of us and this was something I could definitely benefit from. I thought maybe my impatience was being perceived as arrogance, which was also a sin. I didn't want God to strike me down because He thought I was trying to be greater than I was, so I added that to the list as well.

"Do you believe in God, Lauren?" She stopped walking, causing me to bump into her.

"Of course I believe in God. What kind of dumb question is that to ask me?" She seemed angry, which surprised me.

"I don't know. I was just thinking. You don't talk much about yourself so I was trying to figure you out."

"And you think asking me about my religious beliefs is going to help you do that?"

"Well no, but it's a start. We've been stuck with each other for weeks and the only thing I know about you, other than that you have a brother in the military, is your last name, and that's because it's printed on your shirt."

"If you want to know something about me, ask me. Don't try to play no head games with me because I'm not into games." She started walking again so I had no choice but to follow her. Even though she opened the door for me to ask her questions, I was hesitant to do so.

"What made you join the military?" I thought it was a safe question to ask.

"I had my reasons."

"What happened to 'If you want to know something, ask'?"

"Anything but that." She walked faster and, as much as I didn't want to do it, I increased my speed to keep up with her.

"Sorry. It seemed like an innocent enough question to me."

"What about you, what's your story?"

"I come from a small town in Mississippi. I wanted more than what my town had to offer, so I came here." I didn't mention that I'd come to find a man; it would've been too much information.

"What about family?"

"It was just me and my dad." Thinking about my father made me sad. I'd yet to talk to him so I couldn't imagine how that conversation was going to go. The first letter I wrote was going to be to him. I owed him an explanation and I hoped I could explain it in a manner he would understand.

"Oh I get it. Spoiled rich kid."

"Spoiled, hardly. Rich, not even close. We made do with what we had but we didn't require a lot." Thinking of home made me depressed. I was still trying to decide if joining the army was the right thing for me and this depression only made it harder to think clearly. When we got back to the barracks it was time for dinner, so we stowed our purchases for later. I had so much nervous energy, I couldn't enjoy our free time.

"So what do we do now?" I asked after dinner.

"We could go over to the firing range and practice."

"Uh, no. My shoulder is still bruised from the other day."

"That's because you're not holding your weapon right."

"Oh, that's right, I forgot. You're the expert, at everything!" I couldn't resist the dig. If anything, she was the one who thought she was better than everyone in our group. After our first rocky week, she was placed in charge of our unit. By far, she was the most athletic, effortlessly going through the drills, while the rest of us struggled. She even qualified on the range the first day.

"Hey, what can I say?" She smiled, conveniently ignoring my dig.

"Boastful pride is the work of the devil." I didn't mean to say what I was thinking, but I did and I couldn't take it back. Her face appeared to lock in place, a grimace on her lips and her eyes narrowed to tiny slits.

"I wasn't boasting, merely agreeing with the facts. You can say what you want about me, but you have issues." She plopped down on her bunk and turned over, letting me know our conversation was over. I wanted to ask her what issues she was referring to but I was not about to talk to her back.

Chapter 5

Lauren Burns

The army was my family—got it. My battle buddy was my sister from another mother—got that. My sergeant was both Mommy and Daddy—okay, I got that too, but I drew the damn line when I was told my rifle was my lover. Fuck that shit. I wanted someone who was going to hold me back when I touched them. We were one month in and the ladies were bugging the fuck out in the barracks. Tempers were flaring and my tolerance for bullshit had been pushed to the limit.

On a more positive note, our squad had bonded and we were working together as a cohesive unit. We excelled in our drills and we were afforded a small measure of freedom for the rest of the weekend. We were allowed to use the phones and I couldn't wait to call my brother James and check in on him. As promised, he sent me a note, practically every day, but he never mentioned any news from home. I wanted to know if he'd spoken to my dad about me. I knew I should have let it go by now, but for some reason, I clung to the hope we could mend our relationship and get back to loving each other.

"Come on, Foster, I want to get at the phone before all them other hoes."

"Jeez, must you be so crude? These women are our sisters, not hoes." She continued fussing around with things in her locker and wasn't moving fast enough for me.

"Whatever, come on." I liked Foster but she could get on my nerves, especially when she wore her holy drawers. When she put them on, I wanted to put my foot on her neck. Part of my frustration had nothing to do with her but she made herself a target by taking her sweet-ass time getting ready. Because there were so many recruits, each barrack was allotted an hour of phone time to be shared. If we were the last ones in line, there was a good chance we wouldn't be able to use the phone at all, and she did not want to be around me if that happened.

"Dag, I'm coming."

"I don't get it. Don't you want to speak to your dad?" She looked worse than a deer caught in headlights. I saw genuine fear in her eyes and it made me wonder what the full story was. Obviously more than the little bit she shared with me about her life before the military. It also made me realize that everyone has a past, and little Ms. Goodie Two Shoes was obviously no exception.

"I said I was coming." She fell into step beside me but I could tell her heart wasn't in it.

"What's up with you? I thought you'd be knocking folks down to get to the phone as much as you like to talk."

"Can you mind your own business please?"

I was stunned. This was the first rebuke she'd given me and it caught me by surprise. "Well excuse the fuck out of me." I wasn't so much mad at her response as I was stunned. We had squabbled far more than this and she never fired back, so I knew whatever it was that got her blood to flowing was deep.

I waited for my turn on the phone and dialed my brother's cell number from memory. I was taking a chance calling him because I didn't know what his schedule was, but if I didn't get him, at least I'd get to hear his voice on his answering machine and leave a message.

"Hello?"

"James? I can't believe you answered! It's so good to hear your voice. How are you doing?" I felt the tears rolling down my face but I didn't bother to wipe them away.

"Hey, shorty. How's my army treating you? Did you get my letters?" James sounded almost as excited as I felt.

"Thanks to you I'm fine, but they sure did try to kick a girl's ass. But I'm holding my own. I qualified on the range the first day and they made me captain of our squad."

"Word, that's what's up. I knew you could do it. Do you have any fuck-ups in your unit?"

"Hell yeah, I'm saddled with one, but she's good people." There were a few seconds of uncomfortable silence because we were skirting around personal questions. I wanted to know about my father but was afraid to ask.

"The food sucks, right?"

"Oh God, yes. How come you didn't warn me about that shit?"

"If I did, your ass might not have signed up. I know how you like to eat." He laughed and I had to join in because he was right. I loved to eat and this bullshit they were serving us wasn't cutting it.

"I can deal with the food but I swear I'm ready to pluck somebody's eye out for a piece of chocolate. What's up with that? Can't a sista have some sugar?"

"You'll get over it; just tell yourself it's all in your head."

"Yeah, right, that shit don't work and you know it. They said we're doing the gas chamber this week. I'm kinda of nervous about it."

"Oh yeah, it ain't no walk in the park. You'll do okay, though. I'm proud of you, sis."

I couldn't take it no more. "Have you spoken to Dad?" My grip on the phone tightened and I had to force myself to lighten up.

"Uh, yeah. He's cool."

It wasn't what he said, it's what he didn't say that stung me. "All right then, look, I got a line behind me for the phone so I got to go. Thanks for the letters, James. You should be getting some from me soon."

"Sis, don't let this shit get you down. You need to keep your head on straight because you still got some heavy shit to go through before this is all over, especially the gas chamber."

"I'm good. It's his loss, not mine."

"Have you told anyone yet?"

I knew exactly what he was referring to and it pissed me off that he even mentioned it. But then again, I was already pissed so it probably didn't matter what he said to me, I would have been mad anyway.

"Didn't I tell you this is my pussy and who I give it to ain't nobody's business?"

"Damn, sis. Get a grip because you're about to fuck up. Let it go. Trust me, he ain't worth it."

I exhaled. James was right. I needed to get it together. I joined the army to prove to my father I was good enough to handle it, but I also joined because I was finally able to serve my country without having to lie about my sexual preference. It was important to me so I couldn't let something like my father's ignorance change my game.

"I'm good, really I am. Thanks." When I hung up the phone, my heart was heavy but I wasn't going to allow it to ruin my life. It pissed me off that the country could accept me for what I was, but my own father gave me his ass to kiss because I refused to be who he wanted me to be. He lived his life, so why couldn't I live mine?

Chapter 6

Anji Foster

Rita took forever to answer her cell phone but managed to pick up before the call went to voice mail. I could feel the sweat rolling down my back and it had nothing to do with the heat outside.

"Anji, bless your little heart. I'm so happy to hear from you."

I relaxed somewhat. "I can't tell; I haven't received one letter from you."

"Girl, I've been so busy filling in at summer Bible School, I haven't had time to write. These children are driving me nuts." She laughed in a nervous manner. I couldn't help but feel a little envious because had I not left, I was supposed to be teaching the kids.

"I thought you said you'd rather die before you spent another day in Bible School."

"You said that, missy. Besides, I'm not attending Bible School, I'm teaching it."

She was right, those were my sentiments, but I still didn't appreciate her jumping into my shoes without regard to how I'd feel about it.

"Did you give my dad my letter?" My heart began racing and I willed it to slow down so I could hear her response.

"Uh yeah, I did . . . Um, have you met any cute guys yet?"

She was stalling. I didn't want to talk about the guys, I wanted to know what was going on with my dad. I didn't want to call him until I knew what kind of reception I would get from him.

"He ah, he said—"

"Why you tripping? Tell me what he said." My heart was pounding so loudly I was positive everyone else in the line could hear it.

"I ain't tripping, I just don't know how to tell you."

My face got hot as my heart skidded to a painful stop. I didn't want to hear any bad news. My mind started working overtime as I imagined my father, in a hospital room, calling out for me, or worse, dead.

"God, you're scaring me. He's all right, isn't he?" I wished I could wipe away my fear like the sweat on my brow.

"No, girl, he's fine, but he's not real happy with you right now."

Duh, that wasn't a big surprise because I expected him to be upset.

"He said you were as dead to him as your mother. But don't worry, I've been checking in on him. He's getting better. "

I felt like I was punched in the stomach by a giant fist. I knew he would be mad but I honestly believed he'd be over it by now, especially once he knew I was okay. Hell, if he acted this way because I joined the army, what would he have done if I had gotten strung out on drugs or begun selling my body? Part of me wanted to call him up and give him a piece of my mind, but the other, darker part of me wanted to go somewhere alone and cry. I was disappointed with myself for taking the coward's way out instead of addressing the situation with my dad.

"But why?" This wasn't making sense to me.

"He said your mother didn't tell him she was sick and concealed her illness until she died. He said she left him the same way you did. Honey, I'm sorry. He's upset right now and I can tell he was hurting, but give him time. I'll talk to him and I'm sure he'll come around. He's speaking with his emotions right now, not his head."

"Why would he listen to you?"

"Well, I . . ." She giggled like a ten-year-old, and I realized she was doing more than comforting my dad and the thought repulsed me. Rita was my age so what did that say about my dad? I hung up the phone. This was too much information to process at one time. I was mad at myself for being selfish and only thinking about myself. I was also ashamed for not being there when he needed me. I tried to outrun the tears that streamed down my face. How could I call myself a Christian if I behaved like such a devil?

"Whoa, Anji, wait up." Burns used my first name, which was rare, but I couldn't stop to talk to her. I heard her boots pounding the pavement behind me. I wanted her to go away and let me have a private moment, but I knew she wouldn't.

"Leave me the fuck alone!" I was ready to take out my anger on someone and if she didn't get up off me, it was going to be her.

"Whoa, you cussed. Good job." You'd have thought she'd seen the second coming of Christ from the shocked expression on her face.

"And?" I shocked my own self too but I wasn't about to let her know it.

"Damn, my bad, I was just checking on your monkey ass to see if you were all right." She stopped walking but she didn't leave.

"I'm fine. I just want to be left alone."

"Newsflash, I can't go anywhere if I wanted to. Battle buddies, remember? So you can stand over there and, me, I'll stand over here."

She turned her back to me and starting humming an annoying tune I didn't recognize.

"Fine, just don't talk to me." I was angry. I was sick of living with a bunch of females, and more than anything I wanted to be home, safe in my own room.

Rita sounded way too comfortable with my life and I could have sworn I heard something else in her voice. I didn't know if it was just me and my insecurities, but she sounded like she was actually interested in my dad! I ran to the barracks and fell back on my bunk, placing my pillow over my head. I was trying to block out the disgusting images dancing around in my head.

"I don't know about you, but I could use a drink."

Normally, I didn't drink. My dad said liquor was the devil's brew. I let the suggestion linger for about two seconds before I agreed to go with Lauren on post. I wanted to get away from the images in my head and thought a change of scenery might do some good.

"Are you gonna do something to your hair before we go?" I didn't mean any harm but she really needed to do something with the tired bun she'd been wearing since we arrived at boot camp.

"For what?"

"We might meet some cute guys while we're there." I had closed the door on my tears and was ready to have some fun for a change. The more I thought about it, the better I felt. We didn't get much down time and I was going to make the best of it.

"Child, please. I'm not trying to be another notch on someone's belt. These guys probably all have girl-friends or wives at home anyway. I'm not about to allow them to put my shit on blast for fucking around with them."

"For twenty-one fucking days, I've been marching around this place looking like a dude. I don't see anything wrong with fixin' myself up to look like a girl and engage in some harmless flirtation."

"Who are you and what have you done with my battle buddy?" Lauren said, laughing.

I rushed into the bathroom and washed my face. I combed my hair from my own hideous bun and let it flow onto my shoulders. For one night, I was going to forget about my strict upbringing and have some fun.

"What are you drinking?" Since I didn't drink, I had no clue what to order.

"I'm having a Long Island Iced Tea." We were still on the base, but could have been on another planet, because it was so foreign to me. Everyone was so relaxed and appeared to be having fun. I wasn't used to seeing my peers in this type of environment and it was a little unsettling because there were no apparent boundaries.

"Make that two." It was about time I found out what all the hype was about. I didn't expect my soul to burst into flames but I was just a little scared God would punish me in other ways.

"Anji, be careful with these. They pack a punch that will sneak up on you if you're not careful," Lauren warned, but I wasn't trying to hear her. If this drink was going to make me forget my pain, that's what I was going for.

"I got this, boo. You do you and let me do me." With drink in hand, I walked away from Lauren because I needed a break. We spent so much time together, she was starting to remind me of my mother.

"Okay, but don't say I didn't warn ya." I could feel her eyes on me as I walked over to a lively game of pool on the other side of the bar. I'd never played a day in my life, but I couldn't resist the lively banter among the men. Looking up at the ceiling, I nervously took a sip from my drink and swallowed. I was waiting for the lightning bolt that was to set my soul ablaze and when it didn't come, I took another sip. It was so good I almost abandoned my straw, but I didn't want to appear greedy.

"You play?" A deep voice spoke near my ear, startling me. His breath seemed to caress my skin and caused the hair on my arms to stand up. It was like standing next to raw electricity.

"No, I like to watch." I felt warm all over and I couldn't tell if it was coming from the drink or the attention. Whichever the reason, I was starting to like it.

"Oh, you're a voyeur?" He chuckled and clinked his glass with mine.

He was cute and I felt myself getting hotter. I took another generous swig of my drink and practically emptied it. I tried to focus on the game but the guy was standing too close. He had to be over six feet tall and I could see his muscles straining against his fatigues. I envisioned those arms wrapped around my waist, and the visual was so powerful I got woozy.

"Would you like another drink, beautiful?"

I looked around to confirm who he was talking to and giggled. "Sure."

"Is that a Long Island?"

"It was," I said, laughing. I had killed the drink in less than ten minutes and my greedy behind wanted more. My eyes followed his butt as he went to order me another drink. He had a nice package and I had to force my eyes away from the tempting sight he presented.

Ashamed of the sexual nature of my thoughts, I looked around to see if anyone had caught my lustful stares and locked eyes with Lauren. She was watching me like a mother hen watched her chicks. This annoyed me for some reason, so I turned my back and slunk deeper into the shadows.

"My name is Trace." He handed me the glass and I took a hearty swallow over the lump that formed in my throat. He had some amazing eyes that reminded me of the muddy swamp waters of Mississippi. I felt compelled to test those waters just to see what lived underneath. He cocked his head and smiled.

"What?" I giggled nervously. I wasn't used to standing so close to a man but I didn't have the willpower to move away.

"I was waiting for you to tell me your name."

I felt my cheeks heat up and I was glad for the darkened room so it wasn't as noticeable as it would have been in broad daylight. "Foster." I ran my finger across the decal of my uniform for emphasis.

"What, a brother can't get a first name?"

"Oh, right, it's Anji." I turned my attention back to the game but it was a lame-duck effort because my thoughts were more on Trace. I wondered what his story was but I couldn't think of a way to ask.

"Where you from, Anji?"

"Jackson, Mississippi."

"Ah, small-town girl." He raised his glass in a salute. I couldn't tell if he was making fun of me and it pissed me off.

"You say that like it's a bad thing."

"Hey, slow your roll, honey. I love me some country women and I see you're a feisty one. I'm from Jackson, Tennessee myself so we're practically neighbors."

"Oh, okay. I'm so used to being teased by the girl in my barracks I assumed you were going to do it too."

"I feel you. I've taken my share of shit too. I don't know why people tend to think country folk are slow. I could outthink any of them bastards in my unit."

I didn't particularly care for the cuss words but I understood where he was coming from. But, then again, men cussed, even my father did it a time or two, but he normally followed it with a "Lord, forgive me."

"We may be small but we ain't slow." I raised my glass to his. I didn't remember drinking the rest of my drink so I was surprised when he handed me another.

"I don't know if I should have another. I'm starting to feel it."

"You're in good hands, homie, I got you." He stepped closer but I wasn't afraid. It was starting to get warm so I rubbed the glass over my forehead. The ice in my glass cooled my head.

"Is it hot in here?" I didn't notice the music playing when we first got to the bar but it got my attention as I allowed my hips to sway to the music.

"It is kinda warm. Would you like to step outside and get some air?" Trace's lips touched my ear as he spoke. It was loud inside the bar but it really wasn't necessary for him to be all up in my personal space like he was.

"We won't be able to hear the music." I was feeling good but I wanted to feel better. I raised my glass in the air and danced like I was alone in my bedroom. Daddy didn't approve of dancing; he thought it was sinful to dance unless you were praising the Lord.

"You looking good, ma."

Trace's voice sounded huskier. I'd have been lying if I said it didn't turn me on. I felt so sexy as I envisioned all eyes on me. I was doing a slow turn when my stupid feet got tangled and I felt myself falling. It happened so quickly I didn't have time to prepare.

"Whoa, you all right there, shorty?" Trace pulled me from behind before I could make a fool of myself. He cinched me in close to him and steered me toward the door. I was too dizzy to protest so I leaned against his arm as he lead me away.

"Hey, Anji, you ready to go back to the barracks?" Lauren grabbed my other arm firmly and pulled me away from Trace. Her fingers dug into my arm and I could feel the muscles in her fingers daring me to resist.

"Oh hey, Lauren. Meet my friend . . ." My mind drew a complete blank. The man's name was entrenched in my muddled head and I couldn't get it out my mouth. My voice sounded strange, as if I were talking in a tunnel. He did not look pleased.

"Oops, I'm sorry, I've forgotten your name." I laughed at my own silliness.

"Sorry, you have to excuse my buddy. She doesn't drink and apparently has had too much."

"Did you see me dancing, Lauren?"

"Yeah, I did. Now let's get you back to your bunk to sleep this off."

"I don't want to go to my bunk, I want to stay here with what's-his-name." I yanked hard on my arm but Lauren wasn't giving up.

"The name is Trace and if she wants to stay, I'll make sure she gets back."

"Trace? I knew a guy by the name of Trace before." I was floating on a cloud of happiness and I wanted Lauren to go away so I could have me another one of those wonderful drinks.

"That's 'cause you just met him, you idiot, now come on before you do something you'll regret in the morning."

I didn't appreciate the way Lauren was manhandling me. I was grown and she was treating me like a naughty child.

"Stop it. You're hurting my arm." Even though I knew Lauren's intentions were good, I wasn't ready to go back to my bunk. I wasn't ready to think about what caused me to get drunk in the first place.

"Part of me wants to say fuck it and leave your ass right here but I'm not getting into trouble because of you. Now if you don't bring that ass, I'm going to punch you the fuck out and drag you. The choice is yours." She let go of my arm but didn't step away. Trace had gone so I didn't have much of a choice but to go with Lauren.

"Fine, fuck it. Let's go." I started marching like I was in formation until I realized what I said. I stopped.

"Two sins in one night. I'm going straight to hell." I felt like crying and I probably would have if all eyes weren't on us as we marched out of the bar.

Chapter 7

Lauren Burns

After last night's debacle, two things were abundantly clear to me: I was head over heels in love with my battle buddy and there wasn't a damn thing I could do about it. Falling in love was not part of my plan and I was going to have to find a way to deal with it. Being confined in close quarters was proving to be too much for me to handle. During the entire walk home, Anji babbled about going to hell for cussing and drinking. If she weren't so serious, it would have been comical. If she felt this way about cussing and drinking, she'd probably bust a blood vessel if she knew how I was feeling about her.

"If God sent folks to hell because of a little cussing and drinking, he's going to need more space 'cause that bitch is going to be crowded as a motherfucker."

"You can laugh if you want to but I don't want to be standing next to you when that lightning bolt comes from the sky and knocks you down."

She was killing me. She acted as if she had God on speed dial but the God I served had much more serious issues to deal with than a little cussing and drinking. "I'm not making fun of God, I'm making fun of your interpretation of His words."

"What's that supposed to mean?"

I had to keep reminding myself she was drunk. We were alone in the barracks but her voice was a little loud for normal conversation.

"I'm saying that too many people construe the Word of God for their own benefit instead of applying the principals of His Word to their lives. Why do you think there are so many different types of churches and doctrines if there is only one God?"

"Haven't you ever heard of false prophets?"

"So who decides which one is telling the truth? That's my problem with most of the churches I have visited. Why should I believe the man who is standing before the congregation, proclaiming to be God's messenger while lining his pockets with money, instead of relying on His own words to guide me?"

"I'm not going to stand here and listen to this blasphemy. God chooses His messengers."

"Okay, if that's the case then why are there so many and why are they saying different things? How do you know they are truly messengers from God? Unless you were listening on the line when they got the call, you don't."

I never talked about my religious beliefs to anyone, but now that I was on a roll, I couldn't stop. "Did you ever play this game in school where everybody got in line and one person was to whisper a sentence to his neighbor, and each person passed on the message, but by the time the story got to the last person it was not anything close to the original sentence?"

"Yeah, but . . ."

"There is no 'but,' Anji. I believe that's what is happening in our churches today."

"Our pastor encourages us to read the Word and attend Bible Study."

"Most pastors do, but at the end of the day, the congregation looks to the pastor to decipher and clarify what you've read. Don't you see it's the same thing as that stupid game if you don't seek the truth for yourself?" I didn't know why it was so important to me that she understood where I was coming from, especially since I never bothered to tell another soul how I felt, but it was.

"I don't even know why we are having this conversation. My head is killing me." Anji staggered from her bunk, going to the bathroom.

"God gave us choice and free will, Anji. It was a gift and we should treasure it. If He wanted us all to be the same, He would have made it so we were incapable of changing it."

"What are you talking about now? This isn't still about religion, is it?" I could tell she was getting angry even though her voice was kind of muffled. I understood later when I heard her throwing up.

"Honestly, I don't know why I'm saying all this but it was pressing on my heart so I said it. Maybe it was for me more so than you, but something told me you needed to hear it too. Perhaps it will help you because sometimes our choices hurt the ones we love. It doesn't make us bad people, it's merely an exercise of free will." I heard the shower come on but she turned it off.

"What are you really saying?"

"I'm not trying to dip in your business but I know you were upset after your phone call home." I could see her pain etched in her eyes when she came out of the stall, and I fought my desire to hold her.

"You didn't act like you were thrilled with your conversation either."

I was hurt but it was an old wound and I was still trying to come to terms with it. "My dad and I have issues. We haven't spoken to each other in years, no biggie."

I wasn't ready to have this conversation with her so I was glad when she finally got in the shower. I was sure I'd never get her to understand, so I wasn't going to try. I didn't realize it at the time, but she'd completely taken the focus off her, and put it on me. If she acted this badly because of a cuss word, she'd probably split her wrist if she knew she was bunking next to a dyke, who had fallen in love with her.

As our time at basic training was nearing the end, our exercises were more dangerous and intense but not everyone was able to handle this amped-up version of training. Tempers were already flaring so it didn't take much provocation for the slightest infraction to escalate into a straight-up, hair-pulling brawl. I think the fighting kept us sane, and the hardest part was doing it without getting caught. We could kick each other's asses in the shower and go to chow acting like long-lost buddies. Some handled these transitions better than others.

Most of our barrack fights happened after mail call but today was a little different. The ladies were already disgruntled from our sensitivity training, so I understood my part in the fight even before it began. The training caught me off guard because I thought I knew everything when it came to training to be a solider. When we were forced to watch a slideshow presentation about homosexuals in today's army, I found it invasive and offensive. As I sat among my peers, I felt myself getting angry and I had no idea what I was going to do with those emotions.

Perhaps if I had known ahead of time there would be an open discussion on the matter, I would have been better prepared. But then again, probably not, because

I believed sexual preference was a private affair and not something that should be dissected in a boardroom by a bunch of crabby-ass dickheads who knew nothing about which they spoke. I was appalled at the way the army chose to handle this situation because common sense told me that if you force feed someone something they didn't want to eat, instinctively they gag and throw it back up, leaving a hot-ass mess on the table.

As we marched back to the barracks I tried to ignore the comments and the crude jokes because I knew they were tempered by the gag reflex, but it was hard, probably the hardest thing I had to do since I got there.

"That's some bullshit right there. I wish a bitch would try to run up on me. I ain't telling shit; I'm just gonna lay the bitch out," one person bragged.

"Yeah, I will beat that carpet-munching skeezer like she stole something," another joked back.

"And if I catch a bitch looking at me sideways, I'm gonna shoot her and claim it was an accident while I was cleaning my gun." It seemed like the whole platoon was laughing and there wasn't a damn thing funny. I walked faster so I could get away from the bullshit.

"Lauren, wait up!" Anji shouted. She was busy clowning with the rest of the girls and I didn't feel like being bothered. I wanted to get as far away from those people making ignorant comments as I could. I allowed Anji to catch up but it was big mistake.

"So what do you think?" She looked like a puppy about to pee on herself with excitement.

"About what?" I knew exactly what she was talking about but I dreaded discussing it with her, or anyone else for that matter.

"The briefing, silly, what else? Do you think they will put one of them homosexuals in our unit?"

I was so stunned, my feet stopped moving. "Are you fucking kidding me?" I never wanted to hit someone so badly as I did at that moment.

"Darn, what is your problem?"

"All you motherfuckers are my problem." By this time, the rest of the platoon had caught up and formed a small circle around us.

"Why are you yelling at me? You trying to get us in trouble?"

"I don't give a flying fuck, just leave me alone." I continued walking but the throng followed me.

"Is this a lovers' quarrel?" The others started laughing, but to me it wasn't funny.

I froze as I tried to control my emotions but I was fighting a losing battle. *Oh no, this troll bitch didn't try to punk me in front of our squad.* "Bitch, please. Nobody would want your rancid-ass pussy if you served it up honey glazed with a side order of collard greens and some mac and cheese." The squad roared at my joke but it must have pissed off the girl because she launched herself at me like a nuclear missile. I hit the compacted earth hard, as tiny pebbles poked through my uniform into my back. I shoved the woman aside so I could get up from the tortuous bed of rocks I'd landed on.

"Bitch, are you out your rabbit-ass mind?" I knew the heifa was pissed but she had to be a little bit crazy too to charge me like a linebacker.

"I got your bitch." She looked around as if she were looking for a weapon or something and I felt the hairs on the back of my neck stand up. This was a bit more than I expected to deal with when I called her out her name, but I couldn't back down now; all eyes were on me.

"Fine, then let's not talk about it, be about it." I pushed forward as visions of every ass whipping I'd ever taken ran through my head. I was about to take this bitch to work and maybe she'd think twice before she played Mr. Bad-ass again. I pulled back, ready to punch her dead in her face, when someone grabbed me from behind and pinned my arms to my side.

"Get the fuck off me," I shouted. I didn't know who all was holding me, but I was almost as mad at them as I was at the woman who bum-rushed me.

"Keep your damn voice down before we all get into trouble." I recognized Anji's voice but she wasn't the person holding me, she was blocking the other woman from charging me again. It made me feel good knowing she had my back but this shit wasn't over. Normally, I was the most peaceable person in the world until you put your hands on me; then, all bets were off.

"We've got forty more days in this bitch. After that, you two can kill each other as far as I'm concerned but I refuse to spend the next two weeks peeling fucking potatoes or running around in the goddamn mud over some dumb shit," someone spoke.

I felt my anger dissipate almost as quickly as it flared up. I stopped resisting and began to feel embarrassed by my behavior. After a few more seconds of heavy breathing, my arms were released. My back was still stinging from the rocks, but I tried to be the bigger person.

"I'm cool." I shook out my arms as I kept an eye on my opponent. I was willing to bury the hatchet, but I was not about to let my guard down again.

"What were you thinking?" Anji acted as if she were mad at me as we walked away from the crowd.

"Excuse me? The bitch attacked me."

"Duh, and you told her she couldn't give her pussy away on a good day. I would have jumped your ass too."

The hilarity of it all started with the giggles and gave way to loud cackles of laughter. A picture was worth a thousand words and this picture was priceless. However, my laughter stopped as I pulled my shirt free of my pants. I winced in pain.

"What's wrong?"

"Something must have cut me when I hit the ground." I turned around to see if I could see my back in the mirror but it was bolted too high up for me to adequately see.

"Let me look." Anji spun me around before I could object. "Oh wow." She gulped in air like she was having difficulty breathing.

"What?" I was alarmed and tried to turn back around to see for myself.

"You got a few cuts. You might want to go over to sickbay and have them clean them up for you."

"Fuck that, they are going to want to know what happened. I'm sure there is something in the first-aid kit I could use."

She got the kit in the corner and took out a few things as I unhooked my bra. At first she gently washed my back with a warm washcloth. Her touch was so gentle, it was almost sexual. It's a good thing I didn't have a dick or my stimulation would have been noticeable. My nipples were erect but I covered them with my arms.

"This is going to sting at little."

"I don't care just . . . Aw shit!" My body jerked away from her ministrations but she followed me, dabbing at my wounds.

"See, I told your ass to go to sickbay." If it bothered her that she was inflicting pain, I couldn't tell. She followed me around the room until she was satisfied. My back felt like it was on fire and I started to get angry again.

"You are going to have to rinse out your mouth before you go to bed."

"Fuck you."

I was enjoying this new Anji but I was still upset about my back. "I'm gonna get that bitch." It wasn't a threat, it was a promise. I wasn't sure when I was going to do it, but it was going to get done.

"You do and all of us are going to end up in trouble."

"She won't even see it coming and she definitely won't be able to prove it was me." I gritted my teeth and waited for her to finish putting on my Band-Aids. I was sure I would be sore for a few days but that only added to my anger.

"When it heals, I'll put some cocoa butter on it so that it doesn't leave a permanent mark."

"I guess I'll be sleeping on my stomach for the next few days." It was a good thing that bitch didn't stay on the same side of the barracks or I might have choked the heifa while she was sleeping.

"I used some Neosporin too and it works fast."

"Yeah, right." I knew I sounded ungrateful so I came back and thanked her. She didn't have to administer to my wounds so it didn't hurt me to say it.

"I still don't understand what set you off. Normally you're so cool, but you kinda flipped out this time."

This was the perfect opportunity for me to come clean about my sexuality and I was scared shitless. With all that I knew about Anji, I was pretty sure what her reaction would be, but wasn't this also one of the reasons why I left home in the first place, so I could be myself? I had no problem telling strangers I was gay, but because I cared what Anji thought of me, I was terrified to tell her.

I tempered my words carefully so I wasn't revealing so much of myself, but a little about what I was feeling.

"First of all, I can't stand judgmental people. And I don't like to hear folks diss something just because it's not their cup of tea. Everybody ain't going to be the same and for someone to stand up and make jokes about something they don't understand, it got me heated."

"But they were just joking."

"Seriously? What if they were joking about niggas and making derogatory slurs about us, would you think that was funny too? Their comments were peppered with ignorance and were offensive."

"Hey, calm down. She didn't call you gay or anything like that so it shouldn't have been so bad."

"But I am gay. Now what? Does that change things for you?" She turned another shade darker and seemed like she was at a loss for words. It wasn't the way I would have wanted to come out of the closet but it was on the table now.

"You . . . You should have told me." She wouldn't look me in the eye and this only made me madder.

"Why? Did you tell me who you like to fuck? It's none of your damn business because at the end of the day, it doesn't change who I am. And don't flatter yourself and think just because I'm gay I want to lick your pussy, because it doesn't necessarily work like that."

"I . . . I don't know what to say. I still think you should have said something."

"And I say again, why, so you look at me like the spawn of Satan, much like you're doing now?"

The last remark was below the belt, but I couldn't help the way I felt. Having folks who didn't know me judge me was one thing, but having someone I spent so much time with and learned to care about was even worse.

"I understand you're upset, but I didn't do anything to you so you need to stop yelling at me." Anji stood toe to toe with me, pointing her finger in my face much like my father when I told him the truth.

It was a déjà vu moment and too much for me to handle, so I did the only thing I could think of doing. I ran. I ran away from the pain, humiliation, and shame I felt every time I told someone I cared about how I felt. As I ran, I cried. I could hear Anji running behind me, but I didn't care. I wasn't ready to face her and I didn't care if my actions led to some sort of punishment.

"Go away, Anji," I shouted over my shoulder.

"I can't, bitch, I'm super-glued to your ass. Now cut the shit and stop running, dammit."

I stumbled. Anji was cussing her ass off and it sounded so natural coming from her lips I started laughing. She walked up behind me and slapped me on the back.

"Ouch, that shit hurt."

"It should. Why the fuck are we running? Don't we get enough of that shit every other day?"

"So you're fucking mocking me now? It's not a joke, Foster." Pissed, I stopped moving.

Anji bent over with her head dangling down near her feet. She didn't say anything for a few seconds, which was just as well, because I was also trying to catch my breath.

"If it were a joke would it be funny?"

"What? You got that shit from the movie the other night. It's not original and it's not even appropriate for the conversation."

"Hey, you didn't start running again, so it worked for me." She sat down on the ground and drew her knees to her chest.

She had a point and I sat down beside her. I was confused because a few seconds ago I was ready to kick her ass and now it was very important to me we at least remained friends.

"Anji, you don't know what it's like having to hide who you are just because you don't want to make other people uncomfortable. It's not like being black in a room full of white people. They know I'm black right off the bat, so there's no need for pretense. But when you're gay, it's a constant struggle to behave in a manner that makes everyone else feel comfortable. If I see a woman who looks good, I can't openly stare at her, and God forbid I approach her 'cause that shit can get crazy real quick. And then it's the damned if you do and damned if you don't thing. There was this girl in school I was friends with. She found out I was gay in high school and got pissed because I never made a pass at her. She was completely straight, but she said I hurt her feelings. It's so damn complicated." I was so emotionally drained, I wanted to cry.

"I don't know what to say. We're going to have to figure it out."

What the fuck does that mean?

Chapter 8

Anji Foster

I didn't make morning formation. I said it was a bad case of cramps but I was lying. They gave me some Motrin and told me to take it easy for the rest of the day.

"Can I see the chaplain?"

"I thought you were sick."

I almost told the nurse to mind her fucking business but it would have been counter-productive.

"Haven't you heard of the power of prayer?"

"Sounds like some bullshit to me."

I might not have fooled her, but she wrote me a pass. I hobbled out of the office like I was on death's door, but as soon as the door closed, I stood up straight and went to find the chaplain. When we first got to boot camp we were required to attend Sunday service, but now it was optional and I didn't exercise that option. My rationale at the time was that the army gave us so few opportunities to make a choice that I almost always took advantage of the ones they gave me. When I was exercising my option I didn't view it as turning my back on God, but in hindsight, I could see where it would be construed as such.

"Private Foster, I haven't seen you in a while."

I felt like a complete heathen and instantly regretted my decision to come. "Sir, I know I've been remiss by not coming to church, but I continue to keep God in my heart."

"And that's a good thing, but remember if you only call the Lord when you're in need, He might not answer. But if you're prayed up you've paid up, you know what I mean? What can I do for you?" He opened his door and allowed me into his office. After he took his seat behind the desk, I started to speak.

"Can I speak candidly, sir?"

"Of course."

"Sir, I just found out my battle buddy is gay and I'm having a hard time with it."

You can tell a lot about what a person is thinking by their body language. The second I mentioned the word "gay," his whole demeanor changed. With narrowed eyes, he sat up in his chair and stared at me. It was an intense look and made me very uncomfortable.

"I see. Have you attended the sensitivity training?"

"Well yeah, but—"

"Private, there are no buts. The army does not discriminate on the basis of sexual orientation. As long as there is no threat to combat readiness, we don't have a problem."

"But about my rights? I feel like I'm being forced to live with a person who could be a sexual predator and I don't have a choice about it. How fair is that?"

"Life ain't fair, private. Now the army's position is clear: either deal with it or leave. You betta not tell. Those are your choices."

"Do you condone homosexuality?" I was getting angry and almost forget myself.

"Whether I condone it is irrelevant." He stood up, signaling an end to our meeting.

"Wait, but I'm not finished."

"You may not be, but I am. You get paid to follow orders, private, and these orders are clear. If you have a problem with your orders, I suggest you run it up the flagpole and see if it flies in your chain of command."

"But what if the next person in my chain of command is gay?"

For a split second he paused, but if he was going to say something he obviously thought better of it and showed me to the door. "Good luck with that." He opened the door and impatiently waited for me to leave. Once I cleared the frame, he closed the door. Even with all the people milling around me, I felt alone.

"Hey, you feeling better? We threw grenades today. That shit was intense."

"Yeah, I'm straight." I flipped over on my bunk. I didn't feel like talking, least of all to her. I didn't care about grenades or anything else army related.

"I got your mail." I felt it hit my bunk but I didn't even want to see what was in it. Probably another letter from Rita bearing more bad news and I had enough of that. With the exception of Rita, there wasn't anyone else. My dad had cut me off so I really was alone. I started crying softly so I wouldn't attract any attention. If Lauren noticed my shoulders shaking, she didn't mention it. What bothered me the most was that even if I decided to leave the army, I didn't have anywhere to go.

"Are you going to get something to eat?"

I wanted Lauren to leave me alone, but she wasn't getting the message. I didn't want to yell at her but she kept on pushing. Frustrated, I got up, knocking a letter from my father to the floor. I was surprised to see it because I didn't expect to hear from him so soon. My dad was stubborn, but he had a forgiving spirit. With my heart beating fast, I tore open the envelope. I felt like God was giving me someone else to talk to when my earlier efforts to talk failed. However, my elation was short-lived as I allowed the paper to slip from my fingers.

"Are you okay?" Lauren was watching me like a hawk.

"My dad is getting married."

"Oh wow. I take it you're surprised?"

"Yeah, big time. She's over half his age and used to be my best friend."

"Shocker! Sounds like you need a drink."

"You ain't lying. I need several of them in rapid succession."

"How 'bout we skip dinner and go to the bar? If we get hungry, we can order some hot wings or something."

I didn't even think about her being gay when I accepted her offer. I wanted to get drunk and I didn't necessarily want to do it by myself. She didn't look gay, so it should have been all right, I reasoned. Even though we'd been out before and it wasn't a factor, now that I knew, it was different.

I was pretty much in a fog as we walked to the bar. I couldn't believe my father would wait until I'd left, then suddenly show interest in a girl who used to come over to my house and spend the night. I was also surprised at Rita's parents. How could they let their only child marry a man so old, unless they were doing it for financial reasons? My dad wasn't rich, but he was comfortably secure. They must have seen dollar signs and with me out of the way, there was nothing stopping them.

It wasn't that I didn't want my father to be happy, I just couldn't understand why he wanted to be with a child. But the thing that hurt me worse than anything was the way he told me. His letter was only two sentences long and he could have written it on a postcard and saved himself a few pennies.

"What did the letter say?" Lauren asked as she handed me my first drink.

"'Rita and I are getting married. She told me to tell you hi.'"

"That's it?"

"Yep. No 'I love you, wish you were here,' nothing." I picked up my glass and emptied it.

"I'ma get you another drink but you've got to promise to drink it a little slower. Remember what happened the last time."

Any other day I might have heeded the warning, but I was looking forward to drunken oblivion, even if it meant praying to the porcelain god later.

"Don't you think it's perverted for a forty-something-year-old man to be poking a twenty-something girl?"

"I wouldn't call it perverted, but I have my doubts about whether it will last. Right now, he's probably thinking he's a stud for getting the eye of a young girl. Was he sexually active?"

"Not to my knowledge, but hey, what do I know? When Mom died, I always hoped he would marry one of the ladies from church. In fact, I used to tease him about it, but he claimed he wasn't ready."

"Girl, your friend probably whipped some of that young-ass pussy on him and made him lose his damn mind."

"Humph, she must have. He didn't even ask how I was doing." I felt like crying again but instead I drained another glass.

"Careful."

The liquor made me bold and curious. "Have you ever been with a man?" I could tell she wasn't expecting the question when she choked.

She emptied her glass and ordered another round. "Yeah, sure."

I was surprised. "I haven't. Hell, I've barely kissed a guy."

"You make it sound like a bad thing. It's actually rare to find a virgin these days. You should be proud."

"I haven't been with a woman, either." She probably already knew that but I said it anyway.

"Okay, and you told me this for what reason?"

"No reason in particular, I just wanted you to know." It was little warm in the bar and I regretted coming in my fatigues. "Is it hot in here to you?"

"A little bit, but it's probably the alcohol that's got you fired up."

"You know my story, what's yours?" Even after all the time we spent together, there was still so much I didn't know about my buddy, and a lot I didn't want to know.

"Not much to tell. I'm a military brat. Been all over the world with my dad. My mom couldn't take it and left me and my two brothers with my dad. Haven't seen her since I was about twelve."

"That's too bad. All girls need their mother." I couldn't help but wonder if not having her mother in her life was the reason she sought other women. However, I instantly realized the fallacy of that premise because I didn't have a mother either and I wasn't looking at girls in a sexual manner. We were on our fourth drink before I had the nerve to ask the question that was on my mind.

"What happened to you to make you like . . . you are?"

"The way I am? What do you mean, gay?"

I nodded my head, suddenly afraid I'd said something wrong.

"Get the fuck out of here. What, you think I was molested or something?"

"I'm sorry if I offended you, but I don't know anything about gay people. You're the first person I've ever talked to about it."

"Well sometimes if you don't know what to say, you shouldn't say anything."

She was mad, but it wasn't my intent to piss her off and since she basically told me if I didn't know what to say I shouldn't say anything, I sat there. She continued to glare at me but I was drunk so it was hard to maintain my stoic expression. I started laughing.

"So, you're laughing at me now? I'm a joke to you?" She got up from the stool.

"Wait, please sit back down. Can't you see I'm drunk? I've got to laugh to keep from crying. My life is so fucked up right about now."

Reluctantly, she sat down but I could tell it wouldn't take much for her to leave again, so I had to be careful not to piss her off any more than I'd already done. We ordered another round and silently sipped our drinks. It was going to be a long night and we were going to need each other just to get home safely.

"I've always related to men better than women because of my competitive nature. As the only girl in a family full of boys, I felt like I had to fight to get my father's attention. He would make such a big deal over my brothers when they entered the army, I just knew he would love me more if I made it in too."

"So that's why you joined?"

"Yeah. My dad and I haven't been speaking because he doesn't approve of my lifestyle. I was living with my girlfriend and he hated it. I thought I could win back his love, but he still doesn't want to have anything to do with me and it's so unfair."

"If you knew he wasn't going to approve, why did you tell him?"

"I didn't, my girl did. She would do stuff when she got mad."

I watched helplessly as a few tears dropped from Lauren's eyes. I wanted to hug her but I didn't want her, or anybody else, to get the wrong impression.

"Please don't cry. I'm such a sucker for tears."

"It's okay, I'm good. Tears are such a waste of time because they don't change shit."

"Excuse me, would you like to dance?"

A fine cup of tall coffee tapped me on the shoulder. When I turned around, I felt like all the air had been sucked out of the room and I got dizzy. The scent of his cologne seared my nostrils and scorched my drawers.

"Damn."

"Excuse me?"

"Hold my spot, I'll be back." I had no business standing let alone dancing, but my feet barely touched the floor. I melted into his strong arms and he held me up in a slow grind. I felt every muscle in his body pressed against mine.

"What's your name?" I had to shout because his ear was so far from my face and the music was so loud.

"Patrick. What's yours?"

"Anji, and that's my friend Lauren." I tried to swing around and point to her but I almost lost my balance.

"I saw y'all slugging 'em back. I thought you were celebrating, so I came over to join the party."

"It wasn't a party until you showed up." I started laughing which did nothing for my balance.

"Careful or we're both gonna be laid out on the floor. Do you want me to send over one of my boys to keep your friend company?"

"Uh." I froze. How was I supposed to answer him? Surely it wasn't my place to tell him of Lauren's preferences.

"What? Is she shy?"

"Yeah, she's shy. She'd kill me for trying to fix her up."

"Oh, okay. I just wanted to get to know you a little better, that's all."

I was torn because I wanted to get to know him a little better too. "Let me talk to her." I gently pulled away from his arms and two-stepped my way back to Lauren.

"Hey, girl, you okay?"

"I'm good. Where's your friend?"

"I told him I'd be back. He wanted to know if you wanted to meet one of his boys but I told him you were shy."

She looked at me real funny and I wondered if I messed up and said the wrong thing again.

"You didn't have to lie for me."

"I know, but that's not why I came back. I want to fuck this guy." I finished my drink and slapped the glass back on the bar.

"Are you serious? You don't even know that nigga. Besides, he might be somebody's husband."

"I don't want to marry him, I want to fuck him. He can go back to his life tomorrow. I felt his dick on my leg and it was big." I started laughing. This was the first dick I'd ever felt and it had my panties feeling all gushy.

"You've had way too much to drink and there's no way I'm going to let you make this type of mistake."

If I weren't drunk I might have appreciated her for looking out for me, but my mind was fuddled with booze. "I don't need no haters." I backed away from the bar, knocking over the stool.

"Fine, you want to be a big girl and play grown-up games, fine, but don't come crying to me in the morning when you can't remember his fucking name, let alone what he looks like."

Lauren threw some money on the bar and left. She was weaving back and forth, but she was more steady on her feet than I was. I was out of my league and too stupid to know it. Patrick led me over to his group of friends and we started doing shots of tequila. They were good too.

"I think I need some air, it's so hot in here."

"My buddy's car is outside. We could sit for a while and talk—"

"Fine, just turn on the air. . . ."

I couldn't feel my legs and Patrick led me out of the bar into the back seat of a car. He leaned between the seats, turned the car on, and adjusted the radio to a soft jazz station. I had this warm and fuzzy feeling in my stomach and I was sure it had little to do with the drinks I'd consumed. Patrick was so nice.

"Is this better?" He ran his hand along the side of my face, causing tiny goose bumps to raise up on my arms.

"Yeah, much better." Despite the cool air, I started to get sleepy. I wanted to go back to the barracks but I knew I couldn't walk that far. I put my head on his shoulder as his hand slipped down to my neck.

"You're so pretty." He brushed my hair from my face and kissed me. It felt so good.

"That's nice."

I felt his fingers on my shirt, but I was so tired I couldn't stop him if I wanted to. He fingered my nipples as I drifted off to sleep.

Chapter 9

Lauren Burns

I knew I should have never left Anji drunk and alone in the bar, but I couldn't sit there and watch her be with someone else. Even though there wasn't a snowball's chance in hell that we'd ever be together, I'd be damned if I watched her give herself to another. If we got caught in a surprise inspection, we'd both get punished for breaking the rules, but I didn't care. If I stayed in the bar, I was liable to make a fool of myself, and to me leaving was my only viable option.

On a practical note, finding a place to fuck on base would be next to impossible. It wasn't like we were allowed to leave, and unless he was an officer, most soldiers slept in barracks just like we did. There was no way she was going to be able to smuggle a dick into our unit. As horny as those girls were, they would smell it before she could get it in the door. I laughed at the thought, but I was still worried. Anji was not used to drinking and she also claimed to be a virgin. Not a good combination, but she was also a big girl who claimed she didn't need me watching over her. So, whatever happened, she was going to have to take it on the chin.

I slipped into a deep slumber and didn't hear Anji when she made it back to her bunk. It wasn't a perfect sleep but I was able to rest easier once I saw Anji was back. Part of me wanted to wake her to see if she was okay, but the other part of me had no desire to hear the gory details of her night out. I slapped my pillow trying to get comfortable, but I was stone-cold sober and wide awake.

"Fuck," I mumbled under my breath. I couldn't get the visual of Anji having sex out of my mind. I wondered where they did it and if he was gentle. I couldn't imagine my first time having sex in something as common as a stall in the bathroom, and even though it wasn't with me, I hoped it was at least memorable.

Getting up was not an option. The barracks were dark and the other ladies were trying to rest. I couldn't turn on the light, so my only other option was to lay there feeling sorry for myself. This lasted all of maybe five minutes and I climbed out of my bunk and crept to the bathroom. I felt my way in the darkened room, thankful for the clear path, and eased the door closed behind me. I waited several seconds before I turned on the light. The first thing that caught my attention was a bloodied rag in the sink. Since we were subject to inspection at any time, it was really odd to see anything out of place.

"Nasty bitches." I turned on the water and washed the rag the best I could with the military-issued soap. Whoever used the rag must have cut themselves pretty badly because there was a considerable amount of blood soaked in it. Curiosity made me search the stalls to see if I could see anything else out of place. In the last stall, I found another rag and a blood-encrusted razor blade. I felt my heart leap inside my chest as I began to put two and two together.

"Oh God." This was no accident and someone in our unit was hurt. I followed the trail of blood into the barracks and turned on the light.

"Turn that damn light out."

"Aw, man. This shit ain't even funny."

One by one I watched the ladies sit up and complain, all but one. My feet would not move as my eyes bucked with realization of who the wounded woman was.

"Anji, no!" I raced over to my friend, fearing the worst. I slipped in her blood but managed to stay on my feet. By this time, the other woman realized something was wrong and had formed a small circle around her bed. Anji was curled up in a fetal position with a sheet practically covering her face.

"Get some help," I shouted. I reached for the sheet, scared what I was going to find. I couldn't believe Anji would harm herself so I reasoned that something must have happened with the guy. But if he did something to her, why was she here, with us? Things were not making any sense.

"What the hell happened?"

"Fuck, are you stupid? Get some damn help! Somebody else get me some towels." I was shouting orders to keep from breaking down even as the tears streamed from my eyes. I prayed, like I'd never prayed before, that it was all some big mistake. However, one look at her pale skin and the red-stained sheets told me it wasn't. My hands were trembling as I tore the sheets into strips to use as bandages for her wrists. Oddly, Anji had taken the time to make four-inch cuffs on the arms of her shirt. She might not have gotten any blood on the cuffs but the rest of her shirt was soaked.

"Is she dead?"

The paramedics arrived and pushed me out of the way. "Does anybody know what happened here?"

"She slit her wrist."

"We can see that, but do you know why?"

I could tell them about her frame of mind and how she was when I left her, but I couldn't begin to tell them what made her do it and I certainly wasn't going to say anything in front of a room full of noisy bitches. "Can we talk about this on the way to the hospital?"

"Save it for your cadre; this one is going to the morgue."

I was pretty sure I didn't faint, but I did zone out for a while. I could hear the other girls crying but I was so far removed from them, I couldn't feel their pain. We lived like a family for eight weeks so it was hard on all of us. Anji's death was so unexpected, I thought we were all in shock. She wasn't one of the girls I thought would crack under pressure, so I couldn't understand what went so terribly wrong.

I watched as they took my friend from the barracks. One of the officers packed up her things and took them as well. Her bed was marked off, much like the crimes scenes I saw on television. They didn't speak to us as they went about their duties as if we weren't even there. I thought back on all the pain and disappointments in my life but none of it compared to what I was feeling now. It was still dark outside so when the medics and the sergeants finished securing the area they turned out the light and left. With the exception of the crime tape, it was as if they'd never come.

Chapter 10

Lauren Burns

In the morning, I was summoned to the cadre's office. Even though I was expecting the meeting, I felt like I wasn't prepared for it. I hadn't decided how much of Anji's story I was willing to tell. As far as I was concerned, some things were better left untold and unless they pressed me, I was going to carry some of them to my grave.

"Come on in, private."

I walked into the office and saluted the cadre and the two other officers present in the room.

"At ease. Why don't you have a seat?"

I relaxed my stance but not my mind. This was my first interrogation and hopefully my last.

"We have contacted Private Foster's father and he is coming to collect her remains but before he gets here, we were hoping you could fill us in on what happened here last night."

"Sir, yes, sir."

"When was the last time you saw Private Foster alive?"

"She was alive when the paramedics got there, sir."

"I think you know I was referring to prior to the incident."

She was right, I knew exactly what she was talking about, but if she didn't ask, I wasn't going to tell.

"At approximately 2100, sir. We had a few drinks at the bar." There was no point in lying about this because I was sure a lot of people saw us there.

"You and Foster were battle buddies, right?"

"Sir, yes, sir."

"And how was that working out?"

I was confused as to where this line of questioning was going but I played along.

"Fine, sir."

"Was there anything different about Foster last night that you can recall?"

Seriously? Does he really think there is anything about last night that I can't recall? Hell, I've been re-playing the entire night in my head ever since I found her.

"She was upset about a letter from home."

"So she decided to drink it away?"

"I guess so, sir."

"You were with her, so is that a yes or a no?"

"Sir, yes, sir." I was trying so hard not to lose my temper but the cadre was pissing me off.

"Yes, she was drinking away her problems?"

"Yes, she was trying."

"Were you drinking too?"

Right, I was going to go to a bar with my buddy and let her drink alone. "I had a few."

"Did Foster say or do anything that let you know she was thinking about hurting herself?"

I didn't have to think about my answer. "No."

"Did you two argue?"

"When, last night or ever?"

"Confine your responses to the events of last night please."

Sarcastic fucker. "We disagreed, but I wouldn't call it an argument."

"About what?"

"I'd rather not say, sir."

One of the other officers said, "Did you two have a lovers' quarrel?"

I had to bite my tongue before I answered because I knew my answer would've been punishable by a couple of nights in the brig.

"Foster wasn't gay, sir."

"What about you?"

"Whether I am or not is a non motherfucking factor. Now if you have some questions for me about Foster, fine, but my personal life is none of your damn business."

"Calm down, private. We're just trying to understand what happened. We're the ones who are going to have to explain to her family so we need to know."

"There is nothing to understand. It's inexplicable. She was not a threat to herself or anybody else."

"Well obviously, something was wrong with her," the same smart-ass sergeant said.

"Sir, request permission to leave, sir. I don't want to say something that I can't take back."

I felt like he was trying to provoke me into saying something that would incriminate me or discredit Foster and I didn't plan on doing either of those things.

"Negative, private. We're not finished yet."

He might not have been finished but I was about done. I waited for the next question for several more seconds while they shared notes. If it was their intention to make me uncomfortable, it was working. I couldn't imagine what information they had on the chart they were not sharing with me.

"Why did you join the reserves, private?"

"To serve my country, sir."

"I see you're from a military family."

"Sir, yes, sir."

"Did Foster say why she joined the army?"

"Sir, no, sir. But I assume she wanted to serve her country as well."

"Private, I'm sure you are aware what happens when you assume."

"Sir, yes, sir."

"Then stop fucking around. That girl's father is going to be here before you know it and we don't know what the fuck we're going to say to him. Private Burns, why did you leave your battle buddy alone in the bar last night?"

Things might not have gotten ugly if the cadre had been allowed to do the questioning but her authority was overruled by the sergeant.

"She wasn't alone, sir." I started to sweat. Either way you looked at it I was fucked.

"Is that so? Tell us about it." The sergeant winked at the cadre like they were boys.

"She met another solider. When I left, she was dancing with him."

"Do you happen to know the soldier's name?"

"Sir, no, sir. She didn't introduce him to me."

"And did that piss you off?"

"I was her buddy, not her mother."

"You didn't answer the question."

"Why do I feel like I'm a suspect or something?"

"I don't know, you got something to hide?"

I had enough. I was leaving and I didn't care what the consequences were. I stood up and marched to the door.

"We're not done, private," the sergeant shouted.

"Oh yes, we are. My best friend is dead. Protecting my battle buddy was the first assignment y'all gave me and I failed. Ain't nothing I can say that will change that."

I fully expected to be detained when I walked out of the cadre's office but for whatever reason, it didn't happen.

I didn't want to go back to the barracks. I knew the other women had questions, but I didn't feel like talking to them. We were cool and they were like family, but they weren't my sisters. Part of me wanted to go find the nigga Anji hooked up with, but it would be like finding a needle in a haystack, since there were so many people who came through the base. I didn't know anything about the guy and probably couldn't pick him out of a line-up if I had to. Fort Leonard Wood was a hub for the National Guard, army, navy, and reservists.

I stopped at the chaplain's office because I literally had no place else to go. I was angry, confused, and hurt, and once I explained to the clerk who I was, I was given an immediate appointment.

"Private Burns, I'm sorry to hear about your loss."

The chaplain was the first person to realize that I'd lost something very valuable. It started the waterworks that I had been fighting so hard to keep away.

"I don't understand. How can this happen? She was fine." I was bent over with my face in my hands.

"Foster had some issues."

I drew back, surprised. He acted as if he knew her personally.

"You knew her?"

"She came to see me recently."

I was shocked. "How?"

We went everywhere together so how was this possible? But then I remembered she'd called out the morning before. Instead of going to sickbay she must have come there instead.

"Yesterday, right?"

"Yes. Normally I wouldn't tell you this, but under the circumstances I think it's appropriate."

"Did she seem like she was a danger to herself to you?"

"No, if she were, I would have referred her to medical. When she left here, she had some decisions to make, but she appeared to be fine."

"Decisions? What do you mean?"

If it were possible to drop a wall around one's face, this man did it. It was a scary look.

"Let's just say she was having doubts about her enlistment."

"Are you serious? Why? She never said anything to me about it." If he weren't the chaplain, I would've called him a liar.

"She didn't agree with the direction of the new army."

"New army" was a term straight from the slide show we watched about homosexuals. It was all starting to make sense. If this wasn't a personal affront, I don't know what was. Knowing Anji was considering a dishonorable discharge to get away from me hurt, and it also explained why she ultimately did what she did. When she got the letter from her dad she must have felt like she had no other options.

"I see." I no longer felt like talking. I stood up.

"The autopsy suggests she was sexually active prior to her death . . . multiple partners. . . . "

"Please tell me that you are not going to tell her father that! Is it necessary to even bring it up? I mean, come on, she's dead."

"We have to know what happened. What if she were raped, wouldn't you want the people responsible for it punished?"

"Yes, but we don't know. I have no idea who that guy was and the only person who can shed some light on the situation isn't here. Please don't ruin what is left of her reputation by telling this to her father. She wasn't a whore so anything else is irrelevant."

"No, I'm not saying that at all. I was merely making a statement. . . ."

He continued to stare at me as if he expected me to explain her behavior but I couldn't. I was too hurt to even think about it.

"Please don't do that to her, she doesn't deserve it." I walked to the door.

"Private Burns, we should continue to talk about this."

"For what? Not only do I have to carry around my shame for who I am, I now have to carry hers, too? Fuck out of here. I can't do it, I won't do it."

"I'm sending you to medical."

"What if I won't go?" I was feeling froggy and about to leap.

"You'll go."

Two armed soldiers waited behind the door to escort me to medical. It could have gone down two ways but I chose the easy one. I didn't have the will for the fight. I was done.

Chapter 11

Lauren Burns

"Private Burns, you are the best recruit I've had in years, are you sure you want to do this?"

"I'm sure, sir. I don't have what it takes. I failed on the biggest mission of my life and I can't go through it again. It's been three months and I still can't get past those twenty-four hours."

"If you continue with the therapy there is a good chance—"

"No disrespect, sir, but a good chance of what? Will it bring Foster back? Will it change the mindsets of other people when it comes to gays in the service? At the end of the day, will I feel better about myself? I'm not willing to take that chance."

"Quitting might have an adverse effect. Have you thought about how this will look? If the army were to prove gay soldiers adversely affect military readiness this law could be repealed. "

"I can't fight that battle. I know this about me now. As long as the army tries to force acceptance down the throat of its soldiers you're gonna have this problem. Gays can be great soldiers. We bleed just like everyone else and we're perfectionists. I can't stand to do any-thing half-assed and I'm so screwed up right now, I don't have anything left to give you."

"I can respect that. Foster's father has been asking about you. When you're up to it, he would really like to speak with you."

"For what? I don't need anyone else pointing a finger at me."

"He doesn't blame you. If anything, I think he blames himself. He's called every week."

"What does he want from me? Absolution? I can't make him feel better. I can't even make myself feel better."

"Think about it." He slid the number across the table and I folded it and put it in my pocket. I was ready to sign my medical discharge papers and go. I had no other friends there, so I didn't have to worry about some long good-byes.

"I will." I picked up the pen from the table and signed on the dotted line. Instead of the elation I felt the first time I signed my name, I felt relief. I was finally going home.

"There's one more person who wants to see you before you go."

I tried to hide my irritation, but I couldn't. I felt like I was being used as a case study and I resented it. I just wanted to go home. I stood up as the door opened.

My dad was the last person in the world I expected to see. My whole body went cold. Why was he here? Hadn't I been through enough? I searched his face for answers but could see nothing through my tears. I thought I was all cried out, but I was wrong. He hesitated for only a second before he came and wrapped me in his arms. I had dreamed of this moment but it was all wrong. In my dreams he hugged me because he was proud of me and what I'd accomplished. I pulled away.

"Why are you here?"

His face turned bright red, but he didn't let me go. He was crying. I never saw him cry even when my mother left. There had to be a reason and the only thing I could think of was that something had happened to one of my brothers.

"Oh God, is it James?" My breath caught in my throat. I'd been so consumed with myself, I hardly thought about my brother at all.

"Sweetheart, no, he's fine. I'm here for you. I've been acting like a big-ass fool and I'm sorry. Can you find it in your heart to forgive me?"

Blindsided, I tried to sit back down but he wouldn't let me go.

"But I failed."

"No, honey, I failed. You didn't have to prove any-thing to me, I should have been proving myself to you. You're my child and I love you . . . just the way you are."

"You do?" This was too much for me to take in. I prayed for this. All my life I felt like I had to compete for my father's affection and approval.

"Yes." He was slinging snot and tears as he vigor-ously nodded his head in affirmation.

"And you're not mad at me for quitting?"

"No, I'm proud of you, babe, I really am."

It wasn't a picture-perfect ending but it was good start on a beginning. I was going home to pick up the pieces of my life. I shook hands with my cadre and the doctors who assisted me through my darkest hours.

I deposited my gear at the door. "Thank you, I won't be needing these anymore."

"Not so fast, solider, you earned them. Hand it here." My dad slung the bag over his shoulder and escorted me out the door. I had no idea what I would do with the rest of my life, but thankfully, my medical discharge wouldn't haunt me. I had nothing to prove to anyone but me. Now that the pressure was off, I was going to take my time and see what happened.

About the Author

Tina Brooks McKinney began her writing career in 2004, with the publication of her first novel, *All That Drama*. Since that time, she has written: *Lawd, Mo' Drama, Fool, Stop Trippin', Dubious, Deep Deception, Snapped, Got Me Twisted, Deep Deception 2*. She is currently working on the sequel to *Snapped*. She enjoys reading and communicating with her readers. To learn more about Tina, visit her Web site at www.tinamckinney.com or www.faceback.com/tinamckinney. You can also reach out to her by e-mail at tybrooks2@yahoo.com.

Other Books by Tina Brooks McKinney

Snapped

Deep Deception

Around the Way Girls 8

Deep Deception 2

HUSH

By Brenda Hampton

Chapter 1

Like always, Aaron was late picking me up for an event that he, himself, said it was imperative to be on time for. I'd gotten pretty used to his tardiness, and for a man who was pursuing a political career, being late didn't look good to his constituents who awaited him. He knew that all eyes would be on him, if not for being late, definitely for how handsome he was. I had to admit that my fiancé was one of the sexiest men I had ever laid eyes on. Throw a black tailored suit on him and you got a taste of Djimon Hounsou with a hint of more swagger. A true professional Aaron was, and he was determined to make East St. Louis a better place to live.

After all, he had been born and raised in one of the more poverty-stricken neighborhoods there was. As a kid, he had witnessed plenty of people being murdered right outside of his bedroom window and had seen many gunned down by the police for no apparent reason. Schools had been vacated because money had been inappropriately used and the dropout rate had skyrocketed. Aaron grew up insisting that he wanted to somehow or someway make a difference. He was on the right path to doing so, and pursuing a political career where he was able to make the difference pleased him in many ways. I was proud of the man I would someday call my husband and he seemed to be everything I had always envisioned. I guess my only complaint was his hectic schedule, but deep in my heart, I knew that the impact his efforts made for East St. Louis was more than worth it. In knowing so, I kept my mouth shut and didn't dare complain about the loneliness I felt at times. I knew he loved me and that's what truly mattered.

I turned the watch on my wrist, looking at the time that now revealed 7:25 P.M. It was getting even later, and if we didn't make it to the community center by eight . . . eight-thirty, we may as well forget it. The invitation stated that dinner would be served at 7:30, and I thought it would be extremely rude to stroll in when everyone was in the midst of eating. I sighed from the thought, then glanced at the phone, debating if I should call Aaron's cell phone.

After standing in front of the tall glass windows that viewed the Gateway Arch in downtown St. Louis, I stepped away. My hand touched the phone, but before I picked up, it started to ring. I quickly answered.

"Sky," I heard Aaron say.

"Yes. Where are you?"

"I'm downstairs in the limousine. I'm sorry for being late, and I guess you know that I don't have much time to come upstairs to get you."

"No problem. I'm on my way downstairs. See you in a bit."

I hung up, then looked around the spacious penthouse for my silk black clutch purse that matched my strapless slimming dress that cut across my chest. A burgundy silk flower adorned my shoulder, matching the high-heeled stilettos I wore. My hair was in a sleek ponytail that was neatly wrapped into a bun. Long diamond earrings hung from my earlobes and the two-karat diamond engagement ring really set me off. Seeing my purse on the granite-topped kitchen island,

I picked up my purse, tucking it underneath my arm. I checked the oval-shaped mirror on my way out, highly approving of everything I saw. I smiled and headed toward the elevator to enjoy the evening in support of my man.

As I exited the elevator to the lobby, I could see Aaron's stretch Lincoln limousine parked outside the revolving doors. The chauffeur saw me coming and quickly opened the back door so I could get in. I thanked him before entering the limousine.

He shut the door behind me, and all I could do was blush at Aaron, who was holding up one finger. He was on his cell phone, smiling at me with teeth as white as snow. The suit on him was what I had expected and his bald head was completed with a shine. A hint of gray peeked out of his goatee that was shaved to perfection on his chin. At forty-two years old, he was a man on a mission. I couldn't wait to compliment him on how much I admired him, and as soon as he ended his phone call, I did.

"I guess I don't have to tell you how proud of you I am, and how fabulous you look tonight, do I?" I said.

"Not before I say the same to you," he complimented. He leaned in for a quick kiss, then squeezed my hand together with his. "You looked striking, Brown Sugar, or would I be even more correct by saying you look damn good?"

I loved the fact that Aaron often referred to me as Brown Sugar. That made me even more comfortable in my own skin, especially since some people always seemed to rave about lighter-skinned black women. I had a lot of confidence in myself, but even more so because Aaron was good at paying me one compliment after another.

"Since it's just you and me in here, I'll settle for damn good. Striking may work at another time, but either way, I'm flattered."

"And you should be," he said, leaning in again to give me another peck on the lips.

"Soooo," I said, crossing my legs. "You know we're late, and would you like to tell me, again, what this event is all about?"

He looked at his watch. "Only a little late, but it's no big deal. A few other politicians and I put together this event to give praises, as well as thanks, to some of our men and women in the armed services. They do so much for our country and I don't think they get the true recognition that many of them deserve. Dinner will be served at five hundred dollars a plate and all of the funds will be donated to help veterans. I'd say it's a very good cause and we're expecting a packed house tonight. We invited many soldiers from Scott Air Force Base, along with their families. I'm excited about you getting an opportunity to meet some of them, especially the ones who will be honored tonight."

"I'm looking forward to it."

By the time Aaron and I made it to the community center, dinner was being served. The ballroom was filled to capacity with soldiers dressed in camouflage, uptight politicians in suits, people from the neighborhood, teachers, and a few local celebrities. The loud noise in the room was from people talking and from the projector that played a PowerPoint presentation of the soldiers who were expected to receive honorable mentions. It was fairly easy for us to ease into our seats without being noticed. Aaron held my hand as we made our way to the reserved round table that was draped with a crisp white tablecloth. Eight people were to be seated there; six of the seats were already filled. As we approached the table, Aaron pulled back my chair. He sat next to me, immediately indulging in a political conversation that took little time to get heated.

"Democrat or Republican, it doesn't matter. I personally think the debt ceiling should be raised, without including any cuts to the deficit. We can deal with that later, and the priority here should be the economy. People need jobs, and unfortunately, the focus has been lost," Aaron said, responding to a Republican politician who was sitting across from us.

"Aaron, you're always entitled to your views, and I will agree with you on one thing. The focus has been lost, only because this president has not been doing what the American people put him in office to do! You can't improve the economy unless you tackle the deficit first. We are spending money that we don't have, and if Obama thinks the Republicans in Congress are going to hand over a blank check to him, that's not going to happen."

Whenever Aaron darted his finger to respond, I could tell he was upset. The inward arch of his brows stressed the same thing, but he always knew how to keep his cool. Me, I just turned my head and refused to comment. These kinds of conversations were not my cup of tea, because I was guilty of raising my voice in anger and using language that may be deemed as inappropriate. I continued to sip on the ice-cold water in front of me and pick at my salad.

"He's not looking for a blank check, especially not the one that was given to Bush," Aaron fired back. "You know there are a lot of hypocrites running around in your party, Paul, and there is no way you can deny it. All Obama is looking for is Republicans who are willing to compromise. Please tell me where the Republicans have compromised on anything pertaining to his agenda."

Paul's wife touched his shoulder, as she could tell he was getting hyped by Aaron's comments.

"Must we talk about this right now?" she asked. "I thought we were here to have a good time, not to argue about our political positions. This doesn't seem like the time or place to discuss the irresponsibility of this president, nor his lack of experience that's a result of running this country into a ditch."

She had the nerve to smirk behind her comment, and the one thing that irked me more were black Republicans who had no problem dissing the president. Paul smiled at his wife, but before he spoke up, Aaron did.

"I think it would be wise to end this conversation too, as I'm in no mood tonight to have this conversation with confused people who want to forget about how we got here in the first place. The ditch was dug years ago, and unfortunately, the only people who have gotten out of it are the ones who drive Mercedes, Rolls Royces, Bentleys . . . you know, the rich or richer. The ones who can't relate to what people are going through, and the last time I checked, Paul, you were driving a Mercedes, weren't you?"

"Just because I drive. . ."

The back and forth between Aaron and Paul was ongoing. Two of the other politicians had joined in, leaving their significant others to either sit there and listen or ignore them. I chose to ignore them, even though Paul's wife kept throwing in her two cents. She irritated the heck out of me, but being at so many of these functions, I'd learned to let Aaron handle his own. He was certainly capable of doing so, and obviously, her husband Paul wasn't.

While cutting into the parmesan chicken that was placed in front of me, I watched the PowerPoint presentation on the widescreen. Slides of a soldier in training named Lela Monroe were on the screen. I kept thinking if she was Sanaa Lathan, because she sure as hell looked a lot like her. Her flawless skin was butterscotch, her smile was to die for, and her shoulder-length thin braids were in a ponytail. Several slides were shown, one during a Heritage Celebration at Scott Air Force Base and another slide where she was involved in a fitness challenge. She seemed proud to be in a position to serve her country, and from the recognition that was given to her in the slides, the army seemed pleased to have her on board. I was impressed, and was quite surprised that Aaron had abruptly ended his in-depth conversation to look at the screen. I saw him nod his head, and he stood when others applauded the soldier for a job well done. She was called to the podium to accept her award, causing the voices in the room to fall silent, with the exception of applause.

"Thank you," she said, smiling and waiting for the applause to cease. "Thank you so much for your generosity. I can't tell you how much it pleases my heart that my hard work and dedication to this country has not gone unnoticed. While serving . . ."

She continued to speak with every single eye in the room on her. Dressed in camouflage, her sculpted, thick body was clearly visible. Her breasts seemed perfect and her thick, muscular thighs made her pants fit tight. I'd be the first to admit that a woman who showed strength was very admirable to me. One who was poised and seemed to handle herself with high prestige was attractive. Lela exemplified all of that, and there was no surprise that her presence had the entire room at a standstill.

Lela finished her speech, and by that time, my palms were sweating and my mind was all over the place. It had been a long time since a woman made me feel this way. The last time I'd suppressed my feelings for another woman was in my interior design class. I chalked it up as being a fad, never pursuing what I had been feeling inside. Then, one day I met Aaron at a grocery store in Fairview Heights, and as we got closer, those feelings for the other woman went away.

As I sat biting my nails, I hoped that Aaron hadn't noticed the lust in my eyes, as I had noticed in his. He quickly shook it off, then excused himself from the table.

"Sweetheart," he said, "I'm going to go mingle for a while. Can I get you anything while I'm away?"

I looked at my filled glass of water and half-empty plate. "No, I'm fine. I'm getting ready to go to the ladies' room. If you get lost in the crowd, you can find me back in my seat."

"Don't be too long," he said, then winked and walked away.

I made my way to the ladies' room, stopping to say hello a few times, and shook hands with many of the people I had known. One lady, Roberta, held me up with conversation for about five minutes, talking about what else but politics. I didn't mind, only because as I looked over her shoulder, I saw Lela laughing and talking to a group of people. A very tall and slender man stood next to her, dressed in a suit that looked to swallow him. In no way was he attractive, and when he eased his arm around her waist, I assumed he was her husband.

"Aaron is going to change this community around," Roberta said. "And who knows, maybe one day we'll be able to call him Mr. President."

I was so caught up with looking at Lela that I barely heard what Roberta had said. "Right. That's ridiculous, isn't it?"

Roberta cocked her head back. "Huh? You think it's ridiculous that Aaron could one day serve as our president?"

I took my eyes off Lela and quickly corrected myself. "Oh, no, that's not what I meant. I thought you said something else. Aaron would make a great president, and who knows? One day it just may happen."

Roberta continued, but as soon as I noticed Lela walk away from her husband, I halted my conversation. I rushed to stop Lela before she went into the restroom.

"Excuse me," I said, extending my hand to her. "My name is Sky Love. I wanted to take a moment to thank you for delivering such an exceptional speech and for your service. You are such an inspiration and it is a pleasure to meet you."

Lela couldn't help but smile. She was even prettier close up and I couldn't believe that being this close to her had not made me nervous. Her sweet perfume had infused the space around us and the look in her eyes was speaking to me, without her saying one word. If anything, the cat now had her tongue.

"Tha . . . thank you, Sky, and what a beautiful name. I certainly do my best and tonight is a night I will never forget."

I blushed from her compliment, but before another word left my mouth, her husband stepped up from behind.

"Sweetheart, I really need to get going. I'll see you later tonight, so don't wait up for me."

He planted a quick peck on Lela's cheek, not noticing the roll of her eyes as I had. "This is almost over, William, and I don't understand why you can't stay for at least another hour. Do it for me, please."

He hesitated for a second, took a glance at me, then turned to Lela. "I can't. Got to go."

Whatever the reason was behind his abrupt departure, it upset Lela. After he walked away, she mumbled, "Men," underneath her breath. Seemingly embarrassed, she said nothing else to me and went into the bathroom. I assumed that I wasn't the only one who felt lonely . . . neglected at times and it was apparent that she and her husband had some issues. I had to use the bathroom, but decided against it. Instead, I headed back to my seat and waited for Aaron to get done mingling.

Nearly an hour later, Aaron had stepped to the podium to talk about the importance of supporting our soldiers and plans he had for improving the community, if given the opportunity. Then he wished everyone a good night. I was very glad when he came back to the table, saying he was ready to go. We held hands as we exited the ballroom together, but were stopped at the door by the chief of police, who thanked Aaron for coordinating tonight's event with the other politicians. As they talked, I noticed Lela looking in our direction. Her stare made me a little uncomfortable, but who was I to complain? I'd been staring at her all night, thinking dirty little things to myself. I had the nerve to have, if not the finest man, then one of the finest in the room, and there I was lusting for a woman. I had to get out of there, and as Lela and I continued to eye fuck each other, I tugged at Aaron's arm. Thank heavens he wrapped up his conversation and we left. I hoped that I would never see Lela again, but my wish was that we would somehow or someway cross paths again.

Chapter 2

Aaron had spent the night at my penthouse, and was still in bed after an extended night in the bedroom. I bent over the kitchen table, thinking about our love-making session last night. It was mediocre at best, but that was something that I had become accustomed to. He was a very passionate man, but there was something in me that caused me to hold back. I wasn't sure what it was, but as I looked back on my previous relationships, I'd never been able to connect with any man sexually like I had hoped to. My friends were always bragging about how spectacular sex was to them, but for me, it had been just okay. Could I do without it? Possibly. Was it something that I had to have every day? Absolutely not. Once a week? No. No man had ever made me crave that deeply for him, and for a long time, I knew there was something wrong with me.

The truth was, Aaron had been giving me and our relationship his all. As I said before, my only concern was his career that took up too much of his time. Since he'd decided to jump on the political bandwagon, our time together was cut in half. Seemed like the only time we'd get together was when there was a function that we had to attend as a couple, as we did last night, when he needed me at his headquarters to help out, or when he had a sexual urge. I had expressed my concerns about our minimal time together, but Aaron promised me that once all of this was behind him, we'd spend a lifetime together. My sadness about the situation prompted him to propose to me. It was his way of guaranteeing me that he was in our relationship for the long haul. I felt as if I was being selfish for not understanding his motivation for pursuing a political career, and once the ring was placed on my finger, he never heard me complain again. That was four months ago, and at thirty-one years old, it was time for me to get my act together. Aaron wanted me to set a date for our wedding, and since I felt like time was running out for me, I suspected that I would come up with a date soon.

I walked over to the stainless-steel refrigerator, deciding to get started on breakfast. I knew Aaron would be up soon, as sleeping past eight o'clock was never something he would do. It was Sunday, though, so I was sure going to church was in his plans. Sometimes I'd go with him, sometimes I wouldn't. I mean, I believed in God and felt truly blessed, but I couldn't get with some of the messages that were coming from many of the churches I had visited. Needless to say, I had my own way of praising God, right here in my home, while driving, at the grocery store, etc. Aaron understood my way of thinking, but for him, growing up, his parents taught him that going to church was the only way to salvation. My parents taught me otherwise, and even though my father was deceased, he was the main one who encouraged me to seek an understanding about religion that satisfied self.

While waiting for the biscuits to rise in the oven, I leaned against the counter and flipped through the *St. Louis Post-Dispatch*. A few reporters were at the community center last night and so were plenty of photographers. I flipped through the pages, finally seeing a picture of Aaron and me standing next to each other. We looked to be the perfect couple and the smiles on our faces said so. There were more pictures in the newspaper of us and a few of Lela while she was at the podium speaking. I paused to take a lengthy look at her, then turned the pages to another section of the newspaper. As I started to read about a pedestrian who had been hit by a car on Locust Street, I felt arms wrap around my waist. Knowing that it was Aaron, I closed the paper and turned to face him.

"Good morning, Brown Sugar," he said, pecking my cheek and not my lips.

I smiled and placed my arms on his shoulders. "I assume that you haven't brushed your teeth yet. I wish you would, then come back with one of those juicy, wet kisses that keeps you on my mind all day."

"All day," he said. "I can't believe you would sit around thinking about a kiss from me all day. Maybe half of the day, but surely not all day."

"Go brush and we'll just have to see about that."

Aaron pinched my butt, and as he walked away, I shouted, "Ouch."

He laughed and headed to the bathroom to freshen up. I hurried to finish breakfast, and by the time he returned to the kitchen, I had breakfast on the table that included biscuits and jelly, eggs, bacon, and orange juice. Aaron also liked hot black coffee, so I poured him a cup as well.

I placed the kettle back on the stove, and that's when he swung me around to give me a kiss. His soft lips felt as if they were melting in my mouth, and as our tongues intertwined, several "Mmmm's" were released from both of us.

At least two minutes in, he backed away and held out his hands. All he had on was a pair of gray boxer shorts, revealing his nicely cut upper chest that displayed not a lot, but some muscles. His lower half was tight, and at 185 pounds, he seemed to have it all together. "Now, how was that?" he said. "Better?"

"Much, much better. And if you don't mind, I want some more of where that came from."

I stepped forward and grabbed the back of his neck. Our lips met up again, and tongues danced for a little while longer. We paused to laugh at the intensity of our kiss and I backed away when Aaron lightly bit my lip.

"Calm down, woman," he said, taking soft bites down my neck. "You're going to make me late for church. Are you going with me this morning?"

"Not today," I said, walking over to the glass-topped square table. I sat in the tall-back white leather chair and Aaron followed to sit next to me. "I think I'm going to stop by my mother's house today to check on her, then go see my sister, Kate, and her family. I haven't seen or talked to either of them in about two weeks. My mother called yesterday, so instead of calling her back, I'm going to go see what she wants."

Aaron turned on the plasma TV that was mounted on the wall beside us. He tuned into Don Lemon on CNN. "Sounds like you have yourself a busy day. I do too, and after church, I have a meeting with the mayor and some people from the neighborhood who don't like what's been going on in East St. Louis. Wish me luck."

"I'm sure you'll be fine, and as long as you keep your cool, you'll have no problems."

Aaron pretty much cut our conversation short to listen to what was happening around the world. Don Lemon was reporting on a story that was breaking in New York. Two gay women were the first to be married since the Defense of Marriage Act had been challenged. The women looked very happy and so did the crowds of people who came out to join them. Several politicians weighed in about finally overcoming such a huge stepping stone with gay rights, but you still had plenty who opposed it. By the look on Aaron's face, he was one of them. I knew he would respond to it, but he didn't open his mouth until a commercial came on.

"What is this world coming to?" he said, putting jelly on a biscuit.

"What do you mean by that?"

"I mean, come on, Sky. This kind of stuff is ridiculous. A woman should never be allowed to marry another woman and the same goes for men. I think it's taking things too far and the Bible clearly states that marriage should only be between a woman and a man. When we start changing laws that conflict with the Word, it's kind of hard for me to swallow."

I was shocked by Aaron's comments; after all, he was considered the liberal one in the room. I was too, but I wasn't the one out here preaching every day to people, claiming that I understood their struggles and would help fight for their causes. "How can you say that?" I asked. "I thought you would be willing to stand by the Same-Sex Marriage Act and support it. What does gender have to do with anything, and who cares who you fall in love with? It shouldn't matter, should it?"

"Hell, yes, it matters," he said. He reached over to touch my hand, as he could clearly see that his words had moved me in the wrong way. "Look, sweetheart. The way I see it, and will always see it is, a man should only be married to a woman. There is no other right way. Many Liberals take the same position as I do, and some are even sterner about it than I am. The Defense of Marriage Act should have been upheld in all states, and it saddens me that some of them are passing laws that say otherwise. I hope that if or when this issue ever comes knocking at my door, I'll be in a position to quickly shoot it down. No ifs, ands, or buts about it, I will."

I slowly eased my hand away from his. "I can't believe you're so stern about this. Do the people who
intend to vote for you know your position on this? A
while back, I clearly recall you speaking at the Jackie
Joyner-Kersee Center and this subject came up. You
said that you supported gay marriage."

Aaron shrugged and looked directly at me. "Well,
what can I say, other than I lied. It wasn't the first time,
and I doubt that it will be the last. As long as you know
how I truly feel, that's all that should matter."

My eyes widened, and saying that I was in shock was
putting it mildly. Had I given him too much credit,
when it didn't seem due? I had always felt that Aaron
would be different from other politicians, and for him
to admit to lying to people made me wary.

"No, Aaron, I don't know how you feel. Tell me. How
do you really feel about gay marriage, or for that matter, gays in general?"

He wiped his mouth with a napkin, then cleared his
throat. "Personally—and I would never repeat these
words to anyone else but you—but I find gay people to
be despicable. The thought of two men having sex with
each other is just . . . just downright nasty and thinking about it makes my flesh crawl. They parade around
looking like damn fools. In no way should they be allowed to do some of the mess that they do in public. It's
confusing to our children and no one should be forced
to answer questions like why in the hell is a man kissing another man. I will never get with the program, and
I hope that any man who decides to go that route with
his life burns in hell."

I wanted to fall back in my chair. These couldn't be
the thoughts and views of a man I intended to marry,
could they? "You . . . your comments are pertaining to
men. How do you feel about gay women? Most men get
a thrill—"

"Well, I'm not that kind of man," he snapped. "Nothing about two women having sex with each other turns me on and it is just as sickening as two men. Now, if you don't mind, I'm done with this conversation. Having it is not worth my time and I don't want to be late for church."

I said not another word during breakfast, and neither did Aaron. I guess he was entitled to feel the way he did, but the hatred he seemed to carry in his heart for gays really disturbed me. It disturbed me so much that there was a pain in the pit of my stomach that just wouldn't go away. I didn't like the fact that he could easily judge another person's situation without having the willingness to look at the big picture. Maybe some people felt they were born gay, and had no control whatsoever over their situation. Maybe they had been sexually abused and that's what turned them away from the opposite gender. Or maybe, they just happened to fall in love with someone who made them feel complete. Who in the hell was I to judge, and where in the heck did Aaron get off, thinking that these people didn't deserve to have peaceful lives without all of the unnecessary challenges and stereotypes that I was positive were setbacks? The only thing that sickened me was that he was on his way to sitting in a church, praising the Lord, with a heart filled with hate. Something about that didn't seem right to me and the shame was definitely in that.

I parked in front of my mother's house on Cote Brilliante Avenue, in mid-city. She had lived in the same house for years, refusing to relocate anywhere else. The neighborhood was run-down and many of the houses that remained on the street were now vacant and boarded up. After my father died of prostate cancer, I figured Momma would move, but she didn't. Daddy had worked all of his life, but driving around in fancy cars and living in a lavish house was never his objective. He was all about saving money and when he died, he had plenty of it. Most of it was given to me and only some to Momma, none to my sister Kate. My parents had a tumultuous marriage, but managed to stay together. I never understood why, especially since she slept in one room and he'd slept in another. They had separate everything, even separate refrigerators where she had her things and he had his. Growing up with such divisions in a marriage, it was very confusing to me and my sister Kate. We never understood why our parents couldn't get along. We rarely witnessed them being intimate with each other, and I can't even recall a time where I saw them kiss. There was nothing but a bunch of arguing and disrespect. You had Momma trying to get you to see things her way, and my father trying to pull you his way. We were always caught in the middle, and when I finally went away to college, it was the best thing that had ever happened. I hated to return home, even though I had nothing but love for my mother. She was the one who had a slight attitude with me about my father's money, but I offered to give her more of it. She declined. So, instead of going back and forth with her about it, I bought my penthouse, decided to work part time with my interior decorating business, and minimized my visits to her house. The only time she really called me was if she wanted something, and like always, I was there.

Dressed in a sleeveless pink and white sundress and sandals, I opened the screen door and knocked. After a minute or two there was no answer, so I knocked harder. Still, no answer. A bit frustrated that Momma wasn't home, I pulled out my cell phone to call her. She didn't pick up the phone, but when I heard noises coming from the back, I proceeded through the long gangway that separated one brick house from the other. When I got to the backyard, Momma was sitting on a white swinging wooden bench on the back porch. Many flowers in flowerpots surrounded her and hanging plants hung from above. Silver-framed reading glasses were sitting on top of her head that was filled with long and healthy gray hair. A magazine was on her lap and a jug of lemonade sat on the table in front of her. When she reached out for her glass, that's when she saw me standing at the bottom stair.

A forced smile covered her face. "Skyyyy," she said, holding out her arms for me to come hug her. I walked up the unleveled, squeaky wooden stairs, making my way to her. She stood, and after a short hug, I took a seat on the bench next to her.

"Why are you sitting outside?" I asked. "It's too hot out here, isn't it?"

Momma fanned herself with a wicker white fan, then teasingly fanned me. "It's hot, but we're in the shade. Besides, it's peaceful out here and I get tired of staying cooped up in that stuffy old house."

"It is rather stuffy in the summer, and let me guess: you're not running the air conditioner, are you?"

"No, I'm not. AmerenUE just had an increase and I'm tired of paying those high-ass electric bills. When the sun goes down, that's when I go back inside to crack those windows and cool off."

"Momma, you know it only cools down to about eighty-something degrees at night. Go ahead and use your air conditioner. I'll take care of the bill for you, okay?"

"You know the last thing I want from you is hand-outs. I'm fine and my electric bill will get paid. I guess you figured I was calling you for some money, but that wasn't the case."

In an effort to prevent an argument about money, I scooted forward to pour a glass of lemonade. When I sat back, Momma reached over and moved the dangling piece of hair in my face behind my ear.

"You look nice," she said. "I love how you wear your hair in a bun like that. It makes you look older, but I guess since you're going to marry that older man, you have to look older than what you are."

Did she just insult me? I took it that way, but I was use to Momma throwing out comments to make me feel less than what I was. "I like my hair in a bun too, but I don't wear it like this to look older. You speak as if Aaron is walking around with a cane, and that's not the case."

Momma pursed her lips a bit, then picked up her magazine. "Have you talked to Kate lately?"

"No, I haven't. Why?"

"She's been acting kind of strange lately. Every time I call her, she rushes me off the phone. It didn't used to be like that. I don't know what's going on."

"She's probably busy taking care of Leslie and Donnell. Kids are a handful, Momma, and with Ray being in and out of town all the time, I'm sure she has her hands full."

"I'm sure she does. I'm so proud of my baby girl for being so strong and taking care of her family. Ray has issues, but he takes care of Kate and his kids. I wish . . . Never mind. Forget it."

I sighed, knowing where this conversation was going. Yet again, Momma was trying to insult me and she knew that giving Kate so many praises would hurt my feelings. I didn't mind her being proud of her daughter, but she had never said that she was proud of me. That truly hurt. I didn't let her know it, especially since I had a feeling it would do nothing but spark an argument between us.

"What were you going to say, Momma? Go ahead and say it."

She let out a deep sigh, then dropped the magazine in her lap. "I just wish I could feel the same way I did about your marriage to Aaron as I did about Kate and Ray getting married. I don't like Aaron, and I don't think he's the right man for you."

Aaron had been nothing but nice to Momma, so how she ever came to that conclusion, I didn't know. I defended my engagement to him and I knew it was just a matter of time before she raised my blood pressure. "Momma, I really don't care how you feel about Aaron. He's going to be my husband and that's all there is to it. If you don't want to be a part of our lives, I understand."

I stood and started to walk away.

"If you didn't care how I felt, my words wouldn't have upset you. Look deep inside of the man you want to call your husband, Sky, and you'll see what I do. Meanwhile, call your sister to make sure she's okay. Report back to me when you can."

Momma lifted the magazine to cover her face and I walked off. After my conversation with Aaron this morning, I knew he wasn't perfect. But after all, he was entitled to his opinion. I may not have liked it, but did I think it was enough for me to give him back his ring? No. Momma was just mad because he reminded her too much of Daddy. He had stability, always fought for what he believed in, and sometimes took an aggressive approach. She wanted a man she could tell what to do, but Daddy wasn't that kind of man, and quite frankly, neither was Aaron.

Instead of going back home, I drove to my sister's house in St. Charles, Missouri. She and her husband had a beautiful two-story home, one that many people could only dream of having. A part of me was a little jealous that my younger sister had married before I did, had children before me, and had found the man of her dreams. She and Ray seemed to have the perfect life, but I knew that was because I was on the outside looking in. Kate didn't share much of her personal life with anyone, so I wasn't sure that if something was really going on, she would tell me. Either way, I hadn't seen her in a while. When I called, she invited me to come over.

The front door was already open, so I pulled on the glass door and walked in. I could smell something cooking, and when I walked into the kitchen, Kate was frying some chicken. The smell of cinnamon and peaches was in the air, so I assumed a peach cobbler was in the oven. I eyeballed the kitchen table that was set for four.

"You got it smelling pretty good in here, girl."

Kate quickly turned around and smiled. "I didn't even hear you come in," she said, walking up to give me a hug. She kissed my cheek and I kissed hers. "Good seeing you, sis. It's been a minute. I was starting to get worried."

I pointed to my chest. "Worried about me? Why would you worry about me?"

Kate shrugged her shoulders and threw back her hand. "You know how Momma is. She's always talking about you, and the things she says makes me worry."

I let out a chuckle, refusing to entertain anything my mother had said about me. I pretty much knew it was negative.

"Changing the subject," I said, walking over to the bay windows that viewed the entire spacious backyard where my four-year-old niece and ten-year-old nephew were playing. Donnell was climbing up the stairs on his playground, getting ready to slide down on a slide. Leslie was swinging on a swing. "How are the kids doing?"

"They're doing fine. Couldn't be better."

I turned around and looked at Kate. "What about you? You and Ray? How are the two of you doing?"

Just by the look in Kate's eyes, and the pause that came before she responded, "Fine," I could tell she wasn't being truthful. I was never one to push, and if there was ever something she wanted to share with me, I was sure she would.

"You know you can always talk to me, right?" I said.

"I know, but there's not much to talk about. The only thing I can think of is when you and Aaron are getting married. Have you started making any preparations at all? If so, how can I help?"

Like me, Kate was good at changing the subject too. I hadn't made any plans yet for Aaron's and my wedding so there really wasn't much to discuss. Either way, I stayed at Kate's house for several hours, playing with my niece and nephew and enjoying the company of my sister. Ray didn't show up for dinner, but by the time he came home, I was on my way out. I said a quick hello to him, and by nine-thirty that night, I was in bed thinking about Aaron, about my insulting mother, my sister who was definitely hiding something, and yes, even thinking about Lela.

Chapter 3

The week had been very hectic for Aaron and for me as well. I'd been busy with a client of mine who was so particular about her decorating that it was driving me nuts. I didn't quite understand why she had contacted me to help her out, if she was the one who told me what she thought would look best. I had never walked out on any of my clients before, but after she tried to tell me that I had no taste, I left her to deal with the tacky décor she had picked out for her living room. Seeing it made me want to puke, and no matter how much money she was supposed to pay me, in no way did I want to affiliate my name with the mess she had made. Then, on top of that, Momma kept calling with her insults about Aaron. She asked about my conversation with Kate, and when I told her nothing was wrong, she didn't believe me. Basically, she chewed me out for not knowing what was going on and said that I was not the kind of sister my little sister could be proud to look up to. Again, her words really stung, but at thirty-one, I couldn't let the words of my mother cause any more harm to me.

On Saturday morning, I got dressed to go to a picnic and air show at Scott Air Force Base with Aaron. He had been invited to come, and since I hadn't seen him since Wednesday, I felt good about us spending the day together. I'd done some clerical work for him at his office on Wednesday, but things were so chaotic that we barely had a few minutes to stop and speak to each other. So many people were running in and out, but that was because Aaron had a lot of people supporting his political run for office. I definitely knew why, as he knew how to communicate with people, he made them feel as if their concerns really mattered and he was passionate about what he was doing. Even admitting that he had lied about a few things, I still couldn't look down on him. What politician didn't lie to get people on their side? I guess in his position, some lies had to be told.

This time around, Aaron picked me up in his Ford Taurus. The only other car that he had was a Chevy pickup truck, but that often stayed in the driveway at his house in Fairview Heights. Once we were married, I intended to give up my penthouse to move in with him, but at this point, I was glad he hadn't rushed me. I really didn't want to live in Illinois, but just so he wouldn't be disappointed, I pretended as if it would be no problem for me. Then there was a little thing called compromise. I had to do so, especially if he won the election. He couldn't live outside of his jurisdiction, and there was no way I wanted to be married with two homes. That situation reminded me too much of my parents, and I surely didn't want to wind up with a marriage like theirs.

We arrived at Scott Air Force Base at a little after noon. The base was highly secured with soldiers who asked for our driver's licenses and requested that we get out of the car. Our licenses were checked for verification and the car was searched from front to back, as well as underneath. We received clearance to move forward and as we drove onto the base; it seemed very active. Some soldiers were to our left, running in place and doing squats. Others were running along a trail that seemed to have no end. Housing complexes could be seen at a distance and what looked to be a fitness center was close by. I couldn't believe that everything was designed like one big community. The entire place was heavily guarded, if not by soldiers, by high fences and cameras. I felt completely safe, until I learned from Aaron that the air show consisted of soldiers in training who would be flying for the first time.

"Tell me again why I'm here," I said sarcastically. "This could be interesting to watch, but also pretty dangerous."

Aaron parked and looked over at me. "Trust me, you'll have a wonderful time. Just make sure you wear those earplugs I gave you earlier, as things will get pretty loud."

I tucked the earplugs in my purse and we headed toward the section of the base where the air show was taking place. Crowds of people stood around, waiting for the captains to complete the pre-flight aircraft checks, prior to take off. I was very much tuned in, and as soon as the first aircraft left the ground, I covered my ears. It was so loud that I thought my eardrums had busted. One after another, the pilots flew the jets into the air, putting on one hell of a show that impressed us all. I was in awe, and by the look on Aaron's face, so was he. We didn't walk away until the show was completely finished and it ended with plenty of whistles and applause.

Once the show was over, the picnic got underway. Many of the soldiers were there with their families and it was good to see that everyone seemed to pretty much get along. The kids were on inflatable playgrounds playing, and as Aaron left my side to go mingle with some people he'd met at the community center the other night, I sat on a bench eating a hotdog and watching the kids play. I wondered how many children Aaron and I would have. The subject had definitely come up, and I questioned him about being forty-two without any children. At this point, he was ready. I was too, and we both agreed that after marriage, we'd get started on having kids right away.

I was in deep thought about our future, but was interrupted by a tap on my shoulder that caused me to jump. When I turned around, Lela stood before me. She was dressed in an army green T-shirt with camouflage pants that had pockets on each side. Her braids were in a ponytail, and without a lick of makeup on, her skin looked smooth as ever. I couldn't help but smile at the sight of her.

"You're, uh, Sky, right?" she asked.

"Yep. That would be me."

"I'm Lela from the other night. You stopped to talk to me as I was getting ready to enter the restroom. Do you remember?"

"Of course I do. I told you what an inspiration you had been to me and I meant it."

"I'm glad that I have what it takes to inspire. You don't seem like, or should I say look like, the kind of woman who needs much motivation to me, but I'm not always a good judge of people's character."

"Neither am I, but I'm sure that I have you pegged out the right way."

Lela blushed—a little. Her eyes searched the picnic area as if she was looking for someone, then she turned her attention back to me.

"Would you . . . Do you mind if we go for a walk?"

I was surprised that she'd asked, and since Aaron was nowhere to be found, I figured it would be okay. I threw my plate in the trashcan and carried a soda in my hand as we began to take a slow walk.

"I've been thinking about the other night, and I wanted to apologize for ignoring you and going into the bathroom. It's just that I was so embarrassed by my husband's treatment, and shocked that he had no respect for me in front of a complete stranger."

"There's no need for you to apologize for his behavior. I thought his reaction was pretty cold, but hey, it wasn't my business. I just had a desire to meet you, to tell you how proud I was to see a black woman handling her business in the armed services. I didn't necessarily say it like that, but it's always good to see sisters who are on the right path. There is something about you that shines above all the rest and I saw nothing but fire in your eyes. I can tell that you love what you do and that's a good thing."

"You would be correct. I do love what I do, but there are times that I would like to spend more time with my family."

"How many children do you have?"

"None, and at thirty-three, I'm not sure if kids are in my plans yet. My husband and I have put children on hold for now. When I mentioned my family, I meant my parents and brother, who I don't really see that often. My job keeps me very busy and I just got back from Baghdad, Iraq three and a half weeks ago. It was a nightmare, but you learn to adjust and do what you have to do."

I was so honored to be in the presence of a woman who appeared to be so brave. I wouldn't last one darn day in Iraq and would probably be somewhere cooped up in a corner with tears in my eyes. Not to mention the missed hair and nail appointments. I just couldn't do it, but thank God for the women who could. "Again, I'm impressed. I know how it is about family, but if you ever need someone to talk to or hang out with, let me know. I live in downtown St. Louis and the base is not that far from me at all."

Lela halted her steps and crossed her arms across her chest. "I would like that," she said. "Before you leave, let's exchange numbers."

"Sounds like a plan. Meanwhile, I'd better get back to the picnic. I'm sure Aaron may be looking for me and I don't want him to think that I ran off without telling him."

"No, you wouldn't want that. But the reason that you ran off may someday be very well worth it."

Lela's comment caught me off guard. I didn't know how to respond, so I didn't. This time, I walked away and when I turned, she started jogging in the other direction. From a distance, I saw her husband watching and waiting for her to come to him. His face was twisted and his mouth was moving fast. I saw her touch his shoulder, but he snatched it away. Several more words were exchanged before he walked off. She followed him. I watched until the two of them vanished from my sight.

The picnic lasted for hours. I was ready to go, but was disappointed that Lela hadn't shown back up to exchange phone numbers with me. I guessed things must have gotten heated with her husband, so I didn't sweat it. What was meant to be would be, and even though I'd felt a little connection with her, I was skeptical about interfering in her marriage. Her husband seemed kind of possessive and controlling to me, but again, I was on the outside looking in. Lela appeared to be the kind of woman who could handle herself, so I wasn't too worried.

Aaron and I stood near a commissary facility, talking to two soldiers who were telling us about their time in Afghanistan. Bin Laden had been killed several months ago and the mood on the base was very upbeat. Many of the soldiers seemed proud, and Aaron and I stressed just how proud we were too.

"Well, keep up the good work," Aaron said. "Hearing of his death was like music to my ears. That night, I had a feeling the president was about to make an announcement that had something to do with Bin Laden."

Just as I was getting ready to add my two cents, a female soldier behind me interrupted us.

"Excuse me," she said. "Can I speak to you for a minute?"

"Sure," I said, a bit skeptical, but walked a few feet away from Aaron and the other soldiers to speak to her.

"What can I help you with?" I asked.

"Here," she said, handing me a piece of paper. "Someone asked me to give this to you. Have a great day."

Before I could thank her, she walked away. I opened the folded piece of paper and it said

Hope you call me soon. Lela.

Her number was written on the paper as well. I eased the paper in my purse, then walked over by Aaron to resume my conversation with him and more soldiers.

It had gotten even later, and when I looked up, it was almost eight o'clock. Aaron and I were given a more detailed tour of the base, and that took up a lot of time. I had never stepped one foot on the base, but had heard a lot about it. Aaron had visited before, but was never given a detailed tour like he'd been given today. I think he'd gotten tired too, and as his conversations started to wrap up quickly, I could tell he was ready to go. We shook hands with several soldiers and began to make our way back to the car. We were only a few feet away when we heard someone yell, "Hey!"

Aaron and I both turned around, seeing Lela's husband charging our way. He slowed his pace, then stepped up to me, completely ignoring Aaron.

"I don't know who you are, or what kind of game you're playing, but you're barking up the wrong tree. My wife is off-limits! You need to know that I intend to watch her every move. If I think you're going to be a problem for me, I will get rid of you. And please don't take that as a threat; it's a promise."

Saying nothing else, in what appeared to be the routine around here, he walked away.

Aaron yelled for Lela's husband to come back and explain himself, and started to move in his direction. I reached for his arm.

"Honey, don't. I have no clue what that man was talking about. Maybe he had me mixed up with someone else. Just . . . Just let it go, okay?"

Aaron's face was twisted and he couldn't stop looking in the direction of Lela's husband. "What nerve. I don't care if he had the wrong person or not, he was out of line for stepping to us like that. I feel sorry for whoever his wife is and no woman needs a man who goes around threatening people."

"I agree," I said, trying to get him to the car. "It's been a long day. What he said in no way interferes with the great day we had here. I'm glad I came with you and I'm looking forward to what the night has in store for us."

Aaron released a deep breath and his anger subsided. He said nothing else about Lela's husband and that was a good thing. I wasn't afraid of her husband at all, but I was skeptical about calling Lela. Seemed like the last thing she needed was more trouble, and there was no doubt that any kind of relationship with me would start something that neither of us was ready for.

I was so sure of it, and the reason why was because of the feelings I had as Aaron lay on top of me that night. I'd been having them ever since I'd met Lela, and when Aaron's hand took a light squeeze at my chocolate firm breast, I replaced it with her hand. When his tongue rolled down my chest and dipped into my sweaty belly button, I wished it was hers exploring me as he was. I counted on his dick to rescue me from my thoughts of Lela, but as soon as he plunged into me, my eyes shot open. I felt her fingers inside of me, and with each thrust, I could not escape my racing thoughts, as my heart pounded against my chest. In pure darkness, tears welled in my eyes because it was now that I realized Aaron couldn't give me what I desired to have. Possibly, only Lela could.

Wasting no time, I contacted Lela the next day. I left a message for her to return my call, which came on a Tuesday afternoon as I was going over some decorating ideas with a client of mine at my small office on Washington Avenue. I didn't want to be rude, but I was anxious to find out if or when Lela wanted to hook up.

"I can't talk long," I said. "But can I call you back or would you like to meet somewhere we can talk and have dinner?"

"What about Longhorn Steakhouse in Fairview Heights? Can you meet me there around six-thirty or seven?"

"Seven would be fine. See you later."

Lela hung up, and for the rest of the afternoon, I felt extremely upbeat. That was, until Aaron called, asking if I would stop by his headquarters to help out for a few hours.

"I just need you to do some cold calling for me. You've been so successful with doing it, and I can't really say that I have anyone else in the office who knows how to communicate with callers better than you do."

I felt horrible, because I had never told Aaron that I wouldn't be able to help him. I knew the reason why I couldn't and that surely didn't make me feel good. "You should have called me earlier, honey. I have to meet with a client at six and I don't know how long it's going to take me. She lives all the way in O'Fallon, Missouri, so I doubt that I'll be finished by ten. I'll stop by tomorrow to make those calls, and if you want me to, I'll do so all day."

Aaron was the kind of person who wanted things when he wanted them. I heard the sigh over the phone, but he said that tomorrow would be fine.

"Are you sure?" I asked.

"I guess. I really don't have any choice, do I? I'll have to ask Beverly, even though she chews gum and often gets too personal on the phone sometimes."

"Sorry. Tomorrow, though, okay? See you early tomorrow."

"All right, Sky. Enjoy your evening."

"You too."

I hurried to find something to wear for my dinner with Lela tonight, as I had no intentions of being late. And by the time I finished getting dressed, I still had forty-five minutes to get there. I decided to wear a mustard-colored halter dress that went all the way down to my ankles. The color meshed well with my silky chocolate skin, and instead of putting my hair in a bun, I let it fall on my shoulders. Momma said that the bun made me look older, and I was starting to believe her. Leaving my hair down did make me look sexier and so did the way I had done up my eyes. They were already round and pretty, but I extended my lashes with Cover Girl mascara. My brows had been plucked and arched to perfection. A hint of nude lip gloss covered my full lips and as I smacked them together, I was finally ready to go.

I arrived at Longhorn almost fifteen minutes early. To my surprise, Lela was already there. She stood up and greeted me at the door.

"Hello, Sky," she said, walking closer to give me a hug. "Good seeing you."

"Same here," I replied. I was a little nervous, so I quickly backed away from our embrace. She took a few steps back to check me out. At first, her eyes shot to my meaty breasts that slightly poked out of my halter. A silver necklace Aaron had purchased for me dangled between my cleavage. I was surprised when she reached for it.

"This is pretty," she said, looking at it. "And by the way, you look nice. I mean really nice. You'll have to excuse me for not getting so dressed up, as I've gotten used to being kind of dressed down."

Lela wore a pair of faded jeans with a button-down pink polo shirt that was tucked inside of the jeans. A white tank shirt was underneath and a black belt was around her waist. Her braids flowed a few inches past her shoulders, and to me, with no makeup at all, she looked awesome. No doubt, she was blessed with natural beauty.

"If you say so. I'm just glad you're on time," I said with a chuckle. "I hate waiting on people and it was a relief to see you sitting there."

"Now you know we don't play that late stuff. I'm taught to be on time for everything I do and the people I work with, and for, will have it no other way."

The waiter interrupted our conversation, letting us know that a table was ready. She sat us at a booth, then told us that another waiter would be with us shortly.

Lela got comfortable in her seat, but I did notice her looking around the restaurant. I intended to inquire about that later, but for now, I had to get rid of the nervous feeling inside of me that kept coming and going. As I found myself looking off too, Lela cleared her throat.

"Can I say something to you, just to kind of break the ice here?" she asked. I nodded. "Please don't be nervous around me. Be yourself, and before we are anything, we can become friends first. I would really like that and it's so important for me to make sure you're at ease."

"I . . . I am, but it's just that . . ."

"Being in the company of a woman you're attracted to makes you nervous? I know and I get that. I assume that this may be your first time pursuing your feelings for a woman, right?"

"Sort of. I mean, it's not the first time I've had feelings for another woman, but you would be correct in saying that I haven't agreed to anything like this, especially without recognizing that my feelings may lead to something else."

"Let's hope that they do. I'm never afraid to tell anyone how I feel about them, man or woman. So here it is, Miss Sky. I think you're sexy as hell, and the first time I saw you at the community center I wanted you. If you didn't come to me to introduce yourself that night, I would have definitely come to you. I had noticed you as soon as you walked in with Mr. Anderson. I watched you for most of the night, noticing that you had something heavy on your mind. All I can say is I'm glad it was me."

"Me too," I said in a whisper. My eyes sparkled with amusement, as Lela had put it out there. I was delighted to know that we had been on the same page that night. Before I responded, I waited until the waiter came to take our orders. He said he'd be back with our margaritas and Wild West Shrimp.

"So," I said, "if you were watching me all night, don't you think your husband noticed? Maybe that's why he left so abruptly, and before I go any further, I wanted to tell you that he approached me at the base on Saturday. I don't know any of the details of your marriage, but he says that he's keeping his eyes on you. Basically, he told me not to get involved and threatened me if I did."

"Sky, William is all bark and no bite. He knows that I've fallen out of love with him, and he's trying to save a marriage that is beyond repair. He's refused to give me a divorce, and to be honest with you, the only reason that we stay together is for show. We are respected by so many people on that base and high expectations have been set for both of us as we move up the ranks. I think a divorce will happen, but not as soon as I would like for it to."

It seemed so soon to discuss all of this, but if I intended to involve myself with Lela, and possibly screw up my relationship with Aaron, I had to know a few more things. "Other than your husband, are you involved with anyone else right now?"

"I was, for almost a year, but things didn't work out."

"Male or female and can I ask why the two of you are not together?"

She smiled and pulled her braids over to the side to rest on her shoulder. "You sure have a lot of questions, Sky. I hope you're prepared to answer some of mine."

"No problem. Anything you want to know, just ask."

The waiter brought our drinks to the table, and after bringing back two more, I was feeling tipsy. Being that way made me loose and bubbly. Lela was too and our conversation started flowing as if we'd known each other for quite some time. I found out that Lela had been involved with several females before. According to her, she had been interested in the same sex since her early teens, but had faced many challenges along the way. And even though she was married, she recognized that it was doomed from the beginning. Trying to hide her feelings had hurt so many, and was now hurting her husband.

"If he knows how you feel about women, why won't he just let you go? That's unless you like men, too."

"I like men, but I have little desire to be with them sexually. I only go there with my husband to please him, but deep down, he knows how I feel. All I can say is don't enter into a marriage, especially if you're sure that you have feelings for women. You will only hurt Mr. Anderson and you don't want to betray or deceive him like that. Even if nothing happens between us, you shouldn't commit to a marriage unless you're one hundred percent sure he's who you want to spend the rest of your life with."

"I couldn't agree with you more, but I do love him. I love so much about him and I envisioned a man like him as my husband. These feelings that I've had for women are rare and they only spark from time to time. I guess a part of me is just curious, but I can't really say if it's more than that."

"Then allow yourself to experience being with a woman one time. If it's not something that you're feeling, you will know it right away. Then, you can put everything behind you, and if Mr. Anderson is supposed to be your lifetime, he will be."

I sat silent for a while, thinking about what Lela had said. She was right . . . I had to see what was up with these feelings inside of me that had lingered on for some time. I didn't think it was normal for me to feel this way, but then again, what was really considered normal?

"Lela, you mentioned your career when we first started talking. Are you worried about what would happen to you if you get a divorce, or is being married a cover-up for you being bisexual or gay? I heard about the president signing into law the policy that protects service men and women from being discriminated against, but does that still worry you?"

"Absolutely. Because we both know that gays and lesbians are not easily accepted anywhere in this country. We're treated like crap and the DADT—'don't ask, don't tell'—repeal may not change much. I think many soldiers will still be discriminated against and there are other ways to get rid of people who some feel don't belong. That's why I do my best to keep my personal life a secret. Hush is the word, and what I do is done behind closed doors. I refuse to be as open about my sexual preferences as I would like to be and I suspect that being so open about it will damage my career. My past lover had issues with the limitations that were set on our relationship and she eventually walked. She asked me to choose, and I chose my career. Had to, as there was no other way."

"I get that. I really do, and it didn't take me long to figure out how important serving your country is to you. Like I said, that's what I admire."

Lela smiled and we continued our conversation for at least another hour. Our food came and we could barely eat from laughing and talking so much. I swore Lela was so down-to-earth. She was like the best friend

I never had, and I shared with her my feelings about my mother and sister. She was much closer to her family than I was to mine, and they knew all about her being gay. If my sister and mother ever found out that I had any interest at all in women, they would probably disown me. I could see Momma now, downing me and telling me what a disgrace I was. That would give her another opportunity to belittle me and I knew she would happily do it. Lela was right . . . hush was the word. Whatever became of Lela's and my relationship, no one would know about it. She would be seen as a friend, nothing more, nothing less. And to me, that would be easy to pull off because she didn't look like a masculine female. She didn't talk with a deep voice like a man. She was so beautiful, and as I sat across the table staring at her, I couldn't help but think where all of this was going. I didn't know if we'd ever get to a point where I would want her to choose me over her career. Her career seemed to make her happy, and with a husband like hers, I was sure it was her escape. I didn't know how I would handle him either, but for now, I was glad that everything appeared to be moving in the right direction.

"Let's get out of here," Lela said. "I'm not eating much of this food and . . . When's the last time you've been to the drive-in?"

"Drive-in? It's been years. I didn't even know there were any left."

"There's one in Belleville. The night is still young and I'm not ready to call it a night yet, unless you are."

I was enjoying myself with Lela, and was not ready to go back home to my lonely penthouse to be alone. I agreed to go to the drive-in with her, and when we left Longhorn, she asked me to ride with her. On the ride there, she spoke more about her troubled marriage.

"I just want you to know that I'm not going to force you to do anything you're not ready for. If me being married makes you uncomfortable, Sky, just tell me and I will not pursue a relationship between us. We can just be friends and I'm perfectly okay with it."

"Are you really? I mean, after getting to know you a little better today, I'm open to whatever. I hope you haven't changed your mind, and did I say something wrong. . . ."

Lela reached over and touched my hand. "No, you didn't. Actually, everything you've said has been right. I just know how difficult it is for anyone to have relations with someone who is married. You seem like a woman who would take issue with that, but I don't know."

"I do, but I understand that a person has to do what they must do, if they're unhappy. At least you've let me know where things stand. I appreciate that."

Lela blushed at me, then turned up the radio. Before we knew it, we were snapping our fingers in the car, listening to Mary J.'s "No More Drama." Once it was over, we laughed and high-fived each other.

"None," Lela shouted. "No drama whatsoever!"

I folded my arms and looked at her. "Are you sure about that? You sound like you got this."

"Positive. Just wait and see."

I didn't believe Lela for one bit, but being with her seemed interesting, and quite frankly, I was willing to take the risk.

The drive-in was crowded as ever. All kinds of cars were lined up on the gravel, with people in and outside of their cars watching *Bridesmaids*. The movie was so hilarious. Lela and I sat in the back of her truck, with our backs against the window, laughing our butts off. A bucket of popcorn was on her lap and we sipped on soda from our foam cups.

"This shit is too funny," Lela said. "That thick chick is out of her mind!"

"Isn't she. But I can see something like this going down for real. We women are so competitive and I remember going at it like that before with one of my friends."

"What about your bridesmaids? Do you know who they will be, or have you even gotten that far yet?"

"Nope. Haven't made any plans yet, but I guess I will. Soon."

Lela set the popcorn bucket next to her and turned to me. "Just make sure it's something you really want to do. If not, turn him loose and move on."

I was so caught up by how close and comfortable we both were. And when Lela leaned in for a kiss, my whole body froze. Her lips softly touched mine, and as she licked across them, I finally opened my mouth. The kiss I'd waited for had finally arrived and it was slow and delicate. Her lips were so sweet and the taste of her tongue had me in a trance. She touched my thigh, squeezing it as her hands crept up my leg. My entire body was tense, but as she made her way up between my legs, I started to relax. I released a deep breath, only to gasp when her fingers touched the silkiness of my panties. She backed inches away from my face and smiled.

"I feel heat," she said.

"That's because I'm hot," I replied. I inched forward to get back to the lips I had wanted to feel against mine. Lela maneuvered my panties to the side, breaking my insides open with the slip of her fingers. Her strokes were smooth and gentle, causing me to feel the dripping juices that were already running through my crack. I couldn't believe how wet I was, nor could I believe that I was allowing a woman to dig deep into me, while at a drive-in movie. Exciting me even more, her lips pecked my neck. My mouth opened to suck in some air, and that, too, was filled with wetness. I hadn't felt this good in a long time and I definitely wanted more. That was, until a drunken-ass man walked by and bumped into Lela's truck. The thud was loud, causing Lela to remove her fingers and both of us to sit up straight.

"Saawry," the man slurred. "But this is so fucking cool, isn't it?"

I nodded, and when I looked at Lela, we both shook our heads and laughed. The man walked off, singing loudly and causing quite a scene.

"I think we'd better get out of here," Lela said. She looked at her watch. "Besides, it's getting late. I have to get up around four, and I must get a little rest, due to my busy day ahead of me."

A part of me was disappointed, but I didn't want Lela to be so tired. We got back in the front of the truck, and on the drive back to my car at Longhorn, things were pretty quiet. I knew Lela was thinking about what had happened, and I damn sure was. I didn't want to come off as being overly excited about it, but when we got back to Longhorn, I initiated a kiss before getting out of the car.

"I hope to hear from you soon," I said to her. "Be safe and thanks for inviting me."

"Anytime. I'll call you tomorrow."

Lela waited until I got in my car before she sped off and onto the highway. I was zoned out in the car, thinking about her touch. This was all so new to me, but whatever was transpiring, I liked the feel of it. I never thought I'd go as far as I'd done, but at this point, I was glad that I'd broadened my horizons and explored what I had always felt deep inside. To hook up with Lela made me feel free. I felt as if I was now living a life in my own skin. I was happy . . . satisfied beyond my own expectations, and no matter how things turned out between us, this was one experience I would never forget.

While singing "No More Drama" by Mary, I turned the key to my penthouse to unlock the door. When I entered, soft jazz was playing, scented candles were lit, and the smell of fresh flowers infused the opened space. The lights were turned down, and as I stepped farther inside, I saw Aaron leaning against the kitchen island with a red rose in his hand. He was shirtless and white silk pajama pants covered his bottom half. Against his midnight-black skin, he looked dynamite. I had stopped thinking about Lela for just a few minutes to give my man the credit he truly deserved.

"Hello, Brown Sugar. It's almost midnight, but where is my kiss?"

"Sorry," I said, a little nervous, but trying not to let it show. I walked over to him, then placed my purse on the counter. I threw my arms around his neck, hoping that he wouldn't smell Lela's scent on me, as he definitely knew mine.

"Damn, you smell good," he said, already nibbling at my neck. I held the back of his head as he lowered it to lick between my sweaty cleavage. My nipples were poking through the halter, and as Aaron lowered his hands and grabbed big chunks of my ass cheeks, I felt horny as ever. Lela had left me high and dry, thinking about what would have happened if the drunken man had not bumped into her car.

"That ass is soft," Aaron said, grinding against me. I could feel his hardness growing at my midsection. And like Lela's, his hands roamed and searched for my panties. He felt my crotch, causing his muscle to grow by the minute.

"You are soaking wet. Let me hurry this up."

"Please," was all I said.

Aaron lowered my panties to my ankles and threw them over his shoulder. That definitely put the smell of sex in the air, but not as much as when he lifted me on the counter and started to feast upon my insides, right next to the sink. My legs were pushed back to my chest, and my insides were exposed to his face. I tightened my watery eyes from the feel of his fierce tongue, but unfortunately, Lela was still on my mind. Even as we made our way to the bedroom, stripping each other naked and screwing our brains out, I just couldn't get with it. All I could think about was when? When I will be woman enough to tell Aaron that I did not want to be his wife, nor did I want to go here with him again?

Chapter 4

Lela kept her word and we talked on the phone or texted each other every single day. Even when she was busy, she always found time in her busy schedule just to call to let me know she'd been thinking about me. I'd been thinking a lot about her too, and even though much hadn't changed in my relationship with Aaron, I was preparing myself to tell him that I didn't want to go through with the marriage. The timing, however, never seemed right. We were never alone at his office, and even when we were, someone would come in and interrupt us. I'd even invited him to dinner at my penthouse, but that was cancelled because he had to rush out of town on business. On two of the days that he was gone, Lela's husband had been called to the Pentagon to handle some business. She'd been to my penthouse and I'd been to her house, which was located on the base. I loved spending time with her, and on Thursday night, we sat yoga style on the floor in her family room, playing Uno.

"You are such a cheater," she said, looking at the last card in my hand, wondering what color it was.

"Don't be mad at me because I have a good strategy and you don't."

"Is that what you think? You think this game is a strategic game, and not about how the cards come up in the deck?"

"No matter how they come up, you'd better know how to play them. If not, I'm afraid you're going to lose again."

Lela slowly drew from the deck, slamming down a "draw four" on me.

"Awwww," I shouted and playfully fell back to the floor. Lela crawled over me, and just as she was about to kiss me, my cell phone rang. Any other time it wouldn't have mattered, but since it was almost nine o'clock, and no one usually called me at this time, I thought something was wrong. I moved away from Lela, and crawled over to the table to get my phone. It was my mother.

"Yes, Momma," I said, holding the cell phone up to my ear. I could hear her crying.

"Where are you?" she asked, then sniffled.

My heart dropped. "I'm at a friend's house. What's the matter?"

"It's Kate. I . . . I need you to come quickly. She needs you."

"Okay. I'm on my way."

I put my phone in my purse and hurried to stand up. "I have to go. Something is going on at my mother's house and she needs me."

Lela reached for the keys to her truck. "I'll go with you. No need for you to be alone on the highway by yourself and I don't want you speeding to get there."

We left, and while in Lela's truck, I wondered what had gone wrong. Had Kate been ill? She didn't seem like herself when I last visited and was quiet more than anything. I felt bad that I hadn't been in touch with her as much as I should have been and it was killing me inside that I'd been neglecting my little sister.

Almost an hour later, Lela pulled in front of my mother's house. The neighborhood was pretty rough, and when we got out of the car, some thugs across the street whistled at us.

"Say, bitches," one of them said. "Can I get a phone number or somethin'?"

The others laughed, but I ignored them. Lela didn't. "I got your bitches. And if you bring your ass on this side of the street, I'll be happy to show her to you."

The others laughed again, but the one who couldn't keep his mouth closed grabbed his dick, telling Lela to suck it. I grabbed her arm, as she looked as if she was getting ready to cross the street.

"Forget them," I said. "It's the wrong time. Please."

Lela tossed her braids to one side and rolled her eyes at the youngster, ignoring his ongoing calls of "bitches" and "hoes." I rang my mother's doorbell quickly, and could see my nephew, Donnell, through one of the glass windows. He opened the door, hugging me around my waist.

"Hi, Auntie. Grams and Momma are in the kitchen. Leslie and I are in the basement playing video games. You wanna play with us?"

"I sure do," I said. "As soon as I talk to your mother, I'll be downstairs to play."

Donnell looked at Lela. "Who is that?" he asked while circling her. "She fine!"

"My name is Lela," she said, extending her hand to shake his.

"Lela, I'm Donnell. And if you everrrrr need a boy-friend," he said, pointing to his chest, "come see me."

"I certainly will," Lela said, smiling. I invited her to take a seat on the plaid sofa in the cramped living room. Momma's house was scorching hot. Even the walls looked like they were sweating and the fan she had on the floor was there to make noise. It was blow-ing out hot air, wasting electricity. I told Lela I would be back soon and turned on the TV so she could watch it.

When I walked toward the kitchen, I could hear Kate and Momma whispering, but I couldn't make out what was being said. As soon as I entered, Kate lowered her head and Momma stood up. The kitchen was barely big enough for a rectangular table to fit, and Momma hadn't made any updates to it since we were kids. The old white double-big sink was in one corner, taking up too much space. A shelf with expired food on it was in one corner and the outdated white stove was in another. I hated that she lived like this, and yet again, I felt guilty.

"Have a seat," Momma said. I eased into the chair, still looking over at Kate. Finally, she lifted her head and that's when I noticed her face was swollen and she had a shiny black eye. I was almost speechless.

"Wha . . . what happened to you?"

Kate fidgeted with her nails and a slow tear rolled down her face. "Ray and I had an argument. He got angry about something I said."

"Looks like the two of you had more than an argument," I said. I was mad as hell, and for a man to put his hands on a woman, that disgusted me. "Has he ever hit you before?"

"That's what I've been asking her," Momma said, leaning against the sink. She was rattled and hurt at the same time. "She hasn't been truthful with me, so I figured she would at least tell you."

Kate pounded her fist on the table. "I am being truthful, Momma! I called him a lying Negro and he got mad! He's never done anything to this extent before and I don't know what got into him."

"Watch your tone with me, young lady. Negro, nigga, loser . . . whatever! He had no business putting his damn hands on you! I think this has been going on for quite some time and you ain't been saying nothing. If so, now is the time to come clean, Kate. You can't go back to this man if he's abusing you."

"Momma's right, Kate. We can get you some help. You and the kids can stay with me. I have plenty of room and you don't have to go back to him."

Kate sighed. "Are the two of you listening to me? I said it's not that serious. I'm going back home tomorrow, and all I needed was to get away from him for a few hours. He was tired and working so hard—"

Momma slammed her hand on the table, her face so flushed with anger it was turning red. "You shut your face, girl! I didn't raise you to be no damn fool and you sitting right there sounding like one. Get your ass out of that house, call the police on that nigga, and be done with it! Do not subject those babies to a bunch of bullshit, ya hear me?"

Kate wiped another tear and looked directly at Momma. She took her anger out on her. "I hear you, Momma, but this is my life! I live it how I want to, and I get tired of you trying to tell me what to do! I didn't tell you what to do when Daddy was kicking your ass, did I?"

Momma reached out to slap Kate hard across her face. Her head jerked to the side, and I was sure her face would swell some more after that. I jumped from my seat, reaching out to touch Momma's heaving chest. "Momma, calm down, please!"

Rage covered her face and her eyes shot toward the doorway. Lela stood with her eyes widened. "Is everything okay in here?" she asked.

"Who in the hell are you?" Momma asked.

"She's a friend of mine. She drove me over here tonight . . . because I caught a flat tire. I invited her to stay in the living room while we talked."

"You know I don't like no strangers in my house. She should have stayed in the car. This is family business, Sky, and she needs to leave."

Now, I was irritated. "Don't be so rude, Momma." I turned to Lela. "If you don't mind going back into the living room, I'll be there shortly. Everything is fine."

"I'll be outside in the car," Lela said. "Didn't mean to upset anyone."

"Thank you," Momma said, rolling her eyes.

Lela left and I couldn't help but go there. "You can be so obnoxious at times and Kate is right. We put up with a lot from you and Dad, and if she's going through something with Ray, I wonder why."

Momma's mouth dropped open. "Are you blaming me because the two of you chose to date fucked-up men! No way will I hold myself responsible for the fuckups you two keep getting yourselves into. I don't care what I went through with y'all's daddy, and whatever it was, you two should have learned some lessons. Lesson number one, don't go around screwing and having babies by abusive men! Number two, don't marry men who are that much older than you, as all they will do is try to control you. And changing the subject on number three! Don't bring no gay-ass women into my house any damn more. Leave your hoes at your house, and that way, I don't have to be rude!"

She tightened her housecoat and left the kitchen. We heard her bedroom door slam, and didn't expect her to come out anytime soon. Kate looked across the table at me.

"Is your friend really gay?" she whispered.

"No," I quickly said, trying to shoot down Momma's accusation that was really the truth. "You know how Momma is. Always trying to make somebody feel less than what they are. We're not talking about my friend, though. Getting back to you. Why don't you and the kids come home with me for a few days? Don't rush back to Ray just yet. Think about what you want to do with your marriage, and whatever you decide, I'm there for you."

I walked across the room to give my sister a hug. She cried on my shoulder and I felt so badly for her. I knew leaving Ray wouldn't be easy, but she had to make her own decision. Hopefully, it would be the right one. I told Kate to gather her things, and for her and the kids to go to my penthouse. She was okay with that, so I told her I would be there later and gave her the key. Afterward, I knocked on Momma's bedroom door, telling her that we were getting ready to leave. She didn't respond.

"Get some rest, Momma. Sorry that we can't seem to have a decent conversation, but I love you."

No response. Kate walked away to get her things and to tell the kids they were leaving. I was getting ready to go downstairs with her, until I heard police sirens. Almost immediately, I thought about Lela going outside to wait in the car, and those thugs who were being rude to us. I rushed to the front door, only to see two police cars outside with sirens flashing. Rain was pouring down and the clouds had turned gray. My heart raced as I pushed the screen door open and ran down the stairs. I almost slipped on the wet steps, but grabbed the rail to catch my balance. Lela was standing on the sidewalk with her arms folded while talking to an officer. The young thug who was calling us names was on the ground, handcuffed, with a busted lip and gobs of blood dripping from his mouth. The others stood far away, watching from a distance. I walked up as Lela was explaining to the officer what had happened.

"Like I said, I was walking to my car, minding my own business. He came up to me and I let him have it. I had to defend myself, and I'm glad I did, now that you all pulled a knife from his pocket."

"Yeah, that and some drugs, too. Good thing you were able to protect yourself and I'm glad you're okay."

"Me too," I said, looking at Lela, who was wiping rain from her face. "Come on. Let's go."

"Are we done here?" she asked the officer.

"Yes. There's a tornado watch, so you ladies need to hurry home."

As we got in the car, we watched as the police put the youngster in the back seat of a police vehicle. His grill was messed up, and all he could do was look over at us and drop his head. The other police officer started waving everybody away.

"Go home and read a book or something. Get off these street corners and find something else constructive to do!"

The crowd became scarce as Lela drove away. She told me what had happened and needless to say, she kicked his ass! He got what he deserved and we laughed all the way to her house, talking about it. I knew there was a reason why I liked her so much, and was starting to like her even more.

Lela drove slowly in the rain, and by the time we got there, it was almost one o'clock in the morning. I wanted to find out if Kate had made it to my penthouse, but when I called her cell phone, she didn't answer.

"Damn it. I wish she would answer her phone," I said as Lela and I sat in the car. We were in her driveway, looking outside at the crackling thunder and hard, pouring rain.

"Try her again when we get inside. Let's get out of this mess and get to a safe place."

With no umbrellas, we got out of the car. She waited for me to run to her side, and when I did, she took my hand. I kept thinking how nice that was of her, but I knew she had learned to be a protector of the people she cared about.

By the time we made it inside, our clothes were drenched. Lela kept flicking the light switch, but the lights wouldn't come on. The wind was picking up, so she suggested that we go to the basement. She stopped in the kitchen to get a flashlight, and we made our way down the stairs and into the pitch-black basement. I could barely see what was down there, but as Lela flashed the light around, I saw a TV, a couch, some workout equipment, and a fish tank. The floor was carpeted and the basement seemed kind of cold. I shivered and Lela put the flashlight on me.

"Try your sister again," she said.

I pulled my phone from my pocket, using the light from the flashlight to see what I was doing. Finally, she answered.

"Did you and the kids make it safely?" I asked.

She hesitated to answer, then spoke up. "We're at home, Sky. I didn't want to inconvenience you, and besides, Ray and I really need to work this out."

Tears welled in my eyes from the soft tone of my sister, who I knew was making a bad choice. I swallowed the lump in my throat, trying not to preach to her as Momma had already done. "If you can't work it out, please go to my place. It is no inconvenience at all, and I'm not even there. You and the kids can have the whole place to yourselves. Don't argue with Ray again, and promise me that you'll leave if things escalate."

"I promise," she said. "Now, I have to go. I'll call you tomorrow."

Kate hung up and I couldn't help but shake my head. I felt helpless and that wasn't a good feeling at all. Lela moved the light away from my face and stepped up to give me a hug.

"Don't worry. She'll be okay. If she was smart enough to leave earlier, I don't think she'll stick around for another fight. Besides, he's probably already regretting putting his hands on her, and doing his best to make it right. I have the number of a counselor she can talk to. Make sure I give it to you before you leave."

I nodded, and as I continued to shiver, Lela rubbed up and down my arms. Her touch always had a way of calming me and it did.

"We need to get out of these wet clothes. I have some clean towels in the washroom. Stay here and I'll go get them."

I stood in darkness, waiting for Lela to return with the towels and feeling a little uncomfortable. Being in the dark wasn't a good feeling, and I could still hear rain pouring down on the roof, along with the gusty wind. Every once in a while, lightning would bring in a hint of light, just so I could see. That helped, but it was still scary.

Lela came back with two plush towels. She placed them on the couch, along with the flashlight. She then stepped up to me, and as she started to unbutton my shirt, I lifted her wet shirt that was sticking to her body, pulling it over her head. She dropped my shirt on the floor behind me and used her hands to cup my breasts, which were covered with my silk and lace purple bra.

"Are you ready to do this?" she asked while massaging my breasts in circles. My nipples were erect and I could already feel my pussy doing a dance.

"Ready as I'll ever be," I whispered.

Lela unhooked my bra, and when she pulled it away, my firm breasts stood plump and at attention. She squeezed them again, then leaned forward so we could kiss. As our lips joined, I reached out to remove her bra. Her breasts weren't as thick as mine, but they sure as hell were pretty. For the first time, I touched them. I swayed my hand across her nipple, taking a light squeeze.

"Your skin is so soft," I complimented.

"Not as soft as yours."

We stood face to face, just staring at each other for a moment. Lela then removed her jeans, exposing her red thong that barely covered her. Her body was flawless and not an ounce of fat was on it. She lowered the string on her thong, and as she stepped out of it, I was back in a trance. I wanted her so badly and the lustful look in my eyes said so. She reached out, removing my capris and panties at the same time. Once those hit the floor, I stepped out of them and brought my body close to hers. Our titties touched each others, our lips went into action, and so did our hands. My hands roamed the curves of her backside and I had a handful of her ass that was soft as cotton. I massaged it, as she massaged mine. When my hand crept around to her pussy, she followed suit and touched mine. We slipped our fingers into each other's wetness at the same time and a gasping sound followed.

Lela was way more experienced with exploring the female body than I was, and at least two minutes into us feeling each other, I couldn't stand still from her touch. My legs started to tremble and I could barely keep my balance as she pinched and rubbed at my clit. I released my fingers from her insides, but when she moved inches over to the couch and lifted her leg on the armrest, she reached for my hand again.

"Is that better?" she asked. With her legs wider, I guess she figured that made it easier for me. It didn't, because her touch was still making me crazy. I didn't want to disappoint her, so I went in again, rotating my fingers inside of her, as she was doing to me. The more I toyed with her clit, the level of intensity would build.

"Right therrrrre, Sky," she moaned. "Keep touching me right there."

My fingers were soaking wet, but so were hers. Juices were already sliding down my legs and I wanted the same for Lela. As her leg remained hiked up on the armrest, I lowered myself to my knees. I pecked her soft, thick thighs, then entered her slit tongue first. She held her lips open, just so I could have easy access to sucking her juicy, hard clit. It was extremely tasteful, and this time, Lela's legs were buckling.

"Ohhhh, Skyyy," she moaned while taking deep breaths. "What are you going to do when I come? I . . . I'm getting ready toooo!"

I couldn't answer, only because my mouth was full: full of Lela's excitement that she had released in it. We were both overly thrilled by what was transpiring, and as our sweaty naked bodies lay on the couch in a sixty-nine position, the lights finally came back on. I was on top, while she was underneath me.

"Wow, this is so much better," she said, touching my ass and taking pecks at my sore coochie. I'd never had a man perform oral sex on me as good as Lela had done, and before the lights came on, I was working on orgasm number three. Lela had only come once, but I could still tell she was enjoying herself.

"Up," she said. "I have something else I want to give you."

I got off Lela and sat up straight on the couch. I watched as she walked away, and was even more amazed by her body. For a minute, I couldn't believe this was happening. I never thought that being with a woman could make me feel like this, and I was glad that my first experience was with Lela. When she returned to the sitting area, she had a strap-on with harness attached to it in her hand. I thought that going there was a bit too kinky, and wasn't sure if I was ready for something like that yet.

"Why are you looking all tense?" Lela asked, sitting next to me on the couch. "It's just a dildo. Haven't you masturbated before? And I know you've had sex with a man before."

I shrugged. "Yeah, but this is kind of . . . kinky, isn't it?"

Lela laughed. "I would hope so." She held the near ten-inch dildo in her hand and squeezed some type of gel on it. As she rubbed it, she asked me to do it too.

"Here. Get familiar with it. See how it feels and imagine it being inside of you."

I touched it and when Lela told me to close my eyes, I did. Teasing me, she started to suck and squeeze my breasts. As I started to tingle inside, that's when I stopped stroking the dildo and got on my hands and knees, while still on the couch. Lela got behind me, but left one foot on the floor for leverage. She held my hips, and seconds later, she eased a few inches of the dildo inside of me. It was so thick, long, but felt so good. Carefully, and at a slow rhythm, Lela took me to new heights. I closed my eyes with each thrust, biting down hard on my lips and doing my best to contain the liquids that were forming in my mouth. When all was said and done, I was pulling my hair out, screaming at the top of my lungs and begging for more.

Lela and I were beat. We had been at it all night, and had even gone to her bedroom to finish our eye-pop-ping sex session. We couldn't get enough of each other, but it was time to get back to reality. Her husband was on his way home, and so was Aaron. I hated to leave, but I surely didn't want to be at Lela's house when her husband got home. We gave our good-byes at the door, and after a long and tender kiss, I waved at her standing by the door.

"Call me soon," I said softly while sitting in my car.

She smiled, then nodded, before turning to go back inside.

On the drive home, I was in another world. I felt so . . . complete. This was the feeling I'd been waiting for, for such a long time. Like Lela said, give it a try and see if you like it. Not only did I like it, but I loved it. I couldn't even see giving myself to another man, and something about it just seemed so yucky to me now. I refused to go another day without talking to Aaron about how I felt, and as soon as he called to say he was back in town, I was going to tell him that I was moving on.

Chapter 5

Aaron was back, but had been putting me off a little. Again, I tried to arrange dinner with him; however, he said we'd get together on Tuesday night. His idea of getting together was attending a neighborhood discussion at the community center. I had no choice, and if I wanted to see him, I had to attend. Maybe we could go home afterward, and I was sure he'd be in the mood for lovemaking.

Meanwhile, Lela and I had been on a roll. We'd been texting each other on a regular basis, and went shopping together at Fairview Heights Mall. She'd sent some flowers to my house, thanking me for bringing her alive. I felt the same way. I made her a beautiful flower arrangement for her house and had it delivered yesterday. She called, thanking me for the flowers, and for being that special someone in her life. There was no doubt that our feelings were getting stronger for each other.

Before heading to the group discussion at the community center, I called Kate to check on her, then had planned to call Momma. Kate didn't answer her phone, so I left a message for her to call me back as soon as possible. When I called Momma, she answered, but with a slight attitude.

"I'm not going to keep you, Momma, but have you heard from Kate? She's back at home with Ray, and I hope everything is okay."

"Don't know, don't care. The two of you will have to learn the hard way about relationships, and whenever you talk to her again, tell her not to come running this way when her world comes crumbling down. I don't like how she spoke to me the other day and all I was trying to do was help. As for you, young lady, what in the hell are you doing running around with lesbians? I pray to God that you're not opting to go there, Sky, and I worry about you going down the wrong path."

"What makes you think Lela is a lesbian? You're just saying things that you know nothing about, Momma, and even if she was, what's so wrong with it?"

"Check the Bible to see what's wrong with it. I know a lesbian when I see one and that woman was a lesbian! I've been around for sixty-one years, Sky, and it's pretty darn hard to fool me. You can say what you want, but you need to get your life in order."

It irritated me like hell that Momma knew me more, at times, more than I knew myself. "If you know a lesbian when you see one, am I a lesbian? Do you see me as being that way?"

Silence fell over the phone before she cleared her throat. "I've always known it, and I hate it, too. You need not to be running around with a woman, and that kind of mess is embarrassing! It's not like you have a better option with Aaron, but whatever you do, don't bring neither of them to my house again. Keep your life outside of mine, and I mean it, Sky. I don't condone that kind of foolishness, and if you come here again with either of them, you will not be welcomed."

Momma hung up on me, and I couldn't help but shed a few tears and wipe them. Her words hurt me so badly, and why was it so hard for her to accept who I was? If she had known, why hadn't she ever said anything to me about it? I guessed that's why she seemed to hate me so much, but I couldn't help who I was or who I was becoming.

I got to Aaron's headquarters on State Street almost an hour early. I had hoped we'd have time to talk, not about my issues, as I didn't want to upset him before going into one of his group discussions. Truthfully, I just wanted to see him. I needed a hug right now, and since Lela worked so many hours too, and she was busy on the base, I had to settle for Aaron. Only a few cars were on the parking lot, and when I got inside, an older lady, Beverly, who did some part-time secretarial work for him, was at her desk. Another man was by the water fountain and two more people were sitting at tables to the left, making cold calls. Beverly told me that Aaron was in his office. When I got there, I stood in the doorway, looking at him on the phone. His finger went up and he smiled, appearing to be happy to see me.

"Yes, yes, I know," he said to the caller. "I'm excited too, and I knew that sucker was up to no good. See what else you can find out, and let's get this information out there. He needs to be exposed."

Aaron paused while listening to the caller. A few minutes later, he ended the call. He stood, plucking his suspenders and smiling with a wide grin. While heading my way, he rubbed his hands together. "Brown Sugar, it looks as if this election is going to be a done deal. Jefferies has been doing all kinds of crooked things behind these people's backs and it looks as if he's going to be out of there. He was the only one who was leading me in the polls, but that's about to change."

I walked farther into the room, but Aaron walked by me to close the door. Before he said anything else, he squeezed me tightly in his arms and kissed my forehead.

"It's like a breath of fresh air seeing you," he said, rocking my body with his. "I missed you so much and I apologize for not being able to hook up sooner. But when I got back from out of town, I had so many things that needed to be dealt with."

I touched the side of his face, feeling awful about what I had to say to him. Now wasn't the time, but tonight would be. I couldn't put this off any longer, and in no way was any of this fair to him.

"I'm so glad things are working out for you, and no worries about not being able to hook up with me. I know how important this is to you. I'm just here to offer you my support."

We kissed, but not for long, since his phone rang. He answered, but the caller didn't say a word. "Hello," he repeated, then slammed down the phone. "That shit has been working my nerves. I'm sure it's been some of Jefferies's supporters, trying to annoy me."

I didn't even know Aaron had been getting hang-up calls. "How long has that been going on?"

"For about two weeks," he said, throwing his hand back. "But I don't have time to worry about that. We need to get to the community center, and you know I don't want to be late."

Aaron grabbed his suit jacket from the chair and reached for my hand. We left his office, and drove to the community center together. My mind was all over the place. I was worried about the phone calls, but not as much as I was worried about spilling my guts to him tonight. Surely, he'd understand and be thankful that I wasn't foolish enough to let us go through with this marriage. I guess he was what I considered a reasonable man; then again, not so much.

Either way, when we arrived at the community center, there was no place to park. We had to park on the street and walk a short distance. I wore a sheer, breezy chiffon dress that had a scarf around the neck. My Jessica Simpson pumps were pretty high, and by the time we got inside, my feet were already aching. I couldn't wait to get a seat, just so I could step out of my shoes and relax my feet. But before I could do that, many people kept stopping Aaron to talk and shake his hand. I didn't want to be rude, so I kept my place right next to him, continuing to smile.

"You're such a wonderful man," one scantily dressed lady said to Aaron while throwing her arms around him. "You smell good, too."

She laughed, then looked over at me. I paid her no attention, as I was so used to women throwing themselves at Aaron, because he had a commanding presence that women admired. It was so hilarious seeing some of them dressed up at these meetings, as if they were going to a nightclub or something. None of it fazed Aaron, and his commitment to me make me feel a bit guilty for cheating.

"Go and take your seats," Aaron said to the crowd of people around him. "We need to go ahead and get started."

Everyone crowded into the meeting room that was filled with several rows of folding chairs. I took a seat in the front row, crossing my legs and watching as Aaron and the other board of directors members took their seats up front. We stood to say the Pledge of Allegiance, then the meeting was called into order. One by one the people stood, addressing their concerns and inquiring about how so many things that were wrong with the city were going to be fixed.

An irate black man with a potbelly and sweat rolling from his forehead stood up, using his hands to talk. "I have a pothole in the middle of my street, this damn big. I've been calling city hall to come out and fix it, but have had no luck. When it was raining the other day, the hole filled with water, and I watched this lady and her kids in a car go right into that hole. The hole flattened her tires, and the bottom of her car slammed against the pavement, shaking up her and them kids. I had to go outside in the rain, just to see if I could get them out of that hole. So somebody tell me: what do I need to do to get somebody off their ass so we can get stuff like that done!"

The people applauded, but one of the board members had the nerve to ask if the lady was speeding. He knew the streets around here were fucked up, but was trying to come up with excuses. The people in the room started to get louder, and that's when Aaron spoke up.

"Before you leave, sir, please provide me with your address so I can come out and take a look at the hole you're referring to. I don't know why that isn't something we can't fix right away, and I assure you that it will get done. It's time to rebuild our city. We've got to get serious around here and the time to do it is now!"

Nearly everyone clapped, and as they continued to bring up issues, Aaron seemed like the only one who gave good answers. His answers pleased many of the people in the room and they seemed to have a lot of faith in his mission to clean up the city and make it a better place to live. I felt as if he was capable of doing so, too, and had no problem with putting my hands together to clap.

The crowd calmed down, and the ones who were standing took their seats. A few minutes later, a man walked in, shouting from the back of the room.

"I got faith in you too, my brotha! A whole lot of faith. But I hear that you have a thing against gay people." The flamboyant man stepped forward, and stood up front so that everyone could see him. "I'm gay, and I cannot and will not vote for anyone who does not respect me as a person. One who does not understand what it means for me to have the support of others, and one who often goes around downing people because of who they are. I hear that's you, but I came here to hear it straight from the horse's mouth. Bottom line is, I'm tired of electing politicians who make decisions about my life that do more harm than good. My partner and I have been together for nineteen years, and we deserve to have the same rights as any married couple does. Are you prepared to take your case to Washington and support Americans like me? If not, I have a whole lot of people in and around this town who will not vote for you. We've been discriminated against enough, and it's time for you, and many others, to come on board."

The room was quiet and Aaron just gazed at the man, speechless. Normally, he'd have a whole lot to say, but this subject was obviously one that he didn't want to touch. He was spared a few minutes, when one man stood up darting his finger. "Get your faggot ass out of here, fool! People like you don't deserve to have any rights! Mr. Anderson should not be required to go to Washington to defend a small group of confused-ass people! We need jobs, our bridges and roads are crumbling, education is failing, and you up in here talking about your rights as a faggot! Who cares, man? Who in the hell really cares when we have bigger fish to fry in this country?"

"I know that's right," one lady shouted.

"Just listen to the man," another said. "He's got a point! All people should be treated fairly!"

Aaron still hadn't said one single word, and as the man walked toward him, he reached out and gave Aaron an envelope. He reached out his hand to shake Aaron's, but he hesitated.

The man shrugged. "What? You worried about me having a disease or something?"

"No," Aaron said, shaking the man's hand. "Good day, sir. You've made your point."

"I hope so," he said, then walked away.

Everyone was asked to calm down, but since they didn't, a fifteen-minute break was ordered. I noticed Aaron getting ready to open the envelope, but I got his attention before he did.

"I'm going to go get some water. Would you like some?"

He sighed, but smiled. "Yes, thank you."

I couldn't help but lean in to give him a quick kiss, just to calm his nerves. He thanked me again, then proceeded to open the envelope. I went into the lobby and got our bottled waters from a soda machine. As soon as I got back to the meeting room, I stalled at the doorway, watching as Aaron inquisitively studied the papers in his hands. His face was twisted and a big frown was on display. Wrinkles on his forehead could be seen a mile away, and as I moved closer, the papers appeared to be photos. His head snapped up and the look in his eyes was one that I had never seen before. He turned the papers over and reached his hand out for the bottled water.

"Thank you," was all he said.

I didn't respond, but looked down again, only to see blank pages. I smiled, then walked back to my seat. I couldn't keep my eyes off Aaron, only because he had turned the photos over again, and kept looking through them. When the meeting resumed, everyone was talking but him. His eyes kept shifting in my direction, but he never held his stare. My stomach felt queasy as I wondered what in the hell was going on. Even when I smiled at him, he placed his finger on the side of his temple and finally stared at me. A blank expression covered his face, and when I smiled, that still got no reaction from him. Finally, he stood up to address the crowd.

"Ladies and gentlemen, I received an important call during our break. I need to go. Please direct your questions to the other board members."

He grabbed his briefcase and walked toward me, motioning his hand for me to walk in front of him. I stood, and with a racing heart and sweating palms, I proceeded down the middle aisle. The man who spoke earlier shouted, "What about that pothole? I thought you wanted me to give you my address so you can stop by to see it!"

Aaron didn't even respond. The man called him a sly motherfucker, but whatever was on Aaron's mind must have consumed it.

I was so nervous that he hadn't said anything to me. When we got to his car, he unlocked the doors for us to get in.

"What's wrong?" I asked in a soft tone. "Are you okay?"

Aaron didn't answer. He opened his trunk, threw his briefcase inside, and slammed the trunk down. It shook the whole car, and when he got in on the driver's side, all he did was turn on the radio and stare straight ahead of him as he drove.

Whatever upset him, I knew it was about me. Maybe the man gave him pictures of me and Lela, but I was so sure that the pictures could be easily defended, if I wanted to defend them. I could easily say we'd been hanging out since I met her at the community center that night, and suggest what the big deal was. Again, defending myself would be easy. And even though I had planned on telling him the truth about where I stood in the relationship, now didn't seem like the appropriate time to do it. His eyes showed trouble, and I was more interested in calming this situation than I was in escalating it.

Aaron parked at his office and I followed him as he unlocked the door so we could go inside. I followed him into his office, where he laid his folder on his desk and dropped back in his chair. He wiped sweat from his bald head and then lowered his head in his hand, squeezing his temples.

"Clo . . . Please close my door," he said. I closed the door, feeling the tightness of my stomach and a knot that was trying to form. When I turned around, Aaron was staring at me.

"Why, Sky?" he said. I'd gotten so accustomed to him calling me Brown Sugar that him calling me Sky kind of threw me off. "How could you do this to me?"

I played dumb. I had to, until I found out how much he knew. "Do what to you, Aaron? What are you talking about?"

"You know damn well what I'm talking about. But I guess you want me to sit here and spell it out for you, huh?"

"You're going to have to, because I have no idea what you're trying to say."

He stood and walked around his desk. His eyes stayed connected with mine until he reached down and opened the folder. He looked at the picture, shaking his head. "I can't believe you had me fooled. All this time, you toyed with my fucking feelings, accepted my proposal, and told me you loved me. I believed you, Sky, but please tell me at what point did you decide that my dick wasn't good enough for you?"

He still hadn't handed over the picture, and the devilish look in his eyes told me to keep with my defense.

"Your dick has always been good enough for me. I don't know what would make you think otherwise."

He shook the photo in his hand, then tossed it at my face. The photo floated before hitting the floor, and when it landed, I could have died. There was a picture of me and Lela, in a doggie-style position. She was kneeled behind me, positioning the dildo on the strap-on to enter me. My eyes were closed and mouth was wide open. I could only imagine the other pictures Aaron had, but the only words that left my mouth were, "Who in the hell took those pictures?"

"Well, whoever it was, thank God they did!"

I continued to look at the picture, and by now, my eyes were starting to fill with tears. I knew Aaron was about to let me have it, and that he surely did.

"How long have you been a fucking lesbian, Sky? Why didn't you tell me, and why in the hell would you accept my proposal, knowing damn well that you love sucking pussy more than you do dick!"

I wiped my tears and spoke softly. "I . . . I was going to tell you tonight. I've been planning to tell—"

"Really?" he shouted. "You expect for me to believe that shit! You made a damn fool out of me, woman, and if you wanted to be with a bitch, why didn't you just say so? Why allow me to waste my damn time with you? I could have found me a decent woman who appreciates a man like me! Instead, you have wasted four years of my life, Sky! Four damn years you've kept this secret from me! Here I am, working my ass off for the betterment of our future! And what are you doing? Around here destroying my reputation and eating pussy! I can't believe this shit!" He swiped his hand across his desk, causing all of the pictures to fly out from the folder. I looked at some of them, closing my eyes and shamefully dropping my head.

"I'm sorry," was the only thing left to be said. I knew he wouldn't believe that I had planned to come forth with the truth, so I left it there.

"Sorry!" he said, moving closer to me. I slightly backed up, fearing that he would hit me. "Your nasty, freaky ass is sorry? Is that all you can say to me?"

Aaron's words stung and he had never spoken to me in such a way. I was angry and scared at the same time. Still, I wanted to get my point across so I pounded my fist on my leg and started to yell over him. "I am sorry, and I wanted to tell you so many times, but I was so afraid by the way you view gay people! I didn't want you to criticize me, but I . . . I haven't been feeling us for quite some time. I tried, Aaron, I really tried to make this—"

I couldn't even finish before he shoved me backward, pinning me against the wall by my throat. His breathing had increased and the grip on my neck had tightened. "Get the fuck out of here, Sky," he said through gritted teeth. "I never want to see your trifling ass again and I hope that sucking pussy will eventually bring you a lifetime of happiness."

He pushed me away from him, and all I could do was cry. My defense had been shut down, as he damn sure didn't want to listen. As I turned to leave, I saw him pick up the photos. He tossed them to me, then slammed the door as I walked out.

Feeling terrible, I wiped the flowing snot from my nose and squatted to pick up the photos. I was so mad that he had seen them, and my anger quickly turned to Lela. Did she set me up? She had to. No one else was in her house that day but me and her. I was getting madder by the minute, and as I walked to my car, I reached for my cell phone to call her. She didn't answer, so I sent her a text message, telling her that it was urgent for her to call me. I put my cell phone back into my purse, and no sooner had I unlocked my car to get in than someone grabbed my neck, holding me in a chokehold. The smell of alcohol was strong and I could tell it was a man by the smell of his cologne. My arm was twisted behind my back, so tight that I thought he would break it.

"I tried to warn you, didn't I?" he said. "You're crossing over in my territory and I won't stand for it. Next time, it's going to sting worse. So, move on, freak, or else Lela will be attending your funeral."

He let go of his grip, but pushed me so hard that I skidded to the ground. I scraped my knees and twisted my ankle, taking a very hard fall. By the time I got up, I could see Lela's husband speeding recklessly off the parking lot and moving like a bat out of hell down State Street. Of course I was wondering what I had gotten myself into, and when I limped back inside to tell Aaron I had been attacked, he just looked at me and shrugged, having no sympathy. "What in the hell do you want me to do? I've been sitting here thinking about how you lied to me, Sky. When that soldier approached us on the base, you knew damn well what he was talking about. You deliberately deceived me and I . . . I don't have nothing else to say. I'm hurting right now and I want you out of here."

I stood, staring at him for a minute, seeing the coldness that I had been responsible for bringing to his eyes. Confusion and pain was running through me, but I couldn't stay any longer and subject myself to his rejection. I didn't bother to call the police, as they were known for taking hours to show up. Instead, I limped back to my car and checked my phone to see if Lela had called. She sent me a text, asking what was so urgent. I texted her back, asking her to meet me at the QuikTrip

in Fairview Heights as soon as possible. Her reply was:
On my way.

I drove to the QuikTrip to meet Lela, and was glad
to see her car parked away from all the others. By now,
I was angry and I needed some answers. How did this
happen when this was supposed to be a hush-hush
situation?

I got out of my car, slamming the door behind me. I
limped over to Lela, who had already gotten out of her
car. The pictures were in my hand and I handed them
over to her.

"Please tell me how or why those pictures exist. We
were in your house, Lela, and I trusted you!"

Lela looked at the pictures, seeming to be shocked as
her eyes widened. "I . . . I'm not sure. William has been
acting very strange and I wouldn't be surprised if he
was somewhere taking pictures of us, or paid someone
else to do it."

I put my hand on my hip, after I smacked away a
tear. "Really now," I said, not believing her. "The pictures were too close-up, and it didn't seem as if they
were taken from far away. How could they have been
taken without you knowing it?"

Lela shrugged, as if she really didn't care. Her ges-
tures pissed me off, as well as her vague answer. I
pointed my finger at her. "You need to find out where
those pictures came from. And if I find out that you had
anything to do with this, Lela, you will find yourself in
big trouble. I wanted to tell Aaron about this in my own
time, and not like this! For you to force me into a situation like this was so wrong and how dare you do this
to me!"

Lela stepped forward to console me, but I pushed
her away and continued to rant. "Don't touch me!" I
shouted. "You have no idea how I feel right now and—"

She interrupted me. "Are you going to listen to what I have to say or not?"

"I will, if you're willing to be honest about those damn pictures. I'm sure there are plenty more where those came from. Do you and your husband get off on this type of shit? That's what it is, isn't it? You screw women in your house so the two of you can sit back, eating popcorn, and watch. I shouldn't have ever gone there with you. How could I be so damn stupid to trust you?"

Lela looked at her watch and sighed. "Let me know when you're finished. I have a busy day ahead of me and need to get my rest."

"Well, rest on this," I said, slapping the shit out of her. Her head jerked to the side, as my slap caught her completely off guard. She reached out to me, gripping my hair so tight and causing my scalp to scream.

"Listen! I don't fight overly emotional hoes, I fight wars! Get your shit together, and when you're ready to talk to me like you have some sense, call me. If not, chalk this relationship up as a loss and be done with it!"

She shoved my head away, and quickly got back into her car. As she drove off, I continued to rant and call her every name in the book that I possibly could. I couldn't believe all of this had happened to me in one night, and at the end of the day, it left me distraught and thinking hard about where I'd go from here.

Chapter 6

Lela was done, and so was Aaron. So, where did that leave me? Without anyone. For the last few weeks, I had reached out to both of them, apologizing to Aaron, and trying to get Lela to explain why those photos had been taken. She stressed through a text message that she had nothing to do with those photos, but admitted that cameras were, indeed, all around her house. She also said that he was glad he'd found out about us, so I suspected that she knew the cameras were there all along. I was appalled to learn that, and when she said that she was making plans to soon divorce her husband, I didn't trust her words. It didn't matter anyway, because she sent me a text saying that she had to move on. Blamed me for not listening to her and allowing her to find out what had happened. Then she said that being with a woman like me, who she felt was abusive, didn't sit right with her. I mean, what else did she expect me to do, and wasn't she the one who called me an overly emotional ho? She seemed as if she didn't give a damn about those pictures, or about the damage they had caused me. When all was said and done, those pictures were taken when the two of us were supposed to be alone. I never would have allowed her to do those things to me if I knew cameras were anywhere near. There was no telling who else would get a hold of them, and all that was left inside of me was bitterness. Being with her was no different from being with a man, and either way, drama existed.

As for Aaron, the election was only a month away and he didn't have time for me and my mess, as he put it. Too many people had been asking questions about us, and it didn't look good that he was having personal problems. I felt so guilty for bringing unwanted trouble to his campaign, but it was a good thing that only a few people knew the real reason why our relationship had gone down the drain.

While sitting on the L-shaped sofa in my penthouse, thinking about all that I had done, I realized that I had no one to blame other than myself. I should have been honest with Aaron from the beginning, but being so wasn't that easy. I had to figure out the new me first. How would being this way change my life? Why didn't I have the kind of desires for men as I'd had for women? That was only a thought, and if that was the case, then why was I now missing Aaron? Missing Lela too, but perhaps my anger wouldn't let me go back to her. Besides, she'd given me my walking papers, with little or no acceptable excuse about those pictures.

I sipped from the cup of Chinese tea that was on the table in front of me. My penthouse was getting kind of chilly, so I stood to turn up the thermostat. Until it got a bit warmer, I gathered my thigh-high silk robe in front of me and tightened the belt at my waist. I put socks on my feet, and just as I got ready to return to the couch, I heard a knock at my door. It was after ten o'clock at night, so I rushed to the door, thinking it was Kate and the kids, needing my help. It could have been Aaron, too, and maybe he was here to talk? They were the only two who had access to my penthouse, but when I thought more about it, Kate had distanced herself from me, so the possibility of it being her was slim. Every time I called her, she rushed me off the phone. I was so worried about her, but she asked me to let her live her own life, so I did.

Looking through the peephole, I saw Aaron standing with his hands in his pockets. I opened the door to greet him.

"Can I come in?" he asked, dressed in a tan business suit, with a soft peach silk shirt underneath.

"Sure," I said, widening the door. He stepped inside, waiting by the door until I closed it.

"What's up?" I asked. "What brings you here?"

"I'd like to have a talk with you. Some of the things that I said aren't sitting right with me and I want to clear them up."

I had a lot on my mind too, so I invited Aaron to take a seat with me on the cushioned seat by the window, so we could take in the awesome view of the city. He removed his jacket, laying it on his lap as we faced each other to talk.

"First, let me apologize for some of the hurtful things I said to you. That night was just downright crazy and I didn't know how to handle what I saw in those pictures. I felt . . . less of a man, Sky, and I never thought, in a million years, that you enjoyed having sex with women. I'm surprised that our relationship went on for so long without you saying something to me about your feelings. Why didn't you say something?"

"Do you know how hard it is for people like me to come clean? I've fought my feelings for so long, and really didn't know what was going on with me. When I realized it, I tried to tell myself that you were the only person I needed, and what was going on inside of me was just a fad. I've always had desires for women, Aaron, but it wasn't until recently that I acted on my feelings."

"I know it's been difficult to come forth, but when did you and this woman meet? I remember seeing her at the community center that night, but how long has this been going on?"

"For most of the summer. I met her at the community center, then again while we were at Scott Air Force Base. I liked her a lot, and decided to pursue those feelings inside of me. We instantly became friends, and I decided to step it up a notch."

"So, do you . . . Are you still seeing her and would you prefer to be with her instead of me? I still love you very much, Sky, and I will do whatever it takes to make this work."

I wasn't sure if I wanted this to work, but I had been missing Aaron a lot. "The relationship between Lela and me is over. I had an argument with her the same night I had one with you. I don't want to say much else about it, but I don't see us ever going down that road again. As for us, I'm not sure about how I feel, and I'm still confused about who I am. I've hurt you so much and I don't know if you will ever be able to forgive me for what I did, or if I'll be able to forgive myself."

Aaron took my hands, holding them with his. "I forgive you and I truly believe this is just a phase you're going through. You'll get over it, but in the meantime, I'm anxious to make you mine again. Maybe I need to step up my game, and I have no problem doing that. Just give us another try, and if you decide that you're not feeling this, let me know. I'll back off, but meanwhile, I would love for you to put your ring back on and become my fiancée again. You don't have to pick a date for our wedding until you're ready to. And even if that's too much for you to do, I do understand. I just want my woman back, and I'm willing to do whatever it takes."

I smiled at the seriousness in Aaron's eyes. He was so deserving of my love, yet I still had some reservations about us, because I didn't see this as being a phase. But for now, I still had feelings for Aaron. I felt blessed that he'd forgiven me, so why not give us another try? "One day at a time," I said to him. "I'm willing to move on with you, again, one day at a time."

"That's all I'm asking."

Aaron's eyes dropped to my lips, and just to see if he still had it like that, I kissed him. It was nice, so there were no complaints. Even when we wound up in the bedroom that night, making love, Aaron was giving it his all. He, indeed, stepped up his game; yet and still, I held back, unable to give him my all. At this point, I wasn't sure if there was something about Aaron that didn't sit well with me, or if it was actually me, thinking about my sexual encounter with a woman who couldn't be washed away from my thoughts. I felt as if I was back to square one with this, but at least Aaron seemed satisfied. I knew that putting his happiness before my own would cost me dearly, and this was what it felt like to be in a struggle for true love.

The election was just around the corner. We had all been running around like crazy, doing our best to make sure Aaron would one day be on his way to Congress to make some serious changes. I had put my career on hold just to go to his office four days a week to help out. Cold calling was my specialty, so I spent numerous hours trying to get out the vote.

My sister Kate had even joined in on the efforts. She'd finally got up enough courage to leave Ray, even though that wasn't until he blacked her eye again. I couldn't believe that all of us thought Ray was all that and treated her like a queen. He wasn't, but he would be the one to suffer because my sister was a damn good woman. She and the kids were staying with me until she found a job so she could move out on her own. Ray had pretty much stripped her of everything, and was trying his best to make life for her a living hell. Then there was Momma, who thought Ray was so awesome until she found out he had been abusing Kate. Momma was glad that Kate had left Ray, but was disappointed that Kate hadn't moved back home with her. She was always trying to find something to gripe about, so Kate and I, both, limited our phone calls, as well as visits. It was depressing talking to someone who was always so negative. Kate had enough on her plate to worry about, and quite frankly, so did I. I had given Aaron a wedding date that was only four months away. I always wanted a winter wedding, and January would suit me just fine. To me, time was running out. I had a someone who truly loved me, and I didn't want to let this opportunity pass me by again. I didn't think that being with Lela was a big mistake, only because it gave me a chance to explore other options. The chances of anyone else coming into my life as Lela had done were rare, and this time around, I would allow no one to come between me and Aaron.

Aaron paid Kate to do some side work for him. She was filing away some papers and I was making some cold calls. The air conditioner had broken, and since the kids were there with us too, I told Kate to get them out of there and take them home. She wasted no time doing as I had asked.

"We'll see you at home," she said. "Don't you stay too long either. Don't want you to pass out, and since you haven't eaten anything all day, I know you're hungry."

"Starving," I said. "But I'll get something to eat in a little bit. See you all no later than ten or eleven."

Kate put her hand on her hip. "That's like five hours from now. I hope Aaron appreciates all that you do for him."

"I do. I swear I do," Aaron said, standing in the doorway stretching. He loosened his tie and wiped the sweat
from his forehead. "Baby, why don't you go get us something to eat? You don't have to stay around much longer,
but I am hungry as hell."

"I was just telling Kate that I was going to. What are
you in the mood for?"

"What I'm in the mood for, I can't say around Kate
and the kids. But for now, how about some White Cas-
tles or something?"

Kate and I frowned. So did the kids. "Not in the mood
for those, but don't some riblets from Applebee's sound
good? I like that spinach dip, too, and I know you love
those boneless hot wings."

Aaron rubbed his stomach. "But, how long will we
have to wait for something like that?"

"It's called Carside To Go, honey. I'll call it in on my
way there."

"Sounds like a winner."

Aaron said good-bye to Kate and the kids, then went
back into his office and shut the door.

"I really like Aaron," Kate said as I walked to the car
with them. Donnell was hugging my waist and Leslie
was a few steps in front of us, kicking rocks.

"I like him too. He's what I need right now and I feel
really blessed."

"Like him," she said. "I hope you love him. I remember when I used to feel the same way about Ray. He
seemed to be the perfect man, but there was something
inside of me that knew he wasn't right for me."

I looked at Donnell, as I didn't want him to listen in
on our conversation. "Go catch up with your sister," I
said to him. "Let me talk to your mother."

He stepped forward and started kicking the rocks
with Leslie. "I do love Aaron, but of course I have res-

ervations about getting married. I just want things to work out, Kate. I don't want my marriage to wind up like Momma's, but I don't want to be an old lady living alone, either. So while I have a few concerns, I'm confident that Aaron will do right by me, that we're going to have a whole bunch of kids, and that we will celebrate our fiftieth anniversary together."

Kate chuckled. "I was there before too, you know, and I'm in no way trying to shatter your dreams. I just want you to be happy, and if you feel Aaron is the one, then that's all that matters."

I gave Kate a hug before she and the kids got in the car and she sped off. Rushing to get my food, I sped down the highway, swerving a bit as I used my cell phone to call Applebee's. I placed my order, then pulled over to a gas station to pump gas. I went inside to pay, and when I came back out, Lela was leaned against my car with her arms folded. Her braids had been removed and her long, feathery hair hung on her shoulders. Like always, she was dressed in camouflage, with black boots that reached above her ankles. The sight of her gave me chills, but I took a hard swallow and proceeded toward her.

"I thought that was you," she said, looking me over.

Pretending as if I wasn't excited to see her, I opened my car door and got in. Before I could grab the door to shut it, she grabbed it.

"Just five minutes of your time," she said. "And I won't bother you anymore."

I left the door open, and she squatted next to me. "I apologize for not reacting to those pictures like you may have wanted me to, but I was so upset with my husband for doing something so trifling that I didn't know how to respond. All I could think about was all of the hurtful things that he'd done to keep me apart from those I care about the most. From my parents to my brother and my past relationships, he's interfered. This thing with you was the last straw and I'm tired of losing out on having relations with the people who I care about the most. I was falling in love with you, Sky. And even though our relationship may have been rushed, we had something so special that I'd been dying to have for years. Not that any of that matters to you right now, but I wanted you to know that I've started to make some changes. He's threatened to go to the army with those pictures and some other stuff that he has on me too. I may be ass out, but I'm fighting every day to move up the ranks and continue to do a job that I really love doing. Don't know how all of this will turn out, but wish me luck."

I couldn't even respond before Lela moved forward and kissed me. I thought for sure I'd back away, if not because of Aaron, because we were actually kissing each other in public for others to see. I guess hush was no longer the word and Lela was finally ready to put it all out there and lay it all on the line. She backed away from our kiss.

"Those lips are still juicy and sexy like I remember," she said. "I'm leaving for Afghanistan in one week. I'll be gone for six to eight months, don't know for sure yet. The administration needs soldiers in there to quickly shut it down so we can all come back home, and I've been ordered to go. Don't make me leave you under these conditions. Come see me later. I've moved to another duplex on the base and I would love for you to stay one night with me before I go. I promise you there will be no cameras, and you don't have to do anything that you don't want to. I just want to keep this on a positive note, and if that's what you want, I hope to see you soon."

Lela placed a piece of paper in my hand, leaving me speechless. She walked away and I watched until her truck faded out of sight. I was so torn about what to do, and how could I had been so confident about my relationship with Aaron? *Why now?* I thought. Why did Lela have to show up now? What if she went to Afghanistan and never came back? I would never have a chance to tell her how I really felt. I had to tell her that I was falling in love with her too, didn't I? Lord knows I was so confused about what to do, and I couldn't hurt Aaron again. I didn't know why his happiness seemed more important than mine, and when I realized that it wasn't, I decided to meet up with Lela tonight.

When I got back to Aaron's office with our Applebee's, I could barely look him in the eyes as we sat in his office and ate. He noticed my demeanor, and didn't hesitate to ask me what was wrong.

I wiped my mouth with a napkin, then laid my fork on his desk. "Nothing. I guess the heat must be getting to me, that's all."

"Baby, you don't have to stay. The heating and cooling company can't make it here until tomorrow and you've been here all day. Go home and take a load off. I'm not going to stay much longer either, so I will not be offended if you want to get the hell out of here."

"Are you sure? I mean, I know there's still a lot of work to be done this week, and I don't want you to feel as if I'm cutting out on you."

"Positive," he said. He reached forward and put my unfinished food back into the bag. Holding it up, he said, "Go."

I smiled and took the bag from his hand. The guilty feeling had already taken me over, and unable to look him in the eyes, I headed for the door.

"Brown Sugar," he said.

I blinked away the tears in my eyes before I turned. "Yes."

He held out his arms. "I can't get no hug or kiss before you go? I know it's hot in here, but damn."

I chuckled lightly, then walked over to give him a hug and kiss. I did the best that I could to hide my feelings, since the thoughts of being with Lela had consumed my mind. Hopefully, he wouldn't trip off how dry the kiss was, and when he smiled, I felt relieved.

"Drive carefully," he said, still holding my hand. "Call me when you get home and I'll see you tomorrow."

"I will."

I left Aaron's office, feeling as if I wanted to throw up. What in the hell was wrong with me, playing around with people's hearts? This was not who I was. I cared about others and had no intention to inflict pain on them. Aaron told me that if I wasn't feeling this to say so. Why was that so hard for me to do? It was as if I was trying to have my cake and eat it, too. Or was I? If anything, it was time to be real with myself. Truth was, I'd kept up this charade, worried about what people in society would think of me. It was all about a man being with a woman, and I wanted to portray myself as being a loving wife to a man who had shown me nothing but love. Standing up for myself was a challenge, and I still didn't know if going to see Lela would make me feel as if I was ready to be me.

I put the address Lela had given me into my GPS tracking device and allowed it to take me to my destination. The subdivision that it led me to was not located on the base, but was nearby it. There were a lot of duplexes on the street, surrounded by a whole lot of trees. I got out of my car, comparing the address in front of me to the address on the paper Lela had written on the paper. This duplex seemed smaller than her other one, but I guess since she was apparently away from her husband, that's all that mattered. I stepped up to the door to knock, but moments later, Lela came from the side of the house. I jumped from the sight of her, but calmed myself once she walked up to me. She wore an oversized T-shirt that was almost at her knees. No shoes were on her feet, and looking very relaxed, her hair was in a ponytail.

"I was in the backyard," she said. "Come follow me."

I followed Lela around back where I saw a patio set with cushioned seats on the grass. A book was turned on the table and one light from the inside had lit up the area. Lela did not stop there; instead, she followed a trail that led into what looked to be a forest behind her house. I stopped, skeptical about going forward.

"Where are we going?" I asked, looking around.

"What's the matter? You don't trust me?"

I didn't respond, but to tell the truth, I did trust Lela. Don't know why, but I did. I was surprised that she knew I'd come, but I guessed it was something in my eyes earlier, or my smile, that convinced her. We continued down the trail, and stopped at a small space that was lit by several tiki candles. An army-green tent was there, too, and when we went inside, Lela had pillows and thick blankets on the ground. A card and red rose were placed on the pillow and two sliced coconuts were next to a bottle of Caribbean Rum. It pleased me that Lela had put forth so much effort to make sure our night together was special. I was almost in tears, but since she had referred to me as being emotional before, I held back.

"Have a seat," she said.

We sat, facing each other, and before I knew it, things were working their way back to normal. We didn't talk much about what had happened, nor did conversations about Aaron or her husband come up. I was glad about that, because I wasn't prepared to tell her that I had reconciled my differences with Aaron and was planning to marry him. That was, until she finally asked.

"Yes, we're back together, and the wedding is back on. He's a good man, Lela, and I don't want to miss out on an opportunity to share my life with someone like him. Now, if you don't mind, I don't want to talk about him anymore. I know you'll never understand what I feel, but at the end of the day, I think it's best."

Lela held up her coconut with rum in it. "Here's to you and Aaron then. You know I wish you well."

I lightly tapped my coconut against hers and we laughed. Moments later, I set mine down and got on my knees. I pulled my shirt over my head, and removed my bra, exposing my breasts. I had missed being intimate with Lela, and when she reached out to grab my waist, her touch set me on fire. My breast went into her mouth, and as she circled the tip of her tongue around my nipple, I dropped my head back. I closed my eyes, so thankful for the feeling that was soon to come my way. Within seconds, all of our clothes were off, and Lela lay back as I straddled the top of her. The strap-on was already on, and as I rode it, Lela used her fingers to fill me up too. I was so excited. My pussy folds were getting wetter with each thrust and Lela couldn't wait to suck them. She pulled the dripping dildo from my insides, and in our favorite sixty-nine position, we turned each other out. I wanted to be sure to give her something she would always remember, and as both of our bodies profusely sweated throughout the night, she provided the most unforgettable experience of my life.

By morning, Lela was knocked out, but I was wide awake. My head rested on her midsection and the bottom half of our bodies were covered with the blankets. All I could think about was how badly I didn't want her to leave, but I knew that her career came before every single thing. She'd made that clear from the beginning, and in no way did I want to complicate her life. Besides, I was still going through with my marriage with Aaron. This thing between Lela and me was something I had to get over, but I wanted her to keep in touch. With her going away to Afghanistan, I figured that wouldn't be easy to do.

While inhaling her scent, I turned my head, puckering my lips to peck her flat stomach. My tongue sank into her navel, causing her to slowly raise her leg. I reached down to squeeze her thighs, and she wiggled her fingers in my hair.

"Haven't you had enough of me?" she said.

I lifted my head, then rested my chin on her upper chest, looking at her. "Never. What am I going to do without you? I don't know how I'm going to make it through the next months without thinking of you, but pray for me while you're away, okay?"

Lela kissed my forehead and smiled. "I will. And you pray for me too."

"Every day. I promise."

Lela and I spent half of the day together. We ate breakfast in the tent, painted a room in her house that she wanted to make a guest room, and drove to one of the commissary facilities to pick up discount items. I hadn't been home or even called to check on Kate and the kids. She had texted me to say that they were going to the mall, but I did want to check in to let her know I was okay. As for Aaron, he had called four times. My calls went straight to voice mail, but as soon as I left Lela's house, I called him. My lie was already prepared, but I wasn't sure how he would receive it.

"I'm so sorry, honey. My mother wanted me to take her to the emergency room last night and I couldn't find my phone to call you. And when I got to the hospital, I was so worried about her. The room we were in didn't have a phone, so I couldn't call. I didn't bother to call Kate, because Momma didn't want to worry her. You know how she is."

Aaron paused before commenting, and obviously, I wasn't good at lying. "I do know how she is," he said. "But it wouldn't have cost you nothing to go in another room to use a phone to call me. I've been so worried about you, Sky, and I thought something had happened to you."

"No, I'm fine. I'm going home to change clothes, and then I'll be right over. Are things pretty busy today?"

"Hectic. The sooner you can get here, the better."

"Be there soon."

I hung up, ignoring Aaron's slight attitude. I was on cloud nine after spending time with Lela, and there was nothing that could make me come down from my high.

Chapter 7

This had to be one of the worst days of my life. I was sad . . . distraught that Lela had left earlier, going to Afghanistan, and I barely got a chance to say good-bye. Actually, it was by text, and the only thing it said was, Hope to see you soon. Luv always, Lela. And if that wasn't enough, we were now at the community center, waiting for the returns to come in for the election. Aaron was down by 7 percent and it was not a good feeling. The night was still young, but many of us in the crowded community center, filled with tables and chairs, were hopeful. Stress was written all over Aaron's face, and the look on it made me uncomfortable. I didn't know what to say to him, other than wait until all of the votes were counted.

And as they were, the gap between Aaron and the other candidate, Jefferies, had gotten wider. He was now up by 9 percent and things weren't looking too good. According to Aaron's campaign manager who kept on calling, there were only a few more ballots to be counted, and he wasn't sure if those votes would put him over the top.

"Something has to be wrong," Aaron shouted to his campaign manager as we stepped into the back room. He was pacing and seemed so out of it. I had never seen him this way, not even when he had seen those pictures of me and Lela.

He kept yelling into the phone, then turned it off and put it into his pocket. "Damn!" he said, reaching for my hand. "I'm going to have to go out there and face all of those people to concede tonight. This is such a disappointment and I surely thought this was in the bag. I don't know what could have happened. I swear, something has to be wrong because there is no way these people voted to put that no-good Jefferies back into office."

I took his hand, offering him my support. "I don't know how either, but whatever happens, it happens for a reason. Like many of the people out there, I'm just proud of you for trying to make the difference. So many people don't step up, but you did. You did your best and sometimes we fall a little short. Don't look at this as the end, but the beginning of something much bigger to come down the road. Barack Obama lost his first bid to congress, too, but he didn't give up. Look at where he is, and if you have the passion and the drive, you can one day end up there too."

Aaron cut his eyes, but nodded his head. We headed to the stage together, and as he stood at the podium to give his concession speech, I felt awful. There was a man who had given so much of himself, only to be let down by others. Especially by me. Was it possible that he'd lost because of me? Maybe there was some corruption going on behind the scenes, because it sure as hell didn't make sense as to how he'd lost. And, by such a huge margin.

The party wrapped up quickly, and around one o'clock in the morning, Aaron and I headed back to his place. Kate had pretty much taken over my penthouse with her and her kids, but I didn't mind. It allowed me to spend more time at Aaron's place, especially since I would soon have to move there anyway when I became his wife.

He sat on the bed with his head dropped in his hands. I had never seen him get emotional, but from his sniffles I could tell he had let out a few tears. I was kneeled behind him, massaging his shoulders and trying to get him to relax.

"You'll feel better after you get some rest. Let's go to bed. All of this will be easier to deal with in the morning."

Aaron rubbed his head, then scooted back to join me in bed. I laid my head on his chest and we listened to music by Sade playing in the background. Aaron didn't say anything for a long time. I thought he had gone to sleep before he spoke up.

"Tell me something?" he said.

"What?"

"Did you ever think I had a chance to win this thing?"

"Absolutely. I had faith in you and I thought you had it in the bag."

"I did too. But the more I think about it, people in our neighborhoods want change, but they don't want to work hard for it. Look at how many of them hung up when you were trying to call, and all for the benefit of them. We had to beg people to come out to help us spread the word, and unless we offered food and drinks, you really never got a lot of people to come out."

"I don't know if I agree with you on that, because you definitely brought the ladies out," I said, laughing. "If nothing else, Mr. Anderson, they were coming out to see you. I mean, many of them supported your campaign, too, but I know some of them would have liked to find out your skills in the bedroom."

Aaron snickered, while rubbing up and down my arm. "Yeah, it was a whole lot of that going on, but you know I'm all about business before pleasure. I believe that's what hurt our relationship so much, but I could be wrong."

"Nothing you did hurt our relationship, so don't be so hard on yourself. It was me, and again, I'm so sorry for hurting you. I'm just glad the election is over and we can now focus on our lives and this wedding. I found my dress and already picked out our cake. When you have time, I want you to go see it too. The samples were delicious too, and I hope you're ready to be my husband, as I am so ready to be your wife."

Aaron slowed his rubs on my arm. "So, if I asked you to marry me tomorrow, you would do it?"

I looked up and kissed him. "In a heartbeat."

We continued to kiss and he lifted himself from the bed so we could sit up. He held my face in his hands and rubbed my cheeks with his thumbs. My eyes were locked with his, and when he backed a few inches away, we held our stare. "In a heartbeat," he said. "You would marry me, knowing that you have love for another woman. Why is that, Sky? Why would you be so willing to put me through the pain and misery of loving a woman, who does not love me?"

"But I do love you, Aaron. My feelings are not the same for Lela and what we shared is over."

He continued to hold my face. "Over as in just this past week? I guess it would be over, now that she's gone to Afghanistan. How could you think I was so foolish not to know that you were creeping behind my back? If you were planning to be my wife, don't you know that your every move was being watched? Your phone calls, text messages . . . all of that was made known to me. I needed you, though. For my own personal reasons, I needed you to present yourself as my loving future wife. You did a damn good job, even though you couldn't stop running back to that bitch to suck your pussy. But now, it's over. I don't need to put on this front anymore, so you can go put on your clothes and get the fuck out of here. If you need for me to call a cab, let me know. It's the least I'm willing to do."

By now, my face was trembling in his hands that got tighter and tighter as he spoke. I was afraid that he was going to hurt me, but instead, he kept a grip on his temper. He let my face go, sighed, and then got underneath the covers.

"Save your lies for someone else, Sky, and turn off the lights on your way out."

I had been busted again, and had no words left to say. Hurting, because I saw none of this coming. Aaron had made me feel so used, and I felt like one big fool. I put my clothes on, and before leaving his house, I did not turn off any lights. I headed down the street, feeling terrible about all that had happened. Time wasted and time that felt as if it was standing still. I'd made no progress, and maybe Momma had been right about me all along. I hated her for seeing that Aaron was no good, and I couldn't see that he'd been using me for political gain. How did she know these things, and why in the hell didn't I listen? I pulled out my cell phone to call my sister Kate. I had to call several times, because she must have been sound asleep.

"I need a huge favor," I said in response to her groggy tone.

"What's wrong, Sky?"

"Aaron and I got into it. I need for you to come get me in Fairview Heights, because I doubt that a taxi will show up this late at night. Meet me at a nearby gas station, and when I get to it, have your phone with you so I can tell you which one."

"I'm on my way," she said.

I walked to the nearest gas station, then waited until Kate showed up. I felt so bad that she had to get the kids out of bed to come with her. She grilled me as soon as I got in the car. The kids were in the back, sleeping, so we whispered back and forth.

"Aaron used me, Kate. He used me as a prop for his campaign and now that it's over, he doesn't need me."

Kate's mouth hung wide open. "What?" she shouted as loudly as she could, trying not to wake the kids.

"Those were his words, not mine. I never saw this coming, and to be used like this really hurts."

Kate squeezed my hand and reached in her purse to get me more tissue. "It'll be okay. I'm really surprised, too, and Aaron didn't seem like the kind of man who would do that kind of mess to anyone. Maybe he was hurt by the outcome of the election and his words came out the wrong way?"

"No, they came out right. He looked me dead in my eyes and told me that he was done with me. Blamed me for all of this and threw me out of his house."

Kate kept trying to look over at me and could barely keep her eyes on the road. "Blame you? How could he blame you?"

I didn't want to tell Kate about Lela, but I had a desire to get all of this off my chest. Who better to tell about this than my sister, who I was sure would understand?

"Kate, Aaron is blaming me for all of this because he knows that I've been seeing someone else. I've been unfaithful to him for months, and when we ended our relationship a while back, it was because he caught me cheating. We were able to patch up things, but now I know why it was so easy for him to forgive me. I cheated, while still making plans to marry him."

Kate shook her head. "I had no idea all of that had been going on. And if you were unhappy with him, Sky, why waste his time? Using you was wrong, dead wrong, but cheating is the ultimate betrayal. I know how hurt I was to find out Ray was cheating on me. I wouldn't wish that feeling on my worst enemy, and I could never see myself being with another man behind his back. I can't believe Aaron would waste over four years of your time, just to turn around to say he's used you. That doesn't add up, I'm sorry."

I was getting so upset with Kate for defending him. I knew what he'd said and I'd seen that cold look in his eyes. Maybe what I'd done had contributed to his behavior, but the more I thought about it, Aaron had this mess planned out all along. He was going to marry me if he'd won the election, and had plans to dump me if he didn't. That was pretty obvious. "Don't you dare defend him, Kate. That's your take on what you would have done and I'm not you. Whether I had sex with Lela or not, the result would have been the same."

Kate snapped her head to the side. "Lela? You've been having sex with Lela? The one you brought to Momma's house? Oh, my God, Sky! You're gay?"

She shouted it as if I told her I was dying or something. And it puzzled me as to why people always reacted this way. I was sure Kate's loud voice woke up the kids, so I waited before responding. She didn't and kept at it.

"Are you telling me you have sex with women? And men too? That's just nasty, Sky, and I don't know what else to say. No wonder Momma feels the way she does about you, and after hearing something like this, I don't blame her. I don't blame Aaron, either, and I would have dumped you too."

I swear, I could have punched Kate in her face for reacting like she did. After all of the support I'd given her, her words were a slap in my face. I was so darn tired of defending who I was that I shouted to her at the top of my lungs.

"So what, Kate! I am gay, and I may even be bisexual! Either way, take me or leave me! I am so sick and tired of people like you judging me. What gives you the right? Nothing! Not one damn single thing!"

Kate put her finger on her lips, spraying, "Shhhhh," from her mouth. She turned her head to quickly look back at the kids, who were moving around. "I don't want them to hear that mess! Watch what you say around them, please! I don't care what you do, but don't talk that funny crap around my kids!"

I folded my arms. "You sound just like your mother. I guess she has really rubbed off on you, and the two of you sure do have a lot in common. Failed marriages, judgmental, selfish as hell, and clueless!"

Kate and I continued to go back and forth in the car, spewing attacks at each other. When we got back to my penthouse, she packed her and the kids' clothes, stopping on her way out.

"I don't trust you around my kids, especially around my daughter. Don't call me anymore, Sky, and good luck on being a lesbian."

I was done arguing about my preferences and all I did was lock the door behind Kate on her way out. No one had to worry about me, and as far as where Aaron, my mother, and Kate were concerned, I was done!

Chapter 8

My life was in shambles and I was lonelier than I had ever been. Basically, I had shut everyone out and tried to convince myself that that would suit me just fine. After all, they were the ones who treated me as if I had some kind of contagious disease. I knew that I was a perfectly sane woman, who simply had certain sexual preferences. What was so wrong with that? I wasn't sure. Still, I needed someone to fill the many voids in my life. Throwing myself into work wasn't cutting it, and to be honest, I hadn't done much work at all. I missed the hell out of Lela, but there were no letters, as I had expected, and I had no way of getting in touch with her. I'd even called her cell phone a few times, but it went straight to voice mail for me to leave a message. None of my texts were returned, and after trying to reach her for one whole month, I finally gave up. If she wanted to get in touch with me, I was sure she would. Obviously, she didn't, so that was yet another letdown that I was forced to deal with.

So, on January 25, which was supposed to be my wedding day, I sat at the kitchen table with a cream short silk dress on and my hair pulled back into a neat bun. A veil covered my face and my flower-print cream shoes were on my feet. A pretty pink flower was around my wrist and diamond earrings hung from my earlobes. The tiny wedding cake that I had paid for couldn't be refunded, so that was in front of me. I crossed my legs,

forking up piece after piece. While having my own celebration, I laughed at where I was, instead of crying. I
picked up the flute glass of wine to toast to myself.

"To you, Sky Love! For always loving you!"

I sipped from the glass and even turned on some music to dance with myself. I hated to wonder what Aaron
was doing on this very day, but the thought did cross my
mind.

"Screw him," I said, taking a few more sips from my
glass. And as the night went on, I had myself a ball. By
ten o'clock, I changed clothes and headed down Washington Avenue to a cozy nightclub on the corner. I could
hear the R&B music thumping from outside and when
I walked through the door, the place was jumping.
There were a mixture of different people inside, but everyone seemed to be having a good time, bouncing up
and down off of Kris Kross's song "Jump." They were
shouting the lyrics and the dance floor was crammed. I
barely made it through the door in my tight blue jeans
and short black leather jacket before one man snatched
my hand. My ankle boots gave me height, and the only
thing underneath my jacket was a black lace bra. Needless to say, I was prepared to have myself a good time,
and do so with the person of my choice.

As I jumped to the music, so did my partner. He was
all over me, but unfortunately, my eyes were not on
him. I had already scanned the room, checking out as
many women as I could. Some just okay, but many gorgeous as hell. None of them made me feel like Lela did
when I'd first saw her, so I shook the thoughts of being
with them from my head. I continued to dance, and
when the DJ kicked up some Nicki Minaj, people in the
club went crazy. Smoke shot down from above, white
lights started spinning, and the music seemed to get
louder. I was already a bit tipsy from drinking a whole

bottle of wine, and when I gulped down two amaretto sours at the bar, I was starting to feel the heat. From the tips of my toes to the top of my head, I was feeling hot all over. I was now grinding on the floor with a new dance partner, and yes, indeed, the man was sexy. Looked like a tall black stallion. Muscles were bulging from his chest that was busting through his ribbed V-neck sweater. His jeans had a relaxed fit and were held up by a polo belt buckle. His dreads were pulled back away from his face and his smile was melting my panties. Maybe because I wanted so badly to like this man, as being attracted to men, instead of women, could easy resolve my problems. We eye fucked each other for a while, then he finally leaned forward to say something.

"What's your name?" he asked.

"Sky Love," I replied.

"Beautiful name. I'm Tony. I'm having so much fun tonight, and I am dying to get to know you better."

Getting to know him better was not something I was interested in. Tonight, I was here for one reason, and one reason only. "Hmmm," I said. "I'm dying for something too, but it's not all about getting to know you better."

He smiled, obviously appreciating my comment. I quickly spun around, and he held my waist, moving even closer. "Well, Sky. What exactly did you have in mind?"

"You know, or would you prefer that I say it out loud?"

"Nah, you don't have to do that, but I think, or at least hope, we're on the same page. I guess the next question I may need to ask is, my place or yours?"

"Not quite. Let me ask the question, then you tell me. My car or yours?"

"Okay. So you're spontaneous. The quicker, the better."

"You said it, I didn't."

"Mine. Because we can let the back seat down in my SUV and have at it."

"You're still talking and I'm trying to get there."

My advancement was like music to Tony's ears. I didn't know what I was about to get myself into tonight, but I sure as hell didn't care. I was supposed to be on my honeymoon in Jamaica right now, but instead I was in the back seat of Tony's SUV with my legs wide open and waiting for him to put on a condom. His dick stretched at least ten inches, but even the length of it didn't excite me. The feel of it didn't either, and as he grunted and fucked me hard, I wanted to scream. Eventually, I did, trying to release my frustrations. He didn't care how loud I was, and all he kept doing was strive for a nut. My voice strained as I ground on him and yelled for him to fuck me harder.

"How hard do you want me to get?" he asked.

"Harder, goddamn it! Don't you know how to follow directions?"

Pretty boy couldn't be called out, especially not by me. He became like a beast, throwing my legs over his shoulders and rotating his hips at a fast pace. Roaring like a tiger, he started slamming into me so hard that my head was hitting against the driver's seat.

"This shit feels guuuuuuuuuuuud! I'm coming, girl. I'm about to let this shit gooo!"

For the first time, I faked an orgasm right along with him. Tony's whole body collapsed on top of me and I could barely breathe. I pushed his shoulder back, and that's when he moved beside me. Our bodies were sticky from his sweat, which had dripped all over me. He could barely catch his breath, and when he did, my jeans were already zipped and my jacket was back on. We stood outside of his car, which was parked in an alley. He pulled me to him, securing his arms around my waist.

"Now, that was awesome. When am I going to see you again?" he asked.

I shrugged, being very careful about hurting his feelings. "I'm not sure, Tony. I'm kind of seeing someone else right now, and since he was out of town, I came out tonight to have a little fun."

"So, it's like that? Get me all hyped about you and then break me down gently. I feel you, baby, but if you change your mind, and you ever want to go a few more rounds like that, call me."

Tony stuck his number in my back pocket, then patted my ass. He asked if he could drive me home, but I declined. I gave him a quick kiss, and told him good night. I walked back down Washington Avenue to my penthouse, turning my face away from the gusty wind. It had gotten colder, so I hurried to get home. But just as I was crossing over another alley, I spotted a car that looked very familiar. I squinted to get a closer look, and sure enough, the car belonged to Aaron. I recognized his license plates from Illinois, as well as a hanging air freshener that hung from his rearview mirror. From a distance, I could see someone sitting on the driver's side, but no one was on the passenger's side. I wasn't sure if Aaron was behind the wheel, but as I got closer, it looked to be him. His head was dropped back on the headrest, but it didn't seem as if he was moving. My heart picked up speed, because I was afraid that something had happened to him. I cautiously approached the car, frowning from the stench of the dirty alley that was pretty dark. A trashcan to my left was pouring over with smelly trash, causing me to cover my mouth and nose with my jacket. I inched closer, and as soon as I reached the driver's side window, my heart dropped somewhere below my stomach. Aaron's eyes were closed, but a longhaired blonde was bent over, giving him head. She had a tight grip on his muscle and was about to break her neck, she was working it so hard. Her saliva was dripping down it and all I could see was Aaron taking long, deep breaths. His hands were tightened in the woman's hair, while holding her head steady. Lord knows I wanted to run from what my eyes were witnessing, but I couldn't. I tapped hard on the window, causing his eyes to shoot open and her head to jerk up. His brows went up and I had never seen him move so fast. Nearly threw the woman to the other side, and hurried to get out of the car.

"Wha . . . Are you following me or something?" he said, standing outside of his car and quickly zipping his pants.

I folded my arms with a mean mug on my face. No, he wasn't my man anymore, but to see him in action like this had my mind running a mile a minute. I had to somehow or someway put the blame back on him; after all, there was a chance that he hadn't been as faithful to me as I'd thought. "Now, why would I want to follow you, Aaron? But at least I now know that I wasn't the one at fault for damaging our relationship. I have a feeling you've been creeping in alleys for a long, long time."

He seemed awfully nervous for a man who was always so confident. "Yeah, well, now you know. Go on about your business, because your business is no long with me."

"I'm so glad it's not. And to think I was supposed to be married to you today. What a big mistake that would have been. I hope you and your blond bitch have a happy, fucked-up life together."

Aaron was very fidgety, and when the woman jumped out of the car, I definitely knew why. She was one ugly-ass black woman, and I'm sure he was embarrassed. "Who are you calling a bitch?" she said, rolling her neck around. "You don't know me, boo, and I will come over there and kick your ass!"

"Jacenthia, get back in the car," Aaron shouted. "She's not worth my time, or yours."

I could have slapped the mess out of Aaron, but since his bitch couldn't keep her mouth shut, she and I continued to go at it. She had the nerve to rush her way over to my side of the car, trying to pull down her short mini-dress that barely covered her coochie. She pointed her long fingernail in my face and twisted her lips, which were glossed with Aaron's cum. I twitched my nose at how trifling, ghetto, and manly-looking this trick was, and then it hit me. My eyes widened and my mouth dropped open. But just to be sure, I reached out and yanked at the woman's hair, pulling off the blond wig. Yes, it was a man! I paid no attention to "it" as he threw a fit and continued to bark. My attention was now back on Aaron, who looked embarrassed as hell.

"Seriously!" I yelled. "You're out here letting a man suck your dick!"

Aaron sighed, blinked several times, and eased his hands in his pocket. "She . . . we—"

"Don't speak for me!" it yelled, putting the wig back on. "Man, woman, whatever! If you touch my damn wig again, I will beat your ass, bitch!"

I quickly turned to it to silence it. "I have no beef with you, okay? Now, back away from me, please."

It rolled its eyes, as Aaron stood speechless.

I chuckled and shook my head. To me, this was so funny, as the one who always screamed the loudest about gays was always the one who had something to hide. Aaron had big skeletons, and they were running out of his closet in every direction. "You know I require no explanation," I said, letting him off the hook. "And good luck to you, Aaron. You know I wish you well."

I turned, walking down the alley and still shaking my head. I looked up to even thank God for not allowing me not to go there with him. Aaron repeatedly yelled my name, but I kept it moving. I laughed when I heard him say, "Please don't tell anyone." He didn't have to worry about that because he had embarrassed himself enough. And in my case, I wasn't one to judge. If that's what Aaron wanted, so be it.

When I got home, I removed my clothes and took a long, hot shower. My coochie was very sore and felt as if it had taken a severe beating from Tony. I was somewhat disappointed in myself for going there like I did tonight, but at least I now knew the answer to a question that had boggled my mind for quite some time. It wasn't Aaron, Tony, or any of the other men I'd dated before . . . I just didn't enjoy any man being inside of me, and at that very moment, I realized that I couldn't be considered bisexual.

The next day, I left my penthouse, being tired of hiding behind closed doors because some people had a problem accepting who I was. My first stop was at Momma's house and it was time for her to hear me out. I'd had enough of being the little girl she could intimidate with her words, which often left me in tears and wondering why she didn't love me. I had to get some shit off my chest, and as I stood on her porch ringing the doorbell, I was there to do just that.

Momma opened the door, said hello, but then walked away from it. When I got inside, I turned to the right where she was sitting on the couch, looking at TV and flipping through several photo albums. Her hair was rolled in pink foam rollers and she had on a muumuu with a sweater on top of it. Several pairs of socks were on her feet, only because her house was freezing. It angered me that she chose to live like this, but I guessed she had her reasons.

I sat on the other end of the couch, crossing my legs. I folded my arms just to rub them from being so cold.

"Don't ask me to turn on the heat, because I'm not. I have an extra pair of gloves over there if you need them."

"No, I don't need them, Momma, but I will never understand why you won't just turn on your heat and air. I told you that I would help you, but you continue to make this about money and it's not."

She ignored me and kept flipping through the photo album. "What are you looking at?" I asked, changing the subject.

She didn't raise her head. "What does it look like?"

"Pictures. But any in particular?"

"Nope. Just looking."

I scooted sideways, moving a little closer to her. She quickly shot me down. "What is it, Sky? Why are you here?"

I looked down at my finger that used to have my ring. Less than a month ago, I removed it and took it to a pawn shop. "Yesterday was supposed to be my wedding day, but as you may already know, that didn't happen. I just wanted to talk to you about that, and a few other things."

"Well, I figured you would never get married, and I guess Aaron had finally shown his true colors. I told you he wasn't for you. Maybe a man would be happy to have him, but not you."

I slightly cocked my head. "Huh? How did you know Aaron wasn't straight? Did he say something . . . anything to you? I mean, I dated the man for four years and didn't know he was like that."

Momma looked up at me. "Vice versa. He didn't have you figured out either, did he?"

"I guess he didn't. It was time wasted on both of our parts, but you live, learn, and move on."

"Some of us do, some of us don't. It only works out for us if we live the way God wants us to live. If you're not, Sky, many hard lessons will follow."

"You know I have a different take on the way God wants us to live, and I've tried to touch this subject before with you and failed. I'm not here to do it again, but I do want you to know that I'm happy being me, Momma. At first, I was very uncomfortable with myself. But yesterday, I realized that I have to start living for me, and forgetting about what everyone else thinks. I love you, and I always want to be a part of your life, but if you don't want that, tell me. Tell me and I will never come here again. This rejection from you hurts so badly, and I don't want to continue to subject myself to it."

Momma didn't answer. She held up a picture, squinted, then put on her glasses so she could see. "Is this you and Kate in the garage, or you and your cousin, Carol? My eyes are getting so bad and sometimes I can barely see anything." She passed the picture over to me. I looked at it.

"It's me and Kate. We had just come from church and were in the garage, trying to start Daddy's car."

"I thought so. You know she . . . Kate and my grandbabies moved to Texas. Ray been running over here looking for them, but he'll never get me to tell him shit. There are times that I want to go back there to get my rifle and blow his head off. But after all I've been through, a man like Ray will never have me sitting in no jail cell. I told Kate to stay right where she's at, and if he never sees them again, too bad."

"Well, I'm glad everything is working out for her. I can't believe she moved without saying good-bye, and I regret what happened between us."

Momma held another picture up high, looking at it. "Yep, she told me. She was very disappointed to find out that you're a lesbian, and to be frank, so am I. I don't get that lifestyle—never have, never will."

"But I do get it, Momma. I don't know why it's so hard for you and Kate to accept, but you're entitled to feel the way you wish. Just don't make me feel like an outcast, or like I'm so dirty or something. I just happen to love women way more than I do men."

"I can't speak for Kate, but I will never accept it. I accepted it for a long time and look where it got me."

I scratched my head, wondering what Momma was talking about. She hadn't accepted anything from me. "I don't know what you're saying, but you haven't accepted—"

She snapped her head up and gritted her teeth. "From that no-good-ass father of yours. He was gay . . . on the downlow or whatever you want to call it. Made my life a living hell, running around with his men on the side and neglecting his family. I did my best to make things work between us, tried everything I could to get him to love me, but nothing changed. Eventually, I gave up and let him have his men. So, no, Sky. I'm not going to accept you flaunting your woman around and thinking it's okay. For me, it's not."

I sat speechless as soon as Momma started to talk. As I looked back on it, it all made sense as to why I had rarely seen my parents show any type of affection toward each other. Sleeping in separate rooms, and him barely ever being here . . . It all made sense. But that was then and this was now. I couldn't help who I'd become.

"I'm sorry to hear all of this now, Momma, and had I known, it would have helped me understand things a little better. I didn't know what was going on with the two of you and I do get why my situation makes you so angry. I'm not going to force you to accept my lifestyle. But I am your daughter and I hope you love me no matter what."

"This has nothing to do with love. I'm your mother and I protected you, didn't I? At least now you don't have to be married to Aaron and go through what I did. The moment I saw him, I knew something wasn't right with him. I could sense it right away, but was surprised that you couldn't. I'm not going to say much more about this, but your father died of AIDS, Sky. I got myself tested, and luckily, I've been okay. Be sure to get yourself tested, and if I didn't love you, I wouldn't encourage you to do that."

Utter shock was written all over my face. What Momma had said explained so much to me, and shame on Daddy for putting her through so much. If anything, he should have just left. It would have been easier for her if he moved on without us. I was feeling even better about not marrying Aaron, and I couldn't imagine being in a situation like Momma was, feeling less of a woman and feeling as if there was no way out. The reason Momma didn't want any of the money my father had left was because she referred to it as dirty money. She didn't want dirty money to pay her bills, so she made it the best way she could.

For the next hour or so, Momma and I looked through the pictures, laughing and trying to remember when many of them had been taken. We hadn't talked like this in years, and it was such a good feeling inside to have this conversation with her. She now knew where I stood, and I knew where she stood as well. Whether she would ever accept me, and whoever I ultimately choose to end up with, I wasn't sure. This was a start for us, and a good one at that.

Chapter 9

Time apart makes the heart grow fonder, and in my case, it did. I'd been living my life as a gay female, but was truly missing Lela. It had been nearly seven months since I'd last seen her, but the feelings I still had seemed like she was just in my arms yesterday. I wasn't sure if anything had happened to her, but I often followed the news and the papers that gave praises to fallen soldiers. Wherever she was in this world, she was surely missed and definitely loved.

Meanwhile, I had dated a few other women from time to time. None made me feel as special as Lela had, but that could have been because she was my first experience. I had gotten along with some of the other women, but held back because I wasn't ready for anything serious.

Getting ready for a date with Faith, a beautiful lady I'd been seeing for two months, I plucked my brows while looking in the mirror. Once I finished, I put on my polk- dot red and white dress and black belt that tightened at my waist. Jessica Simpson's Francesca pumps covered my feet and they were worth every penny. Checking myself in the mirror, I touched my flat stomach and smiled at the shapely curve on my backside. Surely, and like always, many men would approach me, but I was proud to say that this body was made for women. I snatched up my purse, hurrying to make it to dinner on time. It was Faith's thirty-second birthday, and I didn't want to be late. She'd been so nice to me, and to be honest, we seemed like the best of friends. We hadn't been intimate yet, but had kissed each other from time to time. After tonight, I was sure that would change. Our conversation this week led me to believe so, when Faith said she was dying to see me naked. I felt the same way about her, and smiled as I got out of my car to go inside of Culpepper's in the Central West End.

I spotted Faith sitting at the long wooden bar that had several TVs behind it. For a Friday night, we were lucky to get seats, and thanks to Faith for saving me one next to her. I walked up from behind her as she was staring at the TV. My lips went up to her ear, and I whispered, "Hello."

Faith smiled and stood to greet me. She was several inches taller than I was, and had a figure that would stop any man or woman in their tracks. The jeans she wore looked as if they were melted on her skin and her gray low-cut blouse squeezed her breasts together, making them bigger than what they were. Her short hair, to me, was gorgeous. It was almost shaved bald, but lined to perfection. Someone at a table behind us whistled, and when we turned, there were several men sitting there, smiling. We waved, but sat at the bar to enjoy each other's company.

"I am so glad you're here," Faith said. "They have been at it for the past twenty minutes. Ughh."

We laughed and Faith sipped from her drink. "Twenty minutes. I thought you said seven o'clock? You must have gotten here early."

"I did. Came as soon as I got off work. I stopped at the bookstore to waste some time, then looked at some necklaces at the jewelry store."

"You should have called to tell me you were ready. I would have come sooner. I wanted to give you time to get off work and get settled. Anyway," I said, digging into my purse. I pulled out a nicely wrapped pink and white package with a yellow bow. I handed it to her. "Here you go. Happy Birthday and many more."

Faith showed her pearly white teeth and opened the package. She pulled out a necklace, earrings, and bracelet set I had gotten her from Charming Charlie, one of her favorite places. I'd seen her glowing as she looked at it last week when we were shopping.

"Oh, my, God! This is exactly what I wanted. Thank you, Sky, thank you so much!"

She leaned forward to kiss me. I hesitated not one bit as we smacked lips together. We heard someone clear their throat, and when we turned, it was one of the men. He gestured with his finger, pointing to Faith and then to me. He crossed his fingers, asking if the two of us were "together."

"Yes," we shouted together and laughed. He threw his hand back and all we could do was shrug. I ordered us some drinks and wings, and we toasted to her birthday.

"How old did you say you were again, old lady?" I teased.

"Thirty-two is not old, so don't put that old lady mess on me. So, here's to me. May I live as long as I can, be as happy as I want to be, and find that happiness with whomever I wish."

"I will drink to that."

We clinked our glasses together, drinking as much as our bellies could handle that night. Ready to go back to my penthouse, I paid the bartender and we stood side by side, hugging each other.

"What a waste," one of the men said. "But I damn sure would like to be headed where they are tonight."

He commented loudly enough for us to hear, and as tipsy as we were, I couldn't help myself. "Would you like to come with us?" I asked the man.

He was surprised by what I'd said, and pointed to his chest. "Who, me?"

"Yes, you. You're the one who wants to see what we're about to get into tonight, don't you?"

"That's if you'll let me. I got a feeling that you're just pulling my leg, but it sure as hell would be nice."

"It will be," I said. "With or without you. Maybe next time."

The man smiled and they all eyed us as we sashayed toward the front door, still hugging. When we got outside, I asked Faith to leave her car and ride with me. I hated driving at night alone, and it was always best to be on the safe side. She agreed, so we made our way down Euclid Boulevard. I stuck my hand in the back of Faith's pocket and she held my waist. She pinched it to make me laugh.

"I hate when you do that," I said, lying to myself, as I really loved it.

She kept squeezing my waist until she got me to laugh. "Stooop," I teased as we made our way to my car. But as we neared it, my steps were halted. Faith stopped in her tracks, and when she looked in the direction of my eyes, that's when she saw a woman standing by my car, who was Lela. No smile was on her face. She was dressed in black jeans that bulged at the bottom and were tucked into her rubber boots. A white V-neck tee tightened around her breasts and a black army cap was on her head, covering her long hair that was in a ponytail.

"Who is that near your car?" Faith asked.

"A friend," was all I said as I slowed my pace. Yes, I was happy to see Lela, but her timing was way off. Since Faith and I seemed to be connecting, I didn't know yet if Lela would remain in my past, as I, obviously, had been put on the back burner by her.

I stepped up to my car and she stepped away from it. "Hi, Lela," I said, showing little enthusiasm. "This is Faith."

Lela extended her hand and Faith reached out to shake it. "Hello. Nice to meet you," Lela said, but immediately turned to me. "You got a minute? If not, I understand."

I didn't want to disrespect Faith, but I was very interested in what Lela had to say. Still, her timing was off. I looked at Faith and when she shrugged her shoulder that's when I turned to Lela. "Only a few minutes," I said. "But that's it."

Lela stepped a few feet away from the car, and I followed. This time, Faith stood by my car and waited. Lela looked me up and down before she smiled. "You look nice. Beautiful. I just had to see you and let you know that I was home. Don't know for how long, but you already know how it is."

"Yeah, I do, Lela. Here one minute, gone the next. Why haven't I heard from you?"

"Because I've had a lot going on, that's why. Too much to talk about right now, but if you'd stop by later to see—"

I quickly cut her off. "No. I'm not coming by later. Been there, done that. Besides, as you can see, I have plans. And how did you know I was here? Have you been following me?"

"Not necessarily following you, but observing you. I've only been home for one day, so don't think I'm around here stalking you or anything like that."

I cut my eyes, thinking about how uncomfortable I was when Aaron told me he'd been keeping his eyes on me. It wasn't a good feeling, and I didn't like being watched.

Lela looked over at Faith and gave her head a nod. "Is that your woman? I see you're very open about your relationships now. I'm glad to see you finally being you."

"She's not my woman, but we're good friends. I am being me now, and it doesn't involve me creeping behind closed doors with a married woman who's afraid to admit that she's gay too."

Lela cut her eyes at me. "I guess that's fair, but it's not like that anymore. But if you don't want to hear how it is, like I said, I understand."

I paused before answering. "Sure, let's hear it. Tell me how it is now."

This time, she paused and swallowed. "It's like this. I can't stop thinking about you, and I . . . I love you."

I slightly pursed my lips. "Is that what you wanted to say? And if so, I sure as hell couldn't tell."

"I told you I wanted to tell you like it is. I'll say it again . . . I love you."

"Forget it. I don't want to hear it. Not now, not never. It's time to move on, Lela, and I've made so much progress with my life these past several months. I don't want to look back and doing so will do more harm than good."

Lela stood silent for a moment, then took another hard swallow. She was so good at not showing any emotions, so it was hard for me to figure out what was really going on inside. As I stood there trying to figure her out, she stepped forward and kissed my cheek. "Good-bye, Sky. Take care."

She walked off, crossing the street and putting her hand out to slow a moving car. The car slowed down and Lela jogged across the street to the other side. When she was out of sight, I walked back over to my car to apologize to Faith, who seemed just a little irritated.

"What was that all about?" she asked.

"It's a long story, and one day I promise to tell you about it."

We got in the car, and I did what I did best . . . changed the subject. Faith and I started talking about everything but Lela. I'd be lying if I said she wasn't on my mind. Actually, I pretended to be interested in everything Faith was saying, but had not heard one word. I was so out of it, and when we got back to my penthouse, and were getting ready to have sex, I couldn't get with it. I had a dying urge inside of me to know what brought Lela to say those words to me. What made her come to me after all of this time, and did she, indeed, really love me? I knew how I still felt about her, but why take steps forward, only to get pushed back? I continued to struggle with what to do, and as Faith was massaging my breasts, I removed her hand.

"What a minute, Faith," I said, moving away from her on the couch. I sat up straight and touched my forehead. "I'm so sorry to say this to you, but better now than later. The woman you saw tonight is someone I have some very strong feelings for. She's been out of my life for a while now, and I don't even know if a relationship between us is possible. But I don't want to start something with you tonight that I may not be able to finish."

Faith's face fell flat and she looked extremely disappointed. She reached for her shirt to cover her breasts. "So, are you asking me to leave? It's my birthday, Sky, and this is really a big diss, don't you think?"

"I know. And I feel so bad about it, but I can't have sex with you. I need to get out of here . . . get some air and go clear my head. Something."

"You know if you do this, you'll never be able to call me again. I don't get down like this, Sky, and I thought you were much better than this."

I was disappointed that Faith felt as if I had dissed her, and true to the fact or not, ending this was the best thing I could do for her. My feelings were all over the place, and after seeing Lela tonight, it would be wrong for me to pursue an intimate relationship with any woman until I resolved my feelings for her.

Faith put her clothes on, slamming the door on her way out. I offered to take her home, but she called for a cab. From my window, I watched her get into the cab, wondering to myself if I'd made a big mistake. Maybe I had, but something inside of me felt as if Lela was worth it. I left my penthouse and made my way to her duplex. I wasn't even sure if she still lived there, but I took my chances.

Lela's truck was parked in the driveway, so I got out of my car to go to the door. I knocked, then rang the doorbell, getting no answer. A few lights were on inside, but not many. As I walked away to go around to the back, that's when I heard the door squeak open. This time, Lela stood with an attitude, as I was the one there to make my case.

"I thought you had plans tonight," she said, not inviting me in yet.

"I did, but things didn't work out, so I cancelled those plans."

Lela put her hand in her pockets and stepped outside. "Sorry to hear that. But what brings you here?"

I had no intention of beating around the bush. "You know what brings me here, Lela. I want to know why you left me hanging. That shit hurt so badly and I thought we had something really special going on. I know how important your career is to you, but I expected you to keep in touch with me. Even though I was planning to get married, I still needed to hear something . . . anything from you."

Lela leaned back and bent her knee where her foot touched the brick. "When I left, Sky, I was so confused. Confused about what I was feeling for you, about my marriage, as well as my career. My husband was making threats to hurt you, and to destroy my career. He sent those pictures to everyone he could possibly think of, put them on the Internet, and hung them in several of the women's bathrooms around here. I was downright humiliated. Everywhere I went, people were whispering, calling me names, and treating me as if I didn't belong here. All my life, I've tried to hide who I was, because I didn't want people to treat me that way. I didn't want to involve you in any of this, so I stayed away. But the pictures actually worked out in my favor. I don't have to hide behind who I am anymore, and I finally realized that it isn't all about who you sleep with, it's who you love that matters the most. I don't have to hide behind that anymore, and I don't have to stay married to my husband, afraid that he's going to expose me. I divorced him, but the downside is my career has stalled a little bit. I don't know if it's because I'm a woman, I'm black, or because I'm now open about being gay. I have three strikes against me, but I'm alive. I made it through my tough days in Afghanistan, but my job isn't finished yet. This is my life, it's who I am, and if you're serious about being willing to do whatever you have to do to make this work, so am I."

What Lela said was like music to my ears. I knew this was going to be a tough relationship for me, as being away from her for long periods of time would have its effects. But I couldn't walk away. Not from a woman who was my true hero in every sense of the way. People said our relationships were different, but I was one to strongly disagree. We loved, we cared, we fought, we marched, we strove . . . just like everybody else. Why we were considered different, I just didn't get it. Someone would have to explain that to me one day, but for now, I reached out to Lela and our tongues threw a party. . . a celebration that had awaited us for quite some time. Hush was no longer the word and I was damn glad about that!

About the Author

Brenda Hampton is an *Essence* bestselling author. She was named a Favorite Female Fiction writer in *Upscale* magazine and was awarded the Best Female Writer by readers and Infini Promoters. When she is not writing, Hampton manages her own insurance business in the St. Louis metropolitan area.

Other books by Brenda Hampton

Two Wrongs Don't Make A Right

The Dirty Truth

Girls From da Hood 5

Full Figured : Carl Weber Presents

Naughty

Naughty 2

Naughty 3

Naughty 4

Don't Even Go There

WHEN DUTY CALLS

By Terry E. Hill

Chapter 1

The dining room table was set to perfection. Crystal goblets and silver utensils sparkled from candles that surrounded three floral arrangements placed at equal distances down the center of the table. Gold-embossed dinner plates that once sat before President Washington were placed in front of each guest.

Three male servers in white tuxedo jackets, bowties, and black pants moved silently around the table with white towels draped over their arms, refilling wine glasses, replacing utensils, and anticipating the need of each guest before they knew it themselves. A succession of courses that included salmon carpaccio, grilled quail, summer chanterelle mushrooms, and roasted rosemary potatoes were served in perfectly timed intervals.

Orpheus Roulette, the host, sat at the head of the table. His wife, Raven Roulette, was seated at the opposite end. The six chairs between them were occupied by some of the most powerful men and women in the country and their spouses. The guests included: Milo Fredericks, the governor of California, and his wife, Estelle; The chair of the Republican National Committee, Charles Richardson, and his wife, Carol; Rachel Maddox, the Republican senator from California, and her husband, Scot, rounded out the powerful party of eight.

"We wouldn't be in the mess right now if the president hadn't wasted the first two years of his administration bailing out corporations," the governor said. "Those billions in stimulus dollars should have flowed into the economy from the bottom up. We've still got Californians and millions of others in every state around the country, losing their homes because of bad mortgages. There should have been a moratorium on foreclosures and every one of those loans should have been refinanced automatically at lower rates."

"I don't want to sound like I'm defending the president," Charles Richardson said, waving a quail-laden fork, "but those people are getting what they deserved. They knew they couldn't afford those loans. Why should other, responsible tax payers have to bail them out because they got greedy? I hate to admit it but the president in this instance was right. We had to save the corporations first. What's your take on all this, Orpheus?" he said, looking directly at the host with a challenging smile.

The table fell silent. The servers instinctively moved to the perimeters of the room and faded into the wallpaper. Chewing slowed and all eyes turned to the handsome man sitting at the head of the table.

Orpheus Beauregard Roulette III came from a long line of military men who never shied away from a challenge, either on the battle field or in the dining room. He was 161 of the 217 four-star generals in the history of the U.S. Army. He was also among the youngest. His grandfather, Orpheus Beauregard Roulette Sr., was one of the first black men to fight in Italy in the Second World War. His father, Orpheus Beauregard Roulette Jr., served with honors during the Korean War. Orpheus, one of the nation's most distinguished military officers, held numerous positions of command, served in Iraq, and in record time rose to the rank of four-star general.

Raven tried to make eye contact with her husband while dabbing her red lips with the cloth napkin, but Orpheus's eyes were locked with his inquisitor. His rich bourbon skin glowed in the candlelight, and the distinguished wisps of gray at his temples pulsed in time with his heart.

Orpheus placed his silver fork on his plate and said, "I'm a military man so I approach this from the perspective of national security. I agree with you, Chairman; this is the one thing this administration did right. Corporations are the backbone of this country, and if the banks had gone under, this country would have been perceived as weak on the international stage, thereby making us vulnerable to terrorist elements that would like nothing better than to invade our shores."

The room exhaled when Orpheus spoke the words. Raven smiled as if her child had just delivered the valedictorian speech to his graduating class. The servers moved back to the table, and chewing resumed at a normal pace.

"I'm glad to hear you say that, Orpheus," Charles said with a broad smile. The student had aced the first test. "I hope you don't mind me saying this, Raven, but I worried about the general here when I heard you all had moved here to San Francisco."

"Why is that?" Raven asked with a confident smile.

"Well I was concerned some of the liberal tree hugging, equal marriage, and global warming politics would rub off on my boy here. You know we have high hopes for your husband in the Republican Party."

Raven smiled. "I can assure you, Charles, Orpheus and I are more staunchly Republican now that we've moved to San Francisco. The more we hear the politically correct chatter from the left the more we're convinced our politics are what's best for America."

"It's not easy being a Republican in California," Governor Fredericks said. "Hell, if voters there didn't like my movies so much I would never have been elected."

The table erupted in laughter. "Don't overestimate your acting talent," Charles said, laughing louder than everyone else. "Your poll numbers consistently say that not only Californians, but also a large swath of the rest of the country agrees with your policies. You're the perfect hybrid. Democrat on the outside and true-blue Republican on the inside. That's why we love you," he said, laughing even louder.

"Well, I don't know about you all," Senator Maddox bellowed over the laughter, "but I think the biggest mistake this administration made was when they repealed 'don't ask, don't tell.' It sent the absolutely wrong message to the country. I don't have any problems with gays. What they do in the privacy of their own homes is none of my business. But this is a national security issue. Our brave men and women don't need to and don't want to serve side by side on battlefield with someone they can't trust."

Orpheus decided to preempt the second pop quiz and responded unprompted. "I agree," he said. Again the table fell silent. "It's been my experience that the presence of known homosexuals is disruptive to good order and discipline of military units. Life in the barracks is highly communal," Orpheus continued in an authoritative tone. "Barrack life creates the camaraderie and unit cohesion that is vital to the proper function of a combat-ready force. In the military, respect and loyalty between members is powerful enough to transcend almost every animosity."

Orpheus's response gradually turned into a speech as he continued. "In the army soldiers are always conscious of the fact that the guy down the hall could very well be the guy who comes between him and death on some dirt road in Iraq. Allowing gays to serve openly in the military disrupts the balance and places our men and women at risk in times of war. Men are naturally uncomfortable with the idea of homosexuality and instinctively know that it's not appropriate to relate to one another in those terms. In the close quarters of the barracks, this kind of tension quickly turns into animosity that, in my experience, cannot be overcome on the battlefield."

Suddenly everyone at the table began to clap. The room was filled with, "Well put, General," and "I feel the same," and "I couldn't have said it better myself, General."

"I'm sorry," Orpheus said, "I didn't mean to get on my soapbox, but this is something Raven and I feel very strongly about." Raven beamed proudly at her eloquent husband.

Milo reached for his wife's hand and held it tight as he smiled and said, "That's the message America never heard. I think if they had, they would have never supported the repeal. This isn't about individual rights, it's about the safety of our boys and girls in the military. It's about the safety and security of our country and all that we hold dear as a nation."

"Orpheus, I was in Washington last week meeting with a few of my colleagues in the senate and your name came up," Senator Maddox said.

"I've also heard your name mentioned in Washington," chimed Richardson.

"And what are they saying?" Raven asked before her husband could respond. "Nothing bad I hope," she said with an ironic smile.

"Just the opposite, dear lady," the governor said. "I don't think it's a secret to anyone here that I'm being encouraged by some members of our party to consider a run for president in 2012."

"You'd be a great president," Carol said.

"Slow down, Carol," Milo bellowed with a broad grin. "It's just talk at this stage. But I have to admit I'm honored and seriously considering it."

"We want him to run," Richardson said. "He's got the looks, he was a celebrity long before he became governor and like I said earlier, he looks like a Democrat but has the heart of a true Republican."

"What does this have to do with Orpheus?" Raven asked, already knowing the answer.

"Well, little lady," Richardson said, "Some of us feel your husband's name should be put on the shortlist of possible running mates. What would you think of that, Raven? Vice President Orpheus Roulette."

Raven ignored the patronizing tone of the chairman. It didn't matter because she was immediately thrust into the position she had worked so hard for since the day she married Orpheus Beauregard Roulette. She didn't have to think about it.

Raven was a prolific fundraiser for the Republican Party and known for the elegant parties she had hosted for military brass, politicians, political donors, and celebrities. She had Orpheus's political path well charted. Her sights had always been on the White House and had demonstrated on many occasions that she would do whatever it took to make that a reality. First vice president, then the Oval Office.

"What do you think, Black Bird," Orpheus said to the contemplative Raven across the table. "Did we give these folks too much wine this evening?"

Again laughter swept across at the table. "We're serious about this, Orpheus," Richardson said with a straight face. "I want you and Raven to give this some serious thought. The country is scared right now. Terror threats, instability and political unrest in other countries; keeping our shores safe and maintaining our nation's position of dominance on the world stage are priorities. A man with your impeccable military credentials might be just what the country is looking for on this ticket."

The guests had all departed, smiling and slightly tipsy, in their government-issued, chauffeur-driven cars. The servers had been amply tipped and the caterer's van loaded with the remains of a signature Raven Roulette evening.

"You looked beautiful tonight, Black Bird," Orpheus said, holding Raven in his arms. "Everything was perfect as usual."

"You were brilliant, Mr. Vice President," she said as he nuzzled her creamy neck and shoulders. Orpheus ran his fingers through her silky coal-black hair. Diamonds dangled from her ears and captured what little light there was in the bedroom. She was beautiful. Some would say even too beautiful to be the wife of a vice president.

"It's just talk, baby," Orpheus whispered breathlessly in her ear. "There are probably twenty people on that shortlist. Don't get your hopes up."

Raven took a step back and released herself from his embrace. "Don't talk like that, Orpheus," she said to his surprised face. "We've worked hard to get you to this point. You have to be positive."

"I know, baby, but we also have to be realistic. I've never held political office. I'm sure there are other, more seasoned politicians on the list. I just think it's a long shot."

Raven turned her back to him and walked to a vanity in the corner of the room. "I won't have you talking like that, Orpheus. Do you know how many asses I've had to kiss to get us this far? How many thousand-dollar-a-plate fundraisers I had to chair? How many times I've had to convince people you walk on water just to get your name mentioned as a possible candidate? Don't fuck this up for me," she said angrily.

"Honey, I just don't want you to be disappointed," Orpheus said pleadingly.

"The only thing that will disappoint me is if you screw this up." Raven looked at her reflection in the mirror over the vanity. "I swear, Orpheus, I will never forgive you if you don't fight for this with me. I can't do it alone."

Raven had been a beauty her entire life. She was born into a wealthy family in Los Angeles. Her father was an attorney. His clients consisted of prominent athletes, celebrities, and politicians being sued for seven-figure divorce settlements. Raven inherited her looks from her mother, who had been a Fashion Fair model who gracefully settled into a life of full-time mother and part-time trophy wife.

As a teenager Raven quickly learned that her looks opened doors that were closed to most other people. She was recruited for the high school cheerleading squad even though she had little rhythm and had no intention of ever trying out. The most handsome men in any room would crawl over dozens of other attractive women just to try their best pick-up line on her. She easily grew accustomed to being seated at the best tables in trendy restaurants regardless of whom she dined with.

The attention grew tiresome until she learned to harness the benefits into a commodity that was meaningful to her. Her father always told her, "You're beautiful, Black Bird, but always remember, without power you're nothing is this world."

After completing her law degree at Harvard, her looks quickly transported her into the upper echelons of politics. While working in Washington as a corporate attorney she was relentlessly pursued by politicians and Washington power brokers, but General Roulette was the only man who caught her eye as she walked down the hall of the Pentagon with one of her clients.

The four stars on his uniform were the second thing Raven saw after his penetrating chocolate eyes. Orpheus took a double take when she passed him in the hall. The two stopped and turned around at the same time. It was if the script had been written for them, and all they had to do was read the lines. They were married a year later.

"Don't we have enough already in our lives?" Orpheus said to her reflection in the vanity mirror. "We have each other. We have the kids, a beautiful home in Presidio. Isn't that enough to make you happy?"

"No, it's not enough," Raven said, removing the diamond earrings. "We've talked about this, Orpheus. You and I both want this, remember? You said you wanted it as much as I did."

"I never said that," Orpheus replied while removing his evening jacket. "I only said I want you to be happy."

"Well this is what will make me happy," she said bitterly. "I hate San Francisco. I hate California. I hate pretending to enjoy lunching with all those dried-up, face-lifted, rich bitches. I want to go to Washington. I want you to be president."

"Vice president," Orpheus snapped.

"Don't be naïve, Orpheus. They wouldn't consider you for vice president if they didn't think you could eventually be president."

"I don't fucking want to be president," he yelled. "You want me to be president."

Orpheus continued to undress. He made every effort to not make eye contact with her.

"Don't be fucking ridiculous. Everyone wants to be president," Raven said, jerking around to face him.

"You know that's not true."

"It is true. But you are one of the few people in this country who actually has a chance to make it a reality."

Raven walked to him as he unbuckled his pants. "Baby, listen to me. This country needs you. Those hollow military sanctions against Iran have failed. They already have the ability to produce uranium. If their race for nuclear power is not interrupted they will have a nuclear bomb by 2014. Do you think some Ivy League asshole who never served a fucking day in the military is going to be able to stand up to them? The country needs a leader like you with balls," she said seductively.

Raven moved closer as his pants dropped to the floor. "I know you have the balls." She said, wrapping her arms around his bare waist. "I've seen them and they're beautiful."

Raven slipped her soft hand under the elastic waistband of his military white boxers and gently caressed his testicles. "You see," she whispered in his ear. "They`re enormous; just what this country needs."

She could feel him growing in her hand as she spoke. "You're the man to do the job. You're the man with enough courage to stand up to terrorists. I wish you had been president in 2001," she said, slowly messaging his engorged member. "I think you would have flown to Iraq on Air Force One and killed Saddam Hussein and any other bastard who threatened your country with your bare hands."

Orpheus began to moan under her touch. His hulking body and broad shoulders wilted in her gentle arms. "Don't do this, Raven," came his weak protest. "We're not done talking about this."

"They want to reduce our military," she whispered into his ear. "You would convince the American people we need to make it stronger."

Orpheus raised his hands to her neck and released the hook on her dress, allowing it to glide over her soft shoulders and fall into puddle of silk at her feet.

"You're manipulating me again and I don't like it," he said breathlessly into her neck.

"I'm manipulating the future vice president and he loves it."

Raven unbuttoned his starched white shirt. "The Democrats want to open our borders to everyone in the world," she said, pushing him to the bed. "You would close them and kill anyone who tried to cross illegally. Make love to me, Mr. Vice President," she said, pulling his white boxers to his ankles.

She gently kissed her way up his legs while removing her panties and bra. "I want you to fuck me the way you would fuck anyone who dared to threaten this country," she panted between kisses to his calves and thighs. "Make me feel safe. The way every American will feel when you're in the White House. Take care of me baby. I need you."

Raven straddled her vice president with one stealth move. Orpheus released a whimper as she slowly lowered her body onto his rigid shaft. The movement of her hips left him powerless to only moan in ecstasy and look helplessly into her eyes as she spoke.

"You would have found Osama bin Laden in a week and cut his balls off," she said while gliding up and down. "America needs you, Mr. Vice President. Don't let us down."

Orpheus summoned the strength to grasp her by the neck and yank her to him. He pressed her face to his and kissed her with such force that she gasped with pleasure. Orpheus forced her onto her back while still deep inside her.

She clamped her legs around his thrashing back and moaned, "Fuck me, Mr. President. Fuck me hard and make me yours."

He stroked and kissed her breasts as she moaned with each downward plunge. Raven clawed at his sweaty back and slapped his buttocks, encouraging him to go faster and harder.

Orpheus groped for the side of the mattress when he knew the end was near. The edges of the large bed extended beyond his reach so he gripped the sheets and braced himself for his reward.

For the brief moments of simultaneous climactic pleasure, their bodies melded into one. The overpowering sensations caused them each to moan with pleasure. Their fevered gasps synchronized, allowing one to exhale at the exact moment the other inhaled.

Orpheus collapsed panting onto his back. Raven tossed her jostled hair from her eyes and rested her head on his still-heaving chest.

"I feel safe now, Mr. Vice President," she purred and curled under his arm.

Chapter 2

It was eight o'clock on Monday morning. The Roulette household was preparing for another week of private schools, war, and ladies who lunch. The two-story house was the largest in the Presidio. It rested at the top of a grassy knoll that looked out over the San Francisco Bay, Golden Gate Bridge, and the Pacific Ocean. It was built in 1856 and had served as the residence of previous generals including John Pershing.

Their home was filled with mementoes from the many countries they had lived in. A Samurai sword presented to Orpheus by the emperor of Japan hung over the fireplace. A South African Zulu warrior shield given to him by Nelson Mandela was displayed in the entry hall. Every room held some trinket that gave testament to his stature as a modern-day hero. A winding driveway led up to the white wood-framed structure. The house and its history were perfectly maintained by an army of groundskeepers who kept the hedges trimmed, the magnolia trees pruned, and lush green lawn manicured. The house was an imposing presence on the old army base with its row of Palladian windows on each floor looking out over the base.

The kitchen was the heart of the home. It was a sea of Brazilian cherry hardwood floors and cabinets. A glass-front subzero refrigerator and a ten-burner Wolf range covered by a restaurant-grade stainless-steel hood catapulted the vintage kitchen with all its original molding and fixtures into the twenty-first century.

The Roulettes' cook, Li Yeng, busied herself at the stove, sending the smell of frying bacon wafting through the first floor of the house. She was a somber, slight woman who arrived, with apron in hand, like clockwork at 6:00 A.M. Monday through Friday to prepare a day's worth of nourishment for the Roulette clan. Li Yeng preferred to keep her head down when the entire family was in the room and to avoid eye contact with the lady of the house. She knew more about the Roulette family than they in fact knew about themselves.

Orpheus IV was the first Roulette to come downstairs that morning. "Good morning, Li Yeng," he said in his usual crisp and precise tone. "How was your weekend?"

Orpheus Beauregard Roulette IV was the compact mirror image of his father. At sixteen it was clear to all who met the handsome and polite young man that he would follow in the Roulette family military tradition. He was socially and philosophically on a trajectory that would lead him straight to West Point Military Academy. Little'O, which he was called only within walls of the Roulette home, had been at the top of his class for two years running at the exclusive and academically rigorous University High School in San Francisco.

"It was fine, Little'O. Thank you for asking," Li Yeng replied in perfect English while flipping a strip of bacon. "I hope you're hungry."

"I'm not really," he replied, reaching for the *New York Times* on the marble island in the center of the room.

Li Yeng looked over her shoulder and said, "You are a growing solider. You have to eat."

Little'O enjoyed being referred to as a solider. He looked up from the headline. "You're right, Li Yeng," he replied with his father's smile. "For you, I will have breakfast."

Reva Roulette, the youngest of the Roulette family at fourteen, stormed into the kitchen. "Are you taking me to school or is Mommy?" she curtly asked her brother, tossing her backpack onto the counter.

"Don't be rude, Reva," Little'O replied. "Father has told you to say good morning to Li Yeng when you enter the kitchen."

"Good morning, Li Yeng," Reva said in a huff without looking at the cook. "Now are you going to take me or not, Little'O?"

"Good morning, Ms. Reva," Li Yeng said without turning away from the frying bacon.

"I can take you, but I have to leave in fifteen minutes so be ready."

"I'm ready now. Let's go."

Little'O looked at Li Yeng's back. "We can't leave now. Li Yeng's made us breakfast," he said to his impatient little sister.

"I don't want breakfast. You know I don't like pork, Li Yeng. Why do you even make it? It's gross!"

"Because your father likes bacon."

"Well he shouldn't eat it either," Reva said, rolling her bright caramel eyes. "Hurry up then. I'll wait for you in the car. I hate the smell of frying bacon. It makes me nauseated."

Reva snatched her book bag from the counter and exited the room.

"Just ignore her, Li Yeng."

Li Yeng placed a plate of toast and bacon and a bowl of oatmeal in front of Little'O at the counter and said, "It's okay, Little'O. Teenage girls are like that. Remember I have two of my own."

"My father always says, 'There's no excuse for rudeness,' and I agree."

As Little'O said the words his mother entered the kitchen. "Good morning, darling," she said with a peck on his forehead. "How did you sleep?"

"I slept well, Mother. And you?"

"Like a log. Where is Reva?"

"She's waiting for me in the car. Would you like for me to drop her at school?"

"Thank you, darling. That would be wonderful," Raven said and placed another peck on his cheek. "Li Yeng, did you remember to stop on your way in this morning and pick up the salmon for dinner?"

"Yes, Mrs. Roulette," Li Yeng replied from the sink with her back to Raven. "It's in the refrigerator. I'll start it as soon as you all have had breakfast."

"Good. I want everything to be perfect for the general tonight."

"Yes, Mrs. Roulette," Li Yeng said without looking up. She reached for a dishtowel to her left and was met by Little'O's sympathetic gaze. She quickly looked away as to not interrupt the rhythm of the Roulette morning.

"Good morning, Li Yeng," Orpheus said, appearing in the threshold between the kitchen and the entry hall. He was in full blue service uniform. Four silver stars rested on epaulettes on each shoulder. Proficiency badges covered the flap over his upper left pocket. Above the badges was a colorful swath of ribbons for medals and commendations. His nametag was worn on the upper right pocket flap. Unit awards and foreign awards were above the pocket, with a regimental insignia above both.

"Good morning, General," Li Yeng said, turning for the first time away from the sink.

"Good morning, soldier," Orpheus said to his son. "Are you ready to take on the world today?"

"Yes, sir," he replied, lifting his right hand instinctively to salute.

"Have you told the kids yet, darling?" Raven asked wryly.

"There's nothing to tell," Orpheus said with a hint of irritation.

"Tell us what?" Little'O asked, looking anxiously between his two parents.

"Your father is being modest, dear," Raven said, reaching for the general's hand. "He's been asked to run for vice president," she said, beaming.

"Raven," Orpheus shouted, pulling his hand away. "I haven't been asked yet. Don't start putting that rumor out there."

"Vice president," Little'O said, jumping from his seat. "Dad, that's amazing. I love Washington."

"Slow down, soldier," Orpheus said. "They only said my name could possibly be on the shortlist. A shortlist in Washington could be fifty people."

"Nonsense, darling," Raven said dismissively. "I'll bet there are twenty names at the most on the list. And I guarantee you none of them will have your credentials."

"She's right, Dad," Little'O said enthusiastically. "You're the third-youngest four-star general in the history of the country. Your military record is spotless. And look at us." Little'O dashed playfully to his mother's side, flashed the broad Roulette smile, and said, "You have the perfect American family. How could you not be at the top of the list?"

"He's right, dear," Raven said, posing with her son and matching his smile. "America is going to love us."

"Li Yeng, don't listen to these two. They're being ridiculous."

Li Yeng emerged from the woodwork and said shyly, "You will make a great vice president, General Roulette."

"Not you too," Orpheus said.

"Listen to her, Orpheus. That's the voice of the common man," Raven said, sending Li Yeng back into the woodwork.

"Is my driver here yet?" Orpheus asked to change the subject.

"Of course he is," Raven said. "He's always here at seven-thirty on the dot."

"Well I'd better get going. Where's Reva?"

"She's waiting in the car for me," Little'O said, returning to his seat. "She claims the smell of bacon makes her nauseated."

"Last week it was the smell of raw fish," Orpheus said to Li Yeng. "I love your bacon. But I have to pass this morning. I'm running late. Where's my briefcase?" he asked of no one in particular.

Orpheus gathered his briefcase and keys from the counter and kissed Raven. "What are you doing today, Black Bird?" he asked.

"Just lunch with the girls," came the dismissive reply.

"Please don't mention any of this business to those two. If you do it'll be all over the country by this evening."

Raven did not respond but instead focused on the morning headlines.

Orpheus then bent down and kissed Little'O on the forehead. "Good-bye, solider. I love you."

"I love you too, Father," he replied, looking up proudly at Orpheus.

The Roulette family went their separate ways for the day, leaving Li Yeng alone and in peace in the now quiet kitchen. She emptied a plate piled with crispy bacon, eight eggs prepared with the individual tastes of each family in mind, and a platter of toast into the garbage bin. It was a routine she had grown accustomed to. The general's wife, as she called Raven to her friends, insisted that a full breakfast be prepared each morning for her family and each morning Li Yeng would toss the food, untouched, into the trash.

The general will make a wonderful vice president, she thought as she shoveled the food into the bin. *But God help us all if that bitch goes to Washington with him.*

Chapter 3

The carpet, walls, table cloths, and chairs provided the perfect beige canvas for the ample-busted trophy wives and jewel-encrusted socialites having afternoon tea at the Laurel Court Bar and Restaurant on the ground floor of the Fairmont Hotel. The beige backdrop was splattered with wing back chairs and San Francisco ladies who lunch. Waiters pirouetted between the tables and marble pillars that reached to the ceiling, balancing plates of finger sandwiches, watercress salads, bottles of the finest California wines, and the latest sparkling water.

Pastels accented by family jewels were the attire of the day. Diamonds that had been passed down from one idle generation to the next sparkled on perfectly manicured fingers and hung from tightly tugged necks. Layers of blushing makeup covered the wrinkles and aging flesh of the dozens of the city's wealthiest women of leisure who gathered in the room on a regular basis for tea and gossip.

The room was filled with chatter.

"I heard she caught him in bed with her sister," was the gossip of the day at a table of four.

"I'm so over Paris. It's like the Disney World of France," could be heard from another table. "Every hillbilly in the country who can log on to expedia.com goes there now."

"The divorce is final today," said another woman to her tablemate. "I got the house in Sea Cliff and he got the pool boy."

Raven Roulette saw her lunch companions sitting at their favorite table. Her perfect skin was immediately the envy of every woman in the room. The rhythm of the gossip slowed and juicy tidbits dripped from red lips with slight stammers as Raven made her way to the table in the center of the room. It was her table on Mondays at 1:00 and everyone in the room knew it. She had earned it by the elaborate parties she had thrown and by the sweat of Li Yeng's and countless servers' brows.

Alice Waters, compared to Raven, was a plain but attractive woman. There was no pretense about her and she was uncomfortable whenever she had to wear an evening gown. She never graduated from college but her IQ was in the top two percentile of the country. She made her husband. Alice had been his secretary at a small Silicon Valley startup company. When she met him he lived in a studio apartment and could barely warm up pizza in a microwave. It was she who organized his chaotic world. It was she who kept the company books and fought off the creditors and it was she who married him before the other gold diggers knew the ideas floating in his scattered brain were worth billions. Alice and Raven met and became the best of friends when they discovered they each were more than trophy wives.

Carla McKinney was a trophy wife and proud of it. Her hair was just as blond and her breasts were just as full and perky as the others. The only difference between Carla and her bleached-blond, silicon-buoyed contemporaries was that she had graduated from Harvard with Raven with a doctorate in clinical psychology. Her husband was an investment banker and their contemporary art collection alone was worth hundreds of millions of dollars.

The three women became the best of friends immediately. They were there for the birth of their children. They offered each other shoulders to cry on when their husbands had affairs. They thought of themselves as better than the empty ciphers whose sole purpose in life was to lunch, plan the next big charity gala, and to hang on to their rich husbands. Yet the three were so skilled at playing the "society" game that the women whom they laughed at when their backs were turned were the very same women who welcomed them with open, bejeweled arms into their worlds of lavish wealth and privilege.

They exchanged air kisses when Raven came to the table. Her usual glass of Sauvignon Blanc was waiting at her seat. A waiter appeared from thin air and held Raven's chair until she made the rounds with air kisses to her two companions.

"Good afternoon, Mrs. Roulette. I hope the wine is to your liking," the waiter said with a thick French accent. "The sommelier has selected it especially for you."

"*S'il l'a choisi je suis sûr que c'est parfait,*" she said settling into the wing back chair. "*Remerciez Bertrand s'il vous plaît de moi,*" Raven replied in perfect French.

"I was in Washington last week and the general was mentioned at several parties," Carla said, twirling an olive in her pink martini. "You've been holding out on us, girl."

"I don't know what you're talking about," Raven replied with a wry smile.

"Save the coy bullshit," Alice cut in. "Is he or isn't he?"

"Is who, what?" Raven replied.

"Oh shit, girl," Carla said, leaning into the table. "Is the general being considered for Milo Fredericks's ticket or not?"

Raven casually took a sip from her glass. She looked around the room to see who was in earshot and said, "Yes, he is," with a broad smile.

The women exchanged high fives across the table with manicured fingertips and diamond tennis bracelets waving in the air.

"Oh my God," Carla and Alice said in unison. "You did it, girl?"

"All those Republican fundraisers and kissing all those pasty asses finally paid off," Alice said, raising her glass to the center of the table. "To Raven Roulette. The soon-to-be first lady. That's my girl."

The clinking of the three wine glasses could be heard throughout the room. Patrons at other tables speculated on the reason for the toast.

"Who told you?" Raven asked Carla.

"Jeffrey and I had dinner with Senator Wilkins and his wife last week in DC. He wanted to know what we thought of Orpheus."

"And what did you tell him?"

"The truth," Carla said with a smile. "I said, Orpheus is cool but you got to watch out for that bitch Raven. If you don't keep an eye on her she'll end up running the whole fucking country."

The three women laughed so loud every head in the restaurant turned to them.

"You know that's right," Raven said, snapping her fingers.

"How does Orpheus feel about it?" Alice asked skeptically.

"Does it really matter how he feels about it?" Raven said with a smirk. "He's going to Washington if I have to drag him by his balls across the country."

"That's my girl," Alice said with another snap. "That was the only way I could get Rufus out of that studio apartment. If it were left up to him he'd still be there tinkering with his computers and electronic gadgets. To this day I don't think he knows exactly how he became a billionaire."

"There's no need for him to know," Carla said. "Keep them stupid and hard is my motto," Carla said, cupping her breast with both hands.

"Girl, you are terrible," Raven said, laughing. "But you know it's true."

"If it weren't for the three of us, our husbands would be nothing," Carla said, joining in the laughter.

"But I don't completely agree with you, Carla," Alice said, trying to control her laughter. "Henry could have made something of himself without you. He'd probably be a branch manager for Bank of America in Modesto."

The laughter continued. "No shame in that," Raven said.

"None at all," Carla said, trying to contain her laughter. "But I prefer Matisse, Picasso, and Warhol on my walls to framed posters of clowns and puppies."

Two waiters arrived with Dungeness crab cakes, charred tuna salad, Peking Duck spring rolls, and an assortment of other delicacies they had ordered.

"Please bring a bottle of Salon, blanc de blancs, Clos de Mesnil-sur-Oger 1997," Carla said to the waiter. "This lunch has suddenly turned into a celebration."

The three women nibbled, sipped, and dipped while the buzz of the restaurant provided white noise in the background. Glasses were raised repeatedly to the newest corporate acquisition of a husband, a son making the honors list, a daughter's successful music recital, a remodeled kitchen, and a new gazebo. Although Raven couldn't compete with her companions' wealth she matched them with her intelligence and shrewdness and surpassed them with her beauty.

"Orpheus's administration will undoubtedly inherit this horrible economy," Alice said, dabbing her lips with a cloth napkin. "There's no way this administration is going to have it resolved by the end of their term. Does he have answers ready for that?"

"I'm sure he doesn't," Raven replied between bites of grilled tuna. "But by the time I get through with him he's going to sound like he has a PhD in economics."

"What are you going to tell him to do?" Carla asked.

"Isn't it obvious? The problem is they didn't anticipate the worst-possible-case scenario," Raven said with authority. "Instead the administration doled out billions in stimulus money and hoped that the economy would miraculously bounce back. And it hasn't. But more stimulus money combined with reducing taxes will allow the recovery to take place in its own due course."

"Come on, girls, let's face it. The economy is going to right itself eventually," Alice said while summoning the waiter for more champagne. "I think the problems in Israel are far more intractable. What do you think of the Israelis continuing to build in east Jerusalem? Their actions will never lead to peace and the issue is going to land on his desk."

"I agree with you on that one, but I'm still conflicted on the issue," Carla said. "I concede that maybe the Israelis are overstepping the boundaries. But how is the Palestinian attitude of opposing everything the Israelis do helping the peace situation?"

"This one is a no-brainer for me," Raven said, pouring more champagne. "Israel is the only bastion of democracy in the Middle East. The United States needs to support Israel, regardless of her actions, because it serves our interest."

"I think it's safe to assume you agree with the governor of Arizona on immigration," Cathy said.

"You're damned right, I do," Raven said unapologetically. "Illegal immigrants should be sent back to their countries of origin, and no expense should be spared to secure and seal borders. We can't continue to spend our country's limited resources to house, educate, and provide healthcare for citizens of other countries. I feel adamant about this one."

The conversation continued to include China's technological contributions to the proliferation of nuclear weapons, problems with their nannies, how the stock market roller coaster had put a dent in their portfolios, and the "hideous" gown the mayor's wife wore to the opera season opening.

"We must host a fundraiser for you at our house," Carla said, reaching for the thousand-dollar check. "Oh yeah, and for Orpheus, too."

The Roulette day had come and gone once again filled with the successes that were the trademark of each family member. Little'O had been informed by the principal that he was selected to represent his school in a national independent school debate competition, while Reva received confirmation that she had been accepted into a summer internship program at the Museum of Modern Art for aspiring young artists.

Raven's day was equally momentous. After a morning at the spa and an afternoon of lunching with the girls she had returned home and called several of her more discrete Washington insiders. Her goal was to assess the viability of her husband being ultimately selected as the running mate for the governor's presidential bid.

"Yes, it is true, Raven," the wife of the Republican senator from Nebraska had said. "Orpheus is on the shortlist. Don't tell anyone that I told you, but according to my husband he is at the top of the list."

"I hear the Republican National Committee has already started the vetting process," went another such conversation. "They're already digging around in his past for possible skeletons. The word is if he passes this first level of inquiries he's as good as in."

"That won't be a problem," Raven responded confidently. "They won't find anything."

It was now past midnight. Little'O and Reva were nestled in their rooms after receiving their nightly kisses from loving parents. The day's victories had lulled them each into blissful dreams of wealth, fame, and power. Raven sat in her bed with the glow from the screen of her laptop providing the only illumination for the dark room. Her nails tapped the keyboard, composing gracious thank you letters to friends, colleagues, and soon-to-be contributors to her husband's campaign around the country who had generously donated to her favorite charities solely based on her compelling requests.

The halls in the house were quiet and dark. The only sounds that could be heard were the occasional creaks of the two-hundred-year-old foundation and the sporadic beep of the security system. Orpheus was the only member on the ground floor of the house. He was in his private study with the door securely locked and the shades drawn. The light on his desk formed a halo around the computer screen that held his attention.

The computer emitted the familiar "ding" and the words, "what city r u in?" appeared on the screen.

"Oakland," Orpheus typed after a moment's hesitation. "where r u?"

"San Francisco . . . the Haight," came the reply.

The computer dinged again. "I've never seen you in this room before," scrolled onto the screen.

"first time here," Orpheus responded.

"i like your screen name, 'Generalone.' what does it mean?"

Orpheus leaned back in the leather chair and pondered his response. He jumped when he heard the howl of a cat searching for a mate outside his window. *Why did I pick that screen name?* he thought. *Someone was bound to ask what it meant.*

The Web site was one of thousands that served as the late-night meeting place for men who preferred the buffer of the keyboard and computer screen to face-to-face interaction. It also provided the necessary cover for the married, obese, shy, and agoraphobic.

"doesn't mean anything," Orpheus typed. "couldn't think of a clever one like yours, Kiss-n-tell."

The conversation went on:

Kiss-n-tell: i hate these rooms. so many lonely people out there.

Generalone: then why do you come here?

Kiss-n-tell: guess im 1 of the lonely ones 2. how about u?

Generalone: i suppose im one too.

Kiss-n-tell: have you ever met anyone here?

Generalone: never. you?

Kiss-n-tell: never, but always hopeful.

The Web site indicated there were thirty-six other chatters in the room. Disjointed messages scrolled rapidly on the screen. Multiple other conversations continued to weave in and out of their chain of messages. "i'm 8 inches. u?" and "gave a cop a blowjob in his squad car last night," to "what are you wearing?" and "nutin but my boxers," went some of the parallel exchanges.

Generalone: what is life without hope.

Kiss-n-tell: a philosopher. i'm impressed.

Generalone: LOL . . .

Kiss-n-tell: i hope you meet someone. you seem like a nice guy.

Generalone: i'm really not looking to meet anyone.

Kiss-n-tell: then why are you here?

Orpheus leaned back in his chair again and stared at the screen. Advertisements featuring bare-chested men with glowing, moist skin and wearing Speedos lined the top and bottom of the screen. The messages continued to scroll as he pondered the question.

Leaning back to the computer he typed, "i'm not really sure."

Kiss-n-tell: are you married?

Generalone: no

Kiss-n-tell: are you sure? lots of married men on here.

Generalone: yes im sure

Kiss-n-tell: how old are u?

Generalone: 45

Kiss-n-tell: in the cyber world 45 means 55.

Generalone: LOL . . . in my world 45 means 45. how old are u?

Kiss-n-tell: 30

Generalone: does that mean 40

Kiss-n-tell: LOL . . . no it means 30

Generalone: ok

Kiss-n-tell: are you any of the following: 400lbs? an amputee? serial killer?

Generalone: LOL again. would it matter?

Kiss-n-tell: the first two no, but I draw the line at serial killers :)

Generalone: you keep making me laugh. The answer is no to all of the above.

Kiss-n-tell: good cause I lied about the 400lbs and amputee. It would matter.

Generalone: i understand. i assure you none apply.

Kiss-n-tell: good

Generalone: your turn. married? obese? wooden leg? jeffrey dahmer wanna-be?

Kiss-n-tell: now you're making me laugh! what if I said yes to all of the above?

Generalone: then i would say good night sweet prince and happy hunting :)

Kiss-n-tell: then we're good cause none of the above apply.

Generalone: that's a relief.

Kiss-n-tell: it's getting a little late for me general. think i should be off to bed.

Generalone: just when we were getting to know each other.

Kiss-n-tell: maybe we'll run in to each other again in here.

Generalone: maybe.

Kiss-n-tell: good night sweet prince.

Generalone: good night sweet prince.

"looking for right now. Anyone interested?" came a desperate message from another faceless person in the chat room. Quickly followed by, "i'm interested. stats?" from another unidentified participant.

The messages from others in the room continued to rush by in such rapid succession that Orpheus struggled to read them all. He could see that Kiss-n-tell was still in the room but he had stopped communicating.

Orpheus sifted through the other messages filled with idle chatter and obscene propositions.

The messages kept streaming by but none were from Kiss-n-tell.

"r u still there?" Orpheus typed.

A series of conversations continued after his query. "is anyone going 2 the Gulch 2night?" to "meet me in the Panhandle in Golden Gate Park in 30," and "any hot guys out there want 2 connect?" were among the abbreviated messages that followed, but there was no reply from Kiss-n-tell.

Orpheus checked the list of people in the room again one last time and saw that Kiss-n-tell had logged off. Orpheus followed suit and logged off as well. The computer screen went black. The hum of the hard drive fell silent and the room was suddenly still.

Orpheus made his way up the wooden stairway to the master bedroom. He could see a sliver of light from beneath the door. Orpheus steadied himself at the door before reaching for the knob.

"You're still awake," he said, seeing Raven still tapping away at her laptop.

"Just writing a few thank you letters," she said, peering briefly over a pair of reading glasses that sat on the tip of her nose. "These are people we're going to need for your campaign. Deep pockets and lots of connections," she said without altering the pace of her flying fingers.

"I've told you, Black Bird, none of this is certain," he said, removing his pants and shirt.

"I spoke with several of my contacts today in DC," she said, ignoring his caution. "They all confirmed you are on the list. Two of them said you are at the top of the list. The RNC has already started a preliminary background check."

Orpheus bolted upright and asked, "Who told you that?"

Raven removed her glasses and asked, "What difference does that make? What's important is that they are reliable sources."

"Because I want to know if I'm being investigated."

"It's not an investigation. It's more like research. They simply want to make sure we don't have anything in our past that could embarrass them later. You don't have anything to worry about. We don't have anything to hide. You have the perfect family."

Chapter 4

Mildred Pierson's penthouse condominium was filled with the country's power brokers.

The San Francisco skyline twinkled through the floor to ceiling windows with the point of the Transamerica Pyramid serving as the centerpiece. A string quartet played chamber music on a raised pedestal in the corner of the living room and servers wearing white coats passed trays filled with hors d'oeuvres of toasted brioche rounds with crème fraîche and caviar, lobster salad on endive spears, and chicken liver pâté with white truffles.

Mildred was the quintessential American heiress and socialite. She was the chief of protocol for the state of California and the wife of a former United States secretary of state, Victor Trugonoff. The guest lists to her parties included visiting dignitaries, foreign royalty, A-list celebrities, politicians, presidents, and the select few who orbited around their individual shining stars. Tonight was no exception.

The occasion was the formal state welcome of His Serene Highness, Prince Ronaldo Alexis Jacques Louis François of Monaco and his much younger wife, Princess Amanda, to the seven mile by seven mile city on the bay. The royal couple was surrounded in the center of the room by a gaggle of overly dressed women and their tuxedoed husbands holding champagne glasses with white gloved hands and laughing smartly at the witty family anecdotes being told by the prince. Smaller clusters of guests assembled around tables piled high with finger foods, at well-stocked bars and in several sitting areas just off the main living room.

Orpheus, Raven, and their hosts, Mildred and Victor, huddled in a square formation away from the others. Mildred was a tall, slender woman. Her face was taut from annual nips and tucks administered over the past twenty years. Beneath the blond dye her hair was salty white and her smile was wide enough to welcome the world to California.

"Milo is impressed with you, Orpheus, and so are a lot of other folks in the RNC," Victor said gripping his champagne flute with hands mangled from arthritis. "You could go far in this party if you listen to the right people."

"I'm not sure just how far I really want to go, Mr. Secretary," Orpheus said firmly. "I'll be happy with whatever course my career takes me as long as I'm able to serve my country."

"Now you see, Mildred," Victor said, smiling to his wife. "It's attitudes like that that make men vice presidents and even presidents."

"Listen to him, Orpheus," Mildred said, clutching her husband's stiff hand. "He knows a president when he sees one. He picked the last four presidents at parties just like this one. When Victor speaks Washington listens."

Raven slipped her arm under Orpheus's and said, "I couldn't agree more. I think the voters of America would love Orpheus."

Victor and Mildred each laughed at the comment.

"So young and beautiful, and so naïve," Victor said. "My dear, there are only ten people in this country who decide who will be president, not the American people.

What you see on the campaign trail and election day is nothing more than theater designed to appease the masses."

"That is fascinating," Raven said, clinching Orpheus's arm even tighter. "And just who are these mysterious ten men?"

Mildred and Victor laughed in unison again.

"Darling," Mildred said with a broad grin, "even the presidents don't know who all the ten men are. But I can tell you, you're talking to one of them right now."

Raven's black pupils dilated when she heard the words. Suddenly everyone in the room vanished. There was no chamber music. No giggling socialites and no inbred potentate spewing diplomatic niceties with a foreign tongue.

"And what do you think of my husband?" Raven said boldly.

"Raven," Orpheus snapped. "Please excuse my wife, Mr. Secretary. As you can tell she is my biggest fan."

"Don't apologize, my boy," Victor said. "I like a woman who cuts to the chase. That's why I chose my Mildred. When she sees what she wants nothing can stop her from getting it."

Mildred laughed, kissed Victor on his weathered cheek and said, "He thinks he chose me, Raven, but I chose him two years before he even met me."

"A woman after my own heart," Raven said, raising her glass to Mildred.

"Son, the way you led our troops in Iraq was nothing short of heroic, and this country desperately needs a hero about now," Victor said. "Now it's a bit early for me to say that you're that hero, but from where I stand right now you're the closet thing we've got to him today and you, Raven, my dear, are running a close second."

"Well we're a team, Mr. Secretary," Raven said, looking Victor directly in the eye. "If you pick Orpheus you also get me."

"That's good to know," Victor said. "I always say, you can tell more about a man from his wife than from the man himself. And, my dear, if my theory is correct then the general here is quite a winner."

"General Roulette, have you been introduced to the prince yet?" Mildred said, reaching for Orpheus's arm. "Would you two please excuse us? Come with me, Orpheus. He's a bit of a royal bore but you might as well get used to it if you want to be vice president."

"Don't worry about your wife, General," Victor said, moving to Raven's side. "She's in good hands. May I get you another drink, my dear?"

Mildred led Orpheus by the arm across the room directly to the prince. The crowd parted like the Red Sea as the two made their way through the room. Mildred directed servers to fill champagne glasses and exchanged short party pleasantries as she passed through the guests with Orpheus in tow.

"So what do you think of all this, Mrs. Roulette?" Victor said as he reached for a champagne glass passing on a server's tray and handed it to Raven. "Do you think your husband has what it takes to make it in Washington?"

Victor was the only man in the room wearing a gray suit and neck tie. All others were in black tails and tightly knotted bowties. The buttons strained to conceal his potbelly and his shirt tail bunched up just above his belt. At seventy-six the toll of political power showed on his sagging jowls and bowed posture.

"I think your instincts are right," Raven said.

"Right about Orpheus or right about you?"

"Both," she said boldly. "I won't be coy about this, Mr. Secretary, because I think you'd see right through that."

"You're correct, my dear. I would. I didn't get to be this age by not knowing when someone was blowing smoke up my ass."

"And I didn't get this far by not knowing when I should and when I should not blow smoke up someone's ass," she said with the slightest hint of seduction.

"You're a smart woman. I like that. Mildred is leaving for Paris in the morning. Are you free to join me for lunch here tomorrow? We can talk more about your husband's future."

Raven raised her champagne glass, nodded her head and said, "Tomorrow it is, Mr. Secretary."

"You were magnificent tonight," Raven said to Orpheus. "Everyone loved you."

"I hate that crowd," Orpheus said, removing his pants. "The prince was pompous and his wife was a silly blond twit. Monaco, and England for that matter, should have done away with the monarchy decades ago. They're a useless bunch of inbreds whose sole contribution to their countries is leeching off the people."

"I think they do more than that, Orpheus."

"Like what?"

"They give their countries a sense of history and identity," Raven replied, turning her back to him for assistance with her pearl necklace. "They do charitable work. Look at what Prince Charles has done for the environment and organic farming."

"Yes, but was it worth the shame he brought to his country with the whole Diana fiasco. It took them a decade to live that down."

Raven removed her black evening gown and hung it neatly in the closet. Orpheus took off his suit and crawled into bed, releasing a sigh of relief when his head hit the pillow.

"I'm having lunch with Victor tomorrow," she said matter-of-factly at the vanity mirror.

"Victor who?" Orpheus replied.

"The only Victor who matters in our world right now. Victor Trugonoff," she said, brushing her silky black mane.

Orpheus looked suspiciously at Raven from the bed and said, "Why on earth would you be having lunch with him? What does he want to talk about?"

"What do you think?" Raven stood and walked to the bed. "He wants to talk about you."

"I don't trust him, Raven. Did you see the way he was looking at your breasts? I thought he was going to keel over head first into your cleavage."

"Don't be ridiculous, Orpheus. The man is seventy-six years old. He's so old I don't think even Viagra would help him get it up," Raven said, folding her long legs under the puffy duvet next to Orpheus. "He's just a harmless old man who wants to help you."

"Help me what?"

"You heard what Mildred said. He's one of the ten men in this country who decides who will be president. He likes you and I'm just going to put any doubts he might still have about you to rest."

"And you believed her?" Orpheus said mockingly. "You've been reading too many conspiracy theories. The American people elect the president. They've done so for the last forty-four presidents and they will again for the forty-fifth."

"I'm not so sure about that," Raven said, reaching for her laptop on the nightstand. "Look at what happened with George Bush in Florida. America elected Gore but Bush moved into the White House. Someone vetoed the American people and I think it was Trugonoff and his fraternity."

"That was a fluke."

"Fluke or not, I just want to hedge our bets. What harm will it do? Lunch with a kindly gentleman. At the very least I can tell him how wonderful you are. Remember he still has tremendous influence with the party leadership."

"Raven, I'm not comfortable with this. I think you need to stay out of it. Trugonoff may appear harmless but he can be ruthless. Let them have their backroom conversations about me. I suspect by the time all is said and done they'll find some other golden boy and forget all about me."

Raven looked at him coldly. "That's the point. I don't want them to forget about you."

"Why is this so important to you? You have a wonderful life. Beautiful children. A lovely home. Why do you always want more? You're never satisfied with anything."

"How can you even compare this life to what we could have in Washington? You would be the second most powerful person in the country. Our children would be exposed to some of the most influential people in the world. Don't you want that even for them?"

"Our children are fine just the way they are," Orpheus snapped. "Why don't you just admit this is more about you than it is about them or me?"

"It's not about me," she said, sitting upright in the bed. "If you can't see I've done all this for you then you're a fool. I've busted my ass just to get you on their radar. Do you know how many millions of dollars I've raised just to get someone else's husbands elected?

How many asses I've had to kiss just so people would know who the fuck you are? And this is the thanks I get."

"Save the bullshit, Raven, for someone else. I know you. I know this is about your sick need to accumulate power. Your father really did a job on you."

"How fucking dare you bring my father into this. He's more of a man than you'll ever be."

Orpheus jumped from the bed in his white boxer shorts and T-shirt and shouted, "Then why don't you work on getting him elected vice president and leave me the fuck out of it."

He grabbed his robe from the foot of the bed and stormed out of the room. Raven could hear the creak of the hardwood floors as he bounded down the stairs. She then heard the door to his office slam.

Fucking coward, she thought. *He's going to be vice president even if it kills him.*

Orpheus paced the floor of his study. His Chinese silk robe flapped behind him with every step he took. The room was dark. He could hear the muffled wail of a police siren in the distance.

Why can't she leave me alone, he thought as he made a figure eight in front of his desk. *I'm a soldier. I just want to be a good soldier, not a politician.*

Orpheus finally dropped the full weight of his body into his desk chair and rocked impatiently back and forth. He looked up and saw the blank computer screen and immediately thought of the pleasant chat he had with Kiss-n-tell the night before. The digital clock on the desk read 12:13.

I wonder if he's online, he thought. *Not likely. He's probably out at some club in the Castro. I'm sure I'll never run into him again.*

Orpheus reached down and turned on the computer. The familiar hum of the hard drive filled the room and the glowing screen covered his tense face in a pool of light. When he logged onto the site he saw there were forty-two people in the chat room, but none were named Kiss-n-tell.

Orpheus began to read the flood of entries on the screen.

Pipper: does anyone have any 420?

Manatplay: im looking for mr. right in all the wrong places.

Tit4tat: got wasted at the lookout tonight and made out with some guy at the bar

Bisanfran: you sound like my father. Is that you dad? :)

And then it appeared.

Kiss-n-tell: hello generalone. How are you tonight?

Orpheus's heart leapt when he read the words.

Generalone: im fine. didn't expect to see you in here tonight.

Kiss-n-tell: just came in from work. Thought I'd check to see who's out there.

Generalone: im glad you did.

Orpheus felt the tension easing from his shoulders and the muscles in his jaws loosen as he typed.

Generalone: what do you look like?

Generalone: in the real, world not in cyber :)

Kiss-n-tell: LOL . . . im 6 foot 4. Blond hair, blue eyes, swimmers build, size 12 shoe.

Generalone: ok

Kiss-n-tell: your turn.

Generalone: 6 foot 4 blond, blue, swimmers build, size 13

Kiss-n-tell: LOL . . . beat me by 1 inch.

Generalone: i guess everyone looks like that in cyber.

Kiss-n-tell: only the liars :)

Orpheus tried to imagine what Kiss-n-tell really looked like. *Probably some fat old man masturbating at his computer with his boxers around his ankles.*

The messages kept streaming and seconds ticked by as Orpheus conjured other, more pleasing, images of Kiss-n-tell.

Kiss-n-tell: are you still there?

Generalone: im here.

Kiss-n-tell: what are you thinking about?

Generalone: how i'd like to know what you really look like.

Kiss-n-tell: funny i was thinking the same about you.

Generalone: may I ask you a question.

Kiss-n-tell: yes but remember its cyber.

Generalone: ok. have you ever been in love?

Kiss-n-tell: yes, once

Generalone: is that a cyber yes?

Kiss-n-tell: no

Generalone: what happened?

Kiss-n-tell: guess he didn't love me as much.

Generalone: im sorry. That must have hurt.

Kiss-n-tell: still does. Your turn

Generalone: yes I have.

Kiss-n-tell: what happened?

Generalone: they changed.

Kiss-n-tell: how?

Generalone: turned into someone i didn't recognize.

Kiss-n-tell: how did you handle that?

Generalone: haven't decided yet.

Chapter 5

The lobby of the twenty-three-story condominium complex appeared to be constructed from the remnants of a marble palace. The severely polished floor seemed liquid and reflected the sunlight pouring through the two-story high glass walls. Roman-styled pillars with gold accents at the base, in equal intervals up the shaft, and at the top on the ornately carved capitals. French provincial tan and white chairs were positioned in clusters in the center of the room, near a marble fireplace, and at the windows.

"Raven Roulette here to see Mr. Victor Trugonoff," Raven said to a gray-suited man behind a white desk.

"Good afternoon, Mrs. Roulette. Mr. Trugonoff is expecting you. May I see your identification please?"

Raven handed her driver's license and waited patiently as he compared the image on the card to her face.

"Thank you, Mrs. Roulette," the man said, returning her license. "If you could just sign here, I'll walk you to the elevator."

Raven had spent much of the morning deciding on just the right outfit to wear to her lunch with Victor Trugonoff. She ultimately chose a two-piece black suit that highlighted the elegant curves of her hips and a white blouse that showed just enough of the full cleavage that Victor was so obviously fond of.

"This way, Mrs. Roulette."

The security guard/concierge/desk attendant walked ahead of Raven to a bank of white elevator doors. The first elevator had a sign over it that read PENTHOUSE.

When the door opened, the man stepped aside and Raven entered the luxurious steel box. He followed her and placed a key in a lock next to the only button on the panel.

"This elevator only goes to the twenty-third floor, Mrs. Roulette. Mr. Trugonoff's assistant will be waiting for you when the doors open."

"Thank you," Raven said politely.

The elevator glided upward through the artery of the building, coming to a gentle stop on the top floor. When the doors slid open a tall, efficient-looking woman with a blond bob haircut and conservative gray wool dress was standing in the foyer of the Trugonoff's condominium.

"Good afternoon, Mrs. Roulette," the woman said with an accent teetering between British and Connecticut blue blood. "I'm Amelia Caldecott, Mr. Trugonoff's personal assistant. Mr. Trugonoff asked that you make yourself comfortable and he will be down momentarily."

Raven detected a hint of suspicion in the precise woman's tone and decided to set the tone early in their relationship.

"If you don't mind I'd like a glass of white wine while I'm waiting. Thank you."

"Not at all, Mrs. Roulette," the woman responded minus the tone. "I'll get that for you immediately. Please make yourself comfortable."

The massive room was as she remembered it from the night before. White sofas and chairs, plush white carpet, flowers and more flowers everywhere, crystal vases, glass top tables, and chandeliers sparkling throughout the room. Plaques, honors, and awards were placed prominently to remind the rare guest who did not fully understand the importance of the home's inhabitants.

Raven saw a wall of photographs that she had not noticed the night before. Victor was in every photograph. Some were with his wife, Mildred, but most without. Him standing next to President Reagan smiling from ear to ear. Victor shaking hands with President Clinton and Hillary standing between them. Queen Elizabeth clutching her patent leather purse and Victor smiling in her direction. President Bush and Victor wearing equally large cowboy hats with horses roaming in the background. Carter, Ford, Nixon, they all were present and accounted for. Victor posing with the who's who from both sides of the aisle. Raven recognized most, but some she did not. The wall was a memorial to the very much alive Victor Trugonoff.

"Raven," she suddenly heard over her shoulder. "I'm so glad you could make it," Victor said, walking toward her with both hands extended. "I see you found my shrine. Are you thoroughly impressed?"

"As a matter of fact I am," Raven said with an outstretched hand.

Victor lifted her hand to his lips and kissed it. "Did you see that one?" he said, pointing to a picture near the top of the wall. "That was taken two days after 9/11 with George. He was one mistake I'll never live down," he said, laughing. "This one over here I'm particularly proud of. Do you know who that is?"

Raven moved closer to the picture. "I'm sorry I don't," she said with a puzzled expression.

"I didn't think you would. You see that man standing behind me. That's was the Mayor of New Orleans a week after Katrina. Mildred and I spent three months down there working on the recovery efforts. Sad, sad chapter in American history."

"Excuse me, Mr. Secretary," Amelia said, approaching them from the rear. "Here's the white wine you requested."

"Excellent idea, Raven," Victor said. "Bring me a glass too, Amelia."

"Yes, sir," she said with a brittle smile. "Will there be anything else?"

"Tell the cook we're ready for lunch when she is," Victor said, turning his back to her. "Cold fish," Victor whispered as Amelia left the room. "But she's been with me for years. Don't know what I'd do without her. I hope you're hungry, Raven. I asked the cook to prepare something very special for you."

"That's very kind of you, Mr. Secretary. Yes, I am."

Victor laughed out loud and said, "Mr. Secretary? Come now, Raven, so formal. We're like one big happy family in the Republican Party. Call me Vic. Hell, everybody else does."

"Okay, Vic. Did Mildred make it off to Paris?"

Victor looked at his watch. "She's somewhere over the Atlantic by now. So it's just you and me," he said, taking her by the hand and leading her to the formal dining room.

The elegant room was consumed by a massive crystal chandelier that hung over a glass dining room table surrounded twelve white chairs. A place setting was at the head of the table and one at the seat to its left, affording the occupant the view through a wall of glass that overlooked the aqua blue bay, Golden Gate Bridge, Alcatraz Island, and Sausalito.

"Please sit down," Victor said, pointing to the seat at the side of the table. "So tell me about the beautiful Raven Roulette. Who is she? What does she dream of? What makes her smile?"

"I'll tell you if you tell me the same about yourself," Raven replied.

Victor released his bellowing laugh. "Quid pro quo. A woman after my own heart. Nothing is free in this world. Right, Raven?"

Raven recounted how she met Orpheus in the halls of the Pentagon while lunch was being served by a portly woman wearing a uniform complete with a white apron and hat. She talked about her two perfect children and their lovely home in the Presidio. The two laughed and exchanged Washington gossip through much of the meal. Each finding the other surprisingly charming and witty.

An hour had gone by. The conversation had turned to politics but Victor made no mention of the vice presidency. Raven was patient. She knew he would get to it in his own time. *Can't rush these people,* she thought. *He might be a hundred but he's obviously no idiot. Just play along,* she cautioned herself.

"Of all the half-baked policies of this current administration," Victor said, tossing his napkin onto the table which marked the end of his meal, "you know which one I think is the most detrimental to our country?

"There's so many to choose from," Raven replied.

"Repealing 'don't ask, don't tell,'" Victor said in disgust.

"Why is that?"

"Because it undermines the very foundation of our country's security. Like your husband said the other night, if our boys can't trust each other in the barracks they'll never be able to trust each other on the battlefield."

"You know my husband and I couldn't agree with you more on that. Orpheus has very strong feelings on the subject," Raven said with passion. "He testified before several congressional committees and personally appealed to the chairman of the Joint Chiefs of Staff to encourage the president to not repeal the policy."

"I know he has," Victor said. "I had my staff do some checking on your husband's position on this and I think he's right on the money."

"Really," Raven said with a measured dose of surprise. "I'm sure he'll be pleased to hear that."

"I'm not going to beat around the bush. I like you, Raven. You're charming. Smartest woman I've met in a long time, and that's saying a lot. You're funny, and beautiful, almost to the point of being distracting. Maybe even too beautiful to be the wife of a vice president. You are the perfect mother, loving wife, and, if you don't mind me saying, virtuous. I think America would love you. They're easily distracted. You're a fine woman and I like your husband too. He's got potential. I'm just not completely convinced he's ready for prime time."

"What makes you think that?"

"For one he's never held public office. Washington has a way of chewing up novices for breakfast and spitting them out. I just don't know if he can handle it. He, to some extent, is an unknown entity."

"I understand that, Victor," Raven said assuredly. "But what you have to understand about my husband is that he's military to the core. And as a result, the more pressure he is under, the stronger and more focused he becomes."

"That's a rare trait," Victor said, waving his hand in concession.

"What's your second reservation? Is it about race?"

Victor smiled and said, "My dear, I am happy to say that this country has finally grown beyond its antiquated attitudes about the race of elected officials, at least on a national level. No, it's just something in my gut. And I listen to my gut."

"What is it then?" Raven asked anxiously.

"I can't put my finger on it," he said, tapping his index finger on his lips. "It might be nothing, but until I'm sure I'm going to proceed with caution on this."

Raven leaned back from the table and said, "I understand, Vic," calculating just how much slack to allow in her reel. She knew it was all a game now for Victor. Her challenge was to continue to let him to think he controlled the rules. A difficult task for a woman of her temperament. "What can I do to allay your concerns, Victor?"

Victor stood from the table and walked to the window and said, "You see that boat over there?" He pointed to a hulking two-story sleek yacht docked at the pier. "It's mine. Mildred bought it for me last year. I'm just an old, poor politician from the backwoods of Texas, but my wife comes from old money. She's worth millions."

"It's beautiful," Raven said, standing next to him at the window.

"Thank you," he said politely. "I'd love to take you out on it sometime."

"I'd like that," she replied, showing no sign of the revulsion that was beginning to well in her stomach.

"Good then. Let's make that happen soon."

Victor took Raven by the hand and said, "Now, my dear, I hate to end our lovely time together, but I must be going. I'm meeting with the governor in an hour and I don't want to be late. Who knows, we may even talk a little about the general."

It was a truly lovely day for everyone in the city. Fog filled the sky over the bay like a gray wool blanket but mercifully left the town crisp and clear. Residents took full advantage of the sun. Golden Gate Park was bustling with helmeted families riding bikes along the wooded trails, joggers pounding the pavement, and picnickers lying leisurely on the acres of green fields. Fisherman's Wharf, Coit Tower, and Union Square bubbled over with tourists clutching bags filled with souvenirs and aiming digital cameras at the city's many beautiful sites.

The San Francisco Tennis Club was tucked neatly into a corner of the SOMA district. Twelve outdoor courts and twelve climate-controlled indoor courts were packed with club members who could afford the monthly fee. The sound of florescent green tennis balls bouncing off rackets could be heard echoing throughout the facility. A parade of people decked in the latest white and pastel tennis attire flailed and thrashed on the courts, sipped fruit smoothies and mineral waters with twists of lime in the outdoor café, and others shared the latest town gossip in the indoor lounge.

"Deuce!" Raven called out after smashing a tennis ball past Carla's whizzing racket. Raven returned to the line and studied Carla's stance as she crouched down and bounced on her toes waiting for Raven's next serve. Raven bounced the ball two times then tossed it in the air. She sent the ball flying across the court with a powerful blow. A slight tap could be heard as the ball passed the net.

"Net," Carla called out as the ball whizzed past her.

Raven delivered another serve, which cleared the net and landed to the right of Carla's racket. She lunged for the speeding ball but missed it by several inches.

"Advantage!" Raven called out.

Carla was able to return the next ball with such force and accuracy that it required Raven to rush to the far left of the court and then to the extreme right with the next. The two women continued the volley with such aggression and precision that other members in the vicinity took notice of the fierce exchange. Two women, equally skilled and prepared for the game locked in a duel to the finish. On one side of the court pampered blond hair tossed from side to side with each blow. On the other, luxurious black locks waved to and fro, challenging with each swing the constraints of an elastic headband.

With one final blow Raven released a grunt and sent the ball streaming past Carla's reaching racket. The ball slammed the court and in a flash crashed into the green fence behind Carla.

"Game and match!" Raven called out to her panting opponent.

A smattering of applause could be heard from the members who had watched the final point of the match. Raven and Carla walked panting to the side of the court.

"Good game, girl," Carla said, raising her hand.

"You're getting too good for me," Raven replied breathlessly and slapped Carla's hand in the air. "You've been practicing I see. You really made me work for that one."

The two women gathered their belongings courtside as the next set of players prepared for their game.

"Do you have time for a drink before you go?" Carla asked, stuffing a towel into her gym bag.

Raven looked at her watch. It was 4:10. "Just a quick one. I have to pick up Reva from rehearsal at 5:30. Her drama club is performing a Chekhov play next week."

"Which one?" Carla asked dabbing her cheeks with her wristband.

"Three Sisters," Raven replied. "She's playing Irina."

Raven and Carla took a table near the courts. A blue canvas umbrella shielded them from the still beaming sun. A waiter in white tennis shorts and a short-sleeved green shirt emblazoned with the club's logo appeared at their table.

"I hope you enjoyed your game, ladies. Would you like your usual from the bar?"

"Yes, thank you," Carla answered for both of them.

"Are you and Orpheus going to Mick and Lucy's anniversary party next week at their ranch in Sonoma?" Carla asked. "Norah Jones is going to perform."

"I'm not sure. It's a busy time for us right now."

"Why, what's going on? Are you packing for Washington already?"

Raven laughed and said, "Very funny. But of course that is part of it. As a matter of fact I had lunch with Victor Trugonoff today."

"How did that go? Did he come on to you?"

"No, thank God. He stopped just short of it though."

"Don't worry, he will," Carla said casually. "Miserable old letch. He's fucked half the women in this town and he's still working on the other half. Where was Mildred?"

"Paris."

"She's no better. That wrinkled old bag will hop on any man who can stay hard after he's seen her naked. Rich as fuck though. Her grandfather owned the largest silver mine in California in the 1800s. Three generations later and the worthless cows are still living off it, at least the few that didn't go insane or blow their brains out."

The waiter returned with two glasses of sparkling water, one with lime for Carla and the other with lemon for Raven.

"What did he want?" Carla asked

"He claims to be one of ten people in the country who select the president," Raven said with a slight laugh.

"Why are you laughing?" Carla asked, sipping her water. "It's true, he is one of them."

Raven leaned into the table. "Why didn't you tell me this?" she asked, looking Carla directly in the eye.

"I assumed you knew," Carla said defensively. "Everyone in our circle knows it. We just don't talk about it."

"Well I didn't know. Why don't people talk about it?"

"Because the last person who started blabbing it around town got a visit from the CIA. Her phones were tapped and their taxes were audited for five years straight by the IRS. Nearly ruined their marriage. Didn't matter in the long run though. He ran off with their nanny anyway."

"Goddamn it, Carla, you could have told me," Raven said angrily. "I've been busting my ass all this time and all along this son of a bitch was sitting in my own backyard."

"Calm down, honey, I didn't know. Anyway it turned out that you were better off not knowing."

"Why is that?"

"Because the group has one simple rule. None of the members can be approached by presidential wannabes. If anyone of them suspects they're being lobbied the person's name is automatically dropped from the list regardless of how viable a candidate they are. If you're presidential material they'll find you and it looks like they found Orpheus, thanks to you.

"I'm still finding this hard to believe," Raven said. "What about all the Democrats who have been president. How did they get into office?"

"Honey, these people operate outside of the party system. They make their decision based on who they feel will be the best person for the country at the time. It doesn't matter if they're a Democrat or a Republican. One word of caution though, Raven."

"What's that?"

"There's always a price that has to be paid," Carla said, lowering her voice.

"You mean money?"

"Sometimes, but not always. The final test for anyone they select is that person has to give up something of extreme value to them. They feel it proves just how badly the person wants to be president. They believe in order to get something you really want, you have to give up something you love." Carla reached across the table, covered Raven's hand and said, "Be careful, honey, you're dealing with big boys now and they can play rough."

It was dinner time at the Roulette home. Li Yeng scooped spoonfuls of fluffy mashed potatoes into a bowl and poured sauce into a porcelain gravy boat. She walked into the dining room carrying the potatoes in one hand and a platter of crisp asparagus doused with tarragon cream sauce in the other.

"It smells delicious tonight, Li Yeng," Orpheus said from the head of the table.

"Thank you, general," she replied, placing the dishes in the center of the table. "I made your favorite entrée."

"Wonderful, I can't wait."

Raven sat at the opposite end of the table with Little'O between them. "Little'O, where's your sister?" she asked. "Please go upstairs and tell her to come down right now."

"Yes, ma'am."

Reva appeared in the threshold just as Little'O stood from the table.

"There's my little star," Orpheus said as Reva took her seat across from Little'O.

"How are your rehearsals going? Have you memorized all your lines?"

"I hate this play," Reva said with a huff. "It's so white."

"We don't talk like that in this house, young lady," Orpheus said.

"I'm sorry, Daddy, but it is."

"Darling, *Three Sisters* is considered by many to be one of the greatest plays ever written. You should be honored to have been chosen to play a leading role," Raven said. "We're very proud of you."

Li Yeng returned to the room carrying a platter of rosemary, thyme, and sage roasted pork loin and placed it in front of Reva.

Reva saw the meat and sat upright in her chair. "I told you I don't like pork," she shouted. "Mother, why do you let her serve me pork?"

"Young lady, I've told you about speaking to Li Yeng like that," Orpheus said sternly. "Now apologize."

"I will not. She did this on purpose. I hate pork and she knows it."

"Either you apologize now or you can go to your room without dinner," Orpheus said, placing both hands firmly on the table.

"Orpheus, don't be so hard on her," Raven interjected. "She doesn't like pork."

Orpheus ignored his wife and said to Reva, "I'm waiting, young lady."

"I can make her something else," Li Yeng said, standing humbly over the little girl's shoulder.

"No, you will not, Li Yeng," Orpheus said firmly. "You've spent all day making this perfectly delicious meal and either she is going to eat it or she's going to leave the table.

Reva looked from her father to her mother then back to her father, whose eyes were now squinting angrily. She let out a huff and pushed her chair backward, causing a screeching noise on the hardwood floor.

"Fine," she said, skirting around Li Yeng. "I'd rather starve than eat that."

"Orpheus, don't you think you're overreacting?" Raven said calmly. "The girl doesn't like pork."

"That's not the point," Orpheus said with his teeth clenched. "She has to learn how to make her wishes known without disrespecting other people. No one was put on this earth to serve her."

"But Li Yeng is our—"

"Stop right there, Raven," Orpheus interrupted. "Li Yeng is a trusted and valuable employee. She is not our servant."

"I wasn't going to say servant," Raven snapped, slamming her napkin on the table. "I was going to say cook. Li Yeng, would you please excuse us."

"Yes, ma'am, I'm sorry if I did something wrong."

As Li Yeng walked to the door she saw Little'O looking up at her. The two exchanged almost imperceptible smiles.

"No need to apologize, Li Yeng. You didn't do anything wrong," Orpheus said, looking directly at Raven. "The dinner is perfect. Thank you and I apologize for Reva's behavior."

Li Yeng quietly exited the room, leaving Little'O sitting silently with his parents. Steam rose between the three from the potatoes and vegetables. Raven and Orpheus eyes were locked across the table.

"What is wrong with you, Orpheus?" Raven finally said. "Is this about last night?"

"What are you talking about?"

"You know exactly what I'm talking about," Raven replied.

"Not in front of Little'O, Raven," Orpheus said through clinched teeth.

"Why? Are you embarrassed?"

"Embarrassed about what?" Orpheus said with a puzzled expression.

"You don't want your son to hear that his father is afraid of being vice president."

"That's not true!" Little'O shouted to his mother. "My father isn't afraid of anything. Tell her, Dad." Little'O looked desperately to his father.

"That's right, Little'O," Orpheus said, still looking at Raven. "Your father isn't afraid of anything. The real problem is your mother has an insatiable need to control everyone and everything around her."

"No, son, your mother only wants what's best for her husband and her family," Raven said coldly.

"And your mother seems to think she is the only one who knows what's best."

"I'm not going to let you screw this up, Orpheus," Raven said, bounding from her seat. "This opportunity will come to you only once in your lifetime. You owe it to your children and to me to not let it pass. Little'O, please tell your father how proud you would be if he were vice president."

Orpheus and Raven never took their eyes off of each other. Little'O looked up at his mother but did not respond.

"Don't say anything you don't feel, son. You have a mind of your own and I expect you to use it."

"What is going on, Orpheus?" Raven asked. "Why are you being so irrational about this? What are you afraid of? This is something we've worked for our entire lives."

"Wrong, Raven. It's something you've worked for your entire life. This is about you. Everything you've done since the day we married has been about you. You are the center of the universe and everyone else simply orbits around your star. I've only worked to be a good officer and a good American, which is what I have achieved."

"A good American would not turn down the opportunity to serve his country in the highest office in the land."

"Second highest," he said scornfully.

"You know exactly what I mean."

Little'O watched the volley of words between his parents like a ball on a tennis court. Each biting observation was delivered with a stone face and icy glare. Raven attacked him from every possible angle—the good of the children, patriotism, courage—but Orpheus was intractable. She was running out of options.

"I know exactly what you mean," Orpheus responded, finally breaking his gaze. "Raven Roulette has made up her mind and nothing will change it. Not even her husband's wishes."

The only arguments left for Raven were the race card and God, and the race care hardly seemed appropriate. With lightning speed her Harvard-trained mind formulated her next move.

"Honey," she said in a non-combative tone. "If it's God's will for you to be vice president, who are you to say no?"

After the military, religion was the one constant in Orpheus's life. Regardless of what army base his father had been stationed at in the world, Orpheus's mother always insisted they attend a church every Sunday. In the Philippines it was the Malabon International Baptist Church. In Germany it had been Hannover International Bible Church. Tokyo Baptist Church in China had served as their temporary place of worship.

Even as a young boy, religion had helped Orpheus make sense of a world filled with hate, destruction, and war. In the context of a higher power and an orderly universe, the cruelty he saw around him had a purpose. It didn't matter that he didn't know what that purpose was. What mattered was that someone out there knew. Even if that someone was a faceless being who stopped speaking directly to his creation after the last word of the Book of Revelation was written.

"You've got to believe in something, OJ," his father had said to him on many occasions. "If you don't you'll end up blowing in the wind like tumbleweed in a desert storm."

The notion of God allowed him to be the man he was and his faith allowed him to be a soldier.

"How can you turn your back on this if it's God's will?" Raven said, firing the last round in her arsenal.

Little'O's eyes landed squarely on his father. The room was silent for what seemed an eternity. Raven waited anxiously to learn if the last bullet had penetrated the heart of her prey. She could tell by the slight twitch of his hand that she had made contact. But was it fatal? Would the blood that signified surrender pour from his veins?

"Dad," Little'O said, breaking the silence. "If it's God's will, would you do it?"

Bull's-eye, Raven thought.

Orpheus looked lovingly to his son and said, "Yes, little soldier. If it's God's will, I would do it."

**

Orpheus, Raven, and Little'O ate dinner together in silence. Little'O was the first to leave the table. "May I be excused now?" he said, while simultaneously rising out of his seat, and quickly retreated to his room. Li Yeng cleared the plates, washed the dishes, and left quietly through the back door.

"It's been a long day," Raven said, standing from the table. "I'm going to bed early."

"That's fine," Orpheus said without looking at her. "I'll be sleeping in my study tonight."

Reva remained locked in the cocoon of her pink and lavender room the entire evening. Her voice could only be heard through the door. "Please leave me alone," she replied sharply to a tap on the door from her mother. "I'm studying my lines."

"Okay, honey," Raven said to the oak door. "I love you."

Raven spent the evening huddled in front of the computer screen in her bedroom. By 11:00 she was an expert on Secretary of State Victor R. Trugonoff. Orpheus closed the door to his office and only exited once to relieve himself in the downstairs bathroom. Raven could hear the creaks in the hardwood floor but resisted the urge to go downstairs.

A stack of folders was piled on his desk, all of which were stamped in bold red letters with either "CONFIDENTIAL," "CLASSIFIED," "TOP SECRET," or "RESTRICTED" on the covers. The country's military secrets were laid out in front of him. Afghanistan, Libya, and Iran could keep no secrets from General Orpheus Beauregard Roulette III. The pros and cons of assassinating leaders who posed threats to the United States and the strengths and weaknesses of American troops abroad were outlined in great detail for the few men in the country who "needed to know." Orpheus was one of those men.

Gifted with a photographic memory, Orpheus easily absorbed the contents of each file. The only distractions were the occasional thoughts of the tense exchange over dinner and Kiss-n-tell.

Orpheus had never had a physical relationship with a man and was repulsed by the public display of affection between men he often saw on the streets of San Francisco. Not because they were holding hands or kissing but because they were doing it out in the open for all the world to see. He appreciated the male body and was routinely exposed to it at the height of its perfection in the military.

Bodies that had been transformed into lean, muscular fighting machines by months of rigorous training in boot camp. Confident, strong, and chiseled bodies were paraded in front of him on a regular basis for his approval. Men standing at attention and saluting whenever he entered a room or passed them on the base. Over the years, his appreciation gradually turned into attraction to the point that he even sometimes thought of them while he was making love to his wife.

As an adolescent he, like so many other boys at that age, would become aroused at the site of a naked man. He sometimes glimpsed at his father's perfect body when he exited the shower or walked through the house in only his military-issued white boxer shorts. He consciously suppressed those feelings, which embarrassed him, and they gradually gave way to the blossoming, giggling young girls on the bases who pursued him because of his solid frame, good looks, and prominent military pedigree.

Life had rushed on and the feelings took a back seat to his career and eventual marriage to a person he considered to be one of the most beautiful women he had ever seen. The children were born and promotions came in rapid succession but only occasionally would an attractive saluting cadet or uniformed Adonis catch his eye. A pattern had developed that even Orpheus didn't notice. Whenever he felt overly pressured or manipulated by Raven, the thoughts seemed to surface, and coincidentally there would happen to be one particular man who would be the center of his latent fantasy.

When she hounded him relentlessly to accept the assignment in Iraq it had been the swarthy onyx private who drove him to the base each morning. When she pressured him to move off base and purchase the $2.3 million home in the Presidio, it was the tanned real estate agent whose $500 jeans seemed to be painted on his muscular body. The men would creep into his thoughts throughout the day. He never touched them or gave any indication that he found them attractive, but he made love to them in his dreams—or when he was intimate with Raven.

It was midnight. Orpheus closed the last file on the desk and turned off the lamp. The room was dark except for the glow from the computer screen. Without thinking, his hands moved to the keyboard where he typed "www.mansdate.com." The familiar images of half-dressed men appeared on the screen and he immediately logged into the chat room.

The usual abbreviated chatter rolled across the screen. He checked the roster of people in the room and saw Kiss-n-tell near the bottom of the list.

Then the words appeared, "good evening generalone."

Generalone: hello kiss-n-tell. how are you?

Kiss-n-tell: better now that you're here.

Generalone: you always say the right thing.

Kiss-n-tell: how was your day?

The ticker tape of communications from others in the room appeared between their messages. By all indications, it was another lonely night for many men in the city.

Generalone: tough

Kiss-n-tell: sorry to hear that. wanna talk about it?

Generalone: not here

Kiss-n-tell: let's go to a private room. pick one at the top of the screen and I'll meet you there.

Orpheus for the first time saw the private room option at the top of the screen. He clicked and entered. Seconds later Kiss-n-tell entered the room.

Kiss-n-tell: this is better. i can have you all to myself.

Generalone: much.

Kiss-n-tell: so tell me about your day. what was so bad?

Generalone: just under a lot of pressure 2 take a job i'm not sure that i'm qualified for.

Kiss-n-tell: pressure from who?

Generalone: from someone who can be very persuasive

Kiss-n-tell: no 1 can make u do something u don't want to.

Generalone: true, but it's a little more complicated than that.

Kiss-n-tell: im listening.

Generalone: part of me wants the job.

Kiss-n-tell: and the other part?

Generalone: the other part isn't sure if im qualified.

Kiss-n-tell: what kind of job is it?

Orpheus abruptly leaned away from the screen. *I walked right into that one.* He tried to think of the best way to answer the question. The seconds ticked away like the timer on *Jeopardy!* He expected to hear a buzzer at any moment.

Generalone: the number two man in a pretty large corporation.

Good answer, good answer! he thought proudly.

Kiss-n-tell: im sure you'll make the right decision but don't let anyone pressure you.

Generalone: thank you. enough about me. what's your name?

Kiss-in-tell: david and your's?

Generalone: michael

Kiss-n-tell: nice to meet you michael.

Generalone: what do you do?

Kiss-n-tell: im a photographer.

Generalone: really. of what?

Kiss-n-tell: mostly fashion layouts and catalogs.

Generalone: sounds interesting

Kiss-n-tell: if you think telling models all day how beautiful they are is interesting, then yes it is.

Generalone: could be a lot worse.

Kiss-n-tell: true

Generalone: just noticed the time. you must be tired.

Kiss-n-tell: a little

Generalone: then we ought to say good night.

Kiss-n-tell: ok

Generalone: i enjoy chatting with you david. i always feel better afterward.

Kiss-n-tell: i was thinking the same thing about you.

Generalone: do you think it's possible to love someone you've never met?

Kiss-n-tell: why, are you falling in love with me?

Generalone: LOL . . . maybe

Kiss-n-tell: do you think we'll ever meet in person.

Generalone: i would like nothing better.

Kiss-in-tell: then let's make it happen.

Chapter 6

The morning rush-hour traffic on Market Street was bumper to bumper. MUNI buses competed with a tightly woven blanket of cars, cyclists, and pedestrians. The traffic lights flashed green, yellow, then red in attempts to bring a semblance of order to the morning chaos. Horns blared from drivers who were already wound tight for their day in the city.

Raven maneuvered her silver Jeep Laredo in and out of traffic. It was 7:46 and Reva had to be in her seat in class at eight o'clock sharp.

"Mother, I'm going to be late," Reva huffed. "Why are you stopping for every pedestrian?"

"Because it's the law, honey," Raven said patiently as she changed lanes for the third time in one block. "In California you have to stop if a person is in the crosswalk."

At 7:58 Raven stopped the car in front of the main entrance to Reva's school. A long line of Mercedes, Lexuses, Range Rovers, and other SUVs similar to hers deposited a school full of expensively dressed, cranky adolescents for another day of reading, writing, arithmetic, and fashion.

"Have a good—" Raven said to the slamming car door. She watched as her daughter fell in step with a group of giggling blond-haired, blue-eyed girls who instantly complimented her on her awesome choice of outfit for the day.

Raven waved good morning to several other relieved parents as she merged back into traffic. Another group of freshly scrubbed teenagers passed slowly in front of cars at the next intersection. As she waited with all the other irritated drivers for the group to pass, her telephone, which was perched in a holder on the dashboard, rang. The caller ID read, "Unknown Caller."

Raven never allowed her telephones to go unanswered. Even if she was on another call she would always put the person on hold and respond to the incoming call.

"Hello," she said after pressing the answer button on the hands-free device.

"Raven, good morning, my dear. It's Victor Trugonoff. I hope I'm not calling you too early."

Victor's voice boomed from the car speakers and filled the interior of the SUV.

"Not at all, Vic," she replied as the children finally passed in front of her to the curb. "I just dropped off my daughter at school. It's nice to hear from you. Thank you again for the lovely lunch."

"It was my pleasure, dear. I'm sorry I had to cut it short."

"No need to apologize, I understood."

"I was hoping you would be free to join me this afternoon and take me up on my offer to show you my little boat. I know it's short notice, but it's turning out to be such a beautiful day that I decided to spend some time on it today. I have the damned thing," Trugonoff's voice bounced off the windows, "I might as well enjoy it when I can. And nothing would make me happier than if you would enjoy it with me."

Raven was surprised that the invitation had come so quickly after their lunch. She remembered Carol's words at the tennis club. *"Be careful, honey. You're dealing with big boys now and they can play rough."*

"Victor, I'm not sure if I can do it today," Raven responded hesitantly. "My day is already pretty full."

The speakers were silent for a moment. Raven feared she had offended one of the ten most powerful men in the country. "Victor," she said to the silent speakers. "Are you still there?"

"Yes, dear, I'm here," Trugonoff replied with a hint of in irritation in his voice. "Are you sure you can't rearrange your schedule? I was hoping we could talk more about your husband's future."

Raven hesitated before she responded. "What time were you thinking of?"

"How about . . . three o'clock?"

Three o'clock was the time she was scheduled to return and pick up Raven. "I think I can make it at three," she said all while devising alternative plans for her daughter.

"Wonderful!" exploded from the speaker. "Come to Pier 39. I'll have my man waiting for you there."

As soon as the phone call disconnected Raven dialed her son's cell phone. Little'O answered in a whisper, "Mother, I'm in class."

"I know, honey," she said apologetically. "I'm sorry. I need you to pick up your sister this afternoon from school for me at three."

"But I have debate club today after school," he said, protesting.

"You can take her home and then go back to school."

"Mother, but if I do that I'll be—"

"Don't argue with me, Little'O. Just pick up your sister at three. I love you, honey. Have a good day," she said and disconnected the call.

Raven questioned whether she was truly ready to play with the big boys while driving along the wooded roads of the Presidio. *You've been working toward this your whole life,* she thought. *Just pay him a few compliments, pat him on his balding little head, and walk off that yacht one step closer to the White House.*

In Raven's world every action was a means to an end. Her life was efficient. There was no room for wasted energy, pointless conversations, or associates who could not assist in attaining her goals. People were disposable to her. Once they had served their purpose, she saw no reason to keep them around. The only college friends she stayed in touch with were those who traveled in the same political circles as her. She couldn't even remember the names of anyone from her high school in Los Angeles. If any of them had become somebody, they no doubt would still be in her life.

She interpreted her husband's reluctance to go after the vice presidency as betrayal. *After all I've done for him, this is how he repays me,* she thought angrily as she drove.

I gave him two beautiful children. I've created the perfect home for him. I've sucked up to every asshole in Washington just to get his name on the map and he wants to just turn his back on everything.

The more she thought the faster the car skidded around curves on the winding road. Anger and resentment welled inside her.

If he doesn't do this, I swear I'll take the kids and leave him.

She felt a slight bump under her rear tire but continued to roll forward. In her wake were the remains of a squirrel that had succumbed to the weight of her barreling SUV. *There would be no point in staying with him. I have no intention of being the wife of the youngest retired general in the history of the country. I want this and I'm going to have it.*

But at what price? Again Carla's words came to her. *"They believe in order to get something you really want, you have to give up something you love."*

A shiver worked its way up her spine. She could think of nothing more repulsive than the idea of sleeping with Victor Trugonoff, but it wouldn't be the first time she had used her body to get what she wanted. The promotion at the prestigious Washington law firm of Bernstein, Cooper, and Frank was had due to her impressive law degree from Harvard, her thorough knowledge of international law, and several nights spent in Cooper's Watergate penthouse.

You're a big girl, Raven, she reasoned. *If that's what it takes you can do it.*

It was 2:50 in the afternoon. Raven handed her keys to a valet in a nearby parking garage and began the one-block walk to Pier 39. Sailboats in the distance the size of postcards glided on the crystal clear surface of the bay. Locals jogged and tourists shopped along Embarcadero Street. Dozens of brown and black sea lions luxuriated in the afternoon sun on floating wooden platforms and barked to throngs of visitors who hung over the pier railing taking their pictures.

She could see Trugonoff's two-story, refrigerator-white floating mausoleum looming in the distance. Rows of tinted windows looked like black eyes watching her as she approached. The sleek lines and pointing bow reminded her of an arrow preparing for flight. She saw a series of wooden chairs and chaise longues with blue striped cushions sitting on the rear deck as she walked closer. A brown lacquered table with chrome pedestal legs held a vase filled with orchids, an ice bucket, and two champagne flutes.

"Good afternoon, Mrs. Roulette," she heard from behind her. "Welcome to the *Agente del Poder*."

Raven turned abruptly and found herself standing face to face with a large man wearing dark sunglasses, a navy blue sports jacket, and gray slacks. "Mr. Trugonoff is expecting you. Please follow me."

"Thank you," Raven replied as she fell in step behind the man.

"Watch your step," he said, extending his hand down to her from the deck. "It might take you awhile before you get your sea legs."

Once onboard the man escorted her into the main cabin and said, "Mr. Trugonoff is upstairs. He asked that you wait here. May I get you anything to drink? The yacht has an extensive bar and wine selection."

"No, thank you. I'll wait for Mr. Trugonoff," she replied.

"Very well, ma'am. Please make yourself comfortable. Mr. Trugonoff will be down shortly." The man bowed his head slightly and exited the room.

The room was surprisingly dark despite the banks of windows on each side. Cherry wood covered much of the walls, including a series of bookshelves that held volumes of novels that all seemed to have nautical themes. A big-screen television was positioned on a wall next to a state-of-the-art sound system. Overstuffed tan chairs and couches were placed in seemingly no particular order around the large space. In the center of one such cluster was a white and brown marble chess set on a round table ready to be played. A wet bar complete with stools and taps was in a corner of the room.

"Raven!" Trugonoff bellowed, entering the room. "I'm so glad you could come. You're looking ravishing as usual. Welcome to *Agente del Poder*."

"Thank you for inviting me, Victor. She's beautiful."

"Thank you," he said, clapping his hands together. "Now what can I get you to drink?"

"White wine would be nice."

"Perfect," Trugonoff said, walking to the bar. "I just bought a case of 1993 Masetto, Tenuta Dell'Ornellaia. I'd love to hear what you think of it."

After handing Raven the glass of wine and exchanging the obligatory comments about its full bouquet and hints of fruit, they embarked on a tour of the yacht. It was 199 feet of floating elegance complete with six cabins, a formal dining room, six-person sauna, Jacuzzi on deck, wine cellar, and had a range of 5,380 nautical miles.

They ended the tour back where they started in the living room. "Please sit down, Raven," Trugonoff said pointing to the sofa. "Let's talk about that husband of yours."

"You know, Raven," he opened. "My little circle of ten are divided on your husband."

Raven listened attentively.

"As I mentioned to you yesterday, some feel he's not ready for prime time. Too green. While others are convinced he is not only vice president material but he'd even be ready for the presidency in eight years."

"And which side do you fall on?" Raven asked even though she was already two steps ahead of him.

"Me? Well I'm on the fence," Trugonoff said, raising his hands to signify ambivalence. "I could go either way at this point. We've already decided Milo Fredericks is going to be the next president. The question is, who will be his second man?"

Enough of the bullshit, Raven thought angrily. *Are we going to do this or not?*

Raven moved closer to Trugonoff, positioned herself on the edge of the sofa, and placed her hand on his thigh. She looked earnestly into his eyes and said, "What can I do to move you to my side of that fence, Mr. Secretary?"

Trugonoff covered her hand with his beefy mitt. "Oh, Mrs. Roulette, you are a naughty girl," he said with a wicked laugh. "I like that in a woman."

Raven matched his toothy grin with her own playful smile. "And I like a man who knows when he's being seduced," she said, moving her hand farther up his thigh. "I think it goes without saying there is almost nothing I wouldn't do to ensure my husband becomes vice president."

"I respect a woman who supports her husband," Trugonoff said in a whisper. "It shows he's worthy of other people's respect as well."

"I love my husband," she said, placing her hand on his chest. "He's already my president."

"Well if he's good enough for you," he said, running his hand up her thigh, "he's good enough for me."

Trugonoff lumbered forward and pressed his lips to Raven's. She detected a slight hint of lox and cream cheese on his breath. *Fat bastard could have at least gargled before I got here,* she thought as she unfastened the buttons around his bulging stomach. A field of bushy gray hair sprang from beneath his shirt as their heads turned from side to side locked in a deep kiss.

Trugonoff slid awkwardly to the floor and raised Raven's skirt only high enough for his head to slip under. She leaned back on the sofa and planted the heels of her leather pumps on the coffee table. She ran her fingers through his salty gray hair and moaned convincingly, "I'll do anything for it, Victor, I want it so bad."

He lifted her by the waist and slid her silk panties down and around her ankles. She could feel the stubble on his cheeks as he slid his head between her legs.

"Your husband will make a fine vice president, Mrs. Roulette," he said, probing her with his tongue and thick fingers. "He's a lucky man to have a wife like you."

After moments of loud gurgling from Trugonoff and exaggerated moans of ecstasy from Raven, he struggled to his feet and said, "My God, Mrs. Roulette, you're a beautiful woman." His face was red and wet and his scraggly gray hair pointed in every direction. Raven saw the bulge in his trousers and thought, *First thing I'm going to do in Washington is outlaw Viagra,* but said out loud, "You're so big, Mr. Secretary."

Trugonoff unfastened his pants and let them drop to the ground. The evidence of his lust pointed her in the face. "For your husband, Mrs. Roulette," he said, looking down at his erect member. "Do it for your husband."

For my husband, she repeated in her mind as she took a deep breath, closed her eyes, opened her mouth, and leaned forward.

"Oh, Mrs. Roulette," Trugonoff moaned. "That's it. Show me how much you love your husband."

She felt the thick bush of gray hair tickle her nose and cheeks with each downward lunge. "I love my husband," she said, looking up into Trugonoff squinting eyes. "He's going to be the greatest vice president this country has ever seen."

"With a wife like you," Trugonoff said breathlessly, "he has no choice, Mrs. Roulette."

Trugonoff pulled her head away abruptly, lifted her by the shoulders, and turned her around to face the couch. "For your country," he said, bending her over and lifting her skirt to her waist. "This one is for your country."

For my country, she thought, burying her head into the cushions on the back of the sofa. Trugonoff entered her without warning and pounded at her flesh mercilessly, pressing her head into the sofa over and over again. She could feel the sweat dripping from him onto her back and legs. And then she finally heard the words she had been waiting for. "I'm gonna cum, Mrs. Roulette. God bless America. . . ." he shouted. His spasms sent shutters through her body as he gripped her waist and jerked his body to completion.

Suddenly the boat stopped rocking and the room was quiet. Trugonoff collapsed onto the sofa next to her still panting. *Don't fucking die on me you son of a bitch,* she thought as the old man struggled to catch his breath.

"Are you okay, Victor?" she said, pulling down her skirt.

Trugonoff laughed and said between breaths, "I'm better than okay, Mrs. Roulette. That was fucking amazing. This country needs more women like you."

"You mean who will sleep with you?" she said with an ironic smile.

"No," he said with perfect composure, crystal clear blue eyes, and the sternest expression she had ever seen on any man's face. "I mean who are willing to sacrifice everything for their husbands, even their own dignity."

Raven body jerked upright and a look of shock took over her face.

"Don't be offended, Raven," he said. "I meant that as a compliment. I'm impressed. I honestly didn't think you had it in you. That, by the way, was my last reservation about your husband. I wasn't convinced that you were woman enough to support him no matter what. And now I have my answer. Congratulations, Mrs. Roulette. You are now the wife of the future vice president of the United States of America."

The controls on the Jacuzzi tub were set on high. A whirl of bubbles traced the curves of Raven's body, making their way to the surface and exploding into a mist over the tub. The scent of eucalyptus, lavender, and jasmine bath gels merged into a sweet, indecipherable bouquet in the steam-filled bathroom.

Raven could still smell Trugonoff on her hands even through the aromatic elixir. Try though she might, Raven was not able to wash the memory of her afternoon on *Agente del Poder* from her skin. Her hands trembled when she thought of the man standing in front of her with his pants around his wobbly ankles. The sounds of his moans echoed in her head above the hum of the Jacuzzi engine. Several times she made a premature dash to the toilet fearing that the contents of her stomach were about to spew from her lips.

However, she had no regrets. *I'd fuck him again if I had to,* she reasoned in the bubbly soup. *Hell, I'd fuck all ten of them if that's what it takes.* For the third time she dunked her head under the boiling water and remained there for as long as she could stand the heat. Her head emerged with a violent splash as she gasped for air.

The words she had longed to hear for so long, *"Wife of the future vice president of the United States of America,"* wiped the image of the wrinkled man's convulsing body from her mind and made her smile. *Small price to pay for the White House,* she thought proudly. *I hope he appreciates the sacrifice I made.*

Raven knew from experience that she had to keep moving forward to not become bogged down in the trauma of any bad experience. She willed herself to other more productive thoughts. Keeping Orpheus on point would be her next big challenge.

Reva stood in front of the mirror in her room. She held a script in one hand and gestured dramatically with the other.

"Oh, I'm miserable," she recited to her image in the mirror. "I can't work. I'm not going to work." She paused and threw the script on her bed, then slammed her body on top of dog-eared papers. "I hate *Three Sisters!*" she complained loudly. "I hate Chekov."

Little'O sat at the computer in his room with his fingers flying furiously across the keyboard. He had been a straight-A student his entire life and this year was no exception. This evening's assignment was an extra-credit twenty-page essay titled "The Role of a Vice President in the Current Economic Crisis."

His room was as orderly as his world. There was a proper place for everything and unless that thing was serving his needs at the moment it was in its place. Perfectly starched button-down shirts were hung in the closet according to color, five whites, five light blues, and five yellows. T-shirts and boxer shorts were folded and stacked neatly in the drawers while socks were rolled into tight little bundles and placed in the drawer beneath them. There was a logic to the room and anyone who entered it would be able to intuitively find whatever it was they were looking for.

The handsome adolescent was a study in contrasts. He was a smaller version of his father. Good-looking and tall, all the girls on campus thought he was extremely "doable" but were hesitant to approach him because of his intense demeanor. He always looked like he was in a hurry to get somewhere and paid little attention to those who tried to distract him. Every year his new crop of teachers were always shocked when they learned of his extreme right views on so many topics, from the abolition of entitlement programs, support for the Arizona anti-immigrant legislation, to pro-life. He was often the topic of discussion in the teachers' lounge. "I don't get it," someone had once said. "How could such a bright kid be such a little Nazi?"

The kitchen was quiet and everything was in its proper place. Li Yeng had gone for the evening. Dinner had been served without Raven being at the table.

"I won't be dining with the family tonight, Li Yeng," Raven had said when she came home that evening just after 5:00. "I'm not feeling well."

Li Yeng had been surprised to see her employer's hair in a not perfect state. She had never known Raven to leave or return to the house in anything but picture-ready condition. Her hair looked fine, but it had obviously been hastily combed. Her makeup was on, but it somehow looked . . . rushed.

"I'm sorry, Mrs. Roulette," Li Yeng said convincingly. "Would you like for me to bring up a tray later?"

"That won't be necessary. I'm just going to take a long bath and turn in early tonight. But please make sure the children are fed at exactly seven o'clock."

Orpheus had decided earlier that day that he would sleep in his bed that evening. *She's only doing what she thinks is best for me,* he reasoned silently. *Hopefully they'll find someone better suited for the job and this will blow over on its own. She'll be disappointed but at least we'll be able to get on with our lives.*

The prospect of talking to Kiss-n-tell in the chat room became irresistible as the evening drew on. The children were in their rooms and Raven hadn't come downstairs all evening. It was approaching midnight when Orpheus turned on the computer and logged into the chat room. *I'll just say hello and then go to bed. He probably won't even be there.*

The first words he saw were, "I hoped you'd be on tonight Generalone."

Generalone: how are you?

Kiss-n-tell: not good. got some bad news today. can we go to a private room? could use a friend tonight.

The two moved into an uninhabited room.

Generalone: what happened?

Kiss-n-tell: my mother died today.

Orpheus was shocked when he read the words. He'd expected to see, "lost my job," or "house went into foreclosure," but not a dead parent. He'd extended the condolences of the nation to many who had lost sons and daughters, husbands and wives in combat, but somehow this was different. Once again he didn't know the rules.

Generalone: I am so sorry David. How did she die?

Kiss-n-tell: heart attack.

Generalone: where did she live?

Kiss-n-tell: Los Angeles

Generalone: are you going there?

Kiss-n-tell: not until the service next week. My brother is making the arrangements

Generalone: do you have anyone here that can be with you tonight. You shouldn't be alone.

There was a pause before the response appeared. "I'm embarrassed to say that's why I'd hoped you'd be on tonight. Sad to say but you're the only person I have to talk to in San Francisco. Guess I'm one of those lonely losers I always felt sorry for."

Generalone: don't be embarrassed. sometimes I feel like you're the only person I have to talk to as well.

Kiss-n-tell: im glad we have each other.

Generalone: so am i.

Kiss-n-tell: i've never felt this alone before. im almost afraid.

Generalone: don't be afraid. you're not alone.

Again the words on the screen stopped. Orpheus waited impatiently for a response, but there was none. "are you there?"

Kiss-n-tell: just wasn't expecting to hear that. It felt good.

Generalone: i meant it.

Orpheus looked at the digital clock on the desk. It was 12:23. Could he do it without anyone hearing him leave? Could he start the car undetected? Could he get back to the house before anyone noticed that he had gone?

Generalone: you shouldn't be alone. do you want me to come over?

Within seconds the word "yes" appeared on the screen.

It was a cold summer night in the Haight-Ashbury District. The thick fog enveloped everything in its path on Haight Street. Cars were covered in a blanket of rolling mist. Homeless men and women huddled under cardboard boxes in shop doorways and every other nook they could find to shield themselves from the damp bay air. Giant white globes at the tops of the antique lamps lining the street were covered in the fog causing the mist to glow like a phantom roaming the deserted street.

Orpheus had left the chat room after he saw, "Kiss-n-tell: 2006 oak street #102," on the screen. He made a stealthy exit from his home in the Presidio while Raven tapped away on her laptop, Reva posed in front of the mirror studying tomorrow's outfit, and Little'O curled in his bed dreaming of life at West Point.

He was the only driver on the one-way street. To his left was the narrow panhandle of Golden Gate Park and on the right was a long block of blue, beige, and pink Victorian houses with neatly manicured yards and white picket fences.

Orpheus slowed the car to a crawl when he reached the 2000 block of Oak Street. He could barely see the addresses through the fog on the blue, beige, and pink homes. Then he saw it. A two-story blue Victorian fourplex with white trim and a dense layer of trees that obscured views into the windows. There was only one light on in the entire building, which he assumed was Kiss-n-tell's unit.

What are you doing, man? he thought, sitting in the quiet car in front of the building. There were a dozen reasons why he should start the car and go back to the Presidio. *What if Raven found out? What if he's unattractive? What if he has AIDS? What if . . .* The list grew the longer he sat in the car, staring at the window with the light on. Then he remembered the reason why he had told himself to come. *The poor man needs me. His mother just died.* This thought helped in easing his conscience. *I'll go in, give him a shoulder to cry on, say a few nice words and then leave. Simple as that. Just a man helping a man through a difficult time.* This notion appealed to his humanity and highly evolved sense of responsibility to his fellow man.

Orpheus exited the car and turned up the collar on his coat. He had been careful to divest his clothing of any military clues before he left the house. He was just a man on a humanitarian mission in the middle of the night.

As he walked to the door, the light in the window turned off. Orpheus stopped on the walkway for a moment, but then proceeded boldly to the door and rang the doorbell. He saw the curtain rustle in the same window and the light turned back on. His heart pounded in his chest when he heard the locks unlatching. Again he was keenly aware of the fact that he was on unfamiliar ground. He didn't know the rules and at that moment the instincts that had kept him alive in enemy territory were nowhere to be found.

When the door opened he saw David for the first time standing in the threshold. He was taller than he had imagined and nothing like what he had envisioned. He was wearing a baggy pair of sweat pants and a wrinkled white T-shirt. David didn't have blond hair or blue eyes and he wasn't six four. He was so much more than that. His skin was a flawless rich mahogany. His brown eyes touched Orpheus's heart so gently that he wanted to turn away in embarrassment. No one had ever touched him in that way before.

"I didn't think you were coming. I was just about to go to bed," he said slowly.

The sound of his gentle voice called Orpheus back to reality. "Are you Michael?" he asked.

"No, Michael," the man in the threshold said. "I'm only David in the cyber world. My real name is Darius," he said, extending his hand. "You're black."

"I know," Orpheus replied with a smile. "And so are you."

"Are you disappointed that I'm not six four, and blond with piercing blue eyes?" Darius said defiantly.

"No. I'm relieved," Orpheus said with a smile. "You are beautiful."

"Thank you." Darius replied as if he had heard the compliment many times before.

"Are you disappointed that I'm not six four, blond, and blue?" Orpheus asked nervously.

"Are you joking?" Darius asked sincerely. "Have you looked in a mirror lately? You're gorgeous."

If Orpheus could blush he would have at that moment. He'd been called handsome many times in his life, even elegant, but never gorgeous. He wasn't even sure he knew exactly what it meant in the context of two men meeting for the first time.

"Thank you, I think," he said, brushing off the compliment.

"So would you like to come in," Darius said, stepping to the side," or should we continue to admire each other here on the porch?"

Orpheus responded by walking into the apartment. The unit was part living space and part photography studio. All but one window was covered by black fabric. The ceiling was as high as those normally found in lofts and the floors were glossy gray cement. One half of the large space was filled with computer screens, expensive looking cameras, lighting devices, and tripods of varying sizes and the other a comfortable living space with a large black sectional sofa, and three ottomans covered in florescent green, yellow, and red leather. Six-foot-high photographs of pouting models, snow-capped mountains, and seductively posed men hung on the white walls.

"So you're a photographer in the real world as well, as in cyber," Orpheus commented, pointing to the pictures.

Darius smiled. "Yes. Some things are the same in both worlds. Let me take your coat. Would you like something to drink?"

"No," Orpheus answered quickly. "I can't stay long. I just wanted to make sure you were okay. So how are you doing?"

Orpheus kept his coat on and the two men sat on the sofa at a respectable distance. Orpheus noticed a trash basket next to a desk on the other side of the room filled with crumpled tissues.

"I don't think I'm doing so well," Darius said, laying his head on the back of the sofa. "I can't believe she's gone. I just talked to her yesterday. I told her I would be home next month. Now I'll never see her again."

A tear fell from Darius's eye as he spoke. "She was my best friend. Now she's gone. I've never felt this alone in my life."

Orpheus's heart melted at the sight of the vulnerable young man. All his reservations evaporated. "Come here, Darius." The words flowed freely from his lips.

Darius melted into Orpheus's arms and rested his head on his chest. "I don't know what I'm going to do without her."

Orpheus wiped the tears from his cheek and gently kissed his forehead. "Go ahead, Darius," he said softly. "Let it out. I'm here. It's good to cry."

Orpheus held him closely until the gentle sobs subsided. He listened to stories of how his mother would send him care packages of homemade cookies and his favorite pastrami sandwiches that could only be found at Johnnies in Los Angeles on Adams and Crenshaw. He continued to wipe the tears as they fell and laughed at the appropriate places and was silent when Darius needed it the most.

An hour went by as if it were five minutes. Time almost stood still for Orpheus with the young man in his arms. It seemed so natural and right. He couldn't tell if it was one in the morning or one in the afternoon. The blacked-out windows separated the room from the rest of the world. The only thing that mattered to him was the beautiful man he held in his arms.

"I appreciate you coming here tonight. I really didn't want to be alone."

"You shouldn't be at a time like this," Orpheus said, stroking his hair.

"I'm feeling better now. It's late. I know you have to go soon. I'll be all right."

Orpheus didn't want to let go. He felt so good in his arms. He was glad he waited all those years to hold a man that close. Darius was the man he was destined to hold. Orpheus lifted Darius's head and looked in his eyes. "You are a beautiful man, Darius. I'm feel very lucky that I met you."

In an instant their lips touched. His sweet breath was intoxicating. The room began to spin as their lips pressed together. It was his first kiss and it felt like he had never kissed anyone before. The kiss was slow and passionate. Years of loneliness, isolation, and confusion melted away. Orpheus removed his jacket while their lips remained pressed together. Orpheus made love to a man for the first time that night, and for the first time his world made perfect sense.

Chapter 7

Three weeks came and went in the Roulette household. Tennis club dates, school plays, debate club happened on schedule, and the ongoing battle over pork occasionally reared its head at dinner time. Li Yeng baked, sautéed, peeled, and diced in the shadows while Raven spent hours solidifying her future in the Republican Party. She never mentioned her time with Trugonoff to Orpheus other than to say, "He thinks you have a bright future in the party."

The words "vice president" were never uttered. Raven instead chose to work behind the scenes to solidify Orpheus's place on the ticket. She knew that when it became fait accompli he would not have the option of backing out. Strategy and planning were critical in her well-plotted world and her political instincts had never failed her. Orpheus would find out he was to be vice president only when she was ready to tell him.

Meanwhile, Darius had become an important part of Orpheus's life. The chat room conversations morphed into text messages, telephone calls, and e-mails. The stolen brief moments turned into lazy afternoons in Darius's bed and walks in Golden Gate Park. To him there was nothing "gay" about his relationship with Darius. It was only love.

On one afternoon Orpheus and Darius were the only people left in the restaurant after the lunch crowd had gobbled down their food and returned to their cubicles.

Crepes of all kinds were on the menu. Young tattooed chefs poured batter on griddles and stuffed the thin shells with mushrooms, chicken, cheeses, and any other filling their patrons desired. The choices were displayed behind a glass shield and all they had to do was pick, point, and pay.

"I never thought I'd say this to a man," went one such conversation over a meal in a crowded restaurant on Haight Street. "But I think I'm falling in love with you," Orpheus said in a whisper. "I never thought it was possible."

"Don't say that, David," Darius had responded. "You don't even know me that well. And I know very little about you. You never talk about your work. I still don't know where you live."

Orpheus was unaffected by the response. "Are you saying you don't feel the same way about me?"

Darius hesitated and then said, "Of course do. I've never been this happy before in my life. But . . ."

"But what?" Orpheus said, touching his hand and then abruptly pulling it away. "Why are you afraid of loving me?"

"Because I don't want to be hurt, David. I've been hurt before and I don't know that I can go through that again."

"I won't hurt you, Darius. I love you. I love you like I've never loved anyone in my life."

The waiter appeared at the table, balancing two steaming plates. "Hello, gentleman. Who had the chicken crepe?"

Orpheus raised his hand, obviously irritated by the interruption.

"And this is the vegetarian," he said, placing the dish in front of Darius. "Can I get you guys anything else?"

"No," Darius said politely. "Thank you."

"Look, Darius, I know I haven't told you much about my life but you already know the important thing."

"What's that?"

"That I love you. Isn't that enough for now?"

Darius did not respond.

Orpheus continued to plead his case, undaunted by reticence. "I promise as time goes on you'll find out everything you ever wanted to know about me. But you have to be patient. I'm new at this and I have to move at my own pace. But that doesn't take away from the way I feel about you. I just need you to trust me."

"I do trust you, Michael," Darius said, looking down at the cooling plate. "That's the problem. I trust you for no reason other than the fact that I love you."

"Isn't that enough?"

A day hadn't gone by that the two had not either talked, texted, e-mailed, or touched. Most days it was a combination of them all. Orpheus was driven to distraction on the base. He often found himself staring dreamily out the window of his office wishing Darius were near him. Uniformed soldiers marched past like images in a video game. Sweating, grunting cadets wearing government-issued running shorts and moist T-shirts jogged back and forth and army green Jeeps raced from one side of the base to the other, all in the name of freedom and the American way, but Orpheus could only think of the sweet way Darius's sandalwood soap made his soft skin smell and the way he walked naked so unselfconsciously around his apartment after they made love.

During that time Raven had found a new lover. A lover who could satisfy her like no man she had ever known. One who caressed her at night and cradled her in his powerful arms until she fell blissfully into sleep.

The quest for power was man enough for her. The sweet, intoxicating smell of victory filled her nostrils as she drove through the city, lunched with the girls, slammed the ball across the tennis court, and lay in bed next to her husband.

Three Mondays had come and gone and each had included lunch with Carla and Alice at the Fairmont Hotel. The usual crew of socialites and a sprinkling of tourists filled the restaurant. The waiters danced across the floor and the wine flowed into bottomless glasses.

"So how did it go with Victor?" Carla had asked over lunch.

Raven had by then washed the smell of him from her skin and the revulsion from her memory. "He was a perfect gentleman," she said, twirling white wine in her glass. "Have you seen that yacht? It's disgusting. I want one."

The three women burst into laughter. "What would you do with a yacht, girl?" Carla asked, laughing. "Nobody sails in Washington. It's going to be concerts at the Kennedy Center, private dinner parties in George-town, and state dinners at the White House for you."

"I can live with that," Raven said, raising her glass. "To state dinners."

The ladies clinked their glasses in the center of the table. "To Washington."

Carla wasn't finished. "So you're trying to tell us that he didn't make a pass at you."

"Not even a hint. If I hadn't been so relieved I think I would have been insulted," she said convincingly.

"Can you imagine having to sleep with that old man?" Rita said with a frown. "His dick must look like a shriveled-up prune."

Carla gagged on her drink and said through coughs, "He probably smells like formaldehyde." More laughter erupted from the table.

"You girls are just being mean," Raven said, playing along with the fun. "I think he's a very kindly old man."

"Darling, you pat kindly old men on the head," Carla said with a smile. "You don't fuck them."

"So what does Orpheus have to say about all of this?" Alice asked. "How is he dealing with all the attention? Must be very exciting for him."

"You know Orpheus," Raven said between bites of her cobb salad. "He's like a stone. Nothing impresses him."

"You mean he's not excited about DC?"

"We haven't really talked about it much."

Carla and Alice looked at each other skeptically. They each privately found it difficult to believe Victor had not come on to Raven. Any man—gay, straight, or celibate—if left alone with Raven, would come on to her.

"So what did he say?" Carla asked. "Come on, girl, spill it."

Raven looked over both her shoulders and leaned into the table. "Swear you won't breathe a word of this to anyone."

The girls crossed their hearts.

"He said Orpheus was going to be the next vice president."

Gasps went across the table. "*Oh . . . my . . . God,*" was the collective response.

"I knew it!" Carla exclaimed. "Once Victor started sniffing around you two I knew it was something big."

"You did it, Raven," Alice chimed in. "Congratulations. You really worked that."

"So what's it going to cost you?" Carla said with a straight face. "There's always a catch with these guys."

"She's right, Raven," Alice said. "I heard they made one president, who shall remain nameless, kill a man before they would choose him."

"Don't scare her, Alice," Carla chastised. "Raven, that's just a rumor that's been floating around for years. I'm sure it won't be anything like that."

As the women shared urban legends, Raven thought, *I guess I got off easy. I only had to fuck an old man.*

Every week the latest progress in the race to the White House had been the main topic of discussion with the ladies at their lunch.

The pork wars raged on between Reva and Li Yeng. At least three times a week the smell of either baked, fried, or roasted pig fill the house. Little'O would give Li Yeng a slight nod of approval when Reva threw her tantrum and Li Yeng would apologize profusely and retreat demurely to the kitchen with a smile on her face.

This was one of several little ways Li Yeng would quietly punish the entitled girl. She had been subjected to Reva's ingratitude and dismissive attitude for so long that she grew to resent the "little princess." Another way she would silently taunt Reva was to always forget to buy any items she would request from the market. Chocolate-covered Häagen-Dazs ice cream bars were Reva's favorite treat and there had never been a bar in the house.

Li Yeng loved the general. *He's a good man,* she had often said to herself, and *Little'O is such a fine boy.* She treated them with the same care and attention that she gave her own family. The meats were always prepared just the way they liked them. The house was always stocked with Little'O's favorite chips, ice cream, and cookies. She was too intimidated by Raven to have any feelings toward her other than fear. She didn't dare attempt any hidden digs or taunts against the woman who had berated her so on one occasion that the sting had lasted for years.

Li Yeng had made the mistake of discussing Roulette family affairs with the cook of one of Raven's close friends. When word got back to Raven the scene was cataclysmic.

"It is very important to me that you understand what I am about to say to you, Li Yeng," Raven had said, towering over her in the privacy of the kitchen. "There is not much I wouldn't do to protect my family. Do you understand?"

"Yes, ma'am," Li Yeng said, slightly confused.

"You have no idea what damage I'm capable of when I hear that my privacy has been breached or the Roulette name has been disparaged. If you ever discuss my family with anyone outside of this house again you will learn first-hand just how destructive I can really be."

After that experience, Li Yeng avoided eye contact with Raven and always met every demand, regardless of how unreasonable, made by the lady of the house.

The Sunday *San Francisco Chronicle* landed with a thud on the Roulette front porch. A picture of Orpheus, in full military dress, was on the front page with the headline GENERAL ROULETTE CONSIDERED TOP CHOICE FOR VICE PRESIDENT PICK. Raven, Little'O, and Reva gathered around the kitchen island and marveled over the news. Li Yeng was off on Sundays, so the family had the kitchen all to themselves.

"Reva, go wake up your father and tell him to come downstairs right now," Raven said excitedly.

"Daddy. Wake up, Daddy," Reva said, pounding on the bedroom door. "Come downstairs. You're in the paper."

When Orpheus finally entered the kitchen in his robe and slippers he was greeted with a rush of hugs from the children and kisses from Raven.

"Look at this," Raven said, handing him the paper. "Isn't it wonderful!"

"Father, this is amazing," Little'O said, reading over his father's shoulder. "I can't believe it's really going to happen."

"Give it to me," Raven said, snatching the paper from Orpheus. "Let me read it out loud."

"General Orpheus Beauregard Roulette III," Raven read, while pacing the floor with her bathroom robe flapping at every turn, "is considered by many to be the top choice for vice president for Republican presidential candidate Governor Milo Fredericks's 2012 bid for the party's nomination. Roulette is a decorated four-star general who rose to national prominence due to his leadership in the Iraq war.

"General Roulette lives in San Francisco with his wife, Raven, and two children, Orpheus IV and daughter Reva.

"'General Roulette is a true American hero,' according to former Secretary of State Victor Trugonoff. 'I believe in these dangerous times he is just what our country needs. I've only met his wife once at a dinner party but in that brief time I was thoroughly impressed with her love for America and for her husband."

"I thought you also had lunch with him that week," Orpheus said with a puzzled expression.

"I did," Raven answered hastily. "Remember, darling, this is just theater. He's only saying what he thinks people want to hear."

Raven continued reading, "Governor Fredericks is the front runner in a crowded field of Republicans who have already declared their intent to seek the party's nomination. 'Governor Fredericks has a proven track record of fiscal responsibility and General Roulette has the experience with national security and international relations. I think they would make a perfect team,' said Secretary Trugonoff."

The article went on to chronicle Orpheus's military career. No honor went unmentioned. It ended by saying, "General Roulette did not respond to this reporter's request for a comment."

"That's a lie," Orpheus protested. "They never called me."

"Honey, I told you it's just theater. They say that when they really don't want a quote."

Orpheus took the paper from Raven. "How did this happen? I haven't talked to anyone about this. Milo hasn't called me and I only met Trugonoff that one time at his house. Something about this doesn't feel right."

"I suspect it's their strategy," Raven said innocently. "They leak the story to the press without you knowing so your response will seem unrehearsed."

"Well, they might be surprised by my response."

The kitchen fell silent. Raven, Reva, and Little'O looked curiously at Orpheus.

"What do you mean, Daddy?" Reva asked. "Don't you want to be vice president?"

Orpheus laid the paper on the island face down. "I'm not sure, honey. I haven't really had time to consider it. Daddy has had a lot on his mind lately."

Darius's suede moccasin house slippers skidded to a halt when he saw the man he knew as "Michael" on the front page of the morning newspaper. The stop was so abrupt that coffee from the mug he held lapped over the side and splashed onto the cement floor. The black fabric had been pulled away from the windows and the room was flooded with light as Darius stood transfixed by what he read.

"Four-star General Orpheus Beauregard Roulette III is rumored to have participated in a series of secret meetings with high-ups in the Republican Party for months now. Party insiders, who chose to remain anonymous, are quoted as saying, 'Governor Fredericks has already approached General Roulette about joining him as VP on his ticket and the General has accepted.'

"Sources close to the Roulettes say they are the perfect couple. Most consider him to be a devoted husband and father, well respected by those who serve under him and a devout Christian.

"Roulette recently made headlines when he testified before congress on the repeal of the 'don't ask, don't tell' policy in the military. In his testimony Roulette urged congress to not overturn the policy, saying, 'It is my firm belief that allowing gays to serve openly in the military would undermine the foundation of trust and camaraderie that are the bedrock of our armed forces.'"

Darius stood confused and dazed in the middle of the room with the newspaper dangling at his side. It felt like someone had punched him in the gut and knocked the wind out of him. The room slowly began to spin around him. He couldn't reconcile the Michael he had come to love with the hate-spewing, right wing soldier he saw on the front page of the newspaper. The Michael he knew was kind and loving. The man in the paper was hard and unforgiving. The man he held naked in his arms on those sunny afternoons had the gentlest eyes that made him weak when he looked into them. The eyes on the front page were hard and intimidating.

He didn't know what hurt him the most. There were so many contradictions and lies to choose from. Devoted father and husband rose to the top of the list.

"You're so secretive. Are you sure you're not married?" Darius had asked him on more than one occasion.

"I'm sure," had always been his simple reply.

Darius had a strict policy against dating married men. Not for moral reasons but rather practical ones. Someone was always hurt in the end. With his luck in love, he reasoned, it would most likely turn out to be him. That coupled with the thought of a scene with an angry wife was more drama than he could handle.

"Two fucking kids," Darius said out loud, identifying the next crime on his list. "How could he do that to them?"

And finally, the hypocrisy of it all slammed him in the face like a fist. It was the thing he detested most in people. Saying one thing in public and living a polar opposite life in private. The politician espousing family values on CNN and fucking his secretary in his office. The televangelist preaching the evils of adultery and sleeping with anything with a pulse, be it man or woman. The right wing zealot who proclaimed that homosexuality was a threat to the very moral fiber of our country, but never missed his weekly rubdown at the gym from the hunky masseur who always promised a happy ending for an extra twenty-dollar tip.

Michael. The lying bastard couldn't even bother to come up with a more original name.

Darius spent the day locked in his apartment, too embarrassed and hurt to face the world. He felt exposed and vulnerable. The sun pouring through the windows seemed to burn his skin as he moved from the sofa to a chair, to the kitchen then back to the sofa over and over again. He had in the time it took to read the article lost his place in the world. A place that had seemed so solid and safe on the day Michael appeared on his doorstep.

***

Orpheus, Raven, Little'O, and Reva sat on the front row of their church, New Episcopal Protestant Church in the city. The choir, decked in sky blue robes, sang the morning hymn.

All things bright and beautiful,
All creatures great and small,
All things wise and wonderful:
The Lord God made them all.

The 11:00 service was filled with some of the same faces that could be seen at the Fairmont Hotel on a Monday at tea time. They all looked the same except they weren't holding wine glasses in one hand or the latest gossip on their lips. New Episcopal Church was just one more place to be seen with those who were worthy of being seen.

The cold wind the winter,
The pleasant summer sun,
The ripe fruits in the garden,
He made them every one.

Raven wore a wide-rimmed black hat that sur-rounded her face like a dark halo. Her black dress showed just enough cleavage and was only tight enough to remind all who saw the mother and wife that she was in fact an extremely desirable woman. Orpheus sat next to her in a solid black suit, white shirt, and red tie. Little'O and Reva looked like the perfect modern-day prince and princess.

The choir was a sea of vocalizing pink faces with a smattering of color in the soprano and tenor sections.

He gave us eyes to see them,
And lips that we might tell,
How great is God Almighty,
Who has made all things well.

The handsome, tall minister with a full white beard walked to the podium at the end of the song. His white robe with gold embellishments glowed from the morning sun shining through the stained-glass windows.

"Good morning, New Episcopal family," he said in a booming voice. "This is the day that the Lord hath made and I will rejoice and be glad in it."

The Roulettes were the most "ethnic" people in the room except for a Filipino usher standing near the rear door and the two Latin choir members. Voices echoed off the walls of the gothic church built in 1816. It had been the place of worship for most of the people whom the streets of San Francisco were named after. Henry Haight, Charles H. Gough, James Van Ness, and Frank Turk had all sat in the same pews and sipped from the same communion chalice.

"We are very proud of one of our own this morning," the minister continued. "Stand up would you please, General," he said, motioning to Orpheus. "I don't know how many of you have seen the *Chronicle* this morning, but you just might be in the presence of the next vice president of our great United States."

For the first time that morning the congregation made a noise. Their applause turned the sedate service into the final moments of a rock concert. The extended applause soon brought members to their feet. In no time, the entire room was giving Orpheus a standing ovation. Raven beamed in her black hat. She knew she could not have planned the moment better herself. Orpheus was moving closer and closer to the point of no return. A place where it would be impossible for him to turn down a place on the ticket.

Orpheus slowly spun around to face the audience and nodded his head humbly. He was greeted with excited faces, pointing cell phones, and proclamations of support. Reva craned her neck to see all the people standing for her father and flashed an embarrassed smile, while Little'O looked up at his father with pride. There was genuine enthusiasm in the room. Everyone felt they had cemented their part in a momentous moment in history.

After the service ended, the Roulette family was surrounded by well-wishers and those who offered advice on the economy, Israel, abortion rights, and every other modern-day concern they felt Orpheus might one day impact. They took their one opportunity to make sure he would make the right decision.

Orpheus shook hands politely and modestly stated that he had not made any definite decisions at that point. Raven accepted kisses on the cheeks and hugs from members all while keeping one ear on Orpheus's conversations.

"This all happened rather quickly," Orpheus said to one gushing woman. "I haven't really had time to weigh all the pros and cons."

"He's just being modest," Raven interrupted. "Don't you think he'd make a wonderful vice president?"

"I do. I really do," the woman oozed. "I hope you decide to run, General. You already have my vote."

The parade lasted for almost an hour after the service. Everyone with a cell phone wanted to take a picture with Orpheus and Raven and the children. "Just one more with me and my wife, General," and "I'm going to send this to my mother. She won't believe I go to the same church as the vice president." Raven felt like she was already on the campaign trail. She signed the backs of church programs, kissed the cheeks of ruddy-faced little babies, and shook the hands of members she would have never spoken to before that day. She was well on her way and nothing and no one would stop her.

That evening Orpheus and Raven lay side by side in bed. In the course of one day their lives had changed. Nothing in their world seemed the same. The article in the newspaper and the reception from members at the church service had caused a slight shift in their reality. It was as if they had become actors in a movie reading the lines from someone else's script. They were still the Roulettes but somehow bigger.

The telephone had rung nonstop the entire day and well into the evening. Orpheus was invited to Sacramento to meet with Milo Fredericks. Raven received numerous invitations from the wives of senators from around the country to sit on fundraising committees and to participate in various charitable functions. Little'O and Reva were invited to birthday parties of rich kids they had never met.

The one call, however, that Orpheus wanted the most did not come. He hadn't heard from Darius the entire day. There were no text messages and no e-mails. Orpheus had called him several times during the course of the day and into the evening, but he never answered.

"Darius, it's me," was the message Orpheus left on his fifth call from the privacy of his study. "Since I haven't heard from you I'll assume you've seen the newspaper. I'm sorry, baby. I didn't know how to tell you the truth about me and then all this happened. I swear I didn't mean to hurt you. Please call me. I love you."

"What are you going to say to Milo?" Raven asked Orpheus in bed that evening.

"I'm not sure."

"Baby, you're going to have to decide soon," Raven said, curbing her frustration. "You can't put this off much longer. People are talking about you all over the country."

"I know. I've just had something else on my mind."

"What?" Raven asked, sitting up in the bed. "What's wrong, honey?"

"Nothing to worry about, just a problem on the base."

"Whatever it is it can't be more important than this."

"You're right, it's not," he said, turning his back to her.

"You haven't said all day what you're thinking about all this. I need to know. The kids need to know. Are you going to run?"

Orpheus sighed deeply and rolled onto his back. "Part of me says no and part of me says yes. I've never been known to turn down an opportunity to serve my country."

"I know."

"And the experience would be wonderful for the kids. They would have a front-row seat for history in the making."

"That's true," Raven said neutrally.

"And I know it's what you want."

"What I want isn't important," she said, placing her hand on his chest. "This is about you."

"The flip side is I'm not sure about the campaign trail. I don't know if I can do it."

"You remember what Victor Trugonoff said. It's all theater. All you'd have to do is learn your lines and stick to them. The decision will have already been made in your favor."

"That's another part of this that bothers me," Orpheus said. "It might be old-fashioned but I believe in democracy for the people and by the people. The idea of ten people overriding the system and making the decision without any input from the people is troubling to me."

"Of course it is, darling," Raven said, stroking his chest. "It troubles me as well. But what can we do? It's the real world. But what people like you can do is make it work in your favor so you can make the positive changes you'd like to see in the world."

"That's true," Orpheus said, yielding a fraction.

"Part of me thinks it would be a bit irresponsible, even selfish for you to turn an opportunity like this down."

"Selfish?"

"Well, yes," she said cautiously. "How many people in the history of this country have had this opportunity? To turn it down would be almost the same as saying you didn't care about the future of America."

Suddenly Orpheus saw images of spacious skies, amber waves of grain, purple mountains, and fruited plains in his mind. Patriotism was hardwired into his genes. For the Roulette men, it was God first, country second, and family third.

"You know I love my country," he said defensively.

"I know you do, baby, and this is the way to show it."

"Maybe you're right."

"I know I am, darling, but this is your decision. I don't want to influence you one way or the other."

Her work was done for the evening. Raven kissed Orpheus on the lips and turned off the light. "Good night, darling," she said, rolling onto her back to him. "I know you'll make the right decision."

Chapter 8

A week had gone by and still there was no word from Darius. Orpheus called him several times a day and even went to his apartment on one occasion but there was no one home. He left a note on the door.

I'm sorry, Darius.

Please call me.

Orpheus

The meeting with Governor Fredericks went as expected.

"General Orpheus Beauregard Roulette, will you join in my bid for the presidency of the United States of America?" the governor had asked.

"I'm honored, Governor. May I give you my response in a week? I have to discuss this with my wife and children."

Orpheus logged into the chat room every night at the stroke of midnight on the chance that he would see the beautiful screen name, Kiss-n-tell. But every night he was disappointed. The inane chatter held no interest for Orpheus. He was only interested in seeing Kiss-n-tell in the roster of people in the room.

Like clockwork, on Friday night Orpheus logged into the room. He didn't expect to see him there but there was always a chance.

Piped: anybody need a blow job?

Bicurious: never been with a guy before. looking for my first time.

Need2now: on my way to the club. hope to find mr. right 2night.

And then the name appeared on the roster. Orpheus lunged for the keyboard and typed.

Generalone: hello

Big14u: hello Generalone. how are you tonight?

One4theboys: what are you into Generalone?

The greetings continued but none from Kiss-n-tell. So Orpheus tried again.

Generalone: im sorry

Onceaday: why what did you do?

Favoriteson: probably couldn't get it up.

Boi4boi: LOL . . .

Generalone: please call me

Kiss-n-tell: go to http://www.xp3bb251-111/gov-8/en-us/room.aspz.

Enter the fake name you gave me as the password. i will call you in exactly 10 minutes

Kiss-n-tell disappeared from the roster as quickly as he had come. Orpheus hurriedly scrawled the Web address onto a notepad before it scrolled off the screen. He was so relieved to hear from Darius that he didn't question the unusual instructions. He carefully entered the cryptic address and waited as the page opened.

The site opened and the screen was totally black except for a white box in the center under which was the word "Password." Orpheus typed "Michael." His heart ached each time his fingers touched the keys to spell out the lie that had driven away the man he loved so deeply. When he hit the Enter key the screen blinked off and on; then his name appeared in the center of the screen in bold white letters, "GENERAL ORPHEUS BEAUREGARD ROULETTE III."

Then instantly a tape of Darius's living room played on the screen. Orpheus's heart warmed when he saw the familiar space. The sectional couch on which he had made love to Darius. The yellow, green, and blue ottomans on which he had rested his feet, and the giant photographs taken by a gifted eye. Orpheus longed to be in the room again.

Orpheus leapt to the edge of his seat with what he saw next. Orpheus and Darius walked into view hand in hand. They stopped in front of the couch and embraced. They were talking but there was no sound. Still in a tight embrace, the two men were looking lovingly into each other's eyes as they spoke. As the tape played on Orpheus knew exactly what was going to happen next. He remembered the afternoon in the apartment as if it had been that very day.

Beads of sweat began to form on Orpheus's brow as he gripped the sides of the desk. His heart pounded in his chest as he prayed the tape would end. But it played on. The two men stopped talking and their lips met in a passionate kiss that seemed to last forever. Their hands probed each other's heads, backs, and down the back and front of their pants.

"No, no," Orpheus pleaded to the screen. "Stop! Darius, please don't do this to me."

His hidden love and forbidden passion was on the Internet for the entire world to see. The gentle probing slowly evolved into lustful gropes and probing kisses on their necks and chests. Orpheus could see the bulge in the front of the khakis he wore that day. He slid his hands under the waistband of the green sweatpants Darius had on and lowered them until they dropped to the cement floor. The man in Orpheus's arms was now naked from the waist down.

"Please don't do this, Darius," he begged, wiping the sweat from his brow. "Why are you doing this to me?"

Darius unfastened Orpheus's belt buckle. Orpheus stood up from the desk abruptly and shouted, "No!"

But the tape continued to roll. Darius unzipped the khakis and put his hand into Orpheus's pants. Orpheus's lips parted and he threw his head back as Darius fumbled and probed in the front of his pants. The weight of the belt buckle caused his pants to fall to the floor, forming a pool of beige fabric around his ankles.

Orpheus dropped down hard into the chair in front of the screen and covered his mouth with his hand.

"Oh, God, please, please make him stop."

But the camera continued to roll. Darius slowly lowered himself to his knees in front of Orpheus and the tent in his white boxer shorts pointed directly at his face. Orpheus lovingly stroked the back of beautiful young man's head that kneeled before him.

"Stop it, Darius. Please don't do this to me," Orpheus whispered to the screen. "You can't do this to me."

Darius slowly tugged at the hem of the crisp white boxers and in one swoop the nine inches of evidence of Orpheus's desire for the man kneeling in front of him bounced on to the screen. Orpheus lunged for the power button on the tower and immediately turned off the computer, and in the process sent the telephone and a stack of files, labeled Top Secret, tumbling to the floor.

He jumped from the chair and began to walk frantically around the room. His hands were shaking and sweat covered his forehead and neck. *How could he do this to me?* he thought as he paced from one side of the room to the other. *I know I lied but I don't deserve this.*

As he frantically walked the length and breadth of the room the cell phone in his pocket rang. Orpheus had forgotten that Darius said he would call in exactly ten minutes.

"Darius!" he yelled into the phone. "What are you doing? Why did you make that tape? You'll ruin my life. Take it down immediately."

Orpheus's demand was met with cold silence. "Are you there? Darius? Hello."

"Do not speak. Only listen," came the reply.

"What?"

"If you speak I will disconnect this call and you will never hear from me again, but the tapes will be made available to anyone in the world who wishes to view them on the Internet. Do you understand?"

"Yes," Orpheus said angrily.

"Good. I'm sure you're wondering why I taped our affair."

"Yes, I—"

"I said do not speak!" Darius shouted into the phone. "My entire apartment is wired. Whenever I invite a stranger into my home I record everything for security reasons. Your trained military eye must have noticed the thousands of dollars worth of video equipment. You should know I have four other videos of our time together. The one, I assume by your tone, you have seen. Two in the bedroom and one in the kitchen. You remember when we made love in the kitchen, don't you, General? As I recall it involved you on your knees and a stick of butter.

"You hurt me very deeply and, unfortunately for you, you're going to have to pay for it. I opened my heart to you and you ripped it out and trampled it under your feet. I want you to feel exactly the way you've made me feel. Humiliated, betrayed and exploited.

"Your indiscretion is going to cost you one of two things. Which one is for you to decide. You will pay me two hundred thousand dollars in cash in three days. If you choose to not pay, I will remove the password block on the Web site and distribute the link throughout the Internet. Is that understood? You may speak now."

"Darius, I understand that you're angry," Orpheus said pleadingly. "But you have to believe me when I say I didn't intend to hurt you."

"Your intentions mean nothing to me. The damage is done. Do you have any questions for me or have I made myself clear?" he said curtly.

"Darius can we talk about this? I don't have that kind of money."

"That is not my concern. Borrow it from one of your rich friends. Take a second mortgage out on your home. I don't care how you do it, just know that I am serious and at midnight on Saturday the tapes go live if I don't have the money. Your hopes for being vice president will be over and your distinguished military career will be ruined. I think I've said all I have to say at this point. I will contact you on Saturday with instructions. Good night, Mr. Vice President."

The line went dead. Orpheus's heart was beating so hard he could feel it in his head. He collapsed onto a leather couch in the center of the room, buried his head in his hands, and cried.

Orpheus remained in the room for another hour before stumbling up the stairs and crawling into bed next to the sleeping Raven. He was physically drained, emotionally exhausted, and dizzy from the loss of love and the sting of betrayal.

Raven stirred restlessly when he pulled the covers to his chest.

"You're just coming to bed," she said, still half asleep. "What were you doing down there?"

"Thinking."

"About what?"

"Everything," he replied wearily.

"Have you made a decision?"

"About what?"

"About what? Are you joking? About Milo's invitation of course," she said, now fully awake.

Orpheus turned on his side away from her and said, "I don't think I'm going to be able to accept his invitation."

Raven bolted upright in the bed. "Why not? We talked about this. I thought—"

"Well you thought wrong," he snapped. "Now please leave me alone, I'm exhausted."

"I will not leave you alone," she said, pulling him to his back. "Why can't you do it? You're perfect for the job."

"I'm not perfect, Raven. Nothing is perfect in my life right now."

"What are you saying? You have the perfect family. A stellar career. They think you're perfect for it and so do I."

"Raven, there's more to my life than the perfect image you have tried to create all these years."

"Is there something you're not telling me, Orpheus? What is going on? I deserve an explanation. Whatever it is we can work it out together. We're a team, remember? There's nothing we can't figure out together."

"Let it go, Raven," Orpheus shouted. "This is my problem and I have to solve it on my own. I don't need your help. Stay out of it. It doesn't involve you."

"That's where you're wrong," she said, matching his tone. "Everything you do involves me. Every decision you make involves me and every fucking mistake you make involves me."

"I'm warning you, Raven. Leave me alone. I'm on the edge right now and if you keep pushing me I think I'm going to snap."

"I don't give a fuck if you snap. You can't make decisions like this without me. I've given up too much to be your wife and done too much to get you this far in your career. You owe me."

"I don't owe you a fucking thing," he said, jumping from the bed. "Everything you've done in this marriage has been for you, not for me. You wormed your way into politics for yourself. I never wanted to be a politician and I'm not going to be one just to please you."

Orpheus walked quickly to the adjoining bathroom and slammed the door shut but Raven was on his heels. She swung the door open and found him dowsing his face with water from the sink.

"You can't run away from this, Orpheus," she said, standing in the doorway.

"I told you I'm feeling very fragile, Raven. Please leave me alone. I can't deal with this right now."

"Well you're going to deal with it. Now tell me what is wrong with you."

Orpheus held his face in his hands and began to weep. "I can't talk about this, Raven. Why can't you just leave me alone?"

Raven had never seen her husband cry before. The hulking man stood hunched over the sink sobbing like a child, but she felt no sympathy.

She positioned herself lower than his chest and pushed him into an upright position. His face was dripping with water and tears. "What is going on, Orpheus? I insist that you tell me this instant."

Orpheus leaned down on the sink and said, "I had an affair, Raven."

The initial shock passed almost instantaneously. *A minor obstacle,* she thought. *An affair never stopped anyone from getting to the White House.*

"Of course I'm hurt, Orpheus," she said gently, "but that's no reason to not run for vice president. You'll break it off with her and that will be the end of it."

"It's not that simple, Raven."

"Is she pregnant?"

"No."

"Then what?" she asked, unable to conceal her anger.

Orpheus bent lower to the sink and said, "It wasn't with a woman."

Raven looked puzzled. "What?" she asked as if she had been presented with a riddle.

Orpheus looked up from the sink into the mirror, into the face of the man he had become. He felt numb and exposed. There was no place to hide.

"It was with a man," he said through the water dripping from his face. "And now he's blackmailing me."

Raven froze, standing over the crying man at the sink. She then turned and walked slowly to the bed. Orpheus came out of the bathroom moments later and saw her sitting on the side of the bed, staring directly ahead.

He sat down next to her and said, "I'm sorry, Black Bird. I don't know how this happened." He placed his hand gently on her thigh.

"Don't touch me," she said, pausing after each word. "How much does he want?"

"What?"

"I said, how much does he want?"

"Two hundred thousand dollars."

"When?"

"Saturday."

Raven continued to look straight ahead. "Pay him," she said coldly.

"Don't be ridiculous. We don't have that kind of money."

"I'll get the money."

"How?"

"That is not your concern. You are never to be seen in his presence again. Make the arrangements to drop off the money and I will deal with him from then on. Is that clear?"

"Yes."

Raven slowly lay down on the bed, pulled the covers over her chest, and said, "It's late and I'm tired. Please turn out the light."

Orpheus did not sleep the entire night. The video of him and Darius on the computer looped in his mind like a nightmare that refused to end. Several times during the night he got out of bed and nervously paced the floor of the bedroom, holding his head in his hands, trying to shake the images from his mind.

Raven didn't sleep either. She lay still in the bed with her eyes closed and the blanket pulled to her neck. When Orpheus's back was turned she would steal a peek at the distraught man walking from one side of the room the other. She was repulsed by the idea of her husband and the father of her children making love to a man, but at the moment that was the least of her concerns.

She could feel Washington slipping slowly from her grasp. *I'm so close,* she thought as Orpheus passed the bed for the twentieth time. *Fucking idiot, couldn't keep his dick in his pants for one more year. If I can fix this mess and we get to Washington, then he can fuck every goddamned White House page and faggot in the city. I won't give a shit.*

Raven could clearly see the strain Orpheus was experiencing as he wore grooves into the carpet. She didn't care. *He deserves to have a breakdown,* she thought, turning her back to him. *If he hasn't already ruined everything, I'll pump him with medication and prop him up with a stick up his ass to take the oath of office. Come to think of it, he might like that.*

In the face of her husband coming to terms with his sexuality, Raven never questioned her desirability. The thought never entered her mind that she could have, in some way, contributed to his attraction to men. It had nothing to do with her, she reasoned. Instead she attributed it to a flaw in his personality. Maybe being around all those soldiers for so long got to him. Her attractiveness and self-worth was never questioned. She had learned long ago that if a man did not find her attractive it was because they either had poor taste or some strange fetish that could not be satisfied by a beautiful woman.

Her world was airtight. Nothing, not even a gay husband, could deflate the bubble filled with self-confidence, superiority, and entitlement that surrounded her. Her world was created by and for her alone. Those fortunate enough to float in her orbit benefited from the residue of privilege and access that accompanied her, her entire life.

I let him into my world and this is how he repays me. By fucking a man.

Orpheus's thoughts raced faster the more steps he took around the room. He couldn't let go of the love he had for Darius even though the images on the screen tried viciously to rip it from his heart. The pain of losing him was only intensified by the betrayal that followed. *I never should have gotten involved with him. Look what I've done to him.*

Orpheus clung to the idea that Darius loved him. He needed to believe that what they felt for each other was real. If it wasn't, then nothing in his life had ever been real. If Darius didn't love him then he had nothing. In the short time they were together the depth of their connection became the measure for all that was good and right in the world. Their relationship suddenly put every medal, every star on his shoulder, and every military honor in perspective. They all meant nothing without someone in his life who loved him apart from all that he had accomplished.

Darius didn't know that he had led the American effort in Iraq. He wasn't aware that he was one of the youngest four-star generals in the history of military. He hadn't been told that the man he held in his arms may be the next vice president of the United States, but he loved Michael anyway. Michael was naked and Orpheus was in full military dress. Michael was vulnerable while Orpheus was a warrior. Orpheus longed to be Michael again, vulnerable and invisible to everyone but Darius.

Saturday morning crept into the Roulette house like a thief through the windows. The night was gone and so was the life that had been theirs for so many years. The telephone started ringing at eight o'clock and continued throughout the day. Orpheus refused to speak to anyone, but Raven answered every call and defiantly accepted every invitation. It would take more than two little men groping each other under the cover of darkness to stop her.

In the dead of night a plan was born. In the morning, Raven would do as she had always done and make everything right again. Now the children were occupied in their rooms and Orpheus was locked away in his study. Raven sat at the island in the kitchen and dialed Alice Waters's number.

"Alice, honey, it's Raven. I know it's early. I hope I didn't wake you."

"No, I've been up since five this morning. The workers are here now. Remember I told you I'm redoing the kitchen."

Raven heard hammering and drills buzzing in the background as Alice shouted to one of the construction workers, "Hey, watch what you're doing. That painting is worth a quarter of a million dollars. If you damage it, you bought it. Sorry, honey. These guys are making a mess of everything."

"I need your help with a problem. Can you talk now?"

"Of course I can. What is it? Are you all right?

"Not really. Alice, you have to promise me you will not repeat what I'm about to tell you to anyone."

"I promise. What is it? You're scaring me."

"Orpheus had an affair."

"Oh my God, honey," Alice gasped into the phone. "You must be devastated."

"I'm not," Raven responded without hesitation. "That isn't the problem."

Alice was instantly confused. "I don't understand."

"He had an affair with a man."

There was silence on the phone as Alice dashed from the house onto a deck off the kitchen. "Raven, you must be mistaken. Orpheus is the straightest man I've ever met."

"That's what I thought until last night. I'll get over that, but here's the real problem. The guy is blackmailing him."

"Blackmail!" Alice blurted, then covered her mouth. "For how much?"

"Two hundred thousand dollars."

"The son of a bitch. Fucks him and then robs him."

"We don't have that kind of money, Alice; can you come up with it? Of course I'll pay you back as soon as possible."

Alice sat down in a patio chair and looked over the Silicon Valley that was sprawled at the foot of her secluded mountaintop. "Of course I can, honey, but are you sure you want to pay him? What's going to stop him from coming back for more later? If Orpheus becomes vice president you guys will be sitting ducks. You'll never get rid of this fucker."

"I realize that, but I don't have any other options at this point. Orpheus is scheduled to let Milo know if he's going to join him on the ticket this week. If this guy does something stupid between now and then, we're screwed. It's over."

"I'm shocked," Alice said with a sigh. "Just shocked. How could Orpheus get himself involved in something like this? And the timing couldn't be worse."

"Exactly. I know by paying him it's just buying time, but it's the only choice I have. With more time I can come up with a more permanent solution, but I don't have that luxury today."

"When does he want the money?"

"Tonight."

"Raven, I don't think you should pay him," Alice said, walking farther from the house to ensure the conversation wouldn't be overheard by the workmen in her kitchen. "I want you to consider using the services of a contractor I have access to. He specializes in situations like this."

Raven stood from the island and closed the kitchen door. "What kind of contractor?" she asked in a whisper.

Alice looked over her shoulder to the house. "He makes problems like this disappear. Quickly and quietly."

"Are you saying with I think you're saying?" Raven said, sitting back at the island. "You don't mean—"

Alice cut her off abruptly and said, "Don't say it, Raven. I'm saying exactly what you're thinking."

The idea had immediate appeal for Raven. Eliminating the problem for good had merits that far outweighed paying a man who would then become a part of her life forever.

"I'm interested," she finally said. "How do I meet him?"

"He doesn't live in this country. When his services are needed we fly him in on our jet. He takes care of the problem and we fly him home the same day."

"You're joking, right? This sounds like something out of a movie."

"No, I'm not joking," Alice replied flatly.

"How much does it cost to . . ." Raven caught herself and stopped midsentence. "How much does he charge?"

"You can't afford it so don't worry about that. I'll take care of it. Just think of it as an early inaugural gift from your sorority sister."

"Thank you, Alice," Raven said with a sigh of relief. "I knew I could count on you. So what's his name? What country does he live in?"

"The less you know about him the better, darling," Alice said with caution. "I'll make the arrangements to fly him in tonight. Meet me at my jet at the Hayward Airport tonight at nine and bring the 'problem's' address and a description of him. Okay?"

"What is he going to do?" Raven asked.

"Don't ask any more questions, Raven, and for God's sake, when you meet him tonight whatever you do, don't ask him any questions about himself or his work."

***

At exactly three o'clock that afternoon Orpheus's cell phone rang. It was Darius.

"Do you have the money?" he said coldly.

Orpheus and Raven had not spoken the entire day but he knew if Raven said she would get the money, she would get the money.

"Yes," Orpheus said.

"Good. I want you to bring it to my house this evening at exactly midnight. Do not ring my doorbell. Do not knock on my door. Put it on the doorstep and leave immediately. Do you understand?"

"Darius," Orpheus said. "You don't have to do this. We can still be together. I'm not going to be vice president. I'll leave my wife. I just want to be with you. Just stop this now."

"It's too late, Michael."

"No, it's not. You can end this madness right now. I want to go back to the way we were. I need you, Darius. Let me make love to you again. Just say you love me."

"I do love you, Michael."

Orpheus sat on the edge of the sofa in his study and savored the sweet words. A tear fell from his eye as the words echoed in his ear. He felt the world would soon be right again and that he would soon be immersed in the life that he had been meant to live all along.

"But it is too late," the voice on the phone said. "The damage is done and we can't go back."

"How can you say that?" Orpheus asked in desperation. "If we love each other it's never too late."

Darius wiped a tear from his cheek. "Why did you have to lie to me, Michael?" he asked through his tears.

"I don't know. At first I was afraid to tell you who I was because I'm a general for God's sake. I'm the one who testified before congress against the repeal of 'don't ask, don't tell.' I didn't want it to get out that I was involved with a man. But then, after I fell in love with you I . . . I liked that you loved me for me, not because of my rank. I loved that you knew a part of me that no one else knew anything about. I was your Michael. Only for you."

Darius curled into a fetal position on his couch. The tears flowed freely now. He wanted nothing more than to be enveloped in Michael's arms at that moment but he could not erase the pain of betrayal.

"Are you there, Darius?" He could hear him sobbing softly. "I love you, baby."

Darius sat up on the couch and wiped the tears from his eyes. "It's too late, Michael. The pain is too great. You've broken my heart and you must pay for that. You have your instructions. Midnight."

The phone went dead. Orpheus found a grain of hope in the weeping he heard from Darius. "He loves me," he said out loud. "He loves me."

For the first time that day Orpheus found the strength to leave the study. The wooden floors creaked as he made his way down the hall to the kitchen where he found Raven sitting at the island.

"What is his name?" Raven asked as soon as he stepped into the kitchen.

"Darius."

"What is his address?" she continued coldly.

"Why?"

"Because I'll be the one taking him the money."

"Don't be ridiculous," Orpheus snarled. "I'll take him the money."

"I've told you already, you can never see him again," she snapped. "Have you spoken to him today?"

"Yes."

"And?" she asked angrily.

"He wants me to leave the money on his doorstep tonight at midnight."

"What is his address?"

"You're not going, Raven."

Raven stood from the island and walked directly in front of Orpheus. "This is not a debate, Orpheus Beauregard Roulette," she said firmly. "I've made arrangements to get the money from Alice and I don't trust you or your boyfriend with it. So either I deliver it or he doesn't get it at all. Now, are you going to give me the address or not?"

The two locked eyes. Raven reached to the counter without taking her eyes off Orpheus and picked up a pad and pen and extended it toward his chest. Moments passed before Orpheus snatched the pad from her hand and wrote down the address to the apartment in the Haight.

"Did you tell Alice what the money was for?" Orpheus asked, shoving the pad in her direction.

"No," she replied tersely. "I told her it was for some reimbursable campaign expenses."

"What are you going to tell her when she finds out I'm not running?"

"That won't be an issue because you are running," she said, walking from the kitchen into the entry hall.

Orpheus followed closely behind her. "I told you already—I've decided to not run!" he shouted to her back.

By the time the words reached her ears, she was already halfway up the staircase. She stopped on the first flight, turned slowly, and said, "You don't get it, do you, Orpheus? Because I've had to step in and clean up this horrible mess you've gotten yourself into, I own you. You'll do what I say, when I say it. The first thing you're going to do is contact Milo Frederick and tell him you would be honored to serve as his vice president. Is that clear?"

Orpheus did not recognize the woman on the stairwell. Her face was cold and hard. Yes, she was still the beautiful black bird, but there was something different about her. He felt a chill in his spine when she looked down on him and his throat became dry under her glare. He could not respond.

"Good," she said, interpreting his silence as consent. "I'm glad we have an understanding."

It was nine o'clock on Saturday night. Raven drove onto the tarmac at the little deserted airport in Hayward. Lamps cast pools of light along the dark runway. She saw Alice's white Learjet parked near a hanger in the distance. The door was open and four steps rested on the ground. A gold glow could be seen from the cabin. Next to it was Alice's black Escalade with the headlights on. As Raven drove closer she saw Alice sitting in the car.

When she parked Alice got out and walked to her door.

"Is he here?" Raven said, stepping from the car.

"Yes, he's in there," Alice said, pointing to the jet. "I haven't gone in yet."

"Why not?"

Alice slipped her arm under Raven's, led her to the jet, and said, "I prefer to not be alone with him. He makes me very nervous."

The women ascended the steps one behind the other and entered the cabin of the plane and Alice whispered, "Remember, don't ask him any questions."

The long, tubular space had six buttery-cream leather seats with high backs, a flat-screen television, wet bar, and refrigerator. Sitting in one of the seats was a man wearing dark sunglasses, a navy blue sports coat, and gray slacks. Raven could see his clothes were a very expensive cut and his loafers were Gucci. Except for a scar on his cheek that ran from his left ear to the corner of his mouth, he was a strikingly handsome man with curly black hair, chiseled cheekbones, pouty full lips, and five o'clock shadow.

"This is your client," Alice said to the man without a greeting. "Raven Roulette."

The man nodded his head in Raven's direction. "*Asseyez-vous s'il vous plaît*," he said, directing her to the seat facing him. "You are a very beautiful woman, Mrs. Roulette. What man in his right mind would offend a woman as lovely as you?" he said with a French accent. "I normally don't do jobs for people I do not know, but for my dear friend Alice, I do it for you."

"Thank you," Raven said softly.

Raven Roulette had had her hand kissed by kings and curtsied before queens. She had dined with presidents and made love to a secretary of state, but she had never come face to face with a shadowy assassin. She sensed something evil simmering beneath the handsome façade. When he removed his sunglasses she couldn't see anything in his eyes. They were empty and vacant like the dead.

"Who has offended you, Mrs. Roulette?" he said, leaning forward. "I will avenge your honor."

Alice motioned for her to speak.

"His name is Darius. I'm sorry I don't know his last name." She reached into her purse and retrieved the paper that contained his address. "This is his address in San Francisco. He and my husband—"

The man abruptly held up his hand. "Please, I have no need for details. Your word alone is enough to convince me that he is worthy of death. When shall it be done?"

"Tonight," Alice blurted. "The sooner the better. A car is waiting for you at the terminal. The plane will be waiting here to take you home as soon as the job is complete."

"How will I know it's been done?" Raven asked.

The man's eyes tightened when she said the words. Alice reached over and grabbed Raven's arm tightly. "Don't worry, Raven," she said nervously. "Everything will be taken care of."

"My dear Mrs. Roulette," the man said coldly. "It has been my pleasure meeting you. I wish you the best in your life. Now if you will excuse me, I must prepare for the night."

Alice and Raven tried to not appear too anxious to exit the plane but they nearly tripped over each other walking down the four steps.

"I told you not to ask him any questions," Alice said angrily when they reached the cars.

"I'm sorry. I was so nervous I forgot."

"It's over, Raven. Go home and put this out of your head. Your problem is solved. Now go and deal with your husband," Alice said and then slammed the door to her car and sped off.

As Raven entered her car, she looked up at the plane and saw the man staring at her through the window. She nodded her head slightly and he responded with slight wave of his hand. Raven prayed that she would never see the man again.

Darius had not left the apartment the entire day. The black fabric was pulled tight over the windows and Nina Simone sang sad songs to him all day. After speaking with Orpheus earlier that day, he couldn't stop thinking of the way he felt when he was wrapped safely in his arms. His kiss made all his fears melt away and the sound of his voice made him feel all was right in the world. Today was no exception. He wept for an hour after the call and longed for Orpheus to come and wipe his tears away just as he did on the night they first met.

Darius desperately wanted everything to return to the way things were only one short week earlier. The long afternoons in bed. The walks through the groves at Golden Gate Park and the kisses on his forehead as he fell asleep in his arms. Darius tortured himself by playing the video of them making love on his couch. He saw their bodies twisted and tangled together, making them appear as one tamed and contented beast that, until that moment, had roamed the earth aimlessly and without meaning. To any other viewer it would have been pornography but to Darius it was the greatest love story ever told, because it was his.

It's sacred. It belongs to me, he thought as the video played. *I could never share this with the world.* Darius succumbed in that instant to the fact that he couldn't live without the man he now knew as Orpheus. Regardless of his name he could never hurt him. He felt embarrassed and ashamed that he had even considered destroying someone who had so freely and lovingly helped him find his place in the world. A man who had made him feel safe for the first time in his life.

It was eleven o'clock at night. Darius frantically dialed Orpheus's number. He would ask for an apology and then offer one in exchange. He would tell him to not bring the money, but bring his love instead and all would be right in the world again.

After four rings he was greeted with, "You have reached General Roulette. Please leave a message at the tone and I will return your call as soon as possible. Thank you."

"I am so sorry, Orpheus," Darius said after the tone. "I don't know what I was thinking. Please forgive me. I love you and never want to hurt you. When you come tonight don't bring the money. I don't want it. I only want you. I love you."

Darius logged into the chat room that had served as the virtual incubator for their growing love. He scanned the list of people in the room for Generalone, but he was not there. All the familiar messages rolled across the screen. He ached remembering the many nights he had spent sending similar desperate messages into the wireless void before he met Orpheus.

The messages were moving so quickly they soon became an indecipherable blur. Minutes ticked by and midnight drew near. When it became apparent that it was too late for Orpheus to log on Darius decided he would meet him at the door and beg his forgiveness when he arrived with the money. They would cry in each other's arms and make love without the cameras rolling.

Darius waited anxiously for the sound of Orpheus's footsteps on the porch. He had instructed him to not knock so he planned to greet him as he deposited the money on his porch. At exactly midnight Darius heard a gentle tap at the front door. He sprang from the computer chair, ran to the entry hall, and swung open the front door.

The man appeared in the threshold. He wore the dark sunglasses and his hands were behind his back.

"Are you Darius?" he asked with the thick French accent.

Darius looked at the man curiously and replied, "Yes, I am. Who are you?"

The man swiftly removed his right hand from behind his back and produced a matt black Beretta with

a silencer attached to the nozzle. Darius tried to slam
the door shut when he saw the gun but it was too late.
The man fired two bullets, in rapid succession, that released piercing whispers as they escape the barrel and
entered Darius's forehead.

When Darius fell to the floor, the man closed the
door, walked calmly away from the apartment and disappeared into the fog as quietly as he had come. One
hour later Alice's Learjet was flying silently over the
North Pole to destinations unknown.

Chapter 9

Orpheus was jolted awake by the sound of a car rev-
ving outside his study window. As he shook the sleep
from his head and his eyes slowly focused, he realized
that he had fallen asleep on the sofa.

When Raven had returned home the night before
she had refused to speak to him.

"Did you give him the money?" he asked as she
walked past the study door.

"I don't want to discuss it," she said coldly. "I'm
going to bed. Please sleep on the sofa tonight. I don't
want to be near you right now." She walked upstairs
and locked the bedroom door behind her.

The first thing he did when he was fully awake was
check his phone for messages. His heart pounded
double-time when he saw that Darius had called. He
quickly entered his code and heard, "I am so sorry,
Orpheus," the message said. "I don't know what I was
thinking. Please forgive me. I love you and never want
to hurt you. When you come tonight don't bring the
money. I don't want it. I only want you. I love you."

Time stopped as he listened to the beautiful words.
He was embarrassed that Darius felt the need to apologize when in fact it was he who had hurt the sweet
young man so deeply. It made him love Darius even
more.

Orpheus left the house without saying good morning
to the children or speaking to Raven. He didn't care

that it was Sunday morning or that they were to leave for church at ten o'clock. The only thing that mattered was that Darius loved him and had forgiven him. He needed to see him and hold him in his arms again.

The streets flew by in a blur as he raced to the Haight. The city was still asleep except for a few hardcore joggers and compact cars depositing the Sunday morning *Chronicle* in corner news racks and on front porches. The red light at Van Ness and Turk seemed to hold Orpheus for an eternity. He looked in both directions and sped through the intersection. When he turned onto Oak Street he immediately saw flashing red lights in the distance. As he drove closer he could see an ambulance and six police cars parked in front of Darius's apartment.

Orpheus slowed the car to crawl as he approached. A police officer standing in the street waved his hand as Orpheus neared and sternly directed him to move his car quickly past the scene. Orpheus avoided eye contact with the officer but still looked to the house and saw that the door to Darius's apartment was open. Yellow tape surrounded the property. Officers wearing blue police jackets with SFPD emblazoned in bright yellow letters on the back walked deliberately around the yard.

He could feel his heart pounding in his ear as he reached the end of the block. Orpheus drove to the opposite side of the Pan Handle onto Fell Street and parked at an angle that gave him a clear view of the house. Once again, time stood still for Orpheus as the scene played in front of him in slow motion.

The officers combed the entire yard, occasionally picking up items and placing them into clear plastic bags. EMTs stood in clusters talking calmly and in no particular rush. Orpheus knew the worst had happened when saw the slow pace at which everyone worked. He had seen death his entire life but this one felt like his own. His body wilted in the car seat as he watched from the distance. Tears fell from his eyes but he was too weak to lift his hand and wipe them from his cheeks.

And then, without warning, Orpheus saw the gurney appear in the doorway with an EMT at each end. The body was covered from head to toe with a white sheet and strapped at the chest and knees. The men rolled Darius down the path to the waiting ambulance at the curb. He could hear the metal legs of the gurney clank as the men lifted his body into the rear and slammed the doors closed.

"No, God," Orpheus said through his tears. "This can't be happening. Raven, what have you done?"

Neighbors stood on their porches and in their yards in pajamas and housecoats. Women with curlers in their hair clung to their husbands and men huddled, speculating on what had happened to the quiet neighbor whose name they did not know. Flashing red lights reflected off parked cars and the faces of people standing in their windows the entire length of the block.

Orpheus watched as the ambulance rolled slowly away from the house and vanished in the distance. He rested his head on the steering wheel and wept so hard that his temples throbbed and his jaw ached. By the time he looked up again there was only one police car remaining at the property. The streets were beginning to fill with cars and bikes rolled past him toward Golden Gate Park.

When Orpheus arrived at his home, he couldn't remember how he got there. As he sat in the driveway anger began to overtake his grief.

I'll kill her, he thought. *I'll fucking kill her.*

Orpheus entered the house like a hurricane.

"Raven, where are you?" he shouted from the entry hall.

Little'O came from the kitchen. "Father, what's wrong?"

"Nothing, Little'O," he said, barely containing his rage. "Everything is fine. Where is your mother?"

Little'O pointed up the stairwell. "She's in the bedroom, getting ready for church."

Orpheus ran past his son up the stairs. When he reached the bedroom the door was locked.

"Open the door, Raven!" he shouted while pounding on the door. "Open this door right now."

When he heard the lock unlatch, he pushed hard, causing Raven to stumble backward.

Orpheus stormed into the room and slammed the door shut.

"You bitch," he shouted. "What the fuck have you done?"

Raven stood firm in front of him wearing only a silk robe. "I don't know what you're talking about, Orpheus. Where have you been?" she replied sternly.

"You know exactly what I'm talking about. You killed him."

"Killed who?"

Orpheus charged toward her and slapped her squarely on the cheek.

"Why did you do it?" he asked as she tumbled on to the bed. "He never hurt you. How could you do this?"

Orpheus stood over her, panting with anger. Raven looked up at him, seemingly unfazed by the assault. She stood up, looked him directly in the eye, and said calmly, "If you ever lay a hand on me again the same thing that happened to him is going to happen to you."

Orpheus stood frozen when he heard the words. He didn't know the woman in front of him. "How could you do this?" he pleaded. "How could you kill him?"

"I didn't kill him, Orpheus. You did."

"I didn't kill him. I loved him."

"You brought him into our world. He didn't belong here and now he's dead because of you. The only thing I did was clean up the mess that you made."

Orpheus dropped the full weight of his body onto the bed. He held his head in his hands and wept out loud.

"It's over now, Orpheus," Raven said, looking down on the broken man. "He was going to destroy everything we've worked for and I couldn't allow that to happen. Now everything is back to the way it was. You are going to campaign with Milo Fredericks. You are going to raise your children to love God and their country, and you are going to be the vice president of the United States of America. Is that clear, General Orpheus Beauregard Roulette III?"

Chapter 10

One Year Later

Red, white, and blue balloons filled the air like bubbles in a champagne glass at the Republican National Convention in Tampa, Florida. Confetti poured from the ceiling, covering thousands of cheering, clapping, and whistling Republicans with a blanket of shredded symbols of patriotism. Blue-eyed toddlers, gray-haired seniors, and every conservative demographic in between waved blue and red placards that read FREDERICKS*ROULETTE to the hundreds of television cameras capturing the euphoria for CNN, FOX, C-SPAN, and every other network in the country. A fifty-foot electronic image of the American flag billowed on the JumboTron screen on the stage.

A woman's disembodied voice cut through the excitement of the crowd and proudly announced, "Ladies and gentlemen, the next vice president of the United States, General Orpheus Beauregard Roulette III." The names "FREDERICKS and ROULETTE" immediately flashed on the massive screen on the stage.

The words were met with thunderous applause that rocked the walls of the arena. No one remained in their seats as Orpheus appeared from behind the Jumbo-Tron screen and walked to the center of the stage. With each step he took the applause and cheers grew louder. He waved to the crowed and the glow of his smile seemed to fill the room with light.

"Thank you, thank you," he said over and over in an attempt to calm to room, but to no avail. The crowd would not be robbed of their chance to acknowledge the elegant general who represented all that was good and wholesome in the country. The man who embodied family, faith, freedom, and country. The applause continued for a full two minutes and forty-seven seconds before Orpheus could finally speak.

After crossing the platform several times and waving with each step, Orpheus finally made his way to the podium at the center of the stage and said, "Mr. Chairman, delegates, and fellow citizens, the people of the Republican Party have spoken. I would be honored to accept your nomination for the vice president of the United States. I accept the call to help our nominee for president to serve and defend America, and I accept the challenge of a tough fight in this election against competent opponents at a crucial hour for our country, and I accept the privilege of serving with a man who has proven he knows what's right for our country and that he knows how tough fights are won. That man is the next president of the United States, Milo Fredericks."

The prophetic words from such a great man caused the crowd to burst into thunderous applause. For the next thirty-five minutes every patriotic proverb that tumbled from Orpheus's lips was met with rapturous delight.

"As I stand before you tonight I can't help but think of all the brave men and women who have lost their lives in the name of freedom." Orpheus paused and appeared to choke up.

There was a hush in the crowd as he spoke passionately of courage, love, and honor. But the tears he fought to contain on the stage were not for his county.

They were not for the land of the free or the home of the brave. The tears were for the love he had lost and the price that was paid for him to stand before the adoring crowd. The tears were for the body on the gurney covered by a sheet that rolled past him on that cold Sunday morning on the streets of San Francisco. The tears were for the gentle young man he once held in is arms and for memory of the sweet taste of his lips.

He could smell the sandalwood soap on Darius's freshly washed skin as he spoke. "Some have given their lives so that I could stand before you tonight and accept this nomination. And to them I say thank you and I love you."

The cameras loved Raven and turned to her often. Her beautiful face and radiant smile served as the backdrop on the JumboTron screen through much of Orpheus's acceptance speech. Trugonoff was right. She was too beautiful to be the wife of a vice president. The perfectly sculpted blood-red dress she wore caused her to strike the perfect balance of adoring wife, loving mother of the two perfect children who stood at her side, and a powerful woman who must be reckoned with. She smiled down lovingly on to her husband and the cameras and audience smiled up at her. Raven Roulette was perfect from every angle.

The End

About the Author

Terry E. Hill has worked in the social services industry for over 20 years. A native of Southern California, he attended Cal State Los Angeles where he majored in Sociology, and B.I.O.L.A University where he trained to missionary. After completing college, Hill was employed as Associate Executive Director for a non-profit agency in Santa Monica, California serving the homeless and battered women with children.

In 1995, Terry relocated to the Bay Area to serve as the Executive Director of a well respected and cherished social services agency in San Francisco. Terry later worked as Director of the Mayor's Office on Homelessness for the City of San Francisco.

When Sunday Comes Again is the second novel in the Sunday Morning Trilogy. The first was *Come Sunday Morning*. Hill is currently working on the third novel.

Notes

Notes

ORDER FORM
URBAN BOOKS, LLC
78 E. Industry Ct
Deer Park, NY 11729

Name: (please print):_____

Address: _____

City/State: _____

Zip: _____

QTY	TITLES	PRICE

Shipping and handling-add $3.50 for 1st book, then $1.75 for each additional book.
Please send a check payable to:
   Urban Books, LLC
Please allow 4-6 weeks for delivery

ORDER FORM
URBAN BOOKS, LLC
78 E. Industry Ct
Deer Park, NY 11729

Name:(please print):_____

Address: _____

City/State: _____

Zip: _____

QTY	TITLES	PRICE
	16 On The Block	$14.95
	A Girl From Flint	$14.95
	A Pimp's Life	$14.95
	Baltimore Chronicles	$14.95
	Baltimore Chronicles 2	$14.95
	Betrayal	$14.95
	Black Diamond	$14.95
	Black Diamond 2	$14.95
	Black Friday	$14.95
	Both Sides Of The Fence	$14.95
	Both Sides Of The Fence 2	$14.95
	California Connection	$14.95

Shipping and handling-add $3.50 for 1st book, then $1.75 for each additional book.
Please send a check payable to:
Urban Books, LLC
Please allow 4-6 weeks for delivery

ORDER FORM
URBAN BOOKS, LLC
78 E. Industry Ct
Deer Park, NY 11729

Name: (please print):_____

Address: _____

City/State: _____

Zip: _____

QTY	TITLES	PRICE
	California Connection 2	$14.95
	Cheesecake And Teardrops	$14.95
	Congratulations	$14.95
	Crazy In Love	$14.95
	Cyber Case	$14.95
	Denim Diaries	$14.95
	Diary Of A Mad First Lady	$14.95
	Diary Of A Stalker	$14.95
	Diary Of A Street Diva	$14.95
	Diary Of A Young Girl	$14.95
	Dirty Money	$14.95
	Dirty To The Grave	$14.95

Shipping and handling-add $3.50 for 1st book, then $1.75 for each additional book.
Please send a check payable to:
Urban Books, LLC
Please allow 4-6 weeks for delivery

ORDER FORM
URBAN BOOKS, LLC
78 E. Industry Ct
Deer Park, NY 11729

Name: (please print):_____

Address: _____

City/State: _____

Zip: _____

QTY	TITLES	PRICE
	Gunz And Roses	$14.95
	Happily Ever Now	$14.95
	Hell Has No Fury	$14.95
	Hush	$14.95
	If It Isn't love	$14.95
	Kiss Kiss Bang Bang	$14.95
	Last Breath	$14.95
	Little Black Girl Lost	$14.95
	Little Black Girl Lost 2	$14.95
	Little Black Girl Lost 3	$14.95
	Little Black Girl Lost 4	$14.95
	Little Black Girl Lost 5	$14.95

Shipping and handling-add $3.50 for 1st book, then $1.75 for each additional book.
Please send a check payable to:
Urban Books, LLC
Please allow 4-6 weeks for delivery

ORDER FORM
URBAN BOOKS, LLC
78 E. Industry Ct
Deer Park, NY 11729

Name: (please print): _____

Address: _____

City/State: _____

Zip: _____

QTY	TITLES	PRICE
	Loving Dasia	$14.95
	Material Girl	$14.95
	Moth To A Flame	$14.95
	Mr. High Maintenance	$14.95
	My Little Secret	$14.95
	Naughty	$14.95
	Naughty 2	$14.95
	Naughty 3	$14.95
	Queen Bee	$14.95
	Say It Ain't So	$14.95
	Snapped	$14.95
	Snow White	$14.95

Shipping and handling-add $3.50 for 1st book, then $1.75 for each additional book.
Please send a check payable to:
Urban Books, LLC
Please allow 4-6 weeks for delivery

ORDER FORM
URBAN BOOKS, LLC
78 E. Industry Ct
Deer Park, NY 11729

Name: (please print): _____

Address: _____

City/State: _____

Zip: _____

QTY	TITLES	PRICE
	Spoil Rotten	$14.95
	Supreme Clientele	$14.95
	The Cartel	$14.95
	The Cartel 2	$14.95
	The Cartel 3	$14.95
	The Dopefiend	$14.95
	The Dopeman Wife	$14.95
	The Prada Plan	$14.95
	The Prada Plan 2	$14.95
	Where There Is Smoke	$14.95
	Where There Is Smoke 2	$14.95

Shipping and handling-add $3.50 for 1st book, then $1.75 for each additional book.

Please send a check payable to:

Urban Books, LLC

Please allow 4-6 weeks for delivery